P9-DGE-001

D0015227

Freeport Public Library

314 W. Stephenson
Freeport, IL 61032
815-233-3000

THE MONKEY SUIT

THE MONKEY SUIT

AND OTHER SHORT FICTION ON AFRICAN AMERICANS AND JUSTICE

DAVID DANTE TROUTT

THE NEW PRESS   NEW YORK

Excerpt on page 2 from *Tort and Accident Law*, Keeton, Keeton,
Sargentich, and Steiner (Second Edition) (1989).

These are works of fiction. Although some of the events described in these stories
may resemble events in history and the legal record of actual lawsuits,
the thoughts, motives, intentions, beliefs and feelings attributed to the characters
portrayed here, including physical descriptions and dialogue, are purely fictional
and should not be regarded as factual in any way.

LIBRARY OF CONGRESS

CATALOGING-IN-PUBLICATION DATA

Troutt, David Dante.
    The monkey suit and other short fiction on African Americans
and justice / David Dante Troutt
    p. cm.
    Contents: Introduction—Glow in the dark—The tale of almost—
        Then bargain—For love of trains—Never was—Junius Dogman
        and the mischief—Bitch, son of a bitch—Tell about tellin'—
        Love space—The monkey suit—Afterword.
    ISBN 1-56584-326-6
    1. United States—Social life and customs—20th century—Fiction.
      2. Justice, Administration of—United States—Fiction.
      3. Afro-Americans—Fiction. I. Title
PS3570.R643M6 1997
      813'.54—dc21   97-213023
                                     CIP

PUBLISHED IN THE UNITED STATES BY THE NEW PRESS, NEW YORK
DISTRIBUTED BY W.W. NORTON & COMPANY, INC., NEW YORK

The New Press was established in 1990 as a not-for-profit alternative to the large,
commercial publishing houses currently dominating the book publishing industry.
The New Press operates in the public interest, rather than for private gain
and is committed to publishing, in innovative ways, works of educational, cultural,
and community value that might not normally be commercially viable.

The New Press's editorial offices are located
at the City University of New York.

PRINTED IN THE
UNITED STATES OF AMERICA

9 8 7 6 5 4 3 2 1

ENLIGHTENED DAILY BY MY MOTHER'S LIGHT,

STIRRED BY MY LATE FATHER'S SPIRIT,

THIS IS DEDICATED TO YOU BOTH,

SO THANKFUL TO RETURN SUCH LOVE,

ALWAYS.

ACKNOWLEDGMENTS

I relied for these efforts on the support, skill, encouragement, wisdom, criticism, and bold true love of a great many people. People who had no business interrupting their own work to make mine their business lined up to amaze me. In the stupor of genuine gratitude, one is always at risk of forgetting names along the way. I begin with the unforgettable.

Profoundest thanks to my mother, whose insights, second thoughts, re-articulations, sheer genius and selfless backup bring my words to mind and all my strength to the fore.

I give thanks to my beloved Shawn for her time, honesty, tender encouragement, and partnership. Tremendous gratitude also to my sisters, Eve and Margot, for always reminding me how the creativity we generate in each of our lives is a vital and necessary sharing of life itself. There is nothing like sister love. Special thanks to my brothers-in-law, Tim and Bill, for their questions and suggestions.

I wish to thank my dear friend and former editor Dawn L. Davis for her loving eye and generous energy. This project simply would not have gone forward without her.

I am also grateful to my family—blood and otherwise—who lent time, stories and inspiration to many of the experiences contained here. In Detroit, I thank especially my uncle George Vary Jr., my great-aunt Jessie Ray, my cousins George A. Vary, the Reverand Juanita Peek Vary, and Jean and Robert Lane. I offer praise to our patriarch, the late Anthony Vary, for his guidance and example. Regina Jackson and Steven Jackson were indispensable in grounding me in history. My loyal friend June Jordan was, as always, indispensable in grounding me, period, then taking me aloft.

A very special gratitude to Jane Dystel, my agent, whose candor and vigilant faith has taught me much. Thanks too for Miriam Goderich's careful eye.

I am deeply appreciative of so many at The New Press, especially André

[ix]

Schiffrin, who believed, and my editor, Joe Wood, who helped to strengthen this work.

To my mentors at Harvard Law School, especially my thesis advisor Charles Ogletree, who gave substance and time to these ideas, and, of course, Derrick Bell, many thanks. I am also thankful for the support of my colleagues at Rutgers School of Law—Newark, such as George Thomas, Charles Jones, Dorothy Roberts and John Leubsdorf, who took the time to read, critique and re-formulate. I extend special thanks to Dean Roger Abrams for believing as only he can. Thanks too for the help of many librarians at Harvard and Rutgers, who often allowed their days to be re-ordered by my requests, and to the Schomburg Center for Research on Black Culture.

Finally, I wish to thank the following friends and readers for their generosity: Cheryl Greene, Keith Coleman, Gloria Rivera, the Honorable Barrington D. Parker, Jr., Yvonne Croft, and Kim Landsman. And to all of my teachers everywhere, everlasting appreciation.

David Dante Troutt

FIRST, WE MUST NEVER FORGET.

That is probably the central idea behind this book and much of the inspiration for these stories about African Americans under law. Exactly who or what we are remembering changes across cases, personalities, doctrines and history. Whatever form it takes, however, retrieval always concerns experience. Experience is the first human element forgotten in the translation of life into law. Starting from that common omission, these stories imagine the possible experiences of characters who, with a few exceptions in this span from 1833 to the present, occupied the familiar bottom of American law.

The stories I have written, therefore, cannot be true. *True* stories—in the sense that they directly recall authentic parts of a narrator's knowledge and beliefs about actual events—are best left to the people who actually lived the events. But my stories do tell readers about what might have been, and this is an important thing to do. When the law works systematically to silence the record of people whose experiences have given rise to vital aspects of our past as well as our daily lives, we are forced either to forget or to reconstruct. I chose to invent.

Perhaps more than a choice, this was an undeniable urge. The process of writing these fictions began within weeks of my first year of law school. I was taking a class called torts where students are first exposed to common law rules of civil liability for harms such as personal injury. We were learning about the tort of assault and battery, which, in "black letter" terms, is the intentional infliction of a harmful or offensive contact to the person of another without their consent. The case was entitled *State v. Davis*, and the state was South Carolina, the matter decided in 1833. My professor referred to whittled-down case excerpts such as this one as "squibbs," and it is in fact brief enough to reproduce here.

STATE v. DAVIS, 1 Hill (19 S.C.L.) 46 (1833). The prosecutor, a deputy sheriff, roped a black slave to himself to prevent escape. The defendant cut the rope and carried off the slave. *Held*, an "assault." "The rope was as much identified with his person, as the hat or coat which he wore, or the stick which he held in his hand."

THUS BEGAN THIS BOOK. THIS SQUIBB MAY GIVE RISE TO MANY PROBlems, but before I could reach any of them, I felt the need to ascertain the existence of the person who appeared to be the only real character without legal significance in this short narrative, the black slave. To me—and this seemed an obvious point—the action of the story did not make sense without knowledge of who the slave was, what he or she was doing roped to this sheriff and why this defendant, presumably Davis, cut the rope and took off. (This, of course, was not the point as far as the casebook editors were concerned; the point was the simple rule that you could assault somebody by touching not them but something connected to them.) I went to the library and looked up the full opinion, which was little more than two pages. Still, the slave had no name and little apparent purpose except that he was the object of a mortgage on which the borrower, the defendant, had defaulted. The deputy sheriff was in effect a repo man. The matter concerned only the white men; the slave was but an object coloring the circumstances.

This is not good enough. But it is a routine oversight—most litigants, even of landmark decisions, are forgotten, a disappearance that begins with the form of legal opinion writing by judges. What happens to the slave in *State v. Davis* happens repeatedly across the history of blacks under American law, coercing and inducing forgetfulness. However, the consequence of such constant diminution is greater for those whose representation in the law comes from the bottom, because it reinforces more general representations of them as regular occupants of the bottom, suggesting by direct and indirect repetition that they belong there.

These were among the ideas I was given the opportunity to explore while still in law school, though well before the genesis of this collection of stories. My frustration about *State v. Davis* and other cases led me to propose writing three legal fictions in fulfillment of my third-year thesis requirement at Harvard Law School. Professor Charles Ogletree generously supported me in this and provided indispensable supervision. He believed in the project yet demanded that each story be thoroughly researched from a variety of legal and historical sources. As years passed and seven more stories were added after the initial project, my research approach changed in accord with different artistic objectives, but research has nevertheless informed all of the narratives. The research, however, was always carried out in the service and support of fiction.

As fictionalizations of circumstances that deliberately resemble situations in American legal history, characters in a story can break away from fixed notions of their identities and become metaphors in the history of African Americans under law. The stories themselves are invitations to reconsider important legal situations with the added benefit of context. In this way, fiction helps bring more to mind. Fictional voices speak to us differently and with more familiarity than legal reasoning and judicial pronouncement; they enter through different points and often gain greater access to our thinking.

Fiction can also substitute the law's traditional characterization of case *holdings* with *ideas*. Although each narrative here attempts to do different things with legal circumstances (readers interested in my specific use of four Supreme Court decisions should see the Afterword), each embraces at least one distinctive idea, broadly speaking. The ten ideas could be put in the following order: freedom, ambivalence, exchange, justice, conviction, self-defense, privacy, speech, union and revelation. The ideas I emphasize often have little to do with the point the judges who originally considered the case were making. Take, for example, the Supreme Court's decision in *Screws v. United States*, which parallels "Never Was," one of only two stories in which I deliberately draw from a lengthy factual case record. The

Court's several opinions (narratives in themselves) focus on the constitutionality of a criminal statute as it relates to the accused sheriff. But from the experience of the people who might have lived some of the events involved, an even more compelling idea may be the conviction with which the black victim clung to his rights to own a gun. So too the conviction of the white sheriff of a Georgia town during World War II to confiscate it. So too the sense of dueling convictions typically at the heart of police brutality cases even in the present day. The point is that, by dispensing with a reliance on established doctrine and even "fact," the narratives may free readers to associate meanings they might not otherwise consider.

Of course, this book is not intended to answer legal questions, but to tell stories. And the stories are a way of not forgetting what precedes us and of which we are inevitably a part. They reflect upon our difference and our sameness. Hopefully, they will touch, embrace and urge us freely to examine voices trapped in that vast realm of life circumstances that lie between black letter and our own broken tongues.

I

BONDAGE, BORDERS AND SUPREMACY

DA ROPE SAID RUN. RUN, NIGGA, RUN, IF YOU AM WHAT YOU AM.

But John Henry wuz in a mess curioser den dat an not so simple. Already he am free compared to da day befo'. Yesteday he am wuhkin feh da fugitives Tom Davis and Wiley Pardee. In da mawnin, he gwine back te Marse Pritchard. Soon as da young deputy sherff Mr. James Robertson wakes, dey off te Hamburg. What am free feh a slave lak John Henry? Das what he has te figure. Ain't feh a rope te know. Rope tied up 'tween sherff Robertson asleep on da bed and John Henry lyin on da flo at da foot. John Henry got on ankle chains too. Onliest way te do lak da Rope say be te steal up offa da flo an murder da man. Den cut da chain and da rope befo' mawnin. Nothin simple bout dat feh a nigga.

Hush, Rope, John Henry whisper hard at it. I ain't wanna hurt dis boy. I see bout runnin tomorruh.

But da Rope ain't interested in dat, been 'round John Henry's waist all day, da udder end tight 'round sherff Robertson. Sherff rode him a horse, whilst John Henry marched on da side. All day da Rope bent an pulled 'tween em over the miles. Now it jes tugged at John Henry, knottin up in a fist te speak wit a debilish mouth.

If'n you don't kill him now, dey gon come back and do da job. Wiley warned him so an Tom Davis too. Dey be back tonight. Dey comin back feh ya.

Da day wuz long an da sherff young, jes a boy rilly, carryin' a gun an him law papers, but scared. Takin a slave back from outlaws am highly risky, an he 'fraid te let John Henry stop an eat on da roads. Pulled mutton from a bag he carried te fix him own hunger, but didn't 'llow John Henry do nothin but drink out da wells, no time te relieve hisself either, jes drink so's da sherff don't kill off da bounty he come for. Bounty belong te Marse Pritchard.

We am da law now, Rope. Sherff told Tom an Wiley dat. See no cause te run off now dat I'm back wit da law of Marse Pritchard. Run 'way an it gwine look lak I run offa bein a runaway.

But da Rope said da law don't matter cause nobody own ya rat now. Tom Davis don't own ya. Dis here sherff sho don't own ya. Marse Pritchard don't own ya gin 'til ye git back. Ain't no law round here but you, nigga.

Night outside wuz blue an still. Night inside wuz black an quiet. Alla sudden, da sherff stirred an snorted lak a pig. John Henry's heart pounded in him chest an tapped time 'ginst the cool floor. The Rope got it wheat strings wrapped up on him keloids. Made him wanna go eben worse.

What kinda nigga don't run from dis here? Rope say.

I sho nuff gotta let dis water outta me.

Jes hasta follow da stars te git North.

I don't eben know where I be, Rope. I could be anyplace. Cain't run from anyplace.

You am near Hamburg, nigga. Now, gwon an git you te da river.

Dere wa'nt no river exactly. Dey seen moss carpets in da woods off da road an thick trees dat made a canopy 'ginst da long rays a sun. Wa'nt north or south, jes hills and purty forest breath in ya lungs. John Henry wuz runnin in his mind dat day, scootin 'cross da earth powerful, leapin rocks an dodgin paddyrollers in da hunt. He broke sweat jes thinkin bout sweat, lost wind jes dreamin bout wind. But most dem dat run 'way from Marse Pritchard am nebah tryin agin, for dey learns da worse suffrin da Lawd give out. Tomorruh be da day te go.

If'n I kill dis young man an git caught, dey will sho nuff beat ma brains outta ma head. Fuhst, dey gwine whup me wit da raw hide, salt ma wounds, den dey gwine beat ma brains out feh every nigga dere te see.

But da Rope had a answer. If'n you don't, dey gwine know bout ye runnin all de quicker. Jes git da hounds afta ye when ye has a fresh scent. You am 'fraid a dem hounds, John Henry. Dey gwine tear ya te bits. Den de paddyrollers gwine cut off ye ear, den Marse Pritchard gwine whup you good an salt dem wounds. C'mon git up an kill dis boy, John Henry.

John Henry am sho 'fraid uh dem bloodhounds. Used te lak em, playin wit em as chilluns. But he seen many slaves dat tries te run come back afta da hounds catched em. Dey find ya in a swamp jes lak dey find ya in a tree. Dey angry li'l faces snarlin teeth 'til all em git dey turn te rip off ye clothes an drink ye blood. Runaway cain't hit a dog neither. Das when da white man'll shoot ya. Ebra time John Henry think te run away he 'memba dem dogs an stay put.

Da lil sherff tossed in da bed above, pullin da Rope's frayed knuckles 'cross John Henry's osnabrigs an scratchin 'ginst him old welts.

As death lak singin, dey love John Henry. Go han in han wit wuhk. He could wuhk any job dey g'im. Eber since he bought off da block wit his mama, he prize nigga. Used te wear da same long shirt as a nigga girl, wuhkin fiels aside grown-uns an mendin fence posts, bringin water from da stream, an helpin wit house chores. A Pritchard nigga might sleep six, seven to a cabin, mebbe a pallet feh a kivver, vermin crossin dirt floors an da nekked fire scapin through da skinny walls. Udder niggas die from da scrofula, goat, 'fection, an syphyllis when de herbs quit. But not John Henry. Prize nigga lak him too big an too busy rakin a rice swamp. Eben da squeeters get tired out bitin im. Rakin, ditchin, sowin, plowin, John Henry left blisters on a twenty-pound hoe.

If Tom Davis am comin back a nigga, he want te be jes lak John Henry in da next life. Tom am trash, come ober to South Carolina a hunnerd year ago when him great-grandaddy wuz a convict servant. Dem Davises weren't neber nothin good, tall and thin from England, Germany an so forth, helpin te eben up da numbas 'tween niggas an white folk. Come feh da rice an slavery, allus wuhkin in da middle of da chain. Lowly Tom Davis wuhked long time for Pritchard, mostly am a oberseer.

But Tom had all he could take a dose bottoms an wanted te climb on top. He found him some swampland cheap an swore beside him buddy Wiley dey could till it, make it give. Jes if dey had dem some niggas. John Henry wuz Tom's mortgage. Tom agreed te pay Pritchard two hundred fifty dollars off da fuhst harvest alone. Fall behin' an he owe da whole thousan. Das how come Gull an Ben got hired out te help work aside John Henry. But it didn't work out lak he plan. Da land wouldn't give. Harder dey whupped John Henry, da less da swamp wanna give. Until dey let da two udder niggas go. But not John Henry. Dey took John Henry an run off.

Wiley don't lak ya, said da Rope an snatched one a John Henry's ribs show he mean it. Neber did. Whatcheh gwine do 'bout Wiley?

When John Henry thought bout Wiley, he grabbed da Rope anddug him nails in. Problem wit Wiley Pardee wuz he am very reasonble. "Trash" Marse Pritchard said te look 'way from, but Wiley allus got him piece. Irish Catholic lak him am no betta den da white convicts in South Carolina. But he ain't 'fraid a nothin. Das what make him so nigga dangerous. He used te could trade Indians feh sale in Barbados, den black slaves in Carolina, allus takin what da law gi'm, gettin him piece. He jes figured out da rules. Might set up planters doin dummy trades wit slaves. Feh dat, local magistrate fine da owner. Wiley'd get him piece feh snitchin. Udder times he find slaves travellin' 'lone on pass, beat em near dead an leave a stick 'side da body. Owner be fined feh a insolent slave dat raise a hand ta white man. Wiley's word, Wiley's piece. Den afta da Vesey plot got Charleston in hysteria 'round spring a 1822, Wiley gon work da roads feh runaways. He am viciouser den a pack a hounds, Wiley am. Laks blood eben mo. Male scalp lak John Henry's might could fetch one hundred dollars back den. Ebra time, Wiley got him piece.

Das when John Henry could see Wiley lak a ghost stabbin a knife down at im face. Him bladder bout to go. Him stomach turnin mean an empty make John Henry almos think he gon crazy or bout te lose him breaf.

Wiley cain't find us where we am, John Henry tol da Rope. Ima run tomorruh. Hush, so's I kin rest feh it.

But da Rope kept gettin rascalier. Ye mama got sick too long, John Henry.

Don't has te say nothin on ma mama.

She been sick too long. Wiley tell huh te come on out te da fiel, she say she am sickly.

She *wuz* sickly, Rope. Couldn't tech huh feh days. Couldn't come roun' huh feh she say we catch it. Made me te get on back te wuhk.

Wiley kilt yo mama, John. Whar wuz you, nigga? You worryin feh rice an Wiley out diggin a hole feh huh. Talkin bout get up, bitch. Black bitch.

Huh thoat wuz kivvered up an she spittin blood. Mama couldn't tell im right. Cause Marse Pritchard gon way dat made Wiley bold.

You s'pose to step up feh yeh mama, nigga. It's you done letta git drop in dat hole Wiley made. You da one standin' off wid a hoe all day long whilst ye mama drownin in dat hole.

She di'nt scream, Rope. How's a nigga gwine know?

Nigga might listen. Nigga might run. Ye mama dead. Run, nigga, if you am what you am.

Lil sherff stirred agin, lak a squeeter bit im an he roused. Dat made da hot air stop sudden. John Henry thought mebbe da sherff can hear da Rope, talkin all loud an rascally. Mebbe da sherff know im plans. Mebbe dis am da time te kill im. He lay still an felt a bitter nectar swim from im belly up into da back of im thoat.

What am you, nigga?

John Henry am off da *Leander*. He one dem few niggas can 'memba Africa eben a lil bit. In 1818, he come te Merica from insurrection on da ship *Leander* carryin fifty-fo live Africans. Da journey began wid bof sides unfit feh dey fate. Him an his mama wuz stole when he wuz ten. Fuhst, dey wuz ditchin rice, den dey wuz chained below da ship. *Leander* wa'nt no slave ship proper. She made so by a captain from da West Indies an his crew. Dey di'nt know bout no slave tradin. Dey searched da sea wid dey backs open. Dey went in bunches down te da hold afta a African died, steada jes one man or two. Dey let niggas roam da decks an pray durn da funrals. All John Henry 'memba was da dark ban a movement befo dawn when men unchain dey chains. His mama hid him behin huh. Dese men lifted

[11]

deyself quietly up inda cabin. John Henry heard heavy coughin and bangin what made da whole ship rock an sway. He watched em thow da white men ober. He saw em bleedin and fallin, fallin down, down te da blue ocean skin, den git sucked inside a white hole an disappearin' wid a quickness under da waves.

Dem Africans di'nt know nothin bout sailin a ship back te Congo. A Captain Marson a da *Norfolk* commanded 'em te Charleston, an dey all get te be niggas an sold.

Ye mama dead, said da Rope. Need te split dis boy's head an run, John Henry. Smite im good an go now!

He gasped on da flo. I gotta pee bad!

Daybreak—am too late! You ret te gwon home, John Henry! Cut me loose an gwon home!

Talk bout home make im wanna sweat an cry bof togetha. What a nigga know from home? Word lak dat one stop an start da blood in him veins. Make you cry up all da dust an spit, den choke ya back inta quiet agin. Whar he gittin can git him te home? All John Henry know te want am some udder udder. Not back on Pritchard's plantation. Not back in da bloodsuckin clutches a dem trash, Tom an Wiley.

John Henry nerves astart ballin up in him arms, sensations danced 'cross him thumpin heart, an him knees shook up and down 'ginst da flo. He stared up at da ceiling an looked feh words te tell da Rope. When none came, da tears welled in im eyes. Pools a saliva collec 'roun im teeth, start drippin ober im lips. He closed im eyes but still see lights flashin. Couldn't stop jerkin, just shook and cried lak a baby all alone.

Don't cry, cut me! da Rope called. 'Fo you become de sharecropper, sinner man, coalminer, factory hand, porter, janitor, minstrel, junkie, gangsta, nigger slave—cut me now!

Den, jes as quick as it started, da seizure stopped. John Henry let im limbs go limp an drop lak fish flat 'ginst da flo. Gotsta rest, he tol da Rope. No mo crazy talk outta ya. The lil sherff snored.

Time's up, John Henry, said da Rope. No mo talk am due.

Dey came 'fo da sunrise upon da stolen hides a fast horses. John Henry heard dey heavy boots weaken da boards outside da door. At fuhst dere wuz no light an hardly no noise t'all. Jes a great big swellin achin up in him loins.

Sherff Robertson woke up wid a terrble start, grabbin da kivvers ober da Rope. Da knot lurched John Henry 'ginst da post. Da chain on him ankle rattled on da floor. Robertson tried orderin dem te stop. Stop! he said, but no gun in sight. John Henry heard da empty lil crystal words fall and shatter by da foot of da bed. Tom Davis wuz already sawin da chain. Robertson's voice turned inta shriek, pleadin anywhere inta da darkness, beggin dem te obey da law, obey da law.

Wiley and Tom had dey rifles at dey sides. "I comes feh de nigger, sherf. Don'tcha move and we be on our way."

When da chain am cut, Wiley orders John Henry te stand. He raise im gun; John Henry could smell da salpeter near him nose an he know de barrel be close in im face. "You jes one savage lot a trouble, ye black bastard. Git on yer feet."

Da moments move lak breakneck. Dere wuz mad bangin an terr'ble commotion an no light to see by. Wiley come behind him wid da strength a demons. He grab John Henry's head wid bof hands an yanks him up. Lil Robertson fella leaped te da udder side of da bed so's he can betta grab hold da Rope. Wiley's tug an Robertson's pull sent big ol John Henry stumblin ober da bedside towards da frighten sherff. Robertson's body lurch ahead, too. Das when da two men met, nigga an sherff, eye te eye in da darkness.

"Cut dat goddamn rope, Wiley!" Tom Davis ordered.

John Henry felt da steel blade cool 'ginst him own chest. Wiley cut deep inta da fibers, tearin away da theads. Dis kilt da Rope. Kilt da voice dat wuz back in da darkness holdin John Henry. Dat Rope wuz jes a rope agin, jes a harness in Wiley's hand.

John Henry started te lift up off da white man's beddin when Wiley squeezed da rope in im fist an yanks John Henry te him. Wiley made da rope grab tighter 'round John Henry den befo'. It dug in him skin below da gut too close on da bladder. John Henry couldn't hold back da water inside him no longer.

"Neber agin, nigger," Wiley told him, told him right up in da deep, perfect blackness of im face, whilst John Henry stood in da night's invisible command, peein, warm urine flooding down down him legs, onto da floor, an on out da door as dey went.

The Tale of Almost

THIS IS A MULATTO STORY. AND THEN IT'S NOT.

Will Kelly was a sixty-four-year-old Negro man when a Charleston mob came to make him answer to his fondness for the milky smooth hand of a child, Miss Lucy Burton.

But he was born a slave and black at that. Except for the leaf-sized birthmark of milky smooth skin hidden on his ribs beneath his arms, he seemed to be mixed with nothing else. There was no evidence of unfinished business in his blood. But sixty-four years later, when most of his body was covered in white, Will Kelly found himself in the grip of a mulatto story.

The story has fifteen facts, no more and no less.

The first fact is how Will Kelly came to know people. He began from Esther, his hardworking mama and only kin after the war took his dad and brother. No special thanks to the Freedmen's Bureau, Esther took care to get schooling for Will and a new daddy. That would be Zeke, a Baptist man of God, who worked an indigo squad under contract in Spartanburg County. Zeke was not a kind man, though he provided well enough. Besides Will, Zeke was about the first to see the patch of white appear on the boy's side and warned him it was the ugliest thing for a nigger to mark that way, even worse than being a nigger. So, Will hid his secret. Last, comes the angel Clementine. She was Will's true love.

BY THE SECOND FACT, MANY YEARS LATER, WILL KELLY CAME TO KNOW death, as any man must. His mother Esther died a natural death some years before, and a year before her, Zeke. When he buried his mother, Will thought about the rumor. By now, he knew he was sick with something, that despite Clementine's assurances, Will had unfinished business in his blood to make him turn white so bad. The patch had grown in two, separated from each other and then gone in independent streaks and stripes to his knees and past the elbows where you could see it on summer days peeking out from his rolled up sleeves. Even Clementine could not cool Will's mind about such things. When Joe Bailey was lynched, Clementine mastered Will's nerves. When Mr. Conrad was shorting Will the year's share of profits, as he had done Joe Bailey before he complained, Clementine begged Will's restraint. And he did. But nothing could make Will quit this worry.

THE THIRD FACT PERTAINS TO THE EXISTENCE OF THE HERBEMONT family on this planet, a fact unbeknownst to the young man Will Kelly. Isaiah George Herbemont was a quadroon perhaps and a free Negro for sure, with a small plantation along the river near Charleston, South Carolina. The Herbemonts had owned slaves for generations, right next to the larger farm owned by Carlton Cato Burton, a white man. The families lived in peace and harmony for many years. They shouldered bad crops together, and they drank whisky during the good ones. Isaiah's wife was a mulatto named Genevieve. She was lighter than sand, with great blue eyes and a favorite host of southern ladies like Mrs. Burton.

Isaiah and Genevieve had two children, Daniel and Constance, both white as can be. They were smart children with good home training, and they carried themselves as though they'd made a compact with the wind. When the war came to Charleston, the Herbemonts helped the widows and children of their fallen friends. They hated Lincoln and they hated his war, especially Daniel. Daniel was the torchbearer, ready to assume the lead when his father passed from the world. He was no fan of slavery, had no deep thoughts to share about its survival, and was timid with the lash. But in Lincoln's war he saw the horror of his own future crushed, the possibility that his inheritance, like those of all the teenage confederate boys like him, would be shorn of slaves and half its value when the final shots were fired.

IN THE FOURTH FACT, CLEMENTINE KELLY DIES. THAT WAS 1895.
How could Clementine ever refute the rumor in Will's head? He

had it on good authority that his problem was "mulitis." A white man told him so. It wouldn't kill him, the white man said, but he'd never be able to have issues. The milky smooth patches were proof of that. Will Kelly was no better than a mule, a beast with blood between the races who'd drown one day forever more.

All those years without a child, Will was convinced of his curse. There was nothing Clementine could do, no magic her brown body could awaken in his to bring their seconds forth.

But when Will buried his mama, his mind changed about it. Zeke had taught him what his teachers couldn't, that God has busy work in store for niggers, that Will had better watch and not miss it. Part of his work was to show his mother chilluns for all her work, Zeke told him. Once she was dead, Will decided to get on with his part.

So, he went to Clementine in earnest. But she was too old to answer him. When she died several years later, Will Kelly was alone, swathed in a milky smooth storm, childless and broken.

One fact later, Will packed up and moved to Charleston, never, he hoped, to miss the sound of his wife's voice sweeping over a field at him again. That was 1896.

ON THE SIXTH FACT, DANIEL HERBEMONT CAME BACK FROM WASH-ington, D.C., in 1899. Many lemon-colored Negroes like himself had fled and returned. Some were businessmen and ministers. Many of the women were teachers, eager to make something of the freedmen. Daniel undoubtedly knew some of them in Washington. He had joined the Blue Vein Society up there and talked tough about maybe going into politics one day. But when he came home to run his father's place, he only took up old ties with white folks like the Burtons down the road. He wanted little part of the Negro Problem.

As for Will Kelly, Will could not find the work he had known when he first came to Charleston even if he'd wanted it. Many years of planting would get him no further than flowers. He pretended to have skills that a man of forty years might possess—fence maker, iron welder, blacksmith, barber. That was his plan. But he had a hard time proving his case. Negro artisans got few licenses to open shop in those days; the cities were claimed by white folks. Plus, Will looked funny.

Charleston confounded and excited him. Will marvelled at the colored women in their pretty clothes. He had never been North to see such things. By then you could find in some Southern cities colored men in black tops strolling arm and arm with women waving lace parasols. Clementine would have humbled queens in such colors. And she would have appreciated the upliftment in a man like Daniel Herbemont, the quiet grace that hid his noble race. Will did. Caught in the middle of his changing skin, Will gravitated to a man of Daniel's hue. By now, Daniel was making his money from a commissary that stored each season's necessaries for his Negro farmers. And Will went to work his store. That was the seventh fact.

ON THE EIGHTH FACT, THERE CAN BE NO DOUBT DANIEL HERBEMONT was passing for white. The Burtons probably had it figured, but kept it out of the public know. The black families on Daniel's land who came to the store to spend their last, they knew a drop of true blood when they saw one. And Will knew.

He was sympathetic, sometimes proud. A man like Daniel was in a bind. The South had become so hard since the separation of the races. Marauders were everywhere burning black men in the night. The Ku Klux Klan had outlasted the federal marshals and had even killed a few in their way during the years. Federal controls required state assistance, and public officials in places like South Carolina could be about as helpful as local juries in prosecuting white men accused of restoring the natural order of things.

So, black men hung from trees, and high yellow burned like the darker variety. Will could only wonder what a man like Daniel did to preserve what he had. He had been forced to flee once before and may have lost his own parents on account of Klan mobs. (They died mysteriously in a fire.)

So, Daniel was OK with Will, not that Daniel needed help. Daniel was rising cream in the cup of Charleston politics. He belonged to the civic club and a prestigious business club, too. One time, he asked Will to drive him to the Baptist church where Daniel was a deacon. It was a grand affair with two stained-glass windows and four white pillars out front. But they didn't let coloreds in there.

God had other work for mules like Will. The mulitis had reached across the undersides of his arms, his buttocks and most of his back. To see him from behind by daylight, he looked like a nappy-headed white man.

WE'VE REACHED THE NINTH FACT, AND THIS ONE TOTALLY UNBEknownst to Will Kelly. While men like Daniel passed into the milky glow of white politics, there were men like W.E.B. Du Bois, a mixed man, milky smooth in his own way, trying from his Northern offices to save what was left of the black flesh on Will Kelly's chest. Will's mulitis had conquered the backside of his every limb. His neck was half white, and he was pale behind the ears. The colony of cream had not yet reached his face, nor his loins, nor his heart. Men like Du Bois were fighting to save Will's soul, if not to keep his rear in check. Du Bois wanted Will to come North.

IT WAS A FACT, THE TENTH IN OUR STORY, THAT THE SOUTH WAS preoccupied with violent control over the Negro Problem at the start of the twentieth century. It had come as a surprise to many white folks to see black folks happily multiplying during those years. They weren't supposed to live on that long. Theories about black folks being dumber on account of smaller brains, lazier on account of no direction, and too damn slow to match the march of progress had failed to materialize. Of course, good niggers who stayed put and worked their shares without question could live to be a hundred, if not forever, for they remained in perpetual debt. But mulattoes like Du Bois and his loudmouthed friends and mulitic middlemen like

Will Kelly were too alive and well. So, it is a fact that a lot of black folks had brought strain too long and would have to go.

Du Bois and his NAACP continued urging the colored man North. Not a week would pass without Will hearing fellas standing around the back of the commissary, talking about did you hear the houses they got up there, indoor jobs and a paycheck?; did you know they payin' Negroes to come to Chicago?; theyse building ships in Brooklyn, say all aboard!—and so on like that. Will didn't know about no Du Bois or men of letters as much as he knew himself to be a son of Southern soil, who preferred to stay by the folkways he knew best. He'd make do. Young men could roam. They could whoop up and down about heading back to Africa in Marcus Garvey's Black Star Line ships. But Will was up from slavery, like Booker T. said, and he would finish his business among the crackers in peace.

NEWS WAS MAINLY LOCAL AT THE COMMISSARY WHERE WILL WORKED for Daniel Herbemont. Crops and lynchings were most on a man's mind. But as a matter of the eleventh fact, white fists started closing in on men like Will Kelly down South. Perhaps Du Bois was right. White men had become wilder and wretcheder than ever before, lashing out at threats to their supremacy from under hoods and over pulpits and behind courtroom benches and jury boxes. Du Bois reported about the fierce riots in Northern cities. But all across the South, they were giving black folks grief with one hand and speeding them off to heaven with the other.

As word of night riders came often to Charleston throughout 1918, even Daniel Herbemont got scared. Friends like Carlton Cato Burton were turning a little colder, talking more about the need to hold back insurrection. May not have been the best time in the North, but in the South it seemed like time itself was running out.

BY THE TWELFTH FACT, WILL KELLY HAD FINALLY CROSSED THE COLOR line. Mulitis had won the war of his heart, and by the new year 1920, his brown eyes sank in the middle of white circles. It wasn't a perfect finish, nor was he milky smooth all over. He looked like he'd been burning under slow flames all these years, which left him ring streaked and striped.

Will had to leave the commissary. His presence raised such questions that Daniel Herbemont let him go. Daniel wasn't all bad though, and Will got a job cleaning up the great Baptist church where Daniel and the Burtons went for worship in grand style.

As sexton, Will Kelly did what an old man does to finish his business on the earth in peace. He basked in the innocent glow of milky smooth children, as though they were the ones he could never have. As age would have it, children understood him best of all.

Polishing pews and pulpits was little different from wiping down stock tables and sweeping the commissary. Will wasn't allowed to linger on the premises upstairs and spent most of his time in the dark basement where he kept his rags and a stool to rest on. In the broom closet was room enough for a small basin that he used to wash in. There was a broken looking glass that Will stared at from time to time, watching his progress toward death and wondering what place God had in store for a man like him. Sometimes Will would read alone from the Bible on his stool, drifting off to sleep on some musing of a heavenly reward. That's where the children would find him, little Andrew Turner, Jeremy Potter, Jeremy's little sister Adora, and Will's favorite, Lucy Burton.

Lucy Burton had been among the first children to love him. She came with her daddy to the commissary when Will used to work there. He watched her grow up, taking pride in every little thing she showed him and giving her candy if he could. When other children were scared of Will, Lucy brought him her smiles. They grew to be friends, and when he became sexton at her church, she would sometimes take the others down to the basement to bring Will dried flowers.

In the spring of 1920, Lucy Burton received a handsome wristwatch for her thirteenth birthday. She was very proud of it and wore it everywhere, showing it off. She and Andrew, Jeremy and tiny Adora would go running off to the church basement several times a week, the children seeking stories and pennies from the old man, and Lucy showing off her watch.

A NEGRO MINISTER WAS KILLED ONE MEAN NIGHT IN APRIL AND colored Charleston was in a stir. That's the thirteenth fact. Will Kelly had gone to a secret meeting at the church of the slain pastor to hear about it. Will hadn't known Reverand Sims well, but he had survived rough years to know joy again thanks to the reverend's calls to faith. Now, he listened and prayed with the rest of them. When sheriffs suddenly broke up the meeting on a riot charge, many of the colored families heard what they imagined to be the sound of Du Bois in their ears. The Clemsons, Dottie Taylor, Charlie and Belinda Banks, and even Rusty Coleman, the esteemed black barber, packed up and moved North in short order. White folks in Charleston might one day regret it, but some of their best Negroes were leaving town.

THE FOURTEENTH FACT CONCERNS THE PLACE OF THOSE IN THE middle of situations where the middle ground is no more, which is what happened in earnest to Charleston's old Will Kelly late that spring. Up until the death of Reverend Sims, Will had been considered a good nigger, "peace loving," vouched Daniel Herbemont. But John Burton had his doubts about the old ring-streaked man, and he didn't like his daughter, now nearly a woman of child-bearing age, running down to some church basement to show off her prized wristwatch to a could-be devil. Clyde Potter and Robert Turner felt the same way about their own children's visits. Where did he get those pennies and nickels to be handing out to white children, anyway? they wondered. What business did a colored man have in giving money to white children? they demanded to know. Daniel Herbemont did his passing best to quell his neighbors' fears. Will Kelly had worked for him for over twenty years without a snip of trouble, and the old man could do no harm, he said. But when the sheriff swore he saw Will Kelly at the secret meeting, Daniel Herbemont had to give his ground.

WELL, ON THE TWENTY-EIGHTH OF JUNE, 1920, THE FIFTEENTH AND final fact, these children disobeyed their parents for the last time. They visited Will Kelly while he was reading the Bible. As soon as he saw them, Will gave the younger children the last nickel he would spare them and told them to head for Mr. McGraw, who worked the commissary now. But Lucy Burton stayed behind while they scampered off.

"That nickel's for you, too, Miss Lucy. Why don't you run off and buy you some candy like the rest of 'em?"

Lucy had something secret in her eyes. "I'm too old for all that candy stuff," she said, being coy. "Besides, my watch is off, Will. It might even be broke. Could I sit down whiles you try and fix it for me?"

Will was nervous. Children were simple things in most ways, but a young woman alone, right here, right now, made him nervous. "I-, I spose so, Missy."

Will gave the stool to Lucy to sit on and sat beside her on the floor beneath the naked white bulb. His eyes were no match for the tiny hands of the clock, and he stretched his arms up to capture some light. Lucy was watching him harder than ever; a secret buldged in her eyes. If he could have seen well enough to know, many minutes passed. He trembled under her gaze and sweat broke out on his brow. Will was ready to give up. He couldn't see the hands, but time was putting a bad feeling in him.

"Will?"

"Yes, Miss Lucy?"

"Why are you so black and white?"

He tried to laugh, but never took his eyes off the watch. "Something the Lord had in store for me, I guess."

"May I touch it?" she asked, pointing at his mixed-up hand. "I'm just gonna touch it a little, OK?"

Lucy didn't wait for an answer. She just reached out and touched the place where his thumb met his index finger, gently pressing the skin with her fingertips.

Will tried to break her amazement. "I can't set your watch, Missy, with you in my way now, can I?"

"Oh, Will, that's OK." She started to stroke the border between the two colors, never taking her eyes off the discovery, just caressing and smiling, caressing and smiling.

"I think maybe you should stop now, Missy," Will said, looking up feebly into Lucy's face. But suddenly, the darkness beyond the doorway moved.

"I think you better hold it right there, old man!" said Clyde Potter, standing in the dark at the foot of the stairs with a stick in his hand. Robert Turner was there behind him, and you could see the whites of their eyes menacing.

"Did that old nigger touch you, Lucy?" Clyde Potter boomed. Lucy looked down and said nothing. "I'm talking to you, young lady. Now stand up and look at me!" Lucy stood and looked into the fire of his stare. "Did that coon bastard lay his hand on you?"

Lucy pouted a little. "Yessir," she mumbled.

That was all and the end for Will Kelly. They took him by his shirt and dragged him into the light of day. As he left the church, the bright sun blinded him. He was marched to the Negro jail and tossed in a cell where his unfinished blood could do no more trouble.

You would think that waiting is no challenge to an old man, that experience teaches him to get the better of time. But within hours behind bars, Will wished that he were dead. He missed his stool and his Bible. He could not wash when he was accustomed nor wake to cornbread before starting his day. There was no one left who might look after him even if he survived prison. His skin had done this to him, a cursed war upon his tired body. If it was fighting he had done 'til now, he was done with the fight.

Daniel Herbemont sat silently near the back and watched the trial. He watched Will Kelly sit motionless at the defendant's table. It took a day to assemble a jury, a room full of blue eyes and white lightening. Daniel was afraid to testify. Charleston had gone mad. John Cato Burton had gone mad. A black man could hardly testify in defense of another, not where a white child's word would be questioned, and Daniel feared that his own blood would be tried. He listened to Lucy Burton tell of a touching, while the prosecutor clammered and quaked. But it was the hue and cry of his neighbors beside him that brought Daniel quietly to his feet. He stood and took a last look at Will Kelly, who seemed to be dead already, there with his striped hands clasped together, dead at the sound of Lucy's voice. Daniel slipped outside the courtroom and went on home.

Will Kelly was convicted of attempted assault with intent to ravish. But witnesses had stuttered on the stand, suggesting that his character was not all one color. Even the jurors seemed to stutter in their thoughts about old Will Kelly, and they recommended mercy with their guilty verdict. Daniel Herbemont went away to Washington. He rode nearly two days under cover, found a white lawyer, and returned with him to Charleston on the fifth day.

When Will Kelly's appeal to the South Carolina Supreme Court came down, the Burtons, the Potters, the Turners, and others had moved on to the harvest season. There had been news of three lynchings in Spartanburg County, which relieved some of the pressure on the people of Charleston. Rusty Coleman, the black barber, had returned to the city, and there was little word of any important new departures. Rusty almost stayed away, but couldn't.

Lucy Burton almost had her watch reset.

Daniel Herbemont almost joined the colored ranks. Instead, he pulled within himself all winter.

W.E.B. Du Bois almost won a convert.

And Will Kelly, according to the state's high court, almost committed the crime of his life. But it was for the fact that, despite what his skin did, Will Kelly had hardly ever moved to cause his rightful stir in life. "The evil thought, which is the criminal intent," said the judges, "only becomes unlawful when he who harbors it proceeds to put it into action." Will's harbor was dry.

The Bargain

FOR A LONE PATCH OF GOD'S EARTH, THE GROUND AT THE CORNER OF South 18th Street and Newbury kept a peaceful demeanor, the house above it and its inhabitants doing little to upset the natural order of things. But all around it lay seismic conflicts. Half-sized lots were cut too small, causing imbalances that visibly disturbed the Ground below. Grass here, none there. Gardens tended, weeds erect. It wasn't the people but what they did; tearing at the soil, subdividing and excavating, drilling beyond good reason, wounding without regard. These were all consequences of urban life. They comprised the chewy kernels of daily talk for people living and dying in Louisville, Kentucky. But for the good Earth down under, it was sheer provocation sometimes, enough to hurl trees, make bargains with windstorms, spit water mains on occasion, and instigate whatever clash of elements might, with the exercise of sufficient force, reach a notion in the minds of mortals to restore a little equivalency. But until Dirt speaks English, the problem for such communications is always with just who is listening and how well they can hear.

It was safe to say that neither man was listening on that particular late spring evening in 1912, and that it would likely take years before either man could. George was distracted by questions in his head and Tommy was hunched over the checkerboard, deciding a fit demise for his new stranger-victim-friend with the boney face, leathery skin and tiny eyes.

They were playing chinese checkers just inside the window at the Hi-Lo Club on Broad Street, a storefront nestled inside a strip of stores spread along a boisterous, man-made avenue. The side streets lined with houses and short lawns just off of Broad, like Newbury, were still the Earth's natural province, just like the roads further on, the paths alongside the train tracks, and the ground spreading for millions of miles into the hills in every direction. Still the jurisdiction

[27]

of natural country. But not Broad Street and, by 1912, a growing few others.

"I like Louisville," George said, looking onto the street as Tommy began to make his move. "I don't know why. Really ain't shit here yet. Not compared to Nashville." George's face filled with smoke and his tiny eyes squinted even tinier as he lit a Lucky Strike and shook the match out.

"You from Nashville 'riginally?" Tommy asked after making his move and pocketing two of George's men. He reached for his glass and emptied the last of his whiskey.

"Maybe."

Tommy's eyes brightened to show the whites and he waved at George. "No reason to be slick or phantom-like with me, mister, because it makes little matter to me where you from. What matters is you here today and you losing now."

Both men looked at each other and started to laugh. Tommy was just a finger of a man, slender and bent slightly at the knuckle from hours behind a desk, with a dark brick complexion and cheek bones that pertruded from his oval-shaped head. He wore glasses of nickel-plated silver over kind eyes that bulged forward in their sockets.

"Can I buy that drink for you?"

"Be pretty hard," Tommy said, pulling a half-empty fifth from his shirt, "unless you plan on buyin' it right outta my pocket." Again they laughed.

"Tell you what, I'll lay you the winner of this game whatever you paid for it," he said, leaning to jump over Tommy's man. "I've noticed you in here a few times before. What's your name, fella?"

"Tommy Lee."

"Hmm. That's a Chinaman name. They make colored Chinese?"

"If they did, I could find trouble going *and* coming, sir."

"I wouldn't worry if I was you. Trouble's overrated." George puzzled over the board. "You play like you got some of the game in you."

"No, no, sir. Don't let my game fool you. Don't have to be Chinese to beat a man of your skill at checkers." Don't even have to be grown up, Tommy thought to himself.

Tommy's next move cleared the last of George's men from the board. George just watched with a disappointed grin, but no hard feelings. "My name's George S. Byron."

"Nice to beat you, Mr. Byron. What's the S for?"

"The S?" George studied Tommy's face for a moment. "Mind if I?" he asked, reaching toward Tommy's bottle of whiskey sitting at the edge of the table.

"You just bought it, George. It's yours now."

George smirked and poured himself a couple of shots. "The S is for a man named Socrates." He raised his glass to Tommy, who raised his in return.

"Odd name. Kin of yours?"

"Doubtful. I don't suppose you've read the Greek philosophy." Tommy shook his head. "Socrates the Greek was a great thinker. A philosopher. A teacher. He even taught Plato who went on to surpass his influence."

"Is that right?"

"My daddy, aided by strong drink I'm pretty sure, but determined to bring flourish to my arrival in the world, wished that namesake on me. Imagine that." He paused and met Tommy's fixed gaze. "Play again?"

Tommy nodded and they began to set up. George was not your everyday game, Tommy thought. Colored or white, most fellows could play better. That was the first difference. But all the same, George was book smart, smarter than most. "I like that," Tommy said. "That's a fatherly thing to do. Do you think it worked out like he wanted it?"

"My wife does. I'm no Socrates, but she thinks I am. Of course, her hands are full keeping the peace in our home. Flattery helps, Tom. Helps a lot."

Men, mostly white, came and went as the evening wore on. They played whist on Thursdays in pairs at long tables near the bar. On

Thursdays it was rare to see men at the board games near the door, but neither Tommy nor George were whist men. A few of the colored players emerged from the rear tables where they liked to play and waved to Tommy as they passed him on their way out.

George and Tommy played and drank whiskey in silence until Tommy won again. George cursed at the board, then looked up at Tommy and grinned. "Hope you're enjoying yourself, Tom."

"There's worse I could feel, so this will do."

They set up and began to play again.

A thick white man with long bushy sideburns called out to Tommy from behind the bar. "It's past nine o'clock, Tom."

"Your wife?" George asked, eyes twinkling.

"No, sir. Nah, she ain't my wife. That's just BethAnn he talkin' about. She worry about me after a certain time. That's her job. She work for me."

"I see," George said, lowering his eyes on his next carefully crafted move. "You live around here?"

Tommy started to say just where, then thought twice to tell this white stranger details he might later prefer were left out. "Yeah."

"Then that's where I've seen you. I live up on the corner of Newbury and South 18th Street. With my wife. Margaret."

"Know the block and the corner. Know the block, the corner *and* the house, come to think of it." Tommy and BethAnn lived not five blocks away on Apple Street. "That's a magnificent house."

"It is indeed. That house belonged to Margaret's father. Son of a bitch is dead a year now, thank the good Lord, but she's from one of those Louisville families, you understand. Folks did fair to middling. Not Rockefellers, but well enough."

Tommy knew something about the woman's father, his money and how hard it was to get any business from him. He wanted to know more without wanting to say anything. After all, he wasn't willing to say all to be said on his side, so it was only fair to keep that part of the game even. The problem was the whiskey.

"It's her old man's house, I see."

"I never said any such thing, Tom. Said it *belonged* to him. Now it's mine. That's why we came from Nashville."

Tommy let the talk drift and studied the game instead. A few moves later and George was once again backing in and out of the same corner of the board like a trapped roach. "What kinda work you in, George?"

"Funny you should ask, Tom." George's expression brightened into eagerness. "The answer to that one is really what am I *aiming* to do."

Whiskey was obviously having its way in places. "All right, George. What are you aiming to do, come here from Nashville and all?"

George bent over the board and spoke just above a whisper. Tommy leaned forward too. "Hardware, Tom. Hardware store. Right here on Broad Street. Tool leasing. Light contracting." His back straightened up as he spoke, and George confidently covered both of his knees with his palms while staring into Tommy's eyes. "Louisville's never seen anything like what I aim to do. Great big place, aisles full up to the extra high ceilings with shelves stocked, crammed with everything a man and his family needs in a modern city. It'll be grand. Nothing like it. Folks'll come from all over like they got no choice."

Tommy didn't know what to say at first; he was excited although not exactly sure why. "You know, George, colored folks will be glad to see that. Folks got homes and needs, too."

"I want 'em, Tommy. My store'll be their home before they get home."

The last colored fellow was gone except for Tommy. Nothing changed. The Hi-Lo Club had its usual few remaining customers for the hour and a weeknight.

"What's your line of work, my Chinese friend?"

"I keep books."

George hesitated as the words hit the air between them. "How's that? You some kind of librarian?"

"Accounts. Books of accounts. That's what I keep. Bookkeeper."

George didn't appear to understand. "Been doing it for many years. If you'd been around, I'm sure you'd probably heard of me. I do all kinds of businesses, big and small, wholesale and retail, even some individuals. Do them all the same. Down to the decimal."

George looked up at Tommy and his face took on a graven expression. "That, sir, is right fine to hear," he said softly. The look became a meaningful gaze, and George raised his hand to meet Tommy's. "I'd like to shake your hand, Tommy Bookkeeper Lee."

Tommy didn't quite know what to make of George for a minute. In thirteen years at his trade no one had ever reacted this way. Colored men might show a quick wince of pride, but mostly as part of the negotiating process for what portion of Tommy's services they could afford; too much pride could drive up the price. White men never figured, because none had ever called on him in that time. Perhaps none knew, except a few of his white Apple Street neighbors.

Tommy reluctantly reached out and shook George's hand. "It's, uh, your move, I believe."

They played in silence as time passed, time in which the bartender with the long bushy sideburns clanged thick glasses about, time in which Tommy knew BethAnn would be scheming some fit response to his inability to tell it. But he played anyway, unable to pull himself from the unspoken strangeness of the encounter.

"How far'd you go in school?" George asked.

"Well, I quit going reg'lar around the sixth or seventh grade. A fella like you might not know it, but there's lot a man can learn outside the school house walls."

"I won't bore you with the schooling I got, but you never get enough of it. Sooner or later, you gotta teach yourself." He took a drink. "Specially if you're colored." George moved a man and relaxed in his chair. "You're a lucky man."

"I don't feel so, but I'll take what the good Lord give me."

George waved Tommy's words away. "Don't gimme that modesty, Tom. You're quite lucky, 'specially for a colored man." Tommy's ears got ready. "My daddy hardly had money. He taught us about making

something from nothing, that this country could be the g
earth if men like me and my four brothers put our hands to
never quit. Well, that's what my brothers are doing. It's what I would
be doing if I'd had to, but me, I got terribly, terribly lucky. Met a
woman with a dowry, and now I can really make hard work pay off."
Tommy nodded. "But you take a colored man. What's he gonna do
to make hard work pay? I say nothing. Just about nothing when you
really get down to the fact of the matter. Sure, you all can scrape and
scrimp and work your little industry job numbers as long as we'll let
you—you know, fellas like me, as you say—but that can't amount to
much."

Tommy nodded falsely with his eyes on the board. "All the more
reason why most colored gents you meet don't know much about
working hard anymore, if they ever did. I gotta believe you did for a
time when you all were slaves, but the point is the fire ain't in your
bellies. Not in an American way, you understand. Americans are
taking over the world, Tommy, you just watch. Negroes certainly
aren't going to take over the world, now are they?"

Tommy sat motionless. "But see, even a poor country boy like me
can't fault them for that. Not really. Then, all of a sudden, Tommy,
I come across a colored fellow like you, and you know what I see?"
Tommy shook his head and gave the slightest hint of a grin. "I see
luck come to a black man. Changes the whole picture, luck does.
Shows me a whole new kind of workin' fella."

Tommy took George's whole face in with his large brown eyes and
tried to get a fix just beyond the whiskey. But there was no getting
beyond whiskey now, and it was his own fault for pouring it. "I don't
know where you get your information, Mr. Byron, sir, but when it
comes to colored men, you're all wrong."

A long and serious silence set in while both men just watched each
other, two pairs of eyes perched at opposite ends of an axis turning
on a needlepoint. Tommy thought about how nice the weight of a .45
might feel hanging from his pocket just in case; how nice it might
have been to be home already telling half of this to BethAnn.

George let his breath go with a sigh all of a sudden and glanced away. "I truly doubt it, Tom. I've been in this world a little longer than you, I'd say, though surely I'll never be a nigger. But I understand them just the same."

"Well, Mr. Byron, George, sir, on behalf of niggers everywhere, I thank you and have to bid you good night," Tommy said, grabbing his cap and rising from his seat. Lest his abruptness stirred something violent in the drunken white men near him, Tommy added, "It's been a privilege being in your wise company."

Tommy made a step past George and toward the door. "But I admit, I could stand to be wiser, friend," said George.

Tommy stood still as the words hung in the musty air in front of his eyes. As usual, he couldn't resist. "What do you mean, Mr. Byron?"

"Just that maybe I can't quite get into the mind of a black yet, Tom. But I'd like to."

Tommy wanted to laugh. He stepped around to look into George's face. George wasn't clowning the least bit, and you couldn't even tell that he was drunk. "Why?"

"Got my own reasons, Tom. What do you think it would take, huh?" George pushed back the chair and stood a foot or so back from Tommy, who assumed all the eyes of the Hi-Lo Club were on him, all the white eyes remaining. George pressed his hands together like he was praying, but he was making a pointer which came out of his chest at Tommy. "There's a difference between true knowledge and other kinds of facts, you know. I don't care to learn all the little nit-picky details of every street Negro's life, Tommy, but I want that true knowledge at the heart of every colored man."

Tommy felt good crossing his arms in front of the strange drunk white man from Nashville. "Can't be done, George. It takes a lifetime you don't have again, but maybe next time." He tipped his hat and turned toward the door. "I gotta get on."

"Care to wager that I can do it to your satisfaction?"

Tommy turned around with a smile. "I'm a businessman, George. I don't gamble much," he said, which was a lie.

"Let me walk with you," George said, pulling a last ounce of charm from somewhere he'd been hiding it the past half hour.

They hit the cool air and Tommy felt the best thing to do was to walk in the direction of George's home without hesitation, rather than divulge where he lived. The corner of Newbury and South 18th also happened to be on the way to Tommy's home on Apple Street. All the while, block after slow block, George bragged of how he could overcome the barrier of skin to attain this true knowledge as if it were a woman he could figure out a way to get sooner or later.

"But I might need your help, Tommy Lee."

"I don't work for free, George, especially on things that are impossible to do. I charge a premium for the impossible."

"I like that, Tom. You know, I've known many colored gents before, growing up especially. You remind me of a boy I knew in Nashville, Grimes. Grimes was all right. You favor him, Tom." George lost his thought and struggled to get it back. "But, Tom, I have never done business with a nigger before, not once in life."

"Well, you can't reach true knowledge unless you're willing to change a dollar with a man. It's that simple, George."

"You may be right, Tommy."

"This I know, George." They reached the magnificent house at the corner of Newbury and South 18th. A light was on in the window at the top of the long stairs. Tommy was about ready to offer to do the books for George's new business when George spoke first.

"I bet your wife BethAnn cooks some mean collard greens, doesn't she?"

Tommy was by now well past giving George every strange look he deserved, but the last comment nearly earned one anyway. "She's not my wife, and BethAnn's mustards are meaner than her collards— although she's pretty mean about most things."

"Tell you what, Tom. Let's do a little business over these greens of your wife's. That'll start us off. Maybe if we do some business, we'll reach a point when I can tell you why I need true knowledge about you folks."

"She don't cooks cheap, George."

"One dollar, Tommy. That's what you said."

"Ain't gonna buy you much, but we'll see what can be done about your yearning."

"See you six o'clock at Hi-Lo's exactly one week from today. With greens in tow."

"See you there."

THE TURN OF A CENTURY MEANS NOTHING TO THE EARTH; WHEN you've been spinning in the millions, dividing by hundreds adds little to your task. But to the Hooselys from Calico, Alabama, the start of the twentieth century and Louisville, Kentucky, meant the beginning of something maybe. That was enough. Just something maybe. Maybe better than Alabama with its growing Klan mobs, peonage and land shares. Good jobs, complacent soil and maybe more. Beth-Ann Hoosely came from a long line of people who listened to what the Earth foretold. They liked what they heard in Louisville. Louisville at least had white and colored living, if not working, side by side. And it was a city, not more than a half-million feet upon it by 1902 when they all finally arrived there, but expanding, full of unpredictable possibility, rich with maybe. Ten years later, the Hooselys had spread out into the neighborhoods of the southeast part, near the river and the factories where commerce and occasional floods mixed with the Earth.

BethAnn got a good job in a box factory, one of the few women near the staple gun. She made steady money. Nothing she knew about scared her. One day, she met a carpenter named Goody, with strong hands who loved her pretty teeth and begged her to smile for him. The very next day she met Tommy, a little man known cordially at the African Methodist Church, shy and without friends, aimless with a hand tool and real bookish. From the start, Tommy wanted to love her if he could. But she never learned how to love a bookkeeper in Calico, Alabama. She tried out her two suitors for a few months, then she married Goody and moved across town. She stopped coming to church. Tommy would inquire about her to the Apple Street Hooselys, who would give him a polite look of heartache and a promise to pass on his regards. A year later, BethAnn, smile dimmed and teeth missing, returned to the mutual aid society at the A.M.E. where Tommy Lee rediscovered her and picked her up off the Ground she knew so well.

Empty-handed, Tommy entered the well-groomed walk to their neat house, 826, just after ten o'clock that night, stepping a little nervously.

If Tommy was a finger of a man, BethAnn was a leg, strong and thick. Her body stood rigid and defiant across from the front door, a slimmed down buddha with dark crossed arms, pretending to lean on the bannister at the foot of the small staircase. The house was really just a main room, almost square, with two windows facing the street and a sofa and chair in front of them, a table set with four chairs in the middle of the room, a cooking area a few steps from that, and stairs leading up to the small bedroom. BethAnn had assumed the position as she heard him cross the porch. She had great diamond-like eyes set in the center of her round, thick-skinned face, eyes that on good days brought a quick calm and on bad ones a far-off hope. This evening brought neither. When Tommy came inside, the dark circles of her eyeballs searched him with the quivering exactness of cap-gun nozzles taking aim.

"Wait a minute, BethAnn."

"Wait nothing, Tommy. That's what you always say, but we been over this one too many times."

"But this time I knew the time, BethAnn."

"What time is it?"

"It's late. I must be an hour late."

"It's quarter past ten," she said. He nodded and pulled his cap off and put it to his groin, still unwilling to walk all the way into the room. "Go 'head, take off your coat, man. Cain't get no fat back this hour." When Tommy opened his coat, the air trapped against his chest escaped into the room, and BethAnn shooed the sudden odor of alcohol from in front of her nose. "Ughh. Tommy, you stank."

"I'm sorry, BethAnn." His sincere eyes atop his body just so, his arms open a bit, Tommy's apology looked for a minute to her like the approach to a suspension bridge she might cross with adequate incentive. "I know I said I'd be on time and that I'd remember to bring the pork home. I know you worry when I stay too long." She nodded and waited for more. "It was a man I met over at the Hi-Lo Club." That quickly, the chill warmed, and Tommy was back in his own house again. "A white man. Beat him in checkers about forty-two times. Didn't make a dime, though. Strange man, BethAnn. Name's George Byron. Married that snooty gal whose daddy owns the big house at the corner of Newbury and South 18th Street."

"What's so strange about him?"

"Says he's from Nashville."

"Nothing too strange about that."

"Maybe not. Maybe not." Tommy was thinking as much to himself as telling. "He wants to do some business with me."

"What kind of business?"

"Your good cooking is all for now."

BethAnn's feet had had enough. She curled her fist in her apron and sat down in a chair, shaking her head back and forth. "Tommy, sometimes I sure would like to tell you."

"Now don't start to tell me just yet, BethAnn. Wait 'til you hear how I have this figured. This George Byron fella is gettin' set to open a hardware business like nothing Louisville's ever seen before. Big, grand place with aisles stocked with everything a man and his family could need. He thinks folks'll come from every place to shop, and he wants to make it special welcome for colored folks."

"When?"

"When?" Tommy had to look away to answer. "Well, that I don't know for sure actually. He wasn't exact. He wasn't all the way sober neither. Had to walk him home." BethAnn had launched a question in Tommy's head, and she knew it. "That's a good question you ask, darling."

"From time to time I can do that. You should try it."

"The girl's daddy left her some money which this fella Byron is gonna put to use. He don't know nobody here yet, I don't think. If this thing is half as big as he says, it's a full-time job for a bookkeeper. Really wouldn't need no other accounts. I wanna get in and do his books." He waited for her reaction, but BethAnn didn't look up from what she was doing. "He'd be the first white man whose books I ever done, BethAnn."

She turned and found his eyes searching her hopefully. "I'm afraid that ain't so, Tommy." His face dropped into a question. "Four-five years ago you did Kramer's, that moonshiner, and before that you know white bookies been by here."

All this was true. "All right, BethAnn. True enough, I did, but that was practically white folks posin' as colored. This man is talkin' about legitimate business, a company, with company books and plenty of employees. He got plans."

Soon Tommy started eating, while BethAnn just watched. "You'd be some kind of race man then, wouldn't you?"

Tommy started to smile, then back down in bewilderment, then grin cleverly almost, then ask a question. His voice softened to a whisper when he answered her, "Quit that stuff, woman. You're not listenin' to me. Listen now. Doin' business with a guy like that . . ."

"Guy like what, Tommy?"

Tommy scratched his head, but held his composure. "A big shot, BethAnn. Something tells me this guy is a big shot on the way up." BethAnn didn't blink, but she didn't interrupt him either. "You learn a lot about a man playing checkers. He's relaxed, he's drinking. If he's lucky, he's winning too. Down there a man like George is surrounded by his own kind. He's at peace. He doesn't have to play the colored guy, see? If he do, he doesn't have to say a word. But this man was full of talk, BethAnn. Says he's a poor country boy, but he's educated. Couldn't help using big words now and again. That's how they are.

Married that rich gal, didn't he? Chest out like a white man all right, but earnest. Like he's really gonna do all that he come here to Louisville to do." Still, BethAnn refused to interrupt or even to offer a contrary look. "Louisville's gotta be prime for hardware, darlin'. All these folks movin' in? Oil refineries? Factories and railroads?" He sat back, stars in his eyes, a big breath stuck in his cheeks, looking at her. "I aim to keep those books. One day down the road, I aim to reach an understanding with the man."

"Why you, Tommy? Why can't he find some other white fellas like hisself?"

"'Cause he needs me. I think he trusts me. And he's one of them's got fascination for the Negro. It's a good thing for white and colored to make things together, BethAnn."

BethAnn neither agreed nor disagreed with Tommy. But she was skeptical, mostly about the creep of Jim Crow underfoot. Her long relationship with the slow stirrings below, Earth's signals, as it were, plus her accumulated gut feeling from the many miscellaneous opinions she heard from folks along the way to the factory twice a day made Tommy's wish unlikely, whoever George Byron really was. What's more, this could hurt Tommy's business.

"None of that explains why I gotta get cookin'."

"I'm comin' to that, BethAnn. It's just a pot of mustard greens, that's all." He put his fork on his empty plate and dabbed his cheek with his napkin. "That's damn good," Tommy added with a whisper.

"Thank you. No, sir. Count me out, Tommy."

"You gotta do this one, BethAnn, you just plain have to. This one we cain't fuss over."

"We just might anyway. Who for?"

"For this man and his wife, George Byron. We don't have to eat 'em with them, you just have to make them. As good as you can, too."

"It's not my turn, Tommy, and you know it. You know it ain't my turn this time. Especially you coming in here late *and* forget to bring me fat back, fat back I don't have to remind you I use for cookin' *mustard greens*."

Tommy stood up. "Come on now," he muttered. She rose from the table, took his plate and soaked it.

"It's your turn," she repeated under her breath.

TOMMY LEE SOMETIMES WONDERED IF HIS LIFE WAS RUINED THE DAY his mother told him to make a list. He was about twelve years old and nearing the last days before summer. After that there was no more school in a classroom, just items on a piece of paper, usually a list. Had the suggestion never come, perhaps Tommy would have gone and worked at one of the oil refineries in Louisville or in a factory, like BethAnn. Once you learn to write a list, you never stop. Everything you do or think goes on a list, until you die and people come upon all your lists and try to piece you together—what you did, what you thought about, how far you got. Tommy sometimes wondered if the whole list thing was a jinx his mother left for ·him, knowing he could never die, he'd have to go on working, afraid if he lost his breath he'd leave his list for another to finish, like BethAnn. And she'd get it wrong.

But BethAnn sure got the mustard greens right for George Byron. The day of green reckoning had come and gone. Tommy left the house with the pot brimming over, then thought better of what a dollar was getting George, and turned back inside to skim a little off for a late-night snack. When he reached the Hi-Lo Club at just past six o'clock, the pot was still warm and George was waiting. Three days later he even came back with the pot empty and a big smile. The transaction was a great success, he told Tommy. George's wife Margaret loved the mustards and so did he.

Two weeks later, the greens were fading from memory and Tommy was into several new lists when he and George sat back down to a friendly evening game in the Hi-Lo Club. This time it was poker. Tommy was letting George win a no-stakes series of hands, and

George was feeling pretty good about it. He bought the first bottle of whiskey.

"We never did toast to your wife, Tommy, after that good cookin' she did. Whaddya say?" He filled their thick glasses and held his in the air.

Tommy folded his cards into one hand and reluctantly raised his glass with the other. "To mean greens." Tommy then deliberately dropped an ace in exchange for a five of diamonds. He pretended shock when George's two pairs beat him.

"Really can't say too much for the right woman, you know, Tom? Take mine. Margaret is just what she's made of, and no more. She's always trying to get me to put us in a certain place, the place where her daddy—may he rest in hell—put her mother, only better. You must be catching the same from your wife, ain't you, Tom?"

"Well, first off, I think I told you BethAnn ain't my wife. But she do all right."

"Colored women don't bother a man to get 'em a new house, buy a new stove?"

"Oh, sure. Not mine, but most. Most wanna run the house."

The two men kept drinking and Tommy kept losing to the point where George had to tell him he wasn't much of a poker player. Tommy played nervously, almost winning a hand by mistake, distracted by trying to come up with something to draw the hardware plans out of George. "Still think hardware's gonna be a good business, if you start up?"

George's eyes shot straight over his cards at Tommy and held him in an icy grip. Then, just as quickly, it melted. "Not if, Tommy, *when*. When I open."

Tommy sniffed hard and nodded. "All right. Fine enough. When. Yessir." He lay three queens down on the table between them. "When you think you gonna open, George?"

George sipped his whiskey, seeing the queens in the clear above the edge of the glass and his own sorry pair of jacks distorted through the bottom of it. He dropped his cards for Tommy to pick up and decided not to answer right away. Another moment passed before George upped and said, "America is a great country." Tommy figured this was the point in the conversation when George would reveal that he was drunk. It seemed to be a pattern. "Isn't it?" George asked.

"Compared to what?" Tommy asked without delay.

George squinted and his face looked shocked at Tommy. As Tommy looked into George's eyes, he realized at that moment that his were so green that you could imagine them full of tears at any minute—including that one.

"Take your goddamn pick!" George bellowed up from his long, thin throat. "Any country. Pick one of them little ones in the Caribbean or the Pacific that we're eating up everyday, Tommy, or don't you read the newspapers. I mean, damn, boy, you know this country can't be beat." Tommy listened impassively. George looked back down at the hand just dealt him. "This is a *helluva* country."

The good Earth below the Hi-Lo Club suddenly began to rock ever so slightly. It picked a point in the dark corner behind the bar, a pipe actually, and moved no more than an inch. It started so many miles down under that Tommy and George, certainly in the whiskeyed state they were in, could not have felt it. But it did.

Tommy didn't feel the Earth change, but something made him think about the time. He didn't need the bartender to remind him that the hour was getting on toward BethAnn's worst mood. He remembered a list in his pocket and reached for it. It was a list of things he and BethAnn agreed they would buy that week. He promised to do the buying. That's how it went with Tommy. One minute he's sitting playing cards, the Earth moves, then he thinks of the time and he consults a handy list. Thanks to his mother.

George suddenly looked up from the game, fascinated instead by the crumpled paper in Tommy's hand. "What's that there?"

"Just a list. Some things I gotta do before—"

"Excuse me, Mr. Lee," George interrupted and leaned forward with a deepening smile. "You, you're the first colored man I ever knew to keep a list. I didn't think y'all did that."

Here was Tommy's opening, and yet he faced it with such absolute mockery for the white man across the table that he almost couldn't bring himself to walk through it. So, he paused long enough to savor the image of George's face with the words still in it. "This," he announced, "is another reason why you'll never know how negroes think, George. Sorry to tell you, but I must."

"Just what if you ain't a normal nigger, Tommy? I mean, not too many fellas like yourself down here at the Hi-Lo. Most of your kind plays a much better hand of poker than you've got in you. The average colored man loves this country. *Loves* it—as well he should, case you ever wondered about life swinging from trees. Ask any of 'em and they'll tell you. Plus, you're lucky as sin, *keepin' books* all day instead of out breakin' your back. Worst of all, you make lists, for crying out loud, Tommy. If your wife didn't cook greens so good I'd tell you to stop trying to be a white man!"

They burst into loud laughter again, this time on the same count, and all the men around them looked over with a smile to see if they could catch a little piece of what's funny. Tommy won the next hand.

"It's gettin' hard on you, Tommy," George added sympathetically. "Maybe all you folks ought to start keeping lists, tell you where you can and can't go." Tommy just listened to the whiskey flow from George's thoughts. "Jim Crow, you know, Tommy?" George leaned back in his chair and lit a cigarette, which made him squint again. Tommy just nodded. "Even in Louisville, which if you asked me, an old Nashville boy, was too close to Indiana to get into the segregation act. But it's going. Just like Indianapolis did, Tom. Same as Indy. So get you a list so you can know which doors to come into and which exits to leave out of." George laughed again. Tommy just listened patiently.

"You should consider startin' your books early, George, even before you open for business. Long before. Get it straight early and you'll never be late and you'll never wonder."

George didn't hear him. "Lists is what kills most men, Tommy, so watch out. Andrew Carnegie doesn't make lists anymore. There was a day when he had to, when he was just starting out. But a successful businessman leaves the list-keeping business to others as soon as he can."

This was the moment, Tommy concluded, and it had crossed the table wrapped softly inside a smoke ring. "Then why don't you leave the books to me, George? That's what I do. I could reconcile your lists whiles you become the Andrew Carnegie of the hardware trade."

"Hmm," was all George said, smiling, eyes on his cards. He dragged long on his cigarette and exhaled in a series of separate puffs of smoke through both nostrils. "Those lists will make you edgy." He studied his hand. George won the next hand easily despite the fact that Tommy didn't let him, Tommy specifically planned to win it himself, and Tommy had three kings. George had three aces. Tommy just stared at the cards. "How 'bout a dog?"

"Say what?"

"How 'bout we do some business over a puppy instead, Tommy? Hounds. Man's best friend. Bitch just gave birth to five little cute ones. You can have first pick. They're out at my house. We can go over there right now, and I'll have Margaret bring the litter out onto the porch. Do it for a dollar."

THE SPRING CAME AND WENT. THE PUPPY DIDN'T LAST EVEN THAT long in BethAnn's house. As soon as it grew old enough to recognize that it was being ignored, it ran away. Louisville had lots of things for a dog to do. Meanwhile, the Ground thrashed up new signals and warnings of its subterranean discontent with the order of things above it. Each change seemed minor standing alone. But large rocks a whole avenue long slowly moved up to where soft soil once was. Trees curled and certain weeds invaded. Over a short period, an insect problem as never before struck, then mysteriously settled in people's minds as being at normal levels. Even the weather started to sour, becoming less temperate, but not swiftly enough to be detected. Louisville simply began to lose favor with the Earth, but the residents, other than a few like BethAnn, never quite caught on. They were busy with what was happening at eye level. Jim Crow was cutting paths in life itself, every year a new this or that. It looked like Tommy might soon have to give up his office, because the buildings around his began changing the rules, not allowing colored and white businesses in the same walls. Little things and big things. Big like having to pick up your whole business. Little like not using rest rooms anymore or nodding hello. Fewer nods couldn't be good. And color-coded as it was, the Ground got topsy turvy.

BethAnn was deeply bothered, but Tommy could not be. She started to hate Tommy's visits to the Hi-Lo Club all the more. He always came home with the latest little deal, none of them making him look particularly shrewd. She developed a personal embarassment about it, which she didn't always hide well. Yes, Tommy could get George to buy guide books from him, things the small businessman needs to know about the city. He even sold him maps. Each deal for about a dollar, sworn to over whiskey, delivery over weeks. But he would never get George's bookkeeping business, she knew. And she didn't believe they were friends. She didn't think they could be.

But Tommy knew George was full of games he liked to play with somebody. Rather than a worry, it was the glue between them. The only doubt that gripped Tommy, the part he couldn't quite figure out, was George's wanting to learn from him how colored folks think. George might mention it in conversation, but then quickly change the subject. Or George would ask a question and Tommy would get cagey with the answer. He was never quite sure what kind of answer George wanted, but whatever it was he couldn't reveal everything. If he gave up all his goods, he'd have nothing left to bargain with once the store opened. So, Tommy might think about one of George's questions for a few days and come back with a new angle, like giving George general information about what Negroes seemed to spend their time doing in Louisville when white folks weren't watching. But George wasn't as interested in that, so the doubt would just linger.

And gnaw. The doubt got especially gnawsome after a deal that had Tommy buying a pair of George's used boots. Cowboy boots.

Worn only a few times the autumn before. George said they were half a size too small, but his wife Margaret gave them to him and at first he had to wear them. Tommy had never owned a pair of cowboy boots. George proposed the sale around the time he and Tommy had turned to chess. Chess is a slow game, and it gave Tommy a long time to think about the cowboy boots. In fact, it was over several days. By the time he finally saw them, he didn't see them. Tommy only saw what he had imagined them to be from George's descriptions, and he had grown fond of that. So fond that he bought them, fifty cents per boot, even though he and George Byron wore exactly the same size, even though the boots were a half size too small for him.

Which at times didn't matter. The feeling of tightness in the boots could mix nicely with urgency, like getting George's account one day. He might be somewhere in those boots, the tightness would squeeze him, he would look down at the pointy toes, feel the pain, admire the leather, and remember the future. Yet at other times, the cowboy boots looked ridiculous. Just the thought of them reminded Tommy how much he knew about white folks, indeed how much George taught him. And it was pitiful. Wearing things just to appease your wife. All the patriotic boasts about America. Trying to turn his ignorance about the black into philosophy. A sucker at every game he tried. But earnest. As earnest as those boots. He felt a little sorry for him. While Tommy knew so much about how whites thought, George was too busy to know anything in return. He only hoped that George wouldn't discover how little he'd learned before Tommy got his hardware store account. So, from time to time, Tommy would give George some hard accounting advice he could make use of.

"I don't know what method of inventory accounting you was planning on, George, but if you ask me, a business like yours needs first in, first out. Depends on things, but that'd be the best most likely."

But George wouldn't go for the cues like "depends on things," and ask what things or why, or seem interested or grateful for more than a minute. So, all the thoughts Tommy might have in private about

George's welfare and his hopes of a role in his success were no more than scrip, notions he couldn't trade anywhere or get a nickel for. So, he stopped wearing the cowboy boots.

NEXT THING YOU KNOW THERE'S A WAR IN EUROPE, A *WORLD* WAR.

"Know how many knots per kilometer a U-boat can travel?" George asked Tommy one evening over a match.

Tommy looked hard at him, watched the smoke clear gradually from in front of his eyes. George, it occurred to him in that moment, looked just like the squinty-eyed Lucky Strike man on the cover of the *Saturday Evening Post*. Tommy occasionally stole glances there, but he was not much one for news in the newspapers. "Nope."

George pretended he'd gone back to the game and studied the board for a few moments. After a while, he startled Tommy with a stern look, "What do you think about this war."

"I think we ain't in it," Tommy answered. "Not the coloreds, anyway."

"That may be, Tom," he said, exasperated, "but y'all make out OK, seems to me. Stay behind and get the jobs, keep the work going and move into the houses."

Tommy couldn't understand where George found his edge all of a sudden and laughed nervously. "I'm not too ready to thank the Germans for all that just yet."

IN OPEN DISREGARD FOR THE RUMBLINGS OF THE EARTH, BROAD Street underwent extreme changes in its character and hue. By the spring of 1914, even the Hi-Lo Club stopped admitting Negro customers. The residential streets flowing into the thoroughfare markedly brightened, as colored neighbors were gently purged by a ground swell of unwelcomeness. They didn't leave the city altogether but moved around town. The races made a game of it, the one hopping over the other and taking over a row of boxes according to the rules of an invisible grid. Like checkers, what was black got blacker, and what was nice got whiter.

Along the way, Tommy was forced to move his offices when his lease ran, which cost him any remaining hope of walk-in white customers, big or small. To his surprise, Jim Crow didn't ruin him because it also had the effect of enlarging his exposure within the Negro business community. He did not prosper, but he did not fail. He stayed stable, which to a man in his line of work meant the same as growing slowly. This fit his plans. Indeed, none of it contradicted the imminent possibility of getting George's business. When the dust settled on Louisville's dislocations, Tommy faithfully believed that he and George would proceed. People spoke of the shifts and turns as corrections, gradual and probably for the best. This order of things would prevent trouble before it could happen. Yet, between George and Tommy, there was no trouble to fear. Only the hope of progress.

George made it so. It was clear from the increasing size of the transactions he proposed. It was there in the way he consulted Tommy about where to actually put the store. And unmistakably, it was George who invited Tommy for friendly games right on his back porch after the Hi-Lo closed to them—even with Margaret's hostile shadow marching in angry heels inside the house. In early July 1914, Tommy finally met her in the person. Margaret was even less descript than he remembered her when she used to stroll beside her father as a girl. Now she barely satisfied Tommy's image of a wealthy man's daughter. She was tall and on the thin side, with very pasty skin, dark blonde hair that curled tightly at the sides of her face, and even more so than her husband, thin eyes and thin lips unsoftened by flesh. No sooner had he tipped his cap to her than Tommy forgot her features, which later confounded BethAnn's curiosity. All he could tell her was that Margaret left the distinct impression of a person with zero fondness for Negroes and who quickly disappeared after the introduction.

"I need information from you," George told him that day. Tommy was about to set up the chess pieces for a second game after defeating his host. George waved him to wait. "Hold on there a second to consider the proposition." Tom folded his hands together and sat up on the bench. "I can't say exactly what it's worth." Tommy grew instantly intrigued. "But I need you to find out for me where colored folks in Louisville go for their hardware needs. Where do they go and what don't they like about it? That's all. Oh, and machine tools. Would they lease machine tools?"

"Who from, George? From you?"

"That's who."

"You might need to look into the law to see if you're able."

George hadn't thought of that, but instantly disagreed. He knew for a fact that white businesses could still sell anything they wanted to Negroes, not always *when* they wanted, but they could—as long as they had what he called the know-how. "You just get me some of this know-how, and I'll figure out the rest."

"You need *me* for that? I thought you knew all there is to know about colored folks."

George didn't appreciate the remark at all. He fixed a stare on Tommy that rose with him out of the chair. When he stood back and crossed his arms, the stare became a glare, from which Tommy took a brief leave and surveyed the backyard. He intended his comment. He had not forgotten, even if George pretended to. "I'd been considering the possibility of hiring a good colored man to handle my sales to y'all if that's what the law says I gotta do."

Tommy didn't know what the law said, he didn't know about selling hardware to George's Negro customers one day, and he didn't care either. "None of that concerns me, George. But this information is gonna be tricky to get. Come back over here and we'll have us this game. By the time we finish I'll come up with a good price for the job."

They played. Tommy was awful, but that was OK with him because he was busy counting in his head. The game passed quicker than usual. George might have smirked at his gains but for the knowledge that his advantage resulted from Tommy devising his own.

"When you need it, George?"

"Right away. Two weeks. No, one week. One week."

"*One week?* All right, twenty dollars."

"*Twenty dollars!?* Are you mad, boy? You could do this in your leisure time, can't you?"

Leverage was precious in that moment, because even though Tommy knew that twenty dollars was quite a sum, he knew George had it and would part with it. So, Tommy's face never moved.

That night, both Tommy and BethAnn wondered about leisure time. The truth was, they admitted, neither really knew what it was, not the way you *know* something, which was good for a laugh at bedtime, and in Tommy's case, it made for a good night's sleep too. Long after his breaths turned to snores, BethAnn imagined that leisure time must have resembled time at the Hi-Lo Club.

THE INFORMATION TOMMY COLLECTED FOR GEORGE MUST HAVE DONE the trick, because George finally opened his hardware store and equipment-leasing business on the first Monday of September, 1914, right there on Broad Street. They called it Byron's Wares and Leasing Co. in large white letters nicely done. In fact, everything about George's grand opening was nicely done, both of them. He had one for the general public and another one two days later specially for colored folk. There was a band in front of the store and circulars full of specials and discounts that teenage boys handed out to people passing by on the street. Tommy joined a group of colored men in the back of the crowd that gathered that day to enjoy the festivity of a sure-fire looking business and partake of a little free food. He was anonymous then, looking in from the rear, chicken wing in his hand, just as BethAnn expected he would be if this moment ever came.

Byron's Wares and Leasing Co. quickly reinvented hardware in Louisville. Snappy advertising and regular discount days made it a popular name in all quarters. Even the serious jobber or carpenter was well served by his equals at the lowest price around. But it was the love of colored folks that crushed the competition. Especially Negro women. George made sure that everywhere they went, his store was mentioned kindly. He stocked goods only a Negro merchant would, dressed up the Negro sales window as special as the white and hired handsome Negro clerks. For coloreds, it was tools and much more, a general store with provision for special shopping hours where folks might catch up with each other over anything from a box of nails to hair-relaxing lye. Word was, George Byron was a friend of the Negro, and they devoted their dimes in return.

One day, some weeks after the opening, George invited Tommy in alone after closing. It was his first hard look around. The clerks that day, all of them white, silently went about their work. The place was grand, many hundreds of square feet wide with every kind of tool and knickknack a man could need if he wanted to do some serious building. It even had aisles, three of them, just as George promised.

"You hit it on the head about colored customers, Tommy," George explained from behind a Lucky Strike outside the stock entrance in the back. Tommy smoked one with him. They took long drags together, sending squalls of smoke in separate directions. "Remember that bet we had way back before the war? 'Bout whether I could learn how the black man thinks?" Tommy nodded, his heart picked up and he let the cigarette fall to his side. George smiled. "'Member I told you one day I'd let you in on why I needed that particular wisdom?" Again Tommy nodded. "I don't think I need to tell you now, do I? I must know something 'bout him or you wouldn't be seeing every coon in Louisville lining up to empty these shelves on payday, now would you? My game, Tom. I won."

George's tight face was no match for the excitement behind it, and loud laughter escaped in all directions. He gently swatted Tommy on the arm, but Tommy just absorbed the blow. "But it couldn't be done without you."

"You saying I showed you how?"

"In a matter of speaking, Tom. That's just what you did."

Tommy soaked quietly in the moment, staring at nothing, nodding gently, taking long drags on the butt. Sometimes words welled up inside long enough elude time when they finally leave your lips.

"It's about time you hire me to do your books," Tommy calmly declared. Such words possessed that air. Had George gone on to raise the subject? Had other words preceded those? Who knows. "I think you need me to do your books now after all these months you and me been talking around it."

The response, unless it's yes, has a way of getting lost, too. "How could you think such a . . . Well, to tell you the truth . . . I had something else in mind. Don't want you to think I forget my friends. Tom, I need a Negro salesman."

"I'm no salesman, George, I'm a bookkeeper, probably the best at any price you'll find. And a businessman. Now, ever since you and me been doin' deals and all and tryin' to get you some true knowledge, so you say, I've had to think about my trade jes like you been plannin' yours." George looked almost hurt in a squinty-eyed way. "I don't mean I don't enjoy keepin' company and, you know, frittin' time on a game here and there. But all the same it seems only right to me that you let me work on your books and don't string me along any further."

George drew sharp. "Are you trying to tell me my business, Tom?"

"You know your business, George. That much is plain to see. But did you know first in, first out when you was plannin' how to do your inventory? *I'm* the one been givin' you that advice for free."

"Nigger, you *are* telling me my business."

"No, George, I'm remindin' you about a deal you oughtta keep." Even Tommy wasn't sure what he meant by that. He wasn't sure all of a sudden where such words might land him with George Byron, but they seemed true enough, whatever they meant.

George paced in a semicircle back and forth around Tommy, trapping him against the wall where he stood without expression. "We never had no deal. Every deal we had was clear from the git. I never promised to let a nigger do my books. Are you crazy, Tom?"

"What's fair is fair, George, and you know it even if you won't admit it."

George was truly aghast, close to exceeding the range of any mood he'd shown Tommy before. He paced some more and found a way to calm down, but it wasn't easy. "Tom, you're an intelligent man, a lucky man, and, yes, you've stood by me. I appreciate that and I'll go to my grave with gratitude. Your kind is loyal. I mean that, Tom. A little kindness and you all sign right up. *You* showed me that. But there is an order to things, I'm sure you've noticed, a natural order of things."

The moment needed to be harnessed, but his own body bucked uncooperatively. George jerked a little and squinted, as if he were trying to read from a script whose words his eyes couldn't make out. "We see this order every day in this fine country. It's no less than progress really. I joined it, with the aid of luck and industry and the best idea first, and here you see what it brought me." He stopped pacing to throw a stiff index finger in Tommy's face. "But don't lose sight too quickly, Tom. Admit what you know. When the white man, the man who's making this country for the good of us all, when that man says you, the Negro, can come on, it means you go second after him. You don't go first. You don't tie for first. If you're allowed to go, Tom, you make damn sure and go *second*. That's the natural order of things. You might even think of it as the secret to a long life." He smiled warmly and winked. "Trust me, my friend. For me to let you do my books, well, that's like you walking in *beside* me. That wouldn't be right. That'd be like lettin' you live in my house and have my wife." George laughed through a peerless smile.

Tommy looked at the Ground, which didn't move or speak. "Now, I will tell you this. Me and Margaret been thinkin' 'bout buying the proper house. She wants to move out of the one her daddy left her, and I told her we would if the business keeps up. I suspect there might be some work in doing those numbers, the ones for the sale, not much but some. Whaddya say you think about helpin' me out with the sale if everything works out?"

TOMMY AGREED. IT WAS ALL THAT REMAINED, FOOLED BY PROGRESS. Although George proved an able hardware man, he had been reasoning with more whiskey than wisdom during the bookkeeping parts of his conversations with Tommy. He'd thought of everything but. By the end of six successful months in business, George realized he needed some additional help with the books. When he opened up, George had retained the services of a full-scale accounting firm, a downtown establishment with a high-post reputation. It was the kind of choice that put him in rare company, but it also set him back. They charged for even the smallest things. So, George did what suddenly seemed obvious to him: he threw Tommy some work. And with the stunning realization of a piece of long-time hope come true, a break for Tommy, a testament to tight boots, a rejection of omen, even BethAnn had to suspend her old doubts.

Just as she did, the Earth under Louisville took a most unusual turn. It quaked. The tremor was so faint many missed it entirely. George did. Tommy thought he might have possibly heard the suggestion of something shifting maybe slightly from the norm. BethAnn knew it unmistakably. It came in response to the city's passage of a special Jim Crow ordinance several months back. Over weeks it built and built into an earthquake. The ordinance said that from the time it went into effect until perpetuity is final, every street in Louisville would be designated white or colored for purposes of who gets to live there. If a street like Apple where Tom and BethAnn lived had a majority colored folks on May 11, 1914 when it went into effect, then it would be a colored street from then on. If the street had a majority white like South 18th where George's house fronted, it would henceforth be white. What would happen to a corner house like his, where the cross-street, Newbury, was Negro, that part wasn't perfectly clear. But the rule had come down. It didn't matter who *owned* the place, just who could reside there. There would be no new mixing between the races, and after enough time had passed, there'd be no such thing as a mixed street at all. Anybody who sold against the rule would pay a stiff fine. The law even created jobs for new building inspectors to check into the order of things.

With the ordinance and each sale of a house or building since it was adopted, the Earth truly rolled over itself. Contracts rendered in its name, families fretting, leaving, losing value in the interest of Order, well, the Earth felt lied to and could not adjust.

If the Earth was frustrated, it wasn't alone. Tommy, who never even heard of the ordinance, was mad that his account with George amounted to peanuts—smoked peanuts, not even regular peanuts. George hired Tommy to do the colored accounts only. Even those Tommy had to square with the downtown firm, scramble across town to check with them and answer *their* questions. They treated him like a bug. As it was, Tommy made more money off of his Negro accounts, which were increasing in the colored quarters where he was known.

George too was frustrated, though not because Byron's Wares and Leasing Co. was fast becoming a Louisville legend. For years the city had been growing. As businesses grew, the population increased. More people meant more houses. Roofs had to stay fixed, doors had to lock, windows had to shut and so forth. The only problem was George's own household—more particularly, his own magnificent house on the corner of Newbury and South 18th. He couldn't sell it.

Tommy learned all about it on a visit *he* decided to make to George's house. That never happened before. In all the months of games and deals, each meeting had always come about at George's invitation. This time, ready to quit over the puney account he'd been keeping, Tommy came calling.

"Just the man I need to see!" George said, greeting Tommy at the door and leading him by the shoulder around to the back. Perhaps the occasional handshake, but Tommy was unaccustomed to the feel of George's touch. "I got a little problem, and I think you might be just the man to help me out of it."

George had spread out a bunch of papers on the card table on the back porch. It was the ordinance and some other things.

"Can I get you something to drink, Tom?" Tom looked a little warily at George and nodded. "Be right back. Tell ya what. Read this page here while I'm gone." George thrust a densely worded page at him. Its edges were wrinkled like worn skin.

The title was "An Ordinance to Prevent Conflict and Ill-Feeling Between the White and Colored Races in the City of Lousiville and to Preserve the Peace." George had pointed to the second part, which said:

> It shall be unlawful for any white person to move into and occupy as a residence, place of abode, or to establish and maintain as a place of public assembly, any house upon any block upon which a greater number of houses are occupied as residences, places of abode, or places of public assembly by colored people than are occupied as residences, places of abode or places of public assembly by white people.

George came back out to the porch carrying a glass in each hand. "That damn thing's what's keeping me from sellin' my own house, Tom! I mean, in't it? In't that what they say there? That I got a colored block?" George was red in the chest and getting that way in the neck. Outrage widened his eyes wider than Tommy had ever seen them.

Tommy kept reading. George paced. The paragraph before that one said the same thing, only for colored people not moving into a white block. Tommy scratched his head, took a sip of the drink George had set down for him and said, "South 18th ain't no colored street."

George was incredulous and red. "What? Of course it is!"

Tommy pointed to the page. "See, right here is where it says what a block is and how you know if it's supposed to be colored or white. It says, 'In determining the boundary of any given block—'"

"*I* know what it says there!" George yelled. "Don't you talk law down to *me*!"

"Well, show me the problem then, George. I musta missed it."

George grabbed the paper from the table in front of Tommy and started to mash it in his hands. He looked down at the words then quickly away, hoping Tommy wouldn't catch it. But Tommy caught it just before it escaped. It was none other than shame on George's face. George hadn't read that part, because he couldn't read that good.

"It's one thing to read Socrates, quite another to make sense of garble," George said, unable to retract the grin his nervous lips gave up.

Time stood still for Tommy as he sat with the realization and George's back to him. He wondered how all this could be. He wondered where George's talk of books and world events and things had come from if he couldn't understand the print.

"Real-estate agent tells me the same thing. I figure yer both wrong. You gotta be."

Tommy stood and walked to one end of the porch and looked out across the back of Newbury Street. "I haven't done no count, but I reckon Newbury Street could be colored." Tommy counted on his fingers, checking the identity of each house in his head. "That's right. Colored. Oh," he paused. "I see. George, your problem is this magnificent house sits right at the crossroads of white and colored blocks. Isn't that some luck? You on the border."

The shock on George's face was unshakeable. "Goddamn your eye! Damn it! Damn it to hell!" Slowly his steely look returned above a smirk forming. "Needless to say, Tom, when Margaret hears it, she's gonna be very upset with your people for ruining her chance of getting the only want she has left in this world."

Tommy snorted, adjusted his cap and turned for the stairs. He didn't even look at George. As he passed he said, "Make sure she's upset about all that business we been givin' y'all, too."

"What?" George screamed. "What'd you say, boy, I didn't quite catch that?"

But by then Tommy had made his way back out to South 18th Street.

A THING THAT MEANS NOTHING SUDDENLY BECOMES A MAINSTAY AS soon as you're introduced to it. No introduction, no matter. But once Tommy heard about the ordinance, he kept hearing about it. And talking about it. Not to George though. He wasn't even interested in George's books in the weeks that passed after the insult. No, Tommy talked with BethAnn about it. She had her ear to what changes the ordinance brought to the men and women down at the box factory. She heard the Ground toss and falter beneath their feet, as mere mortals presumed they could rectify the natural order of things.

George thought better of his way with Tommy. After a few days, he regained his cool. After a few weeks, he sort of missed him. And Margaret laid into him for what he did. More than anyone else, she was the reason George found reasons to make up with Tommy. In fact, it was her idea to invite Tommy Lee and BethAnn for dinner at the magnificent house itself.

BethAnn didn't want to go and dragged herself bitterly, almost to the minute. She believed that if Tommy was truly offended by this white man who was supposed to be his friend, he ought to have no trouble turning him and his wife down.

"I'll tell him," was all Tommy would answer. "I'll tell him in my own way."

They arrived in Sunday clothes at six P.M. sharp. Behind the pleasantries and greetings, nothing made sense right away. Margaret's smile was quick and timely and false. BethAnn was not charming and found herself rocking on her toes a lot. The house was magnificent, full of detailed appointments that George said were Margaret's touches and hobbies, her pride. George would point things out, reflecting on her good taste. Tommy would politely agree. But Margaret refused to tell the story about each item when George asked her to. BethAnn, after marveling momentarily to herself at the cost of it all, wouldn't speak and thought Maragaret's taste was awful. Nothing connected. Tommy and George were not friends. Margaret and BethAnn were not interested. BethAnn and Tommy were not supposed to be there. Even the men couldn't pretend.

So, they broke bread. The table was a rectangle covered with multiple settings. George and Margaret occupied the long ends, while Tommy and BethAnn sat at the sides. George began to talk loudly and incessantly. He interrupted every private thought in each of their heads. He besieged them with banter and encouraged everyone to just eat. But as they ate food Margaret had prepared in a form much drier and blander than either of her guests were accustomed, there would be momentary silences.

"I know George has something he would like to discuss with Mr. Lee." Margaret said. That meant the meal was done. "We gave the servants the night off." That meant Margaret expected BethAnn to help her clear the plates. But BethAnn desperately did not want to; her desire to stay by Tommy was bigger than her curiosity about how the kitchen looked. Besides, BethAnn was a factory hand, not a domestic. Margaret stood up. "Shall we bring you gentlemen some tea?"

They all had tea, but it was only to hear whatever George was going to say. BethAnn returned to her chair as soon as the tea cups were on the table. She and Tommy shared an unmistakeable observation in one small glance: These folks meant business.

"Tommy, I'll get right to the point. You know that I've encountered a might difficulty selling this magnificient house of mine. You're the one saw the ordinance with me. You and I go back some ways now. I credit you for giving me knowledge I could use in doing business here in Louisville and it's been a very profitable one." He paused to make sure everybody was in the right spot. "Well, Tom, Margaret and I have got to leave this place, and I want *you* to buy it from me. I think you and BethAnn should have this magnificent house."

BethAnn's hand shook and spilled the hot tea on a forgotten finger below, which in turn made her snatch her hand back. With all the eyes upon her she smiled in embarassment, but once smiling she launched into a giggle. Tommy couldn't hold back a little snort either. Their hosts were not amused.

"George, there's just one problem," Tommy told him politely. "We colored."

"Ordinance don't say nothin' about owning," said George. "As a colored man, Tom, you got the same right as a white to buy this house from under me. And I know you, you wiser than most white men and would know to give me the right price." Margaret shot George a look that plainly sought a little forbearance with the facts.

BethAnn was overcome by a feeling and stared hopefully at Tommy across the table. His brow was furroughed and he rocked the tea remaining in his cup back and forth. She loved him. It was crazy, but that was it. In this light, among these people, everything about Tommy was suddenly very agreeable to her. A cleverness in his eyes. The shine on his cheeks. His hairline. BethAnn had never seen her man play cards before.

"True enough," Tommy said. He wanted to know what kind of price George had in mind; George stammered and tossed out a figure that was entirely too high. Tommy's eyes only briefly looked up from his cup to see what Margaret was doing with her face, then returned to the tea. George said that was the real-estate agent's price, but naturally he thought that too high. Tommy agreed and said, "No matter. According to the ordinance, if a colored man was to buy, you probably won't find a real-estate agent who'd handle the particulars anyway."

"We never needed no go-between before, Tommy."

"Yes, sir, we did. When you hired that accounting firm to do books for you—"

"Aw, Tom—"

"They is a go-between for business you and me shoulda done directly."

"What are you tellin' me?"

"I'm sayin' I'm wonderin' how you expect you can sell me this house without a go-between now."

"'Cause it's my goddamned right as an American, that's why!" He slammed his fist down on the table, making BethAnn look down at the table and scoot back in her chair. Tommy thought about moving, but he didn't. "Excuse my language, ladies. But, Tom, there's a constitution out there says I got the right to do with my property whatever I want. Can't no one tell me who or when or why I can or can't sell my own house! Can't make it so I can't sell to the highest bidder, can't make white men walk away from here, turn away decent buyers. Can't do that! I won't stand for it, Tom. I'd sooner die than let that happen in this country."

To BethAnn, George's rage could make the floor shake. She heard Calico, Alabama, in his tone, his sure-fire outrage, and immediate alarm. His voice echoed to the beams above and hung like a threat in the air. Used to expect certain trouble when you were within earshot of a white man so mad, she recalled. Now, she just listened and kept her eyes on her own man, who sat firmly in the middle of the rage. She glanced occasionally at inanimate fixtures in the background, the stairwell partly visible in the hall, the thick panes of the windows, and the soft cushions of the seats, the chandelier, the great mantle, and what seemed like a lifetime's worth of detail. Such a magnificent rage could only be perfected inside such a magnificent house.

"I would like to buy this house from you, George," said Tommy cooly. Margaret's expression deepened in her eyes. George's redness pinkened and paled slightly. BethAnn's heart stopped. "There's lots to consider, need to talk things over with BethAnn here. Might want to look around some more. But, as you know, I'm a businessman. This house is only good to me if'n I can live in it. Ownin' doesn't make me no difference but to walk by and admire the thing empty. You at least, maybe you can't sell it, but you can live in it. I ain't buyin' nothin' I can't live in. That's what needs to be thought through."

"Would that be the only obstacle?" Margaret asked.

Tommy almost stammered. "I mean no disrespect, ma'am, but next to death the law is about as big an obstacle as they get."

She did not smile with him. "I understand. It's just that George and I need to move on."

BethAnn felt it would be polite to add something. "Tommy tells me y'all have your sights on a larger house."

"It's not the size so much," Margaret answered matter of factly. "It's the neighborhood." BethAnn strained to look like she understood, but she didn't. "This area has changed since I grew up here—"

"My wife's in a family way."

"—There's more mixing than is due," Margaret added without looking at anyone.

Slowly, as if paced by the rotating Earth itself, BethAnn slid back in her chair, bowed and turned her face in the general direction of Tommy. That's not so, Tommy wanted to say. Maybe for you. But we used to mix even more. He never said that.

"I don't mind sayin' this with the ladies present, Tom. I'm gonna have us a contract of sale drawn up."

"Have you got a lawyer?" Tommy asked.

George looked irritated, then shrugged. "I do. Of course I do."

"We gonna need one."

"How's that? I thought you didn't want any go-betweens."

"'Cept that we fittin' to break the law, and you the one bent on fighting for your rights."

George sat back and squinted into his hands for a minute. He had not quite thought this through, though he was not inclined to share that fact with Tommy, certainly not in front of their wives. "I'll look after it."

"I just need one right for myself now, George."

"What's that, Tom?"

"Make sure you tell him the Negro won't buy unless the Negro can live in the house."

George reached out his hand, and they shook on it. BethAnn and Margaret pretended to smile at each other.

"That Washington fellow has nothing on you," Margaret said, speaking of Booker T. Washington. "You are a credit to your race, Mr. Lee."

OUT ON THE STREET, BETHANN'S REACTION WAS SIMILAR IN A WAY. "You a true race man now, ain't you."

Tommy stopped and looked over his shoulder. "Not really, Beth-Ann. Ain't no way we ever gonna buy that house."

BethAnn realized she must have been playing in a game up until then. She stopped playing. She wanted that house. She wanted to come down those stairs and go up to wherever they led. She wanted to cook in that kitchen and lift heavenly voices to those high ceilngs. Stand warm inside those windows and look out, stand tall against that mantle and look at the fire, she wanted to marry Tommy in that house. "Can't afford it?"

"Oh, I suspect we could. You know, business has been so good since all these changes. That house is big enough—I could work right out of it and wouldn't need no office."

"Then what is it?" she pleaded, unable to hide her desire.

"Law won't allow it, BethAnn. And even if it did, that man can't find no lawyer to help him. They 'fraid of the law more'n anybody. They the ones who understand why."

BethAnn walked in silence, staring ahead at the familiar yards on Apple Street, hating each and every one. "What about them new lawyers for colored peoples we heard talk of at church? The ones just started out here. The association or something."

"National Association of Advancing Colored Peoples?"

"Them."

Tommy laughed. "Naw, darlin' that'll never work on George Byron. Most of them lawyers I hear is colored. George don't want to do no business with colored men."

BethAnn kept walking, wishing there was a way, hoping to stretch the blocks into miles in order to come up with something. Tonight she had discovered two wishes in one at the same time she discovered Tommy's cunning with somebody other than herself. Tommy was gonna string George along right back for all the stringing he did to him, and he knew it would be a long ride. Only it would mean stringing her along too, which is really how it all began between

Tommy and her seven years ago. Him in love with her, her never quite ready, stringing him along. BethAnn decided to go with Goody, the other man, the one from the mutual aid society where they met, a man larger than Tommy by many pounds and inches, a man who beat on BethAnn's smile. They were married, she got pregnant, then he slipped away. Tommy stuck by because he said he would. BethAnn lost the baby, painfully, almost dying pain. Most folks thought Tommy stuck by because the child was his. Mutual aid, he called it. No longer love, just duty. That's when they started doing things by turns together. He had loved her, she would not. She would love him, he could not. But the duty held. At last she wanted a change.

What she didn't know walking and wishing that night, what Tommy couldn't foretell either in spite of his designs, was that the NAACP would be the one to find George a sympathetic lawyer, while the NAACP defended Tommy. George got a white one and Tommy a black. It wasn't really a lawsuit, but it took a lot of trials. George's lawyer said Tommy had to pay up on the contract; Tommy's lawyer saying not unless he could live in the magnificent house. That demand rankled every judge who read it, upsetting the very natural order of the Earth itself, they said. Not until the case reached the United States Supreme Court did a judge see it George's way and the Ground settled down. That killed the ordinance. The judges there told Tommy to pay up. And move in.

But he and BethAnn knew no such thing walking home on Apple Street that night. October chill between them. Bland food in their bellies. Crickets madly giggling. Earth beneath their feet.

"I want that house, Tommy," she said very softly, almost in prayer.

"Is that right?"

"Quite right."

"I just don't see no way, BethAnn," he said, as they turned up the walk at No. 826. "It's not like it used to be, you know. You can't just one person buy a big ol' house and shack up with a woman. Nowadays, you gotta be married or they won't let you sign. But you're not supposed to be married unless two people in love. Makes it a real riddle. Even if we could get the place by the one law, the other one won't let us. Ain't that a riddle?" he laughed more to himself than to her.

BethAnn was not amused. Nor was the Earth. She sighed heavily and stepped onto the porch ahead of Tommy. "Wouldn't be a riddle if you asked me."

Just then the roof fell in.

THE DEPRESSION & WARTIME

For Love of Trains

THE LORD HAS NO PATIENCE FOR COLORED BOY-CHILDREN, AND
neither should Janie. I tried to tell her. 'Specially Haywood. My sister
wasn't fond of listening, which only encouraged the boy to disobey us
both. We had time for many arguments about that one because I was
a permanent visitor in my sister's home. My husband died some years
past and left me no children of my own, so living in close quarters
with Janie, Claud, and their four children, I did what rearing I could
on a sometimes basis. In Elberton, we all worked an acre on halves
together for the sharecropper boss down yonder. But mostly my job
was to worry on their souls.

After Claud had trouble with the boss, we stole off for Chattanooga, Tennessee, and left Georgia for good. The shack on Poplar
Street looked mighty decent to a bunch of fresh green country folk
like us. It was in the Negro section, where Claud and the mens went
to work at the American Brake Shoe Company. In the good years, he
didn't let Janie work outside the house. I went to cook for a white
family on the other side of town, the Hendricks. After '29, things just
got so bad for colored folks 'specially, and everybody had to try for
work. Haywood got himself a job making deliveries for some Jewish
merchants. Cebelle worked in a home like me. Julian did something,
I can't recall. And my sister Janie took the baby Ollie with her and
went out washin' white folks' laundry.

But Janie didn't like workin' all day for white women, and that set
a bad example for the boy. Each morning before the sun come up she
had to stand in the slave mart. That's what we called waitin' on the
corner of Third and Thomas for white ladies to drive by and give you
a day's work cleaning they houses. On the same day the lady she was
workin' for refused to give her carfare home, Janie also discovered the
lady was turning the clock back on her. Typical, a fire started in Janie
and burned quickly. She was like Haywood that way. Next day, she
quit and took to laundrin' at home again.

By that time it was too late to find the Lord in Haywood. He was about nineteen and man enough to do as he pleased. He lost his job with the Jews and started running with the gutter rats from Blue Goose Hollow and Tandry Flat. Sometimes he would stay gone for several days ridin' trains, most dangerous things known to man. He bragged to me about the places he knew—Florida, Arkansas, back to Georgia, and as far north as Ohio—because he knew his auntie didn't like him hoboin' around with all the Godless hooligans who lived in those jungles. Janie explained he was lookin' for work, and wouldn't stay in the house to take meals from out of his younger siblins' mouths. He was grown and liked to bring his mama money when he could. Janie said it was right for a boy of his make to measure the size of the world for himself. Jesus was watchin' Haywood 'specially. Of course, I could not agree with her on that.

But it would be the last time I pressed. The spring of 1931 did the most terrible thing to my younger sister. The news didn't reach us until the first of April. Mrs. Hendricks told it to me when she let me go.

The state of Alabama had taken Haywood.

That was how we knew it, that he got caught by a state that would never let you out. It was for fighting with white boys on a train and rapin' two white girls, Haywood and eight other colored boys. The world stopped turning for us. Claud slumped his whole body down in a chair like it had turned to worthless stone. He cried a long, long, silent cry. Janie's deep brown eyes searched the room furiously, lockin' on to things, her children, Julian and Cebelle and Ollie, then forced to look off again. Her body wouldn't stop shaking. The news brought the end of something too precious, and she wasn't ready yet. Cebelle filled our little house with long moans. Julian froze up nervous and scared. In all the commotion, even the baby started throwin' up food. We'd been struck by white lightening.

The hardest thing that night was we had no information. No one sent for Janie or Claud to tell of their boy. This world expects that colored folks will know these things from time to time, suffer some and that will be all. The law and white folks is one, we knew. Colored folks were nothing but niggers in Alabama. The mountain folk of Jackson County I knew for a fact called colored people no-tail bears. And Haywood was just a boy in that place, Scottsboro or Paint Rock was all we knew, accused of the worstest thing a colored boy could ever dream to do. He loved always to talk smart, but I knew the boy. Somebody needed to be there to hold him. So, that night we hardly slept, just hugged everybody together without lettin' go and prayed for deliverance.

The church had the newspapers waiting for Janie, and I read them to her and Claud as best I could. Some of the other sisters there stood behind us like it was a funeral, all ready to bury another Negro boy. The papers called Haywood all species of inhuman sorts and described the boys as a gang of brutes. They talked about the lynch mobs that cried for blood all through the night outside the jail, but praised the good white people of Scottsboro for keeping calm. We read the names of the two white girls, Victoria Price and Ruby Bates, saw their pictures in front of the vicious mob. We read the other boys' names, Clarence Norris and Charlie Weems. They were the oldest, just twenty and nineteen. Willie Roberson was seventeen, and Ozie Powell was sixteen. Olen Montgomery was seventeen. Then the paper said three of them were from Chattanooga along with Haywood, Eugene Williams, only fifteen, and two brothers, Andy and Roy Wright. Roy was only thirteen. Paper said they were all part of the same gang, acting in cahoots to terrorize the white boys and girls on the freight train. But we never heard of them boys or their families.

"We have to go to Scottsboro, Reverend Maples," Janie told our minister. "I got to see my boy."

Reverend Maples tried to calm her. "Word of these boys is traveling all over the country mighty fast, and white folks are fixin' to make a quick mess of it."

"That may be so, Reverend Maples, but my boy needs me now, and I'll have to go with the Lord's protection."

Reverend Maples looked nervous a little, and the sisters stepped aside to let him closer to Janie. "Sister Janie, Haywood needs his mama and daddy to be safe. You'll reach him soon enough. What he needs is a lawyer to defend him."

Reverend Maples is a strong pastor and commands my faith to the fullest. But Janie was my sister and Haywood was my nephew, and I had to disagree. "Reverend, they say the trial is just a few days away," I said. "Janie must see her boy before . . ." I left it at that, left it as the matter of time.

Claud went to the local NAACP to find a lawyer. He wanted to fight any way he could, but law was hard on him. If he could, this would be a matter for his hands, not somebody else's words.

The boys had already been in jail for over a week. The trial was set for April the sixth. The NAACP men had to work fast. They got on the telephone to headquarters in New York for help. The lawyer man they got, name of Mr. Stephen Roddy, said he'd go to Alabama and defend the boys. Mr. Roddy came dressed in a three-piece, pin-striped suit, had a gold watch hanging off the vest and was sure to keep a distance between him and all the colored folks there. Mr. Roddy talked down to us from on high. Great big law words rolled off his bushy mustache and fell at our feet where we had no use for them. But they sho nuff were law words, and he promised he'd go and put things in order. I could feel a smile coming out of me. But not Janie.

"You, sir, you alone is gonna handle the whole state of Alabama on account of nine colored boys?" she said. Claud looked sharp at her.

Mr. Roddy looked at Claud about his wife and said, "I'd better be on my way. There's work to do."

The lawyer took the one hundred dollars the church raised to pay him, took it up front, and left without asking any of the parents anything about the boys. Claud had hopes, but Janie had other feelings.

"Ruth, we need to go down there, I can feel it," she told me later. "Claud and I need to see our boy for ourself."

And they did. I stayed behind with the children. The thing was so big now that we could hear about the trial right away. Mr. Roddy had told us falsehoods that day he took our money. The newspapers said he hardly even met the boys, and he pretended to the judge that he wasn't the correct lawyer or something. Big crowds had come out for the trial and probably scared him, just like Janie said. That Monday was First Monday in Jackson County, Alabama, and all the mountain people were down to swap horses and watch the Scottsboro niggers get the chair. They had a big brass band playing, "It's Gonna Be a Hot Time in the Old Town Tonight," and National Guardsmen were everywhere on the scene, holding back the stir-crazy people. They had a prosecutor by the name of H. G. Bailey who told the jury that the boys were runaway zoo animals that needed to be hanged so decent white people in the South could live in peace. The jury took two hours to find all nine boys guilty. Two days later Judge Hawkins came back and sentenced all of them to die in the electric chair on July the tenth, except for the baby Roy Wright. Judge gave him life in prison.

Janie and Claud never did get to Scottsboro to see Haywood. The law barred all Negroes from the town. When Janie found some colored folk, she told them who she was, said she was the mother and father of one of the Scottsboro Boys. Claud said those words lit 'em up, and the poor people opened up their home to 'em. They had to steal their way back to Chattanooga, but they had heard the news along the way. I never seen Janie dazed as that before, all her wits drained from her by that Scottsboro jury. And Claud became like a hopeless kind of iron, just thickening and hardening under flames he couldn't put out. First thing I could do was get them full of warm food, Janie 'specially, and hold them. We hardly would sit with nobody else at first, just gathered as a family for holdin', eatin', kneelin', and prayer. I sang quite often with the children. Every day was like a death in the family. The sisters brought us food and donations from the church, and Janie would send what she could on to Haywood with a letter. She had not seen her boy in almost a month, and the nightmares that filled her sleep stayed fresh for days on end.

Then one day while we were all in the kitchen eatin', a great big white man knocked at the door of the shack on Poplar Street. It was rare indeed to see a white man in the Negro sections of Chattanooga, 'specially on a weekend. Claud opened the door, and Julian went to the back to fetch a shotgun. Janie stopped him quick and serious, thinkin' the man could be the law as easy as any other kind of trouble. But this was no ordinary white man. He smelled different. He was tall as the door itself and wide as the road behind it, with spectacles and a black mustache even thicker than Mr. Roddy's.

"Mr. Patterson?" he asked in a thunderous voice. Claud looked back at Janie, who was as surprised as him. This oak tree of a white man was not from anywhere we had ever been. White people didn't call no colored folks Mr. or Mrs. anything. Just boy, girl and nigger. "My name is Joseph Brodsky. I represent an organization called the International Labor Defense. We've been following the wretched and unlawful treatment of your son and his co-defendants. I've come from New York City to offer you help. May I come in?"

Mr. Joseph Brodsky had said about thirty-three things never before spoken from a white to a colored man, and he had not even crossed the threshold.

Janie came straight to the door, took her husband by the arm and spoke right up to the white man. "Please come in, sir," she said. Then she touched him. She just reached out and laid hands upon his coat to pull him into the sitting room.

"Thank you, ma'am." He sat comfortably and looked us all in the eyes. "It's the strong belief of my organization that the current attorney of record for your boy and the others, Mr. Roddy, has utterly failed to adequately represent the defendants. With pressure from comrades of mine, he at least filed motions to request another trial based on blatant miscarriages of justice in the way the first trial—a racist lynching party, I should say—was handled by the court, the jury commissioner of Jackson County and the local press."

When he spoke about the court things, his eyes squinted very angry-like, and his lips curled his words into one corner of his great mouth, like cannonballs for him to fire out, spittin' a bit, too. "But we have decided that there's nothing to be gained by waiting for the judge to answer his motions. The I.L.D. has authorized me to offer you representation of all matters, and we are further prepared to launch a worldwide protest against the state of Alabama and the continued attempts by the racist, capitalist power structure to divide Negro and white in a class struggle that will only end in blood."

So many words caught Claud and Janie by surprise, such unlikely talk out of the mouth of this white man from New York. But while Claud sat back and listened like he was still makin' up his mind about the man, Janie sat at the edge of the seat beside him and asked the white man question after question. Information streamed out of his big old face. He said that what they call affidavits were signed by people who saw the train pass and saw nobody gettin' raped, people in the jail that night who overheard the two white girls talkin' about havin' a conspiracy, people around the hobo jungles who say they were prostitutes. He said the I.L.D. was taking action to show the court that all the commotion and fanfare with bands and mobs and yellow journalism made the trial unfair to be held in that place. Mr. Brodsky also said that he and the I.L.D. were communists, and they would bring the strength of the world down on Alabama. "We have the power to bring Alabama to its knees," he said, with thunder like a minister. "And we will."

Janie didn't skip a beat. "Sounds like you ain't need to ask for nothin'. You tellin'. Right?"

That's when things in the room started to change. Our visitor gave a long, respectful pause. "It was an emergency. You couldn't be located. Some of the boys agreed."

It was all too nervous for me to worry on, so I came from out of the doorway and offered the man a plate of food. He smiled very warmly and took off his coat. Things changed some more. We never had a white visitor in our home before.

"You were eating. I interrupted. I'd like to join you, if I may."

We all started back for the kitchen, nobody sure how to act precisely. But when this man took off his coat to eat our food like a colored man might do, when we could see power and courtesy in his eyes as he smiled at my Janie, we grown people in the room took a different approach to the matter.

"Mr. Brodsky, is it natural for you to eat greens so?" Janie asked. Praise God, I thought to myself and almost spit out my food. Even Claud let his brow wonder at her. Truth was, I was never natural eatin' greens in front of white folks. But watching this Jewish man from New York eatin' greens and cornbread with his hands like he lived next door, I guess Janie couldn't help herself.

"Every chance I get, Mrs. Patterson," said Mr. Brodsky, looking up from under his spectacles with a handful of greens right up under his lips.

One after another we started laughing, which pleased me no end. It was the first laugh we had since Alabama took Haywood away.

"But, Mr. Brodsky, sir, if y'all are so for poor colored folks, what about working with the NAACP? The NAACP is supposed to be all riled up about my boy too. Aren't y'all workin' together up there in New York?"

Mr. Brodsky started at the question and spoke very politely about the NAACP so's not to offend other colored folks, it seemed. But he told us that he was a lawyer himself and very familiar with fightin' racist judges in Alabama. The NAACP were not, he said. He said they couldn't cut through white mobs, and he, Mr. Brodsky, had white mobs of his own that he could bring from the struggling masses all over the country and the world to fight for the Scottsboro Boys. He also said that the I.L.D. would make sure the boys had everything they needed in prison and he'd look out for us families too.

"Mr. Brodsky, sir—" said Claud, but he got cut off.

"Please," Mr. Brodsky said, holding his hand toward Claud. "I'm not your sir, Mr. Patterson. I'm your brother."

Claud had to work on that one for a minute. Janie put her hand on his knee. "The NAACP say they can get two of the top professional white lawyers to defend my boy, a Mr. Clarence Darrow and a Mr. Arthur Hays, I believes. Now, pardon me for asking, sir, but why can't y'all work somethin' out together? You be twice as strong, wouldn'tcha?"

"I understand your concern, Mr. Patterson. We're working through that right now. But unless the I.L.D. can put the full force and magnitude of its workers into this very important case, there might not be an opportunity for the gentlemen you named to defend anybody."

Janie was all for it, she told Claud after Mr. Brodsky took his coat and left. I agreed with Claud about the communism part. There was no telling what the hillbillies in Jackson County would do when a bunch of nigger-lovin' communist Jews from New York came marching through Scottsboro calling white girls liars and prostitutes.

But Janie took heart after Mr. Brodsky's visit. It was as though an angel had come to remind her how God's light shines on her. She began to sleep again. Sometimes I would come upon her holdin' Claud, not just in comfort but for the sake of a huggin', wantin' to love on her man despite it all. When Mamie Williams and Ada Wright would visit with their children, Janie would love them too. She fed them a good fight and led us all in constant prayer. In the place of Haywood came a strict purpose to return him. The purpose got behind all things, like being bothered that she couldn't understand all the words Mr. Brodsky said. She wanted to better understand what the yellow newspapers were telling about the case, so she started workin' on her reading. Then she would have to pray that even on death row at Kilby prison there was someone kind enough to read Haywood her letters to him.

But the purpose ain't a child. Haywood was supposed to be executed in July. During most of the month of May there was no word from the judge, and we still could not get to Scottsboro to see Haywood. Sometimes I'd be lookin' around for her. I'd look and look, 'til I'd find her hiding almost inside the curtain over the front window. I could hear her whispering to herself pleading real fast, "Such a fine boy, Lord, and you know I teach him to love his color so, all people really, but to love his own color, Lord, I teach him, protect that young man of mine, Jesus, hold him in Your arms, that fine boy of mine, let me see him smile again, dear Lord . . ." Then she'd fall to crying, surrendering her whole tiny body like a fluttering whisp ravaged by storms. She'd see her baby in that electric chair and lose all faith in the purpose.

Not long about that time, the gentlemen from the I.L.D. sent a telegram to Chattanooga askin' Janie was it all right if they send someone for her. Claud too was having his up and down days thinkin' on his boy in an Alabama jail, and he was against his wife travelin' all the way to New York, 'specially with mobs gathered all over the South to do in the Scottsboro Boys. Janie listened carefully to him. She reckoned he was right. But Julian told her later that he thought it was a good idea. The telegram said Harlem, not New York, and he heard that black folks up there were so many and so fancy that white folks couldn't touch 'em if they wanted to.

Once again, those fellows at the I.L.D. asked second and acted first. They sent a dark-skinned young man named Ben Davis on the very wings of that telegram. He was a smart looking gent. Seeing him at the door, you could tell he had been to a university, but it was hard to know he was a communist. He got there while Claud was out workin', and by the time Claud got home, Janie seemed like she'd made up her mind to go.

"Well, Janie . . ." Claud started to say. But he didn't know what to say. Claud needed time for the right words to come, but he didn't have time. He couldn't slow her down. So he turned to the communist. "Som'in happen to my wife up there, young man, I'll have no problem killin' *you*, y'understand? I ain't lyin, boy. I find ya."

"I understand, Mr. Patterson," said Ben Davis, still holdin' his coat by the door. "She'll never leave my side. I won't let nothin' happen to her, sir."

Claud turned back to Janie again. "You has to go?"

Janie looked down, then she looked up at me of all things. "Won't you come with me, Ruth?"

Right there's when the baby sister order of things changed forever with us. She was tellin' me. "Of course I will, Janie."

"All right then, Mr. Davis. We'll go to New York with you."

It took us one full day travelin' by bus to New York City. Janie and I never been no place outside of Georgia and Tennessee before. Each state seemed to be a whole United States, flat and green and endless.

"My Lord, Ruth, can you imagine?" Janie kept saying once the bus reached New York City. There was so many smokestacks and automobiles and buildings tall as mountains clumpin' down on countless white people, no thanks, it was frightful. For a while we refused to get out the bus. Ben Davis kept sayin, what do ya think, what do ya think? But words are too tiny to describe that place, and it was fittin' to swallow us up. They could put all of Tennessee in one of those office buildings downtown. We never left Ben Davis' side. We held on to him, and we held on to each other, making sure we didn't get lost where surely Jesus could not find us.

Ben Davis took us to see a whole pack of I.L.D. characters, including Joseph Brodsky. A lot of white men came around to take an interest in Janie. They wanted to like her right away. I sat back on a nice cushioned bench with Ben Davis. A lawyer man named Walter Pollack introduced himself and started talking about the case.

"The Alabama courts think shotgun justice will carry the day. They tried everything they could to deny your son a fair trial, Mrs. Patterson. Haywood and Clarence Norris and some of the others were coerced into implicating each other, but we know their confessions were beaten out of them."

Janie fell cold. I couldn't see her face, but I know my sister's shoulders when they slump like that. At first she lost her breath. "I'm afraid I don't understand what you mean by implicate, Mr. Pollack, sir."

"Oh, I apologize. In layman's terms, it means the boys told on each other in court. The prosecutor got them to say they had seen the others commit the rape."

"My son was beaten, sir?"

The men got real silent there. "I'm afraid so. But he's all right, Mrs. Patterson. We're doing what we can to keep him safe."

Janie turned 'round to me then. Her cheeks couldn't hold the thought of Haywood gettin' beat on, and I had to search quick through my purse to get her my handkerchief. That little white handkerchief looked like all we had from the world we knew.

"Mr. Pollack, why would these people want so badly to do harm to my boy?"

All the communism words couldn't answer my Janie's plea right then. Communism just got as dumb as every soul on earth. All we needed was the Lord's sweet mercy on us.

"They don't know your son, Mrs. Patterson," said Ben Davis from beside me.

"The evidence is all against the state, Mrs. Patterson," a man named Mr. Taub stepped in to say. "We know for a fact that several of the boys on the train that day could not have taken part in any criminal act even if they wanted to. Roy Wright and Eugene Williams are mere children. Olen Montgomery has only one eye. Willie Roberson has been suffering from advanced syphyllis for many months. We think we're getting close to getting a new trial, and if we do, we will bring the state of Alabama to its knees."

That was their favorite boast.

"But we need your help," said Mr. Pollack.

The I.L.D. arranged for Janie to speak to the audience at the Apollo Theater in Harlem. After that they wanted her to be in the lead of a march.

Janie bowed her head for a minute. "I don't know what you want me to say, sir. But I will surely do it for my boy."

When we left, Ben Davis took us in a taxicab up to Harlem. We were to stay in the YMCA on 135th Street. Janie was very quiet, and Ben Davis did all the talking. He showed us where Harlem started, and we could see hundreds and hundreds of colored folks makin' their way around the place like they owned it all. They wore such pretty clothes, and when white folks passed them, it could have been wind. Never had I seen such things.

"These are the struggling black masses," he kept pointing out. "In Harlem, the colored man owns only one out of every five businesses. White folks come up here to play and gamble and exploit colored women. I'm sure it looks real different from Chattanooga. But let me tell you, ladies, colored folks are hurting up here, too. The North enticed all these people here to work its factories and to scrub floors for white families. But what does the capitalist power structure answer when people ask for work in hard times? Go on home. Here, take some welfare if you can find it."

"You sound like an NAACP man, Mr. Davis," Janie said.

"I'm afraid not, Mrs. Patterson. I'd rather fight in the class war than sit idly by in some bourgeois parlor sipping imported cognac."

"Is that so?" I asked. Ben Davis caught his words and took a long breath toward the window.

I was glad to be in Harlem, though I truly wish Janie and I could stay on the ground floor. Instead, the man down at the desk put us up in the air on the fourth floor. Janie and me huddled by the window after Ben Davis took his heathen talk away someplace.

"Will you look at those children down there, Ruth. Mm, mmph, Lord have mercy. Playin' so close to saloons and such. No wonder the NAACP say there's so much juveniles runnin' around up here. Doesn't nobody watch out for 'em?"

"We need Jesus more'n ever, Janie," I told her.

"I think you right, Ruth. I think we just have to stand fast to it, and we come out all right."

Then we knelt down beside the bed and prayed.

The next day Ben Davis took us to 125th Street where the Apollo Theater was at. Colored folks going back two centuries came out to see Janie and another mother they called up from Monroe, Georgia, Mrs. Viola Montgomery, whose son Olen was the almost blind one.

They put us in back of the stage whilst some other people were out speaking to the audience. That was the first time we ever heard jazz music up close. The Apollo had an orchestra with colored and white playing beside one another. Janie was grippin' my hand so tight I thought she might wanna take it with her on the stage.

"Listen to that music, Ruth. So pretty and sad all at once. The horns sound like boys horsin' 'round and playin' one minute, then they start to wailin' as if they bein' hurt the next."

I couldn't hear the music, I was so panicked for Janie. But that was no use. They called her name, and a man in a smart suit came back for her. It seemed like she walked all the way from Elberton and the great many miles in between to get to the big microphone on that stage. She walked right up to it, and all those colored folks began to whoop and cheer and holler so loud I thought the chandeliers would land on their heads. It was just Janie under those lights, my little Janie in the cotton dress from Chattanooga, standing like an orchid at a mountain's feet, ready for the mud to slide or the sun to shine.

Her voice came out tiny. "Thank you very, very much, and God bless you all. I'm no speaker or nothin' like these other good folks, and I'm not sure just what to tell you all, except my son Haywood is a fine boy. We have not been able to reach him in Alabama, you know. But my boy, I can surely tell you, is a Christian boy who never would do none of the terrible stuff those people keep wanting to say he done." Janie looked out into the dark crowd and up to the balconies. There was not a sound in the whole place. Except when she giggled into the microphone. "Boys must love the rush of those great trains, you know, just bein' boys and all. Rush, rush, my Lord, they just love them trains, don't matter where they take 'em, just gotta rush, rush in such a hurry . . ." Seemed like she went on about the trains for some time. I didn't know she had such feelings. But all of a sudden her voice got real faint. Janie turned back toward me like she forgot she needed my hand some more, and Lord knows I wanted to run out to her. Tears startin' to stream from her eyes, but the man backstage asked me to hold on. "I need my boy back with me," she said, this time stronger and reaching out with her hand and pointing. "It is not right to snatch a child from his mama. It is not right to give false testimony. We mustn't let the law step between us and divide kin from kin like we slaves. Help these young men. Please!" she said, and her voice hit a peak and cracked. "All of you, please pray for these poor boys. Tell Jesus you want these boys to be free. Tell Him. Ask Him with me, every day until we hear Him answer yes."

And the people gave Janie a standing ovation.

THE JUDGES IN ALABAMA WAITED UNTIL JUNE 22 TO SAY THAT HAY-wood would not be executed in July. He and the other boys could live on in prison until their trials were appealed to the Alabama Supreme Court. Janie went on writing letters all the time. She wrote to President Hoover and to the state politicians in Alabama. She wrote to Haywood at least once a day, because she wasn't sure he was receivin' her letters. The I.L.D. was tryin' to make it possible so Janie and Claud could go see Haywood at Kilby. They told us that the prison always let white folks into the death row to gawk at the condemned children. Many papers covered stories folks told about how they met the famous Scottsboro Boys. Haywood was Janie's Scottsboro Boy, and she had not seen him since he had crossed into that God-forsaken land.

In mid-July, Janie and Claud, Cebelle and Julian, and the baby and I, we got our first chance to go visit Haywood in Kilby. The I.L.D. helped us get a car once we got off the train in Birmingham, but from there we was on our own in Alabama country, fearing the worst at every turn. Claud drove and said absolutely nothin', 'cept for askin' Julian about directions from the map. The rest of us just rode very quietly, the women and the child in the backseat, too afraid to even look out the windows for long. We didn't want to disturb nothin', too scared of this land.

Alabama white folks looked to be the meanest, nastiest white folks ever made. The closer we got to the prison, seemed like the meaner they looked. At Kilby, the over-sized guards recognized us right away:

Nigger family of one of them Scottsboro niggers, they kept callin' us. Bein' frisked and searched rough, it was hard to recall Mr. Brodsky's tough talk about bringin' Alabama to its knees. Alabama stood on all fours right now, lockin' doors behind us so loud it made your shoulders jerk. But the last thing I would've wanted was to be a man right then, watchin' poor Claud prepare to see his son among all those sons. He was trembling somethin' awful. The horrible odor in the place was making the baby sniffle. Julian was burning. His eyes seemed blind. He began to sweat right away and grind his teeth, to keep from smoulderin'. It was the hardest place I ever seen to be a colored man.

They crowded us into a high-security room with cubby holes. There was room for one, maybe two people on the visitor side, but they crammed us all in just the same. They had a thick wire screen in the middle, so thick you couldn't hardly see through to the other side. We waited. And we waited some more. Then, another terrible steel door broke open, and the biggest guard you ever saw stepped out first and pulled Haywood out behind him.

Janie lept back in the seat and caught her hand over her mouth. Cebelle screamed. The guard was holdin' Haywood by his collar, almost draggin' him over to the chair, and then he just hauled up and threw him in it like the boy was a sack of feed. His handcuffs hit the table hard. Claud's heart was really pumpin' hard and fast now. This was Haywood at last. They'd beaten him across the left side of his face, and his eye was swole up. But when you looked deep into them, there were the brown, tender eyes of the boy. It was Haywood. We all moved right up to the screen to be closer, and a guard behind us smacked his billy club against the cement wall. His mama and daddy started talkin', talkin', sayin' little things all at once. Haywood just leaned forward as far he could and smiled. His large, soft lips broadened across his face in the same old way. He tried to whisper something, to reach for a sound, but his lips were struggling against tears. They trembled so fierce he couldn't smile, tinglin' and crackin' until tears rained down over them. Janie started weepin', too.

"You all right, mama?" Haywood asked.

"Yes, yes," she cried. "What happened to your hair, baby?"

"They cut it off, mama. They don't like niggers to have hair in here." He put one hand up to his mama's and the other up to his daddy's. "You know I didn't do what they say I done. It was a frame-up, mama. It started when one of those white boys on the train stepped on my hand and said he was gonna throw me off. That's all. That's what happened. We in here 'cause we fought them white boys off the train. I didn't even see them girls on the train."

Janie comforted him, told him we all knew he would never do such things. When the guard made him put his hands back down Haywood tried to calm himself. He asked us each how we were makin' out without him. We said a little, but it's so hard to come up with the right words when you're on short time like that. Janie told him everybody was prayin' for him, and that the lawyers were fightin' to get him home. She said not to worry and to be good and to pray.

"I go to prayer three or four times a day, mama. The preacher-trusty give me a Bible, and I be readin' it all the time. I'm workin' on my readin', mama, after all you tried to do gettin' me to learn, I'm learnin' now, how to read better and how to talk right."

"Good, baby, good, baby," Janie said, reaching her fingers out to touch the screen. "Do you get my letters that I send? I write to you every day."

"Get some of'm, mama. I think they like to take our mail a lot. But I hear you in the Book, because that's where you always said to go, mama. I'm in a cell, but I'm livin' in the house of the Lord. That Book's what connects you and me, mama."

Claud cleared his throat and asked him about the cuts on his face. Haywood just searched across each of us, his eyes dartin' and checkin' each face like he was makin' sure to have pictures to take back to death row. "I'll try to write you, daddy, and tell you 'bout how L. J. Burrs likes to whup on niggers, 'specially Scottsboro Boys. If I don't make it home from here, you know it was him that did it."

"You runnin' outta time, nigga," said the over-sized guard, slappin' his hand with his stick behind Haywood.

"Mama, I been thinkin' 'bout somethin. Remember when we lived in Elberton, and I used to never listen to you?"

"Oh, precious, don't you fret over any of that. You know your mama loves you."

"Yes, mama, I love you. But remember that confusion we had one time when you asked me to bring you flowers from out back, and I went to playing in the mud instead?" Janie just nodded and sniffed. "Mama, I'm so sorry. I tracked mud through the house then, now I'm trackin' mud again, and mama I'm so, so sorry." He couldn't control his tears again. "Please, mama, please don't be mad at me."

"Mama's not mad at you, sugar," Janie tried to say. "It's, it's just white lightening hit us, son. That's all. It ain't you."

The great bull guard behind Haywood came up and snatched back the chair. "Time's up, nigger," he shouted, liftin' Haywood out of the chair by his prison coveralls.

We couldn't help screamin' when he touched Haywood's body. "Be careful, son!" Janie hollared. "You gettin' your money, Haywood?"

Haywood was almost out the door again, and the guard wouldn't let him answer. "Yeah," the guard called back, "these Scottsboro niggers got more money than they got time to spend it."

We was all numb after they threw us out of Kilby prison. They gave us 15 minutes with him after missin' him almost four months. Claud told Julian to drive and not to stop until we reached the state line. The whole way we didn't talk again, only this time we just cried, each of us to ourselves, lookin' at the road, feelin' guilty about escapin' Alabama without Haywood.

For more than a whole year, nothin' happened in Haywood's case. More Jewish lawyers joined the I.L.D. in fighting for the boys. There was a trial again. When we lost that one, the lawyers took it to the highest court in the state. When that one sentenced the boys to die again, the Jewish lawyers took the case to the Supreme Court. But Haywood was nowhere near to home with his mama.

One day Janie stopped me as we was walking home on the street. "You always thought I was soft on Haywood and you think that's why he's in the trouble he's in now, don't you, Ruth?"

"Now, Janie you know I would never say such a thing."

"It's not important what you say, it's what you think, Ruth. You think I helped make Haywood's fortunes?"

"I would never even think such a thought, sweety. You and Claud raised the boy to demand respect and to respect the human form in kind. That's what I think."

Janie stood for a minute beside a parked car. "My feets hurt," she said all of a sudden. Then she just took off her shoes right there and started walking in her stocking feet.

"Girl, what in heaven's name are you doing?" I said. "Put your shoes back on."

But Janie couldn't hear me. She was talkin' about our mama and papa. Daddy was a Black Creek Indian. He had long, straight black hair, pretty hair like Haywood's, and a awful temper. Mama could be severe, but she was usually following papa's orders when she whupped us.

"Ruth, I swore, yes I did, I swore to myself some thirty-some odd years back when me and that man got married that I was not going to beat my children like we was."

"Janie, dear," I pleaded. "Please put your shoes back on." People were passin' and lookin' funny at her. Janie paid them no mind. She was havin' her own conversation with herself and me.

"All I could do was lay down rules so's they could follow. I know each o'm has they own spirit. I know each o'm have to figure out the right way accordin' to they own insides. So, that's what make my treatment of Haywood look so special to you, I guess." Janie stopped and looked into my face. She was grindin' her teeth badly. Her eyes welled up. "Maybe I was wrong, Ruth," she whispered. "Maybe you was right all along." Then she collapsed into my arms.

Two weeks before Thanksgiving 1932, all the Pattersons got good news. They had it in all the papers and on all the radio programs. The

United States Supreme Court said the first trials were no good and unfair. The Scottsboro Boys would get another chance. Joseph Brodsky had come through on his word. Looked like the state of Alabama was down on its knees.

Things really started moving fast. The I.L.D. sent for Janie again to meet with Ruby Bates, one of the two white girls that lied on Haywood. She told Janie she lied 'cause she was a minor crossin' state lines on account of a married man. Ruby and Janie and some other Scottsboro mothers even went to visit Eleanor Roosevelt in the White House. It was a tour, the I.L.D. said. They wanted the world on notice about Haywood and the others. People everywhere knew about the Scottsboro Boys in that Alabama jail, even had protests in other countries that broke out into riots.

But none of that helped Haywood none. Try as he might, the new Jewish lawyer, Samuel Liebowitz, couldn't turn those Alabama crackers around. They convicted the boys again, gave 'em each a life sentence. Mr. Liebowitz took the trial right back up to the Supreme Court. Again the Supreme Court said Alabama had to get its rules right, had to have some colored people on the jury. Four more years had passed, but still Haywood rotted in Kilby Prison. He wrote his mama to say he gave up God.

That's when what starvin' strains of laughter we still had left the shack on Poplar Street for good. It was February 10th, in 1936. Janie was home about a week from one of them tours, and it seemed like Claud was returnin' to himself. We just got through readin' a letter from Haywood. He learned such somber words to tell of his despair. Me and Janie kept up the conversation about it while Claud drifted off to sleep on the sofa. Over these six years Claud seemed to sleep extremely hard or not at all. Couple of times Janie went over and stroked his head, but mostly she and I kept talkin' late into the night about what to tell Haywood. A time passed, the sun set and darkened the sitting room. We fell asleep, me and Janie, right there in our chairs. Then mornin' come and Janie woke me. It was terror across her face. Look, look! she said. Claud wouldn't stir and his arms were stiff. No, no! we screamed but nothing could make the terror go away. There was nothin' we could do to bring dear Claud back to us.

The Lord comes regular with the live long day, providing food for our bodies and spreading glorious life eternal in every crevice on this earth. He gives us Mr. Brodsky and Samuel Liebowitz. He gives us the support of many strangers along the way. Jesus even brung truth to Ruby Bates' lips. And I am thankful. But when the Lord took Janie's Claud from her, faith stood on shaky ground where we lived. Some womens look around when their love is taken and find a reason in God's will. Some mamas lose one boy only to gather a living child with one hand and hold His with the other. But not Janie, not with Claud dead and Haywood gone, she was losing her grip on the Lord. After all, the judge was white, she'd say. The lawyer men and all but one of the jurors was white. The po-lice was white, like the National Guards was white. Janie said the law is white. It struck like white lightening. Lightening come down from above. Jesus is white, she said, pointin' up at the cross of him we had nailed against the wall. That's all she said.

Cebelle had already moved to Ohio by the time of Claud's funeral. She came back to find Ollie runnin' 'round with wild boys, actin' like missin' his daddy was baby stuff, tryin' to be a little man and all. Julian was too sensitive to act tough; his quiet turned to silence after his daddy died. And Janie wouldn't eat or pray. So, Cebelle begged her mama to come up with her to Ohio to live.

"Can't go now, baby," Janie said, lookin' off somewhere. "Can't go no place 'til I git Haywood." She took a deep breath. "Gotta tell your brother his papa's dead."

I come home from the store one day. It was just a few weeks, maybe a month since Claud was in the ground. Cebelle went on back alone to Ohio. I come in the door and find Janie on the sofa in a winter coat. She was shakin' like she was chilled, but the weather was warm.

"Child, why you have your coat on?" I asked.

"Had to pay a visit, Ruth," she said. The crucifix on the wall was missing. The whole wall was bare.

"Janie, you shakin', honey. Where you been to, shakin' so?"

"Oh, I'll be all right." She was cookin' a broth, a special kind. It was hoodoo stuff, a herbal potion.

"Janie, girl, it smell like death in here." I said, but I didn't dare ask her what it was. I knew. Conjurin' scares me in my bones.

"Well, there's been enough of that, Ruth. Lord seem to have a lot of that in store. But we see if we can't ask it to go away for a time." She wouldn't look at me.

"Aw, honey," I put down the bag of things and moved over to hold her. "Let's not—"

"No, Ruth. Please don't touch me. This is work I'm doin'. Gwon now." I stepped away scared. I didn't like this one bit. "White man's religion . . ." I heard Janie say as I shut the door behind me.

The next day Janie told me we had to go to Alabama to see Haywood at Kilby Prison. He was in the hospital there. The leg problem he suffered as a boy got hurt in a accident when he was picking cotton on the Kilby farm. We wasn't sure he was gonna be all right; we had to go now and make haste, she said, so's they don't mistreat him. It was the onliest thing left to do.

We sat in the colored coach and rode the train out of Chattanooga. The countryside looked grand at times and beautiful, I had to say. With the windows down a bit, a warm breeze seemed to rise up off the flowers in bloom and from out of all the sweet crevices of His earth. Farm hands workin' they fields, and we could see out to rows and rows of new life slowly comin' up for spring.

Janie looked hard at me. "Why you smilin' so, Ruth?"

"Was I smilin', honey? Maybe I was expectin' good things to come."

"You like these trains?"

"I think I might."

"You like this time of the year, don't you, Ruth?" Janie just kept starin' at me, like I was a child with no sense.

"This is a fine time of year, Janie."

"Yes. Yes. This is March, for sure. And do you know what this little town here is called?"

I wasn't sure whether to take Janie serious. Of course I didn't know.

"This here is Paint Rock, Alabama, Ruth. This is March in Paint Rock. Pretty soon we'll be in Scottsboro. This is a train, rushin', rushin', and there will be others comin' soon. Some carry coach and some passin' freight." Janie's legs started to shake against my side. "Colored boys love this ride, love their trains. And these Alabama white folks just loves them some niggers." Then she stared back out the window. "I hope I never live to pass this way again."

When we reached Birmingham, Janie and I took a taxicab out to Kilby. At the infirmary, they had Haywood in a bed in the corner near the door. You wouldn't think any of the poor men there were criminals, wrapped liked nobody cared and afraid as they looked. Haywood's bandages barely covered his whole leg, and the boy looked sickly. I kissed him and took my place in a chair nearby so's his mama and him could have a little time to themselves.

"They have to keep you in chains even when you hurt, boy?"

"They wish I be dead so they can use these chains on someone else, mama."

Janie looked weary and her shoulders were shaking a little. Haywood asked her about that. He wanted to see the hoodoo necklace she had on, but he didn't ask nothin' about why she had it. Just ran it over his fingers. They had an understanding. Janie slowly reached her hand toward him. She had not touched her child in six years. She had not been allowed the precious smoothness of his skin. So, she did it carefully. She put her hands on his shoulders, like she was checkin' the muscles for wear. She ran one hand along his ear and stroked his hair, while he just watched. The worlds in his tender brown eyes turned on the sight of his mama alone, but at times when the feel of her touch reached warm inside him he closed them lightly. Janie brought her hands up to his cheeks and held on to them, leaning slowly down now and again to kiss him, and smile at him, and hold his cheeks again.

"Son."

"Yes, ma'am."

"Your daddy's gone."

"My daddy?"

"Yes, baby. Daddy passed on last month."

I don't know what Haywood ever did there in that prison without his mama. He was not grown. He didn't know 'bout losing his own before. I watched how Janie stared into his eyes inches away from him, how they just looked at each other while his tears quietly flowed from his eyes. Not a word more. Just taking each other in and gently having the cry. Until Janie sniffed and leaned over to hug him. That's how they stayed. Wrapped around like missing pieces finally found. I don't know how long. But it was the most natural thing. So necessary. And I could not imagine how she could ever leave that boy again or how Haywood had survived this long without her.

"Try not worry now, boy. Your mama loves you so much. You know how much I love you, don't you?"

"I love you, too, mama," he whispered.

"We got to have faith in the I.L.D. The I.L.D. is workin' to get you out, they workin' every day." Janie tried to explain things that they were doin' to help. Some things she said was true. Some was just hopes, things she would do if she could. But it all started Haywood's face to get rude with anger again, and the tears dried up against his skin. Soon as it come Janie stepped up to meet it.

"We countin' on you now, Haywood. Cebelle and your brothers. We all love you, and we gonna keep doin' the best we can, you hear? But we countin' on you just the same as always. That's what your daddy would want from his young man. Can't give up. You hear?"

"I know, mama. They ain't never gonna get me. I'ma come back which'yall soon enough. They can beats me if they want. But just so's I know you safe."

"You'll survive."

"I'll survive."

"You will."

"Yes'm."

Another burly white Kilby guard came bustin' through the door, almost topplin' me in my chair. "That's enough now, niggers! Time's up!"

Janie got so startled she began to shake even more than before. The guard motioned to another one who was standin' some ways over to step closer. He had a red face and no expression whatsoever and came up alongside the gurney Haywood was on. Janie turned to him and said plainly, "I needs a little more time with my boy, sir."

"You needs to take your black ass outta my jail, else this is the last time you'll ever see the nigger."

I never seen Janie so mad. I never seen evil rush to her eyes like that as she jerked her face up toward the guard. Her mouth grew firm and she sized him, sized him like a child. Haywood groped toward her hand before she might raise it. But the guard settled back on his heels.

"You're wrong," Janie told him dead in his face. "There will never be a greater wrong than you and you and *all* of you. Take a good look at me, 'cause I want you to remember my face while you rot in hell!"

The guard reached out to grab Janie's arm, and she smacked it down and stuck her finger to his face. "Ah ah!" she yelled, catching him before he could so much as blink. "*Just* a goddamned minute!" Janie held the cracker in her stare a moment longer. He didn't move. The hate fixed steady in his eyes, but somethin' kept him still. She turned back to Haywood and smiled.

"Mama loves you, precious. Don't you forget it." Then she kissed him.

As we walked quickly from the gate, Janie was shudderin' all over. The fight had settled in her cheeks, and her teeth began to grind out loud. The driver had to help me lift her tiny body into the cab, and I held her tightly against me. When she wouldn't stop shakin', I wrapped my coat about her. There was sweat on her brow and phlegm rising in her chest.

"Janie, what's wrong, honey? What's wrong with you?" I begged.

"I can't see, Ruth," she mumbled.

"Driver, please, is there a colored hospital close by? Please, my sister is very sick." Janie started breathin' heavy and loud against my neck. I looked down and her eyes were flickerin' up and down. "Oh, no, God. Oh, no, please, God!"

Spittle started drippin' from Janie's lips. I tried to rock her, but everything was flinchin' so powerful. "Driver, please! Please get us to some help." I could feel him speedin' up, sayin' OK, OK, I'm tryin', ma'am, I'll get you some place. "Janie, talk to me, baby. Baby?" But Janie couldn't answer me. Her fists were clenched and her chest was heavin' somethin' terrible. "Oh, God!" I screamed. "Oh, Lord, help this poor woman!"

With Janie in my arms, I tried everything I could. Every time she shook against me, I tried to hold it all in. I didn't know. Lord, I didn't know what to do, to try to hold in what was hurtin' her or let it escape, I didn't know. "Oh, God, she's not movin'. Oh, Lord, don't take my Janie. Lord, please don't take my Janie away from me!"

We seemed to go a long way at high speeds, but all the fury was inside her. For miles and miles, Janie suffered silently against my breast. I tried to pass my life into her. I thought of Haywood lyin' alone in that bed back there. I pleaded with the Lord to take me instead. The driver kept sayin' the hospital was not too far, not too far, but a colored hospital is hard to find. It was Alabama. It was Alabama at work again.

At St. Margaret's hospital in Montgomery, they rushed my Janie inside. She was havin' a stroke, they said. I sat and waited. Sometimes they come over to ask me questions, wonderin' was I really correct about her age. Then I would just wait some more endless waiting, praying 'til I was silly, and hopin' to see my Janie again.

THE LORD GIVETH AND TAKETH AWAY. HE SETS HIS PLANS ACCORDIN' to no man's wishes. His blessings are the only way and the cure for injustice. Cebelle came down from Ohio, and took Janie back with her at last. She gave no resistance. Only Julian stayed behind. Janie would lay all day in the bed weak, listenin' to Haywood's letters between naps. We would not laugh again, nor praise the light of day together. In the days before His birth, I asked Christ what miracle He might bring us. But my sister couldn't wait. Early in the morning, December the 23rd, Janie Patterson passed from this world.

Never Was

IT WASN'T JUST THE WAR, THE ORGANIZATION, HIS CHILD, OR THAT gun that brought Bobby Hall to the end.

But it indeed started with the war. A war so large it refitted every tool, swallowed all belief, threatened to change the tomorrow of a continent or the yesterday of a country. Georgia gave its men. Not including Bobby Hall. His brother Lemuel got called, but not Bobby. Selective Service denied most colored men the chance to fight. Rather than join all a man's grit with all the world's muscle, Bobby stayed home with his young wife Annie Pearl and their baby; rather than be swept up by the truth of America's guns of freedom, he stayed near his father Willy to read the letters from Lemuel and cheer a Negro in uniform when he returned home on leave. Otherwise, he fixed Newton's cars and led the organization.

IT WAS THE ORGANIZATION. THE FEW COLORED SOLDIERS THAT SERVED were left on the fringe, sent to quartermaster corps and overhead where they hardly saw combat. Most never left the South. It was hard enough that angry rednecks commanded their hours with spit and vulgarity, but townsfolk tried to keep them in their place, too. Then the military itself might cheat their families or not allow enlisted men to look in after wives, children, or sickly parents left behind in the fields. When they'd come home dressed in their brilliant green, trouble would start. White folks did not much appreciate the sight. Trouble wouldn't end until some time later, after the soldiers had left, when a business would dry up suddenly, or farmers couldn't fetch a fair price for the same crops as the year before, or the tax levies seemed askew. So, some who remained started an organization, the Negro Betterment Society, to make claims on behalf of the Negroes in Newton and across Baker County. Bobby, not even a farmer himself or a soldier's wife, led the way.

"How you doin', suh?" Reverend Clark might ask him. The reverend called him sir. Or Jimmy Keys, a carpenter. Or one of the farmers, Gilbert Rhoades. Men nearly his father's age.

"I'm handy 'til I break," Bobby might tell them in his peculiar hushed tone voice. "Handy 'til I break." But everybody knew Bobby wasn't about to break.

Bobby's father Willy Hall never liked being cheated, and even as an old man wondered how the white folks of his small town could jeer and taunt a colored boy defending his country. But he wanted Bobby to stop making demands on the local sheriff. "Quit standing under this cat's tree," he warned. "There's shade enough to go 'round."

Willy was wrong, and Bobby tried to explain it. "The only reason he's in the tree is to keep the peace. It's only right he keep some or climb down out of it."

IT WAS THE CHILD. ANNIE PEARL WANTED TO NAME HIM NEW. HE WAS born in the summer of 1942. Bobby thought he was perfect and started looking for a name in the Bible. He struggled over the names of disciples, Paul, Mathew, Luke. He switched to kings.

"I change," she said one August night on the porch, Bobby in the flat chair, Willy snoring on the stoop.

"Better not, please."

"Jes think how I do, Bobby." Annie Pearl swayed gently in the rocker, the baby boy at her breast. Bobby leaned his wiry brown arms on his big knees and listened, admiring every copper pound of her softness. He liked to love the irregular beauty of his bride's auburn lips spread out like a permanent butterfly kiss. He waited for the words to rearrange her cheekbones and thicken her coal-black eyebrows. "I don't know if I'm gonna be the same girl next year as I is today. I cain't hardly remember who I was last year, and I don't truly miss her." She expected him to say something, but he kept listening. "Let's name this baby New."

Which they did. New went into town and New went to meetings. Except in Bobby's auto repair shop, the child, like his mother, was a small fixture beside a square hulk of a man. Everywhere Bobby liked to go, they liked to go with him.

At that time, Annie Pearl was the kind of woman split between the tenderness from which she'd come and the glory she seemed headed for. Just twenty-one, she was a spunky sidekick to the man who believed you stand for something. Her airs begot jealousy among those who were young enough to want the same. Older colored folks' eyes tried to speak for white folks' minds and cast weary looks at the spectacle they made. Stop flaunting it, said their faces. But Bobby and Annie Pearl had time, New, her cotton dresses, his business and, so it seemed, color on their side.

IT WAS THE GUN. BOBBY HAD A PEARL-HANDLE AUTOMATIC THAT FOR a while he carried in his waistband. Bobby liked how the cool blue steel felt against his palm when he held it, the precise lines flowing up and down the thickness like something crafted in a different time and place. Most men liked the creamy, marble-colored handle the best. Bobby only let them hold it away from Annie Pearl, who didn't like having it around at all.

"Where'd you git it?" Manley Poteat asked him. Manley tore his gaze from the gun just long enough to meet Bobby's eyes before he was back admiring the chamber again.

"That's not a fit question, Manley," Manley's father Walter said. They lived in Albany where Walter ran a Negro mortuary with his boy and came down to Newton for meetings. "Don't be askin' Bobby to give up his goods."

Bobby had no problem being asked. "Lemuel bought it off an Indian in Savannah."

"It's army issue?" Manley asked.

"No," Bobby laughed. "I think he said it's German. I don't rightly know."

The Germans had little to do with Bobby's pearl-handle pistol. He had the gun because it was the thing that says, I am. His brother stood ready to die to protect freedom abroad. He himself would serve in a minute. Bobby and Lemuel had decided together, many times over meals, it takes freedom before anything that works can last. You had to die to protect something that precious. If you can bear arms against the enemy in Europe, you can protect yourself against your enemy anywhere. For the colored man, to serve was to serve. He had a child, a wife and a business. With responsibilities came certain dangers, which he would stand against. Where freedoms were at stake in Newton, like the right to be left alone, Bobby would be ready. He didn't invent these rules. The president himself announced them for the world to know. White folks had lived by them for years. The rules seemed clearer to him now, as though he had finally discovered something that *they* had been trying to teach. No, Bobby saw no wrong in owning the thing.

Being a mechanic also gave Bobby a peculiar appreciation for the gun. Both a farmer and a mechanic do a business of the hands. But a mechanic unites his soft fingers with the hard grooves of cold steel. He diagnoses and adjusts and overcomes the resistance of angry metals in disrepair. A good mechanic has eyes on his fingertips and patience in his knuckles. You have to make the machine give in. When Bobby lay beneath a Chevy he'd do small battle with the angles. A Packard might find another way to fight him or a Chrysler or a Ford. But not the gun. The gun only had to do one thing, fire. He never knew it to fight. As long as he cleaned it, the handgun stayed perfect, beautiful, its little parts never changing, power in his pocket. So, Bobby carried a pistol because he needed it; he owned that one because he loved it.

FOR SHERIFF CLAUD SCREWS, THIS WAS NOTHING BUT BIGGETY REA-soning possessed of nonsense. When the world came to Newton, it had better climb the stairs up the courthouse steps and ask his permission. Otherwise, it was just words on a newspaper.

Screws was a man in his late forties with no significant property.

He lived in a rural county yet knew little about farming, harvesting instead the courtesies of farmers and the control that came with his badge. He and Deputy Frank Jones kept order. Frank was a big dumb kid of a man, with a build drawn up like a V. The shorter Screws hung just the opposite way, wide at the bottom with a small head. He wore thick black framed glasses, above his premature jowls, and a flap of flesh had developed on his throat from years of tugging at it. They allowed no drunks or Hitlers to invade the good sense of Newton, swiftly hauling them to one of the jail cells behind the office. When Bobby Hall, representing the Negro Betterment Society, came to the sheriff's office and asked him to arrest the men who were harassing black soldiers on leave, Screws threatened to lock *him* up.

By the new year 1943, Screws was convinced that the Negro man in arms posed more than a nuisance to real soldiers in the field. Too many of them thought a uniform made them better, as if the suit could change the flesh it covered. He heard of rallies by Negroes up North in cities like Chicago and New York where they demanded Double Victory: freedom abroad and freedom at home. For a long time he blamed their false hopes on Roosevelt, until that January when he read in the papers about the "Murder on the Mainline." A young blonde newlywed traveling by train to California with her husband had been viciously murdered in her sleeping bunk, her throat slashed and the life bled out of her. She was the bride of a navy ensign. The murderer was a colored navy cook. It was more than the president, but their own nature at work. After that, Sheriff Screws decided to take away the guns from Negroes in Newton.

"Sheriff, I don't need me no warrant, if'n you jes say so," Frank Jones told him, sitting, boots up in the chair. "What's the boy gon say, anyway?"

"That really ain't a matter of your concern now, Frank, is it?" Screws said, looking up from the black Royal typewriter he liked to pluck at. His light blue eyes could shoot razor looks sharp from the tight lines around them. To Screws, presenting a warrant, even a false one, spared him the trouble of explaining the new law. The warrant was like an official seal around the words and made the law legal.

"This boy thinks he's got just about every damn thing figgered out. He's a right cunning bastard, and we gonna put a halt to this today. You hear me, Frank? You take this here piece a paper, tell Bobby this is from the justice of the peace on account of the new ordinance just passed, ain't allowin' concealed guns and weapons carried on the person—or anywhere about him. Y'understand what to say? Tell 'im it's a warrant."

"All right, I will."

"Good. And you bring that pistol straight back here to me."

Frank was a child beguiled by his own size and duty. He needed to be led. Putting his great weight on somebody in the name of the law was job enough, and he could do it over and over all day. But he worked better when he was led to it. Sheriff Screws was a leader. His unspoken love for the town and its families was passionate and strict. Screws served with such purpose, and it was the purpose for which he served.

Though the January air is mild, its rain has soaked Newton's red soil. Frank nearly slips on his way down the courthouse stairs into the square where the cruiser is parked. The drive out to Butler's garage where Bobby usually worked alone took ten minutes in good weather, but twenty on muddy roads. As he drives up, Frank can see Bobby under the grill of Bruce Jenkins' Chrysler.

"Come out from under that auto, boy. Wanna have a word with you," Frank tells him. He cocks his head sideways to view the thick body half under the grill. Frank is also doing a little something with his tongue against his teeth, like he had snuff in his gums, but it's just attitude and a fondness for these moments.

Bobby recognizes the boots and cannot deny the voice, much as he'd like to. "How ya holdin' up under all this rain, Frank?" he asks, rising to his feet. He and Frank are about the same age.

"Enough of all that, Bobby. I got quick business with you." Frank holds the paper across his chest, other hand on his hip next to his holster. "Says here you betta gimme that pistol you been carryin' around."

Bobby wipes the sweat from his greasy brow with his forearm, then pulls a rag from his grimy pocket and starts cleaning oil from his fingers. Keeping a safe distance from the nervous deputy, Bobby says, "That some kind of a warrant?" Frank just nods. Bobby squints. "Don't s'pose you let me take a look at it?"

"You've seen everything you need to see, Bobby. Now don't waste my time. Where's your gun?"

Butler's garage is just big enough for two small trucks side by side, with a work space lit up by a single light bulb. Outhouse out back, space in front for several more cars. Right now there's only the Chrysler, the lightbulb, Bobby and Frank, separated by about ten feet, and that piece of paper.

Bobby scratches the back of his head hard, as if something there really itched, and squints again. "Why come I gotta give up my gun all of a sudden, officer Frank? How's it against the law me havin' a gun around here?"

Frank relaxes his teeth and remembers what the sheriff said. "Been a new law passed, ord'nance, says cain't be concealin' weapons no more. This here warrant is for your gun, boy. So lemme have it, and you can go on back to work."

Bobby weighs in his head exactly what he wants to say. Finally, he chooses. "Ord'nance only applies to niggas?"

This becomes Frank Jones's unfinished dream, the one he keeps having for days afterward, wondering why he didn't lay Bobby flat with his fist, pistol-whip him, shoot him right there, how the adrenaline nearly blinded him, but his hands forgot to move. Instead, heat wells up on his forehead and races down to the hard curve of his mouth. "That's the last thing you gonna say to me now, boy, ya hear me? Where you keep the gotdamn gun?"

Bobby walks slowly toward the wide opening of the garage and points to his Chevy parked outside next to the road. Frank motions to him to walk to the car and follows close behind him, hand firmly around his holster. When Bobby reaches the passenger side, he steps back, points to the map compartment, and lets Frank have his way. Bobby starts shaking his head slightly. A little ice chills in his veins. Frank opens the compartment, smiles at the gun, motions Bobby to head back into the garage. Then he captures the blue steel pistol and takes it back in the rain toward Newton and the sheriff.

That was supposed to be the end of the gun incident, but it wasn't. Bobby had dreams too. They were war dreams, made from the details of Lemuel's letters. Bobby imagined men in their green fatigues running over hillsides, machine guns in their arms, pistols in their waistbands. The hills were Newton's hills with magnolias rising in between them, but the enemy was German, white like Newton's white folks, but foreign in their talk and all wearing spectacles, like in the newsreels. Bombs exploded everywhere and dirt and shrapnel rained. Lemuel's combat drills turned to real combat in the dreams. The sergeants and company commanders were white men from Baker County, men you'd see in town, now fighting as one, Negro and white. They yelled to the soldiers to hold a position and fire, and the soldiers, Lemuel and the Negro battalion, would hold and fire. But they didn't spray their machine guns, they shot the Germans' eyes out with their pistols, always with their pistols. They opened their chests and they ripped off their limbs, but always with pearl-handle pistols.

"I gotta get my gun back, Annie," Bobby said suddenly, waking in the middle of the night.

"Careful, Bobby, you gon crush the baby!" New slept between them on the bed. "You already got a gun," she added trying to get back to sleep.

"What gun?"

"Shotgun." She pointed in the darkness to the shotgun behind the bed.

"No, no, baby. This is important. The man had no right to be takin' my pistol offa me." Bobby put his hand against New's bare side and felt his sleeping heart beats. Without thinking, he stuck his nose down and took a deep breath of his skin. "I'ma git it back."

He was surprised to look up and see Annie Pearl fully awake and staring at him. "You got betta to think on," she said and slid New's body up to where it was right in their faces. Then she sighed like she was taking in a deep breath and snuggled down lower in the bed. With his face full of baby skin, Bobby could feel her reaching to raise her night dress, then the heavy warm wave of her thick thighs on his. She wet her lips and buried them in the tough curls on his chest. Smiling in the dark, Bobby lowered himself a little more down the bed and stuck the bridge of his nose against the baby's backside. Annie Pearl let a hand drop slowly over his lower body, and he started to grow straight and weightless in her touch. He opened his legs and found her hips with his fingertips. New didn't stir. Baby smell and baby sleep around him, he gasped as Annie Pearl lifted her bottom side to side, stirring him up a little more, baby sleeping so perfectly. In the morning, they were all a tangle puzzle of bodies locked in slumber. But all day Bobby carried a vivid memory of the dream.

So, he decided to ask his father to have a talk with Sheriff Screws and try to get the gun back that way. Willy Hall grew up just ahead of Screws. They had years of polite understandings between them.

"Heard talk they gon send colored troops to fight," Willy said as he poked randomly at things sitting on Bobby's work table. A long metal tube caught his curiosity and he held it close to his cataract eyes and stared down it. "Heard they might send Georgia boys."

"Is that right?" Bobby asked from halfway under the Chrysler. "To Europe?"

"No, no. Heard say Africa. Mebbe Liberia."

"Is the Germans there too?"

"It's not just the Germans, Bob. Could be Japs. Could be Mussolini. They all workin' together."

"Mm hmm," Bobby said. He scooted out from under the car and turned to work on getting a pin into a tiny T-bolt that was supposed to fit somewhere in the middle of a Packard strut. Willy stood next to him at the table, watching Bobby's fingers move ever so slightly. "I know it was Screws behind this thing," Bobby said, like he's telling the pin.

Willy spoke quietly. "Probably so. Frank's dumb as mud, so figger he ain't 'bout to invent no law and come out here to tell yeh 'bout it."

Bobby grunted a laugh so as not to disturb his fingers. "I was wondering if maybe you'd go have a word with Screws, pop. Just you and him. Ask him for my gun back."

"The man ain't interested in what I got to say. He's hot for you, I think." Willy's eyes found a crack on the floor and began studying the detail. Bobby kept his eyes on the T-bolt. Willy snapped his focus out of the crack and he turned back around to where Bobby was concentrating under the light. "Mebbe that's all the more reason I should talk to im."

SHERIFF SCREWS' CONFISCATION OF BOBBY HALL'S PISTOL LACKED THE power of B-29s over Berlin, but it did him proud. It had none of the majesty of a hundred-thousand troops ready to do battle on the ground in France or gunships ablaze over the sea. But it was good enough for Newton. In a way, he liked to think he held the homefront. He held the ground out by the town square and protected the homes that faced the well in front of the courthouse and the stores there. These were his streets, threatened not by jackbooted brownshirts, but Hitler's unintended soldiers, Negroes in arms.

Around six every evening, Mavis Bailey, old and widowed, invited passersby for a neighborly moment to chat on her porch overlooking the square. Sheriff Screws' talk with her had been about other things, like the unusually warm weather, until Joe Ledbetter came up with his wife, Elizabeth. Sheriff Screws mentioned the pistol then.

"Matter of fact, I just wrastled a pistol offa that Hall nigger durin' the storm today." He spoke almost under his breath, which mixed with the clean, moist evening breeze that followed the rain. Mavis Bailey and the Ledbetters let the breeze linger in their noses awhile before acknowledging what he said.

"Willy Hall, sherf?" Mavis asked.

"Nah," he laughed, one leg up on her porch step, one big arm leaning down on it. "Old Will's all right. Talkin' 'bout his uppity son, Bobby, the cowboy."

Minutes passed and dimmed the sky a little. "Reckon the darkies are startin' to carry guns on 'em, sherf?" Joe Ledbetter asked, turning a skeptical glance toward him.

"I know it to be so. Young ones," he said, low key. "Ain't legal to conceal a weapon."

Edward Ellis and his daughter Alma made their way over to Mavis Bailey's porch from their own house three doors away. Elizabeth started talk of the war, as someone always does. They trade imperfect information, and leave the questions in the air. Alma, looking younger than her sixteen years, sat alone in the rope chair, blonde, cherub cheeked, listening to talk of guns and calibers. Screws turned things back to the enemy in town and warned folks to be on lookout.

"Say you found the gun on 'im?" Ed asked. "That boy's got my Packard in there."

The sheriff looked off into the square. "Nah, not on 'im," he laughed, raising up to light a Chesterfield he pulled from his shirt pocket. "He carries the damn thing around in his car. Ed, you've seen that boy rollin' around town in that big Chevy."

Mavis Bailey started to hum quietly from a corner of the porch.

"That ain't exactly concealin' to me, sherf," said Joe.

The exchange began to rile him, but he was out of words. 'Some o'm would kill us all if they could,' he wanted to say. "Trust me," Screws told them and walked on into the night.

Frank Jones was having a little better luck over at Johnny West's, a small liquor store about half mile away that doubled as a saloon.

Josephine Price was there with her dyed red hair and exaggerated laughter for the things Frank managed to say. She loved to dance with or without music. She came to Johnny West's with Velma Mintner and Velma's husband Jack where they liked to drink wine with Frank in the back room.

"Some of these darkies nowadays will definitely take a mile, you give 'em an inch," Jack was saying. Josephine ran her tongue over her lipstick, which she knew Frank was watching carefully out of the corner of his eye. "I'm not sayin' Bobby Hall is one of 'em. I don't rightly know this boy. I'm jes sayin' he could be like some of 'em I *have* seen."

That marked a good time in the talking to swig again, and all four threw back their heads to drain their glasses.

In Frank's first version, Bobby didn't watch his distance and Bobby didn't ask if the law applied to white folks too. But Frank tells it too many times. In his latest version, he added that Bobby stood inches from his face, so close Frank could smell his breath. Bobby was still holding a crowbar he didn't think Frank knew he had on him and maybe also had the gun in one of the pockets of his overalls. *Then* Bobby demanded to read the warrant for himself.

Jack leaned over his wife and stared hard past Josephine and into Frank's eyes. "Ja break his jaw, Frank? Did ya butt him in the mouth and break 'is goddamned jaw?"

Frank's bad dreams started happening for real.

WHEN WILLY HALL CLIMBED THE COURTHOUSE STAIRS THE NEXT DAY to ask Sheriff Screws if he would return his son's pistol, Screws flat told him no.

"Likes to hep yeh, Willy, you know I would. You and me go way back an all. But your son carryin' guns around and incitin' niggras, well, then it becomes just me and my bi'ness. Cain't gi'yeh no gun back."

Words were harder to find there in the pale flourescence of the jailhouse, as he stood cap in hand beside the sheriff's desk. Willy wanted to reason with him, but he knew the sheriff would take offense if he could tell that Willy was being reasonable with him.

"Sherf, Bobby ain't plannin' on usin' no gun."

"What's he carryin' it 'round for then, Willy? Pheasant? He want to stop by the side of the road and kill him some pheasant with a six shooter, I guess. That it, Willy?"

Frank Jones walked heavy booted past the vestibule and into the main room where the two men were sitting around Sheriff Screws' desk. Frank was followed by two men, Hoke Gilly and Samuel Hart. Hoke was drunk, and Frank directed him to a cell in the back to sleep it off.

"Say, Frank," said the sheriff. "You was in on this pistol-totin' Bobby Hall thing. He got his daddy in here askin' could he have it back."

Willy turned around and bowed to Frank. Frank smirked, trying to get a laugh out. "Law's the law, old man." Frank continued on to the rear with Samuel Hart and the drunken Hoke.

"Don't want to take up too much o'ya time, sherf, but lastly I was just wondrin' could *I* be the one responsible for the gun and makin' sure that Bobby don't never carry it in his car or on 'im, ceptin' mebbe jes keep it in his own home?"

Sheriff Screws leaned back, but didn't laugh this time. He tied his lips up to one side skeptically, but kept his thumbs rotating in his lap like he was considering the suggestion. "Nope. Cain't do that for ya, boy. Sorry. 'Sall there is to it. Now let me get on back to work."

LEMUEL HALL'S ALL-NEGRO BATTALION WAS SENT TO LIBERIA SOME time in late 1942—they didn't know exactly when because the letter which arrived in mid-January did not specify. He was in Africa, he wrote. As far as he knew, he was among the first colored troops to serve anywhere alongside white soldiers. The white soldiers were all officers in command. He wrote a little about the bush and said he hadn't seen any jungles yet, but had heard tell of it and couldn't wait to go. Lemuel found it odd that such a modern war, a war that produced the aircraft that flew him and hundreds more such a distance, a war that made the whole world small, made him feel like nothing changed. Except for the way the women and little children dressed, the Africans looked just like him. They spoke English at pointed angles like the British, but they looked the same as he.

His mission was to protect Firestone rubber plants from invasion by the Axis powers coming down from North Africa. They would probably deliver shipments themselves, not just loading cargo like every other Negro in the service. On those trips north, they might even see some fighting. *Miss you all but proud to serv,* he wrote.

News of his brother fighting alongside white men in Africa was enough for Bobby. When Willy told him what Sheriff Screws said about the gun, Bobby tore into a rage right there on his porch. "This cain't stand, pop!" he yelled. Annie Pearl looked up at him with the baby in her arms, hoping to restrain him some. "The man cain't swoop down on me and take what's mine," Bobby bellowed, looking back at his wife. "If he can take my protection, he can have anything he wants. No, sir. I'll take it up to Albany. I'll ask the whosie-callit, the attorney general to see about this ord'nance."

"Don't ask the snake nothin', boy," Willy said, twisting his cap in his hands. "The rattle only tells you what the bite already knows."

"Well let the cracker rattle away then! I ain't gettin' bit. I got no cause to get bit. I ain't broke no law, daddy. I ain't done nobody wrong. This man is foul, thas all." He knew if his voice reached a certain pitch the baby would start crying. Bobby paced and tried to think it through calmly. "He don't wanna round up no rednecks callin' names on hardworkin' colored folks. He won't protect colored soldiers who gone and pledged to protect all *they* have, layin' lives on the line. Lemuel's in Africa, you know. *Africa.* No, sir, there's got to be a point where it's clear even in *they* eyes. He just plain wrong on this. We ain't no goddamn animals."

"Shhh in front of the baby!" Annie Pearl snapped.

"This is *for* the baby, whatchoo talkin' 'bout?"

Annie Pearl rocked for a minute and stood up suddenly. She

stepped in front of Bobby and handed him the bundle. "Hold im."
Bobby looked at her like she was crazy. "Hold im!" Bobby took New.

"Where you goin'?"

She sat down again. "I be right here wit your daddy on the other
side of sense. When you figger it out, come on over here wit us."
Bobby started to talk, but she interrupted him. "Nuh uh. Right ain't
always right, Bobby. You the one like to preach that. Makin' these
men mad at you only gonna put all us in a world a danger, Bobby.
You *know* that. You do." She held him in a fierce stare, until he
looked away and pulled the baby closer. "They don't need no reason,
but you wanna give 'em one anyway."

"They might sure want to beat my brains in, babygirl, 'cept they
don't believe I got none," he laughed.

Bobby declined to live what he called the hell of fear. It made no
sense to give in to the sheriff's whim. He wasn't asking for something
beyond his due. It wasn't a question of gaining some whites-only
privilege or access to their things, their homes, their businesses. Bobby's demand fit nicely inside what was regular and hardly pushed a
boundary. What's mine is mine. And if my blood can stand and fight
for this country, if my brother, my kin, should leave on this nation's
ships and planes, lay down his life and perhaps never come back, then
at least preserve for me the honor of my private bounty. So, Bobby
had to seek out the grand jury in Albany. He had to.

BOBBY WAITED UNTIL SUN-UP BEFORE RETURNING TO NEWTON FROM
the grand jury. The twenty-mile drive is perfect in the early hours, the
sun shining in the tiny branches of naked trees along the highway,
and safer too for a colored man traveling alone. He spent the night
with the Poteats, above their funeral parlor. Fresh with some of Mrs.
Poteat's good eggs and grits in his stomach, Bobby drove with all of
the events of yesterday still turning in his head. Every now and then,
he'd glance off into the thick woods that flanked the highway. He
wondered why Lemuel was so eager to get to the jungles, and now he
remembered why. They enchanted the eye, drawing him deeper into

the thickness where light couldn't reach. Occasionally, Bobby checked the windshields of oncoming cars, looking for Sheriff Screws approaching from the opposite direction. Sheriff Screws didn't always take the police car and sometimes used his own car on police business. Bobby knew the sheriff had police business before the grand jury that day in Albany.

Grandest thing about this jury to Bobby was that they made him wait all day to see it. He'd paced the marble floor of the courthouse most of the morning, twisting sweat into his cap, practicing what he might say to all those white men in there. A bailiff said the grand jury had a lot of business on Tuesdays and Wednesdays, because it didn't convene on Mondays or Fridays and only half days on Thursdays. Head prosecutor for the state that day couldn't be bothered with a Negro trying to challenge a sheriff to get his gun back. But the head prosecutor had indeed reviewed the complaint Bobby signed that morning. Around four o'clock the bailiff told Bobby that the prosecutor was explaining the law about concealed weapons to the men on the jury, and that he should get ready to come in and say whatever he had to say with a quickness. A few minutes later, he did.

It was easier than any time he'd ever been before a pack of white men in Albany. Other times he'd gone up on business for the Negro Betterment Society, the county people were always urgent and hostile. It was the same assortment of spectacles and suspenders. But this time the white men looked sleepy, and he saw one with his leg hanging out of the jury box. He was wearing jeans, not trousers, like he was taking a break from his yard to come hear Bobby's dispute with Sheriff Screws.

When Sheriff Screws arrived the next day, it was a whole different picture. Screws occupied a large brown leather chair in the center opposite the twenty-odd men in the box. The prosecutor was Maston O'Neal, the solicitor general himself, dirty blond and red-mustached, medium-sized but built with a slight hunch. He walked in comfortable little circles while he spoke, mostly so the jurors could hear him. He seemed to know them all.

Screws knew O'Neal and knew some of these men too. Sleepy would be familiar, and Screws would have liked that. But in the room with the high ceilings and a long day ahead, that's not what Screws found.

Explain to us the precise manner in which the Negro carried the pearl-handle pistol on his person, Claud. Who witnessed this? What justified the issuance of the warrant? Claud, we called your deputy and still couldn't find no record of the warrant, you happen to fetch a copy with you today?

Each question burned a little deeper red into Sheriff Screws' face, until all hope for the familiar turned to flames behind his eyes. The anger filled all the thickness of his cheeks, planning its escape. They sounded like they didn't trust him. They sounded like they were no longer on the same side of the law. "You gentlemen startin' to wear me out with all this talk about some Negro's rights to pack a pistol in my jursidiction, an' I just about listened to as much as I care to hear today."

"Claud, now you know we have to resolve this thing. Man come up here asking for his gun back."

"There ain't nuthin' to resolve that ain't already, Maston. You fellas are jes wastin' your goddamn time and mine over this triflin' nigger bi'ness." A court stenographer tried to catch the heat on paper, but it started moving too fast for her. The more Sheriff Screws cussed in front of the young woman, the more anxious the expressions on the jurors' faces. "Who y'all think you in here tryin' to protect? When our boys left for Germ'ny, ya think they asked me could I please leave armed coloreds in charge of they wives and kin? No, sir, you are mistaken. I'll take the guns off the niggers, and I'll do it alone. Somebody try to make me give that damn nigger back his gun betta be ready to take it out ma hand." Sheriff Screws stood up and put his hat back on his head. "S'all there is to it, men. See ya when I see ya."

THE GRAND JURY IS NOT SO GRAND AFTER ALL, BOBBY LEARNED ON Friday. Just because they decided Bobby wasn't unlawfully carrying his pearl-handle pistol didn't mean he got the right to retrieve it from the sheriff. It takes a justice of the peace to sign that order, and the one presiding in Albany, Judge Carl Crowe, was in and out that week. Maybe he'd sign it, maybe he wouldn't. It takes Maston O'Neal to write up the request. Neither man did it. The justice of the peace over Newton was T. A. Riley. That old man was a rubber stamp for Screws, if it wasn't Screws that signs all his papers anyway.

Willy Hall found it hard to believe that the grand jury had sided with a colored man over a sheriff. But Bobby didn't stop to take much joy from it. He wanted his gun back. More than anything in the world. He faced the familiar chorus on the porch, Annie Pearl's flammable disbelief and Willy's wizened old fear.

"What's this thing to you, Bobby?" Annie Pearl asked him. "Which sun won't rise, which dog won't bark, which meat won't cut if you don't get your pretty little gun back?"

Bobby smiled first because he loved the rich bottom of her voice, and also because he didn't know what to tell her. His own mind was a jumble, yet it was clear. The jumble had an army uniform in it, Selective Service not selecting him, Liberia, faces black as rubber, white faces jeering at Lemuel, wanting so much to fight, folks getting ripped off, prices suddenly rising, America. The clarity had something to do with a new day coming. After all, the grand jury sided with him. "I'm just trying to make somethin' outta nuthin', baby."

"Son, if you ask me," Willy said from the stoop, "the fish that gets away oughtta be thankful to the hook and git."

Bobby chuckled and patted his dad on the shoulder. "Mebbe so, but remember: I ain't no fish. Seems to me the only thing a man needs to thank a hook for is supper."

So, on Tuesday Bobby took the road to Camilla to see a lawyer named Robert Culpepper. Culpepper once represented a merchant farmer named Vincent, who owned one of the largest acreages in the southern half of the state. Bobby remembered him as the only fair lawyer up against the Negro Betterment Society when it was demanding an accounting from Vincent last spring. But the first day

Bobby showed up, Culpepper had disappeared. Bobby grew impatient and decided to come back on Thursday. He wanted his gun back, and he wanted a justice of the peace to sign the paper making Screws give it back. He started seeing that moment, the fresh ink on the paper, the presentation to Screws, who would doubt it, turn red studying it, and finally have to end the matter by returning the pistol.

Culpepper was in. He was a gold watch and suspenders man, the very picture of a lawyer in Bobby's mind. Spectacles in a hip pocket he pulled out from time to time. Grey suit. Coins shaking around in his pockets. Venetian blinds in his office and a pretty white girl at the desk in front.

"Came to see Mr. Culpepper, ma'am," he said without first ascertaining what business he might have walked in on. Luckily, nobody was doing a thing, not the woman, not Culpepper. She took his name back to Culpepper's office. Bobby turned the hat in his hands, wanting to sit down. Instead, he stood and waited.

The ten-mile drive from Newton didn't take as long, but Culpepper finally came out. The woman sat down at her desk to do nothing again. Culpepper approached with his hands on his waistband. His square face was crowded by salt-and-pepper locks of thick hair, and his large brown eyes fixed so powerfully that Bobby took a step back. "How are ya, boy? Name's Hall ain't it? Think we've met. What is it you want me to do for you?"

He tossed a finger toward a bench by the door for Bobby to sit on. Bobby looked at the bench, then at Culpepper. "Won't we be needin' some privacy, sir?"

Culpepper cut a broad grin, which relieved Bobby a little to see. "Miss Jackson's my assistant. Not to worry. Only my clients meet in the rear, and, well, you're not a client as yet."

So, Bobby told it in a whisper. When the outrage bubbled up, he thought of his wife and settled down. Culpepper kept staring hard at him, like his words and Culpepper's eyes weren't connected by the same purpose.

"Well, I can start by writin' Sheriff Screws a letter, lettin' him know you've retained me and that we're interested in the return of the gun, based on the grand jury and all." Bobby stopped to savor the sound of that *we* and how lawyersome it was. In all that he heard, he didn't hear no. Culpepper sighed. "It'll cost you fifty dollars for me to start this ball rollin' for you, son. Twenty-five right now if you want me to start today, other twenty-five middle of next month. I can dictate your letter right now and get it out tomorruh. Whaddya say?" Culpepper extended a stubby hand. Bobby stepped forward and shook it.

"Thank yeh, sir. That'd be just fine," Bobby said.

ROBERT CULPEPPER KEPT HIS WORD. HE WROTE THE LETTER TO Sheriff Screws and sent it by courier Friday afternoon. It was short and crisp in lawyer words that marched off the page like little black soldiers. With reference to regaining possession of said automatic pistol . . . Be advised . . . Presume your intent . . . Rightful owner . . . Meet in person . . . At once.

That day, the state of Georgia switched to official war time. The clocks were reset.

When Sheriff Screws read Culpepper's words Friday evening, he decided he was going to get Bobby Hall that night. It took a while for him to know what getting meant; the lawyer words both riled and arrested his thinking. It was a kind of blasphemy of trust, how another white man, a man of the law like Culpepper, dared from his position on high to side against the meek lives below. Invasions start like that. So, getting just had to be something sure and powerful, if not final. Right then he only knew he had to get Bobby Hall good.

Like the man of action he always wanted to be, Screws started at the typewriter in his office, still holding Culpepper's letter in his fist. He shuffled around the desk for T. A. Riley's ledger and found the heavy red book. Then he pulled a form of warrant from a drawer and rolled it into the Royal. Back and forth, Sheriff Screws made careful work filling out the ledger in fountain ink and then copying the information on the typewritten form. It was for the arrest of Bobby

Hall. The charge was tire theft. He typed that. Complaint made out by Mr. George Durham this twenty-eighth day of January 1943. George wouldn't mind. Where it said "sworn to" he squiggled a line with a hill here and there where the consonants might be. Over on the ledger, at the usual place, he wrote "so ordered: T. A. Riley" and dated that too. When he noticed the heavy sound of his own breath against the black keys, he sat back to examine his work. Done, he ripped the sheet of paper from the typewriter and leaned an arm against the armrest.

Frank Jones accidentally walked straight into his gaze, and the deputy was forced to slow up and grin nervously. "Howdy, sherf."

Frank was accompanied by another fellow, Jim Bob Kelley, a lean man with shirt hangers for shoulders visible through his plaid jacket, bead-like eyes, and worry cliffs on his cheekbones that looked calloused by the sun. Jim Bob waved to the sheriff and kind of smiled nicely. He was there to get Screws' consent to testify to certain facts that would get Jim Bob title to a piece of property near his farm, so he came with extra courtesies.

Sheriff Screws saluted both men with his chin. "C'mere, Frank. Somethin' I wanna show you." Frank stepped carefully over to the desk. "This come today by post from Camilla. Says we got some work to do tonight, boys. We bringin' in one smart nigger. Bobby Hall." The sheriff's voice dropped suddenly, and his eyes went cold. "Bobby Hall. The boy got hisself a *law-yuh*, and this here's a letter from 'im tellin' me I betta give that darkie back his pistol. Can you 'magine that! Gonna sick the law after the law! Who that boy think he is, Frank?"

Frank sat against the edge of a desk with a dull grin across his cheeks and couldn't answer.

"Fellas," said the sheriff, "you know this here is *my* town. Been that way for quite some time." Both men nodded. "Might be war everywhere else, but there's peace 'round here. Now this biggety nonsense gone on just about too goddamn long, and we 'bout to put things back to order, see." That's the moment when Sheriff Screws convinced himself how he was going to get Bobby Hall. "Wanna be a dep'ty tonight, Jim Bob?"

THE DAY WEARS SLOWLY, DRAGGED BY THE WEIGHT OF EXPECTATION. The three men have an early supper in the courthouse, discussing plans, then nazis. The beef is fresh, the steak delicious. Sheriff Screws instructs Frank and Jim Bob to meet him out at Mamie Wrights' filling station later that evening. Along the way, be prepared to round up some more deputies, he says. He wants to see a mob out by Bobby's house that night.

Alone, resolved and wondering how to put the finishing edges on time, Sheriff Screws reaches once more into a desk drawer and pulls out a fifth of whiskey. His blackjack hangs from a hook on the side of the desk, and he grabs that too. He pulls a .38 special from his holster and makes sure it's loaded before heading for the police car parked out back. The sheriff gets in, takes a long swig from the bottle, and drives away with the hot vapor still washing down his insides. He hums quietly to himself as he sets out for the intersection just out of town where Butler's garage sits on one side of the highway and the Wrights' filling station and drink stand on the other. There's a dip between the roads there like a shallow ditch, and he turns in there. From his vantage, he can look out and see both businesses. At Butler's across the way, to the right and under the light bulb is Bobby Hall, working on a truck. Screws stares, he drinks; he stares, he drinks, until the bottle is empty and his upper body is full of heat. Bobby's sporadic movements in the shop provide a guessing-game theater, growing blurry with alcohol. He wonders about Bobby's arms and legs, sees him twisting heavy metal and banging against a two-ton truck's resistance. Bobby's young; he shows no respect. Fear occurs to Screws, so he burns it with whiskey.

Around half past seven or eight o'clock, Bobby closes up the shop, turns out the light, and climbs into his Chevy. Sheriff Screws cranes his neck to see him drive away. Once his taillights are out of sight, Sheriff Screws opens the door and lifts himself awkwardly out of the car. The steak supper and whiskey still settling in his stomach, he walks over to the Wrights' filling station and goes inside. Mamie Wright is in there along with her husband and a couple of other men finishing dinner.

"Evenin', folks. I'm lookin' for Joe Whitlock. Any a y'all seen 'im lately? Mamie?"

The sheriff holds the doorway for support, his face bright red and his shirt halfway sticking out of his pants on one side. Mamie turns a hollow, tight face toward him and looks concerned. "No, sheriff. Why?"

"Don't matter none," he says with fresh authority. "I need me some men tonight. Any you men got guts enough to come wit us tonight? Gonna round us up a black s'ombitch and kill 'im. This one done lived too long already. Whose wit me, eh?"

By ten o'clock, the sheriff's posse remains Frank Jones and Jim Bob Kelley, and they are back together buying wine at Johnny West's place. A small crowd of white planters fills the front room where Johnny is serving behind a counter. The three men head for the empty room in the back. Johnny's got a jukebox there, and Frank wants to dance. Along in the doorway come the Mintners, Velma and Jack, with Josephine Price, the women dressed in bright colors for a Friday night of fun.

BOBBY'S TIRED WHEN HE GETS HOME TO ANNIE PEARL. HIS ARMS ARE caked with grease and his fingernails are black. With just a single lamp on, Annie Pearl heats the buckets of water for Bobby's bath. New lies in a makeshift day crib that he is almost too big for. Bobby stands naked over him going ga-ga, while Annie Pearl draws the tub water.

She walks over and guides him over to the bath with her hand on his buttock. "Git in. Wash up. We eatin' soon." Then she fixes a piece of fish for their supper.

At Johnny's, Josephine Price shows Frank Jones new dance moves she says are the rage of Atlanta these days. Smiles turn to glaze as the drinks go down. Sheriff Screws reaches for his gun sitting on the table. Aimlessly, he spins the chamber against his palm.

"You comin' wid us, Jack?" Jim Bob asks.

"Cain't tonight, boys. You know I work niggras." Jim Bob nods and drinks. Sheriff Screws keeps a hard look trained on the gun he's holding in both hands. Jack Mintner finishes his bottle and adds proudly, "I don't rightly go with arrestin' officers."

Suddenly, the gun goes off in Sheriff Screws' hands. Josephine jumps into Frank's arms, and everybody twitches. The bullet lodges in the thick wooden floor near Jim Bob's feet. He examines the hot lump while the others watch. Then he runs his fingertips over it, pretends the heat makes him snap them back and kisses them. "Hoo-wee, sherf! Reckon yer gun's sure clean!" And everybody gives up a great laugh.

BOBBY SITS AT THE TABLE IN JUST HIS BRITCHES, ANNIE PEARL IN HER night dress. They eat while the baby sleeps at last in a makeshift crib beside the bed.

"Why you didn't go to the dance tonight over at the school?" she asks.

He bites into the cornbread in his hand. "Tired. You the onliest one I wanna dance wif, and I sho don't feel like standin' around wid all them old guys talkin' feed."

"Like yo daddy?"

"Pretty much." He smiles across the way at her. Puts his big toe on her calf and strokes her skin. She giggles slightly and pulls a bone out of the fish on her plate.

"On top o' dat I seen Sheriff Screws watchin' me out at Butler's tonight." Annie Pearl stops chewing. "Probably best to stay off the roads." He looks up and Annie Pearl's studying his face. "You done cooked the devil outa dis meal, baby. "

JOHNNY WEST COMES RUNNING TO THE BACK.

"Who's dead?" he asks from the doorway.

"Nobody yet," Frank tells him.

Sheriff Screws asks Johnny if he wants to come along. "We fittin' to round up a s'ombitch nigger. Why don'tcha come along, Johnny? Make yeh a dep'ty."

"What'd he do?"

Sheriff Screws looks a little surprised by the question. "He disobeyed the law, Johnny," he says, turning up his eyes at him. "Wants to make a career of it, too."

"No, sherf, I cain't go wit y'all tonight. Why don't y'all wait until tomorruh?"

"No thanks for the advice, Johnny," says the sheriff, grabbing his hat and fitting it back on his head. "We ain't lettin' this bastard get away."

Frank convinces the others to make one more stop at Loreat Hatcher's place to buy beer. Thirty minutes later, beer in their veins, they pack into the sheriff's personal car. It's nearly eleven o'clock and the roads are barren black. Only the first few minutes draw conversation, and only that between Frank and Jim Bob. The sheriff quietly smokes a cigarette as he drives them closer to Bobby Hall's house. About a half mile away, the conversation stops, and the loud motor of the sheriff's late-model Ford fills the air. Despite the chilly temperature, each man wears a light coat of sweat on his brow.

The headlights flood the dark yard with sudden light. Chickens scamper and squawk. Sheriff Screws turns to face his deputies; he mutters and they huddle. Then Jim Bob gets out his side, pulls his gun from his waistband and leans on top of the car. Frank walks up to the house and bangs his heavy fist on the door.

Inside Bobby stirs first. He unwraps Annie Pearl's sleeping arms and reaches for the shotgun beneath the bed. Crouching near the floor, he sets the gun upright against the wall beside him and moves toward the door.

"Who's that?" he calls. Annie Pearl wakes with a fright at the sound of Bobby's voice. The absence of his body next to hers starts her heart beating wildly in her chest.

"Frank Jones, Bobby."

"Whatchoo want now?"

"Wanna talk witcha, boy."

Bobby thinks of the shotgun sitting ready. Before he can decide, Annie Pearl lights the lamp beside the bed. Their eyes meet and freeze. She sees in him a fear she never knew he was capable of. He sees a fear in her equal to a great longing. She reaches for his arm. He reaches for the dirt-brown pants at the foot of the bed. There's a new knock at the door.

"Hurry up, Bobby."

Bobby goes to the door, opens it and steps back. The headlights pointed at the porch blind him. Frank Jones's silhouette steps forward into the little house. Annie Pearl grabs the blanket and covers herself. With the white man in the room, standing armed and anxious, a forever distance seems to open between her and Bobby. New begins to cry. She cannot comfort him without exposing herself, and she cannot expose herself.

"What's the matter, Mr. Jones? What y'all need with my husband this time o' night?"

"Takin' him in, Annie Pearl. Got a warrant for you, boy, on account o' you stealin' a spare tire."

Annie Pearl gasps and covers her mouth. From his stance in the doorway, Frank reaches for Bobby's arm. "Well, I declare, Mr. Jones, I never stole no tire."

"No damn short talk about it!" Frank commands, and New's cries turn to wails. Bobby wants to go to him. "Git yer clothes on, boy, and let's go."

Bobby puts on a faded yellow shirt, and turns to Annie Pearl. His eyes caught unprepared between certain fear and the pain of wonder, he takes leave of her and walks ahead of Frank out the door.

Frank sees the shotgun just as he's turning to leave. "Hey, boy, whas that over there?" Frank steps over toward the bed, throws a suspicious glance at Annie Pearl, and suddenly jerks the shotgun to him. He holds the long gun up near Annie's thigh and cocks the handle. The gun spits a red shell out of its side, which falls to the floor. "This here's comin' wit me." New's unattended lungs tear into the height of screams. Frank closes the door behind them.

Annie Pearl rushes to the window. On the stoop, Frank pulls handcuffs from his waistband and slaps them around Bobby's wrist. Annie Pearl watches Bobby's body lurch in discomfort as the cuffs close. Words are exchanged but she can't hear them over the motor. Frank pushes Bobby into the backseat. The deputies get back in. Annie Pearl leaps toward the baby and snatches him up in her arms. She kisses him, squeezes him too harshly, desperately, and props him on the bed while she dresses in a panic. As she hears the car turning onto the road, she grabs New and dashes out the back of the house and down the road one hundred yards to Willy's house. The sheriff's car heads over a hill and disappears.

"What'd somebody say I done, sherf?" Bobby asks from beside Frank in the backseat. He tries to keep his voice from trembling, tries to ignore the thick smell of alcohol, hopes to reason through a misunderstanding.

"Shut up, yeh black s'ombitch!" the sheriff says, staring at the road. "Smart nigger like you always wants teh know somethin'. Teach 'im a little somethin' teh keep 'im quiet, will yeh, Frank?"

Bobby feels a brief space open up between his body and Frank's arm. A large shape hovers in the dark periphery, then suddenly a loud *whomp*! Frank smashes his elbow into the side of Bobby's head and knocks him against the other side of the car.

All the men are quiet. Sheriff Screws smokes another cigarette. Jim Bob smokes one too. Bobby, hands shackled behind him, leans forward and stares down at the floorboard. He asks for clarity in his thoughts and begins to pray.

At half past one in the morning, Newton is asleep. The sheriff drives down Main Street to the square. He parks the car a few feet from the well that sits near the courthouse steps. Once the sheriff turns the motor off, Jim Bob gets out and comes around to Bobby's side of the car. Using the barrel of Bobby's shotgun as a cane, Sheriff Screws turns to face Bobby. "I'm about to finish you up, nigger."

The sheriff is inches from his face. "You're wrong, sherf," Bobby says. "I ain't took nobody's tire."

At the sound of the words, Sheriff Screws's eyes squint to an angry boiling point while his hands grapple madly to pull the blackjack from his belt. Staring deep into Bobby's eyes, Sheriff Screws blasts him in the face with the blackjack.

The hard rubber crushes a bone in Bobby's cheek; the heavy steel inside the rubber seems to lodge in the flesh under his eye. Then again and again, until his face feels wet and Bobby loses all sense of who's striking him. When he tries to move away, somebody kicks him back. When he tries to put his arms up, the blows rain from an unprotected side. They're figuring out how to kill him as they go.

"Hep 'im up, Jim Bob. Git 'im out where I can get a betta lick on 'im. Don't let this nigger bleed all over ma car."

They drag Bobby around to the front of the car, catching his body in the space between the fender and the stone sides of the well. Under the street lamp, he can barely make out Jim Bob to his left, Sheriff Screws carrying the shotgun upside down and Frank to the right wrapping his own blackjack tighter in his grip. The sheriff is panting, maybe smiling. Bobby can't see him. "Open 'im up, boys," the sheriff spits. Jim Bob and Frank hold Bobby steady. The sheriff raises the butt of the shotgun into the light.

"Nuh!" Bobby tries to yell and turns his head in vain.

The butt crashes through his skull and the blood escapes in all directions. The two men at Bobby's sides tear at him with fists, passing his body off to each other, against the side of the car, into each other's blows and against the well.

"C'mon! Git 'im good!" The sheriff yells, tired, blood on his fists, blood escaping into the square. "Hit 'im again! Hit 'im again!"

Bobby can't feel the blows anymore. He loses sight, hope, smell, touch. Only sound remains. Each blow of the blackjack against his head and neck, each kick in his groin and back as they stomp him comes together in a chaotic rhythm of thuds. Nothing can protect him. The Lord's back is turned. Thuds keep coming through the night. The fury of blows from one side rests momentarily while the other heats up. Then a new side takes over. Then another. And again.

After about forty minutes, the beating stops. Bobby lies in a pool of blood about a half-inch deep. The street light exposes the redness of his flesh. Twisted arms facing west, legs caught running east, Bobby's body is still, heavy yet weightless, exhausted but tranquil. The three men carefully record the image in their minds like souvenirs. They stand over their work, proud and tired, catching their breath. Sheriff Screws crosses his arms atop his great stomach and stares into Bobby's open eyes. On his toes, he rocks in and out of their distant focus. Finally, Screws turns and Jim Bob and Frank grab Bobby by his feet and follow the sheriff up the stairs. Bobby's chest, then his head, scrape the ground, then each step, bouncing against the hard edge of cold stone, leaving a trail of blood back down to the well. Inside the courthouse, they drop Bobby's body in a small dark cell in the back. An ambulance arrived from the Negro hospital in Albany, but Bobby died before the doctors saw him.

WHEN ANNIE PEARL REACHED WILLY'S HOUSE WITH THE BABY, SHE met all caution. He held her, waited for her to control her crying, then questioned her.

"Say dey was in Sheriff Screws's personal car? Dey was three o'm? Put de cuffs on 'im? Say Frank had alcohol on 'is breaf? No, baby girl. We ain't gon to de jail jes now. We go at sun up."

And that's what they did. At sun up on the morning of January 30, Willy Hall, Annie Pearl and New drove into Newton and headed to the square. There they saw Bobby's sock, pieces of his yellow shirt, a shoe and the dry lake of maroon blood that leaked from him and trailed up the courthouse stairs.

The road to Albany proved too long for Annie Pearl. New couldn't distract her. Hope couldn't fool her. Willy couldn't even save himself, except with silence. How could he be dead? she screamed at him.

Why would they have to kill him? How is it fair? she wanted to know. But no question comes all the way past her lips before another, more terrible question jumps it, and as its horrid answer takes shape, it is cut off by the blind swipe of another. All the way to Albany.

Annie Pearl waited in the car while Willy rang the bell at Walter Poteat's funeral parlor. She watched to see if Walter was expecting them; she hopes that the stop will be brief on their way to the hospital. Walter will be surprised to see Willy. The two will laugh goodbye and slap each other on the back. They will be two old colored men with living sons promising each other a better meal than the other can make. New rocked on his mother's knee bouncing anxiously. She whispered chants of nothing into the baby's delicate curls. She squinted from the road as the door opened. Walter Poteat steps out and holds Willy by the shoulder. She sees Willy's head look up as the first words were exchanged, then down quickly, down and not up again. Walter is severe. He is sorry. Bobby is inside. From her window, Annie Pearl screamed and New joins her in earnest.

THE WAY YOU GET A WHITE KILLER MASQUERADING AS A LAW MAN IS to show up all the sickness in him. Claud Screws didn't know that, and in the end it didn't matter. If you'd asked Claud Screws what should happen now that he beat Bobby Hall's brains all over the square, he'd say what any white killer who masquerades as something else will tell you: Nothing. Which is almost what happened. Everybody in the houses out on that square knew somebody was getting lynched that night. They *liked* Bobby Hall. They liked his daddy, they liked Lemuel, and many of the Hall family. But they took Screws's word and Frank's word and even Jim Bob's word, even though Jim Bob got his property out of it. Screws said the nigger took the tire, the nigger was a thief. Screws said the nigger pulled a shotgun, the nigger had to die. If it took forty minutes to do it, well some niggers' lives take longer to snuff. Especially how they fight back.

There never was an inquiry into the sickness in the man. Beyond the obvious, nobody questioned how a man like Screws goes on about his business in peace after dashing a young man to bits. They never asked how you could drag a dying body up the stairs in the name of justice. They never asked why Screws wouldn't protect colored soldiers from angry rednecks. They never asked him what the pearl-handle pistol meant to *him*. If you want to know what's in a man's state of mind, you have to find out what he's thinking.

Spring returned to Newton. The magnolias bloomed and Claud Screws again walked merrily among the jasmine and crape myrtles of a generous earth. He satisfied himself with righteousness. He restored order to his delinquent soul.

What surprised him was the FBI's interest all of a sudden. The agents who came to Newton investigating the death of Bobby Hall seemed to be doing the work of the Negro Betterment Society. But they weren't. They weren't because they represented the same federal government that had sent Lemuel to Liberia and was bombing Dresden and claiming triumph on the globe. They weren't because they didn't once ask about the sickness.

At Sheriff Screws's trial for the deprivation of Bobby Hall's constitutional rights, many in Newton stepped to the witness stand. They were asked and they answered about what Sheriff Screws and his posse intended to do to Bobby on the night of January 29, 1943. That's where the problem got away from them. Not because Screws would win there. He didn't. A Georgia jury convicted him, Frank Jones and Jim Bob Kelley for conspiring to take Bobby's rights away along with his life that night. But the facts they wanted and the ones they got only told about visiting the grand jury in Albany and what was said there; about being drunk and rounding up men to catch a Negro thief; about shooting into the floorboards at Johnny West's; about words overheard from the ruckus by the well that night; and about waking up on Saturday to hear the three talk of the rough night before.

The conviction—just a couple of years and a fine—was appealed all the way to the U.S. Supreme Court where the justices had quite a battle over it. All beside the point, all of it. Not a single solitary word having to do with what killed Bobby Hall and why. They sent the case back down for a new trial to see if Screws and his men did indeed "willfully" take Bobby's rights away. By then it was too late. The new jury was probably tired of all the interference by the federal government in the affairs of a small town, so Screws and the rest were acquitted.

BUT ONCE IT KILLED BOBBY, THE SICKNESS BECAME HIS FAMILY'S LIFE. The first thing that happened to Annie Pearl, even before she could see it through her grief, was she and New became poor. From then on, she would always be poor or nearly poor. Eventually, anger transformed the scrappy sweetness of Bobby's copper sidekick with the butterfly lips, and she all but quit smiling. She became a survivor because she was the one left alive in the house that night. After the acquittal, Annie Pearl found her shoes and left Newton to complete her bitterness in New York City where she hoped it would be different. It was that. There Newtons appeared block upon block; the town's black sections teemed in high-rise projects, locked into the sky. It was not freedom. Every time she'd hear of another death, down the street, across the country, her whole body would wince. The brutality of memory made it impossible to accept whites, and Annie Pearl lived a palpable legacy of distance and mistrust. She made do.

And New inherited his father's lynching. He marked the growth of his own body against the image of Bobby's officially desecrated flesh. Muscled squares and squares at torn angles. More than what his mother said or his grandfather or anyone else let slip, his own body reminded him of what he was too young to remember. No one would explain to him exactly what happened; no one really tried. Just for his body, he had to assume the rage, his own, his father's and Screws's. Just for the body, New could never forget. He wondered how to sustain it, where to put it, how to honor it. How was he his father? Was New's strong-willed mind like his daddy's, the tilt in his stride, or the gestures he made? Would New some day share his bludgeoned head, his tortured trunk? So, New wore him in a certain sullenness. He maintained the daily demands of cool detachment. Like battle fatigues, a hard, mournful style obscured the quiet passions coursing through him. He got good with his hands. And as soon as he could, New carried guns, somehow, he figured, to avenge him.

III

MID-CENTURY

Junius Dogman and the Mischief

AFTER YOU DECIDE YOU GONNA KILL YOUR FIRST WHITE MAN, YOU have to fight to stay real calm in yourself. Because it's a mighty little feeling that wants to well up in you and keeps trying to get out too soon. It got away from me the first time.

I was a young man in my twenties and very strong. Better be a boulder 'cause a rock ain't had nothin on me. We was six colored men on a day job digging ditches 'cause the river was breakin. Wasn't my regular work, but don't take much to teach a nigger how to go from plantin crops to diggin ditches. Two white men, both crackers, mean and stingy, were in charge. One standing over me name was Jim Crow, I ain't lyin. Jim kept tellin me to keep up, promised he gonna whup me if I don't. Bunched up his lash in his hand and kept showing it to me. I didn't look. He took a shovel and starts stabbin at the ground beside my feet, faster and faster, tellin me that's my pace, that's gotta be my pace nigger and so forth. Shovel got plenty close to my feets, too. I'm bending low to lift the dirt, and next thing I know this cracker's shovel comes down real hard on my left hand. I look down and my pinky's hanging by a gutstring, not a bone in sight. That's when I haul up from my crouch and bury all a my fist in Jim Crow's face. All of it. I can feel his eyeballs against my knuckles. His nose is gushin all the blood in his head. Man's face just caved in. But I didn't kill him. The devil musta run off with the purpose 'cause I let up. For that I did four years pickin cotton for the state of Mississippi at Parchman Farm. But I swore that I would never lose another finger and I would surely kill a white man. I got one right.

The other thing about killin a white man is if it don't rise from honor, it ain't never gonna come. Honor is tricky. That's why so few men really have it. Honor brings impostors to make you think it's honor, but maybe it's just your pride. I'd take one man with honor over one proud-ass army any day. Honor knows just what to do when it comes to killing a white man. It contains that feeling until it can really do some good. Honor visits with it, see, asks about it, brings it refreshment. And you gotta refresh the feeling every day, just like a man's bed. Most especially the pillow where he lays his head to rest at night. If you don't fluff and spank the pillow every day, there's gonna be a build up where the head has to sleep. You can't live without sleep, and you can count all your days by needin it. That's why you must refresh it. And that's the same with your decision to kill a white man. It's livin in the days of your time on earth just waiting, each day it gets a little refreshment, moves on, then it becomes the whole thing—nerves, plan, target, confidence—until one day, the day it's supposed to wake up, it wakes up and goes to work. Bang. You take him out.

Another thing makes the difference to me: I never feared the horror white folks is. Fear'll make you crazy and proud so you do things you ought to know better and come to regret. Lawyer at my trial told white folks I was insane, said a nigger had to be crazy with fear to kill some white po-licemen. Not this one. This my daddy taught me when I was small: the law ain't in for colored people, it's out for 'em. So you gotta take it into your own hands.

WE COME FROM LOUISE, MISSISSIPPI, JUST BEYOND THE FLOOD LINE, low end of the Delta, where trees grow bigger than shacks. Not much law in the country. Lots of cotton, though. I am the son of Isaac and Lucy. I was raised as much by their words as the backs of they hands. Rough hands and sun burnt, 'specially from September when the bolls burst white and we all of us, my brothers Delaney, Joe and Ray-Ray and my sisters Ella and Janine, worked the cotton fields. My daddy worked us hard for the furnish. Bossman gave you furnish against what your shares might bring you that season. The furnish opened up his store. Daddy would get what we needed plus a little of what we didn't need. I'm pretty sure the bossman shorted him, too. But if you can't truly count, why talk when you got mouths to feed?

So it went like that. I liked the workin best. That's when we was all together as one family.

More usually daddy was away at Parchman with his brother Luther. Luther understood about fightin and killin better than most, and I think my daddy watched his back. When I got to go to Parchman that one time, Luther was a caller there. Right away that put me in. Sure I got whupped in front of other men, but the trusties let me be mostly. 'Cause Luther had that voice, see, and just the right rhythm to keep the other men workin them rows in chains. Right behind him was my daddy. Somewhere else was me, with the dogs. Mainly 'cause I could run my ass off. I was a dogboy at Parchman, catchin' runaway convicts with hounds.

That's where I saw my first white man leave here for the next world. His name was Sam so and so. There was a trusty-shooter also by the name of Sam so and so. I had the dogs near the shooter. Sam ran for it and the dogs and me took off. Bullet screamed right past my shoulder and into the back of Sam's head. In a bang and a zip it went from Sam to Sam. But usually it was colored fellows crossing over. The men of my family were in that line of business, which is how they wound up married to Parchman. My father got too drunk and killed a man in a blind tiger. Luther musta killed a whole line. But words from my mother, I would not.

For that I might be crazy, I know. I understand that some of the best killin there is goes down between one nigger and a blacker one. I couldn't bring myself to it. I was gonna once, had my knife out and him where I needed him to be, but my back tightened up way down at the spine, just when I was heating up, just when I was really about to enjoy feeling his flesh puncture, my back gave up some poison, a smell like formaldehyde come over my nostrils, and the poison seemed to wrap around my backbone and snap me so quick I couldn't move at all. I had no breath. I thought I was gonna die. I couldn't see his face no more, but I knew it was his turn to try and do to me what I couldn't get it together to do to him. Just a couple a pair of eyes staring each other down but not seeing the other person. Seeing yourself, at least that's what I saw, me and me alone, me not ready to die just then, not that way, not at his hands, but not even ready to save myself. No. I don't consider killin brothers for long.

When I finally got ready to kill my first white man, it was two of them and it was easy. By the late 1950s, Claudette and me had been married several years. I don't know exactly how many, only that legally we were probably one by then. No preacher declared it, but every man and woman in Louise knew it. The two po-licemen there, Brent Avery and Vernon Sellers, they knew it. And Claudette's cousin Boonie better know it. I didn't much care for Boonie. He was a rascal and ugly about it. I can't think of a good thing he ever did no one, but somehow he used to get right into Claudette's head. And that night he was. Claudette and me was at Jelly's. It was a Saturday. Jelly's is a nice little place, not too dangerous like The Ginny. A dead nigger was seldom seen at Jelly's 'cause Jelly didn't allow no card playin for cash and no dice. There was music though, and Claudette and me was enjoyin it as usual. I had that kind of wife, the kind you wanted beside you and your first free dollar when you finally got your first free hour. Honey, she is, dark honey and thick, with a wide mouth like my mother's and Chinaman eyes. In those days still had an ass on her like quittin time.

Only thing that happened was the whiskey and the wonder. Claudette and me was having a go at one of our favorite wonders. What's worse? What's worse, I'd ask her, gettin beat with a branch or beat with a belt? We both agreed on belt. What's worse, she say, a fever or a rash? Depends on where the rash is. Under something. Well, the rash, we decided. And it went on like that all night. Mosquitoes or a rat? A Monday or a Wednesday? Syphilis or gonorrhea? We was having quite a roll when something Boonie musta been tellin her spoke up. What's worse, hurricane or a flood? By that time, I was feelin footsteps in the back of my head. Jelly kept my kind of whiskey and I probably had enough. But this one was easy. You can't live off no Delta without knowing it's flood. Claudette said hurricane. How you gonna say hurricane, I asked her, when everybody in the county know somebody done died in a flood? Your own auntie got washed off in a flood a few years back. I do believe Claudette was drunk. But, Junius, she tells me, floods just get a few at a time. If a hurricane come through here right now, it'll take us all with it. That's a world-size if, I tells her back. And pretty soon it got very nasty between me and my wife.

Jelly come over talkin 'bout I gotta settle down or go on home. He was interfering in my family business and I told him so. Jelly's a good man, and he begged my pardon, saying would I please at least finish this outside. It was May and cool, so I said OK. Outside Claudette just got louder. She started tellin how Boonie told her such and such about hurricanes down in Biloxi. I knew for a fact that Boonie ain't never been nowhere near Biloxi. My beloved was irritatin me no end with that Boonie shit anyhow. All a sudden I got so mad I struck her right out there on the porch. Claudette ducked a bit when she saw the blow comin, so I only caught her shoulder. But I caught it good and knocked her down. I seen what I done and reached down and tried to help her back up, but she wouldn't let me. That's when here come the old cracker po-licemen Avery and his cricketty sidekick Sellers. Most times Avery don't care to get in between a man and his wife, even a colored man, but that night he had it in for me special. He come swaggering out the squad car, and in the headlights I can make out his square face, the part separating the white hair on top from what's on the side, and truly beady eyes. He's working on some chewing gum, makes his thin mustache move.

"Look like the fun's gettin a little out a hand, Junius."

After that I just remember his cold tiny eyes. Avery's eyes were so mean, you almost could admire him for it. They had no room for fear in them whatsonever. Luther had that; not me so much. But I wasn't about admiring nothin that night. Sheriff Avery was first gonna talk me into tryin something, so he could kill me, I figured. Either way he was gonna take my wife away from me, 'cause he said so. Claudette looked very tasty in her pink and white dress that night, and there was no tellin what Avery and Sellers might wanna do. But that's where the honor struck gold for me. I wouldn't let the devil run wild with my feeling right then. I decided I would have to kill these white men, and I was gonna do it right. Wait here, nigger, Avery said before they drove off. Said something about takin' Claudette home, then coming back to take care of me once and for all. I was willin to wait. I didn't move.

Soon as they drive away though, I head to Boonie's house, which is where I knew I kept my shotgun last. I damn sure wasn't drunk no more. Boonie was in there messin with some little girl, but Claudette wasn't. He jumped up when I rushed in. You seen Claudette? I ask him. He said no. I couldn't lay eyes on him, just fetched my shotgun. He wanted to know where I was goin. I wasn't gonna tell him 'til I figured maybe Claudette would show up and wanna know. I'm goin home, I told him. Ain't nothin suspicious about a nigger takin his shotgun home with him on a Saturday night.

My house was about half a mile away, and my car was low on petrol. I decided to leave it a few hundred feet from the shack, just to throw 'em if they came. They came all right. Both of 'em. Alone. No Claudette. My problem was they came too quick for me to get the shells loaded up, so I had to keep them in my pocket. These old fellas sure meant business that night, cause they left that po-lice car on the road next to my car. I watched from the front stoop and they checked the hood to see if it was warm. Next thing, Sellers turns off the headlights. Then I hear 'em comin. I know they got rifles out 'cause once they get past the first tree I can hear 'em cockin. They must still got pretty good eyesight even in the dark 'cause Avery calls out I better drop the shotgun. He couldn't see that good, 'cause I wasn't holdin it in my arms. I had the butt on the floor and was holdin on to the barrel. I lifted it off the stoop and banged it on the boards so's he could see better. That was my mistake. All I see next is the light flash outta Avery's gun. The two of 'em blink like shadows. And I got a burnin hole across my backside. That dropped me for sure. Another blast comes flying just over my head. That one mighta been Sellers. I'm fumblin in my pockets for the shells, and they can hear me I guess 'cause more shots start for me. My ass was a bloody mess, but my spine was fine, and as I fired into that night, I opened my eyes just in time to see Avery get cut in two.

Just like that I'm on the lam. I didn't bother tryin to bring God into it, because I figure He knew all about it already. Maybe I was doin somethin that just needed to get done. Only He knew. So off I went. Seems like I went everywhere and nowhere. I drove and drove, expectin' to see the mobs loosed on me any time. I headed west, called by the river. Best thing for me was it rained all day Sunday. I made it to the banks along the backroads near Vicksburg, got out to watch the rain fall on that mighty Mississippi and dress my wound. Seemed like I could see that hungry river rising, and the current chopping here and there like dog teeth roughin up a bone. Didn't mind gettin wet. Wasn't scared neither. I figured the sight of this big grey river would be one of my last, and I felt like a king on his throne. Only the water knew what I might tell it. For that moment we was both masters. The river of rain and me of men. I know I was s'posed to be hanging from a tree someplace, or burnin alive in front of the county's meanest, dirtiest crackers, but I felt like a king all the same.

When the rain lightened up that evening, I needed cover, so I decided to get away from that wandering river and try to make it over the state line. Something in my head made me think Biloxi, and I started off thinkin I could really get there. Find me a boat to Mexico or somethin. What the hell, with my luck, maybe a hurricane come and wipe us all away. I got as far as Gulfport. I was miles from the mobs now. My brother Delaney told me that. That's how come he avoided gettin lynched once. You need rain, a car and ya need to pass enough different jurisdictions that dumb white folk can't catch up. Then at least you get to see what law they got for ya. For us, that used to mean Parchman.

I have never been in a courtroom when white folks was conducting they own business, so I cannot tell the goings on of justice and all.

But whatever it is, they must surely take the day off when we inside. It's like they on all fours again. A Negro don't stand a chance. Especially then. I killed the only policemen they had, maybe the onliest ones they ever had cause they was so old. We heard talk in other parts of Mississippi where what they called Freedom Riders had come down from the North to shake up the crackers. There was talk about a new law on the books sayin colored and white had to go to school together. None of this pleased the mean and dirty white folks of Louise much. Fightin it just made 'em madder. The little courthouse they had me in was quite out of the way of news for the papers, but somehow I knew I had stepped right in it all.

Here comes this lawyer fella from Jackson. He was nice enough. Appointed to represent me. Scared shitless, you could tell, and what smarts he had he hid good. Thin guy with a city haircut, prob'ly never worn coveralls a day in life. Country white folks scared his type, and I can't see why not. They packed the courthouse so bad it bulged, the whole posse that had come searchin for me in the rain. They was tired and bug-eyed, mean and had a evil smell about 'em. Put the victims' sorry lookin families in the front row. I knew 'em. I knew 'em all, but I didn't expect no mercy. The jury was a bunch of the same hooligans mad 'cause they couldn't have me on a rope. Lawyer fella, can't remember his name, tried to explain my case to 'em. He said it all came down to a darky goin wild on a Saturday night. Some of the jurors nodded. He said I was insane at the time, I had to be, holdin a shotgun in front of the law. He disagreed with the prosecutor, who said I ambushed Avery and Sellers. My lawyer said I acted in self-defense. He told the jury they gotta see how the shots were fired at me, how I got hit on my own stoop, and how I was just tryin to protect myself and my home.

If lawyer fella had talked to me about all that first I coulda told him no one was gonna buy it. But true enough, he was tryin to keep me out of the place where I've been ever since. The thing is, it just made no kind of sense. Self-defense is what it was. If Brent Avery didn't kill me that night, old Vernon Sellers would. It was them or me. But lawyer fella had to add in the part about me bein insane. This was s'posed to save me from the electric chair. If I was insane too, then the jury might could send me back to Parchman so I could be a trusty-shooter forever. All the trusty-shooters was insane. Well, maybe so, but not so far as that jury was concerned. We was in and out of the whole mess by lunchtime. They gave me the chair. But I didn't have to go to Parchman waitin for it.

When I first got here and they put me on the death row I did indeed wonder maybe the lawyer fella was right about me. Maybe I was crazy to do what I done. Death row make a man think sure 'nough, maybe even drive him mad, but it don't go back into time and change what used to make sense. Nothin may ever make sense again, but what used to make sense still makes sense. That was my puzzle. Lawyer fella started out thinkin I was too dumb to know what insane was. So he repeated it for me a few times. Man has to have a mental disease or some kind of defective wiring in his brain. Then he's not supposed to be able to tell right from wrong. Inside that cell alone, very little light in there, slop jar stinkin up beside me, flies and big-ass bugs everywhere, steel mattress, I confess to wonderin if that was me out there that night, a looney with a shotgun and a ripped up butt.

Along one day comes a visitor. The prison had real guards that worked for the state by now, not trusty shooters like they had at Parchman. This guy come tellin me to get my ass up and clean off, 'cause somebody from the victim's family wanted to see me. This was the first true visitor I had. I thought the man say it was somebody *for* the families, so I tried to stall and take my time before they dragged me in there to hear what they was gonna take from me this time.

Well, very much to my surprise it turns out to be Sellers' boy. Said his name was Charlie. Charlie looked to be about my age. Still had most of his hair unlike his daddy, but had the same large eyes deep in his head, a cheekbone like someone took a chisel to it, and the same nose, heavy with thick red skin. I have always known this boy turned man, but he only now decided he was gonna know me too.

Charlie sat across from me behind a glass, tryin to hold me in his stare. There was nothin to hold, as far as I was concerned. But Charlie come out to the prison to find out for himself was I crazy.

We got to talkin. Seems like when a white man comes to see you, they give you all the time he needs. Later on when my people came, we got 'til they get tired of lookin at us, which is awful quick, even now. Charlie wanted to hear me tell it. I obliged. Said that it was dark and I was shot. Avery I knew was dead 'cause there was nearly two of him. Sellers mighta been breathin. He mighta been waitin for my back to turn so he could finish me off. I bent low and followed around to the other side. He was still near the car, lyin curled up on the ground. I could make out Sellers' bald head, and I felt like it was facing me and he was takin aim. I hid behind the tree and loaded another shell. I counted to three, stepped out into the path and fired at that bald head. That's what I told Charlie. Next I made sure Sellers was dead, and he was. The next part surprised me, I told Charlie. 'Cause in the next part I decided to reach into Sellers' pocket and take his money off a him. He had twelve dollars. That's how come they tried me on the armed robbery, too. Somehow they figured out that I got Sellers money. I never woulda gone near Avery's pocket, even as a dead man, but they didn't ask me about that.

"You stole the car next?" he said, tryin to stay cool.

"Sure I did. Mine was outta gas."

I could see it all startin to get to the man, so I tried tellin him about ridin around in the po-lice car. I told Charlie about the radio and the specialized engine, how that baby was really made to go. I knew this guy knew of all these things them cars have, I knew he took to the siren buttons and lights and gizmos and things as much as any boy ever would, but especially him 'cause Charlie was the son of a deputy. I used to watch him get to play in that car.

"Why'd you have to kill him, too, Junius?"

This wasn't the big question it was supposed to be in his mind. I had my answer right away. I told him how Sellers and Avery had been killin niggers and helpin others kill niggers and catching niggers and jailin niggers since before him and me was born. I told Charlie how Sellers and Avery started out on my grandaddy, makin' up crimes and pickin him up and sellin him. Just sell him to sell him. Just to make him work for free cause you could do that under the convict lease. You just needed a nigger, and you could be his bad luck. For the rest of his life, servin time on some white man's farm, breakin his back layin railroad ties, killin him slow from some Delta swamp disease before he could pay off some term wasn't never meant to be paid off, answerin for some crime wasn't never no real crime nohow. Sellers and Avery been smack in the middle of it all. Sad to see that game go when it did. But they come back with new tricks. Got Ray-Ray. Got two of my wife's brothers. Mighta got me. But they lived a long life, I told Charlie. Both of 'em died old compared to what they done.

I had to thank Charlie for comin by that day 'cause that was the day I decided I was never gonna be insane. Used to be that a colored man on death row had a ritual they beat into him before he died. Some been beat so bad so often that when the time come he didn't have to be beat. Just stepped up and did it. I was supposed to do it for Charlie, and I think that's really why he come. First, I was supposed to confess my crime; next, tell him how sorry I was I took his pappy; and then beg the Lord's forgiveness. Never even occurred to me. Took me weeks later pacing that little cell of mine to figure out that's what Charlie musta wanted. The old three-step passed down from the original sorry nigger. Not this one. That's how come I knew I wasn't insane. Not then, not now, not ever.

Claudette finally got to see me a year or so into it. A letter or two I could hardly read got through, but that was the first time I saw those eyes again outside my dreams. I expected her to tell me her and some fresh new slim was leaving for Chicago or something. Everybody we knew had family go up to Chicago at some point or another. No, but that's not what she said. She said she still loved me, even said she was sorry about the hurricanes. That's finally when I cried. That was the first time I cried in that whole affair that became my life. I didn't hardly cry for what happened; it felt like I was cryin 'cause I never did get to tell her how sorry I was to hit her like I done. I never hit her before (though I sure wanted to on occasion), and I never would again, I told her. Claudette said then everything would be all right. Just like that: All right. She was busy tryin' to get my sentence changed. She told me my pappy was dead and Luther too, but she was tryin' to get me out in time to see my mama go. And to be with her. Some place else. Not to lose faith, Boonie was helpin her.

But word already got 'round about my not layin down a sorry nigger's life for the Sellers' boy-man. White men was startin to be put in prisons more by that time. Mine had many, even on death row, and they musta knew about me. My crime was rare; most of my kind never made it to no prison. One guy especially wanted to be my huckleberry. Cyrus Willie McDougan. He was a big one of them what you call black Irish bastards with rotten teeth, tattoos all across him and dark matted hair. He had killed many men, most of 'em Negroes, and he just didn't want to give one of us any respect. He's goin to die like I'm going to die, yet of all the no-count, mountain trash, go-fuck-a-mule crackers, he don't wanna look straight at a colored guy. He wanted to look sideways at ya. And they told me Cyrus Willie was gonna do me in.

Well, he did not. I don't know if he got his orders from the Sellers' boy-man or what, but he mixed 'em up one day. They was makin some of the death row convicts clean out the insides of a ceiling over at one of the prison buildins where they mostly kept guards and offices. They was fixin to put in electrical air conditioning. Gave us slices of metal, maybe alluminum, that fit just so in your hand. This thing let you scrape off the paint and splinters from the walls up in there like a spatula. The ceiling had to be hollowed out, they said, before they could put the system in. All of us was tired by the third day of it, and I was not watchin as careful as I used to. I'm workin alone in a corner, sweatin' like swine, and I know they was just about to call break. All a sudden Cyrus Willie comes runnin over to me. I barely see him but in time to get my hand up over my face. Slam!

Slam! His arm comes down on me with this spatula thing. It's a lot of commotion as I'm tryin to right myself and fend this fool off a me when I hear drop, drop. Something tells me it's two fingers on my good hand. Gone. Chopped off and dropped at my feet. That was it. I had been here before though, and this time I knew exactly what to do. I killed him. I held his face out with my bloody hand, and I cut his throat with the other. But mostly I remember his body fallin through the ceiling to the cement floor below and the sound it made. It was a thud, a thud that echoed through the whole dead body as his last breath escaped him.

I did very hard time for that one. I couldn't see no visitors and they kept me in the hole for twenty-three hours out of more days than I care to remember. But after that they let me alone. Nobody in particular missed Cyrus Willie, and I did save the state an execution. Killin him musta convinced the last holdouts that I was crazy. There was nothin more to know about me. But on account a me losin as many fingers as I killed white men, I couldn't work the same as other convicts no more. So they gave me the dogs to take care of until it was my time to fry. I don't rightly know just how come this prison keeps dogs. They don't got no dogboys standin in the fields after convicts like they got at Parchman. Musta been a tradition. And I am very grateful, cause I do loves me some hounds. They made it my job again, to love 'em and take care of 'em for the warden at the time, name of Everlie Ferguson, and he liked to put 'em in dog shows around the state. From then on I was a dogman. *The* Dogman, they called me.

ONE DAY ABOUT TEN OR TWENTY YEARS INTO IT, CLAUDETTE VISITS ME and says, "What's worse?" That was the fuckin game that started all this, I tell her. Didn't wanna play neither. But she wasn't smilin like regular. Claudette was very good at smilin when she come to visit, and it truly is the little things that matter. But this time she had none for me. What's worse, she says, life or death? Took me a while to answer, to be honest. That's when she told me they had sentenced me again, this time to life in prison. No gas. No chair. We hardly spoke after that. Me and her just looked down. I think she was starin at my hands clasped on the table. I was lookin in the glass too but at myself in the reflection, the parts I could see, just beneath my neck. My chest, my arms, my hips, legs. This was how much of me I would keep after all. All a me. 'Cept a few fingers, the state of Mississippi would let me take the rest of me to my grave myself. Claudette said she'd wait.

Wouldn't you know it, but Charlie Sellers musta found out about it somehow and comes to see me. That's what I figured. A lot was changin in Mississippi by then, and I could see it on Charlie. He wore a turtleneck and had long sideburns going grey like my own. I'd never seen glasses like the ones he had on, almost pink they looked to me, and it made it hard to follow his eyes. He told me I was gettin old. I said him too. He said he come for "closure." Said he and his needed it, he wasn't gonna lie. I told him I had nothin for him, closure or anything else. Then he said he hated me, just said it. When nothin else was said, I told him I always figured he did. That was all right. I never figured much else was possible between his kind and mine. No, I was way off, he told me, because some things had changed since I been away. I figured if I said anything or asked him what he meant, he'd only lie. He was fightin somethin inside himself, I don't know what. I asked him did he ever remember seeing me growin up. Skin on his face squinted up in a question. Charlie had no idea. So, I told him some memories I had about him and his sister playin in they front yard, and how me and Ray-Ray and Ella and Janine used to pass by they house sometimes on Sunday. We just saw him, that's all I told him. Nothin' else.

The whole thing bothered him, I think. He scooted back in the seat a little like he was gettin ready to leave. Then he said, "You're a cold-hearted bastard, Junius, but you ain't crazy. I only feel sorry for your soul, because the Lord prepares hellfire for men like you and you will surely fry in eternal damnation!" That's just how he put it, gettin hotter in the face with each extra word.

I expected that to be it. Maybe an apology from me might have changed things. But he just gave me a long look from behind those pink glasses. It doesn't bother me one bit where I'll end up, I told Charlie. I have no doubt. Heaven is where I'll be. Not a word back from God neither. I'll just get sent. Automatic. Already paid up. Because heaven I figured out is a very big place, much bigger than a universe, more than you imagine. White folks are always tellin me such and such about not being allowed to go there, because God doesn't have room for everybody or I'm too bad. This is a lie for certain, Charlie. Heaven is the most infinite possible space there is. I'll go there at the end of this life, and when I get there I'll know to walk. Walk up into the bright horizon there. People will pass me. I'll come up on animals and fish and insects heading up the horizon too. Me, I'll just keep on walking along the length of heaven. Walk and walk, walkin, walkin, almost until forever. But at the end of this movin sidewalk motherfuckin universe called heaven I'll come to a point and step off, Charlie. Then I'm pretty sure I'll wake up. Somebody will be slapping my ass and making me cry. It'll be the start of this life again. My trophy for never givin up. Which is why I'm quite sure my ass is going to heaven. Shit, heaven just ain't that big a deal when you think about it, man.

I got beat up pretty good for that one. Charlie told somebody before he left that day, and I sure 'nough got brung back to this cell they like to take you and got my ass whipped for over half an hour. But you couldn't beat this outta me 'cause I already started believin it. I wasn't just sayin it to Charlie, though I was just sayin it to him at the time. All my life white folks been tellin me where to go and not to go. All my life they try to say how things really are. Call me crazy. Call me bad. Well, if I am an evil nigger, then it seems to me I'm just doin a small part to even the score in a big-ass game. And it must be a game to God. I'm quite sure He couldn't take all this as serious as we want to. Weeks and months are probably like seconds for Him. Most times our voices are probably too small for Him to hear anyway. We're down here runnin 'round like ants, how's He gonna make out when one of us loses a few fingers or a head or somethin? Naw. God permits a certain amount of mischief to go on among the men of the earth. If that ain't so, He woulda stepped in for niggers a long time ago. Niggers didn't start out wantin white folks or trouble. We just got 'em. So I say it's mischief. God figures enough is OK for one life, then back we go to try again next time.

Could be that's the way forgiveness works, if there is such a thing. Or the closure. That was for me and the dogs to find out, and the hounds weren't sayin nothin about it. Just had babies, played, ate, ran, barked, won prizes, got old and died. Over the years, me and the dogs got very close. After Everlie Ferguson died, the new warden came on and liked dogs even more. His name was Winn Grigsby. Grigsby was what they called a penologist, not really a warden by training. Mean, of course, and didn't think much for the passions of niggers, but crafty and organized as any white man I ever knew. He liked me, let me stay at my job with the dogs. Even gave me and Claudette conjugal visits at our age, which was gettin pretty old. Somehow the word traveled about me and them dogs and being The Dogman, because I started gettin visitors and having journalists come 'round to take pictures of me and the hounds. White folks, it seemed like, was startin to forgive me.

The older I was gettin the more white folks liked me, or at least gave me attention. Come to find out they made a picture of me with the dogs that got on the cover of the Sunday paper in Jackson. Called me The Dogman and caught me lookin old. It got sent to me by some Avis Henley lady, a dog lover wantin me to autograph the thing and send it back to her. She put in a picture of her poodles, five of 'em, looked like rats in wigs. But I sent it back anyway. I sent it because I was amazed. I *was* amazing. I had to be. I was the only nigger I knew in the world or at least Mississippi that killed three white men and was not very, very dead. Instead they liked me, maybe even loved by white folks, *loved*, on account of I lived long enough for them to forget what I done to them. Like a dead nigger walkin the earth just over the side of the prison wall from them.

You would think now that my mama's dead I would be through wantin to get out of here, but that ain't so. Now I think maybe I'm ready to go along with them and do the three-step. Claudette thinks it can get me pardoned, and I reckon we ain't got much time. Took me a long time to get curious, but I am. I wanna see for myself what come over people. I wanna slip outta Mississippi for a minute and wonder what. Nothin dishonorable about walkin away now. I done already confessed the deeds. I know what God's got for me. I guess I could tell 'em I'm sorry.

The only problem is the dogs.

Bitch, Son of a Bitch

AS CERTAIN AS BETRAYAL, VONETTA, DEEP IN A MOOD, WISHED THAT her first footer of 1959 would be a man. She wished this backwards over their New Year's meal of black-eyed peas, hog maws and greens. She made Rachel say it with her. "Male be him let." Then they ate. Then two days passed. Gwendolyn almost came up from the apartment downstairs, but Vonetta yelled down no. Another day passed. Life almost went on as normal. The bad mood stayed fresh inside her. Then, common as betrayal, he stepped first through her door. He was answering the ad for the upstairs room on Bleeker Street. Cecil, she'd learn, was right but so wrong.

Vonetta charmed the beginning, he obliged and it went famously enough. It helped that they were both the same height, five feet six inches, and eye level. This was her home, both floors, she explained. He could have what had been her bedroom and he would have to share the bathroom with her and Rachel. She was a woman, Rachel a girl, so he would have to be a gentleman and promise to be neat. He swore to all that, as if it were his business. She believed him. Not minding his business, Cecil soon wanted to know how a reasonably young colored woman such as herself owned this house and if so why she now needed a boarder. Strict terms, was all she answered, I'm not your cook, rent's due on the first, don't settle in with all them bags you got because there is no telling when I'll need that room back. Soon, she thought. Gwendolyn waited less than one full day to ask her if she was gonna fuck him. This was her home, Vonetta told her.

Rachel took instantly to him. He was off a note or three. He cropped his hair very short, with a wave in it, and groomed the edges sharp and precise. That it was done so was cool. That he did it himself in the bathroom with the door open was the end for her. His voice was gentle and unequivocal. Cecil talked all about the city as if it was inseparable from him. All the features of his face looked drawn with a fine-tipped instrument. He saw you out of the wide corners of his eyes. His lips were very, very full, like bags containing the second half of his face. His face was just a little bit darker than the rest of his body, which was of dark chocolate *inside* the bite and threw no glare or shine. Nobody looked like him; people were always looking for him. For that alone she could love him. Rachel was fourteen.

They talked about that once he had gone off to work one day and before Vonetta had to start her own shift. Rachel sat in one of the two wooden chairs, applying nail polish, one long leg hanging to the floor, the other held close against her body. They both wore robes only, like before, except that Vonetta still made Rachel wear a brazier; his presence made them flesh aware. That morning was a rest.

"What do you think of Mr. Richards?" Vonetta asked, as she prepared eggs and grits at the stove.

"He's OK," Rachel said, managing disinterest.

"Is that all?"

Rachel was in a bind to lie well. She was large, with abundant breasts and long legs that only recently got that way. If she wasn't careful, her body would give her away at any moment. But her long, elegant neck rendered lying impossible, because it instantly straightened up whenever a lie reached her mouth. "OK for a *fine* man," she laughed.

"That's what I figured you meant."

"What do *you* think of him?"

"I think we need some new rules around here, that's what I think. I think you're gonna have to close doors and wrap things up and stay to yourself when he's in the house, you hear?"

Rachel pretended to offer no resistance, nodding like it was her own idea. "He's fine, though, ain't he?"

"No, he ain't, girl. He's a man, he's clean all right and hopefully we won't have a problem with him and the rent." She went back to the stove, but could feel Rachel's eyes hard on her. "What?"

"You know what."

"I'm sorry you're so crazy, Ray. I truly am. We'll have to find a way around it. How much grits you want?"

"He told me you have great lines."

Vonetta nearly slammed the spatula down on the counter and turned around. "He said what?"

"I think he wants to take a picture of you."

"That's what he said?"

"I talked to him at the bus stop. I can't say for sure he meant anything by it. But it's a compliment, isn't it?"

"Could be. He shouldn't be sayin' it though, not to you, Ray. C'mon. He say anything else?"

She finished a nail and admired it. "Told me I have great hands. *Delicate* fingers. I think he has a good eye."

Vonetta listened carefully, made a judgment, and turned back around, satisfied to finish serving breakfast. "I'm not even sure that he is what he says he does. I don't know too many photographers. I don't even know one, come to think of it. But still and all, seems like a real photographer would—" She lost her grasp of the spatula, and it fell to the kitchen floor. "Truth!" she said. Then she returned to her thought. "Seems like a real photographer would have a real camera. Far as I could tell, Mr. Richards has a little old instamatic, which, by the way, is up there when he's supposed to be at work."

"You think he's lying?"

"It's not uncommon."

"Didn't you tell me something the other day about how it's dangerous to speculate on people?"

"Yes, and today I'm gonna teach you the difference between speculating and investigating." She carried the plates to the little table and set them down. "This man is living in our home."

"How old do you think he is?"

"He didn't tell me," Vonetta answered, turning to the food as if to signal the end of this round. "How old do *you* think he is?"

"About thirty, but that's just speculation."

"He's not thirty." That would make him older than her, she thought. "Let's pray."

"How come he's not married, you think?"

"Rachel, we're going to pray now. If you want to see about marrying him, I'll talk to him this afternoon."

HAVING CECIL BOARD THERE SETTLED AS MUCH AS IT UNSETTLED FOR Vonetta. It was not what she wanted to do, yet it fulfilled a wish. The home she had on Bleeker belonged to the bank. She also owed it to the urge she followed to leave her family some years before. In Rachel, she had adopted a daughter with the same need for sanctuary. Her wages and tips at Pharaoh's, where she worked as a cocktail waitress five nights a week, might have been enough for the bank but not for Rachel too. She planned in time to make as much as the white girls there. This she promised Gwendolyn after Vonetta got fired from the phone company. Pharaoh's had never even hired a Negro waitress before. The job had a little glamour to it, but the hours could be late since she wasn't allowed to work mealtimes. Cleveland was starting to change; a lot of whites were leaving to live just outside the city. Enough came through Pharaoh's though, which is how Vonetta met a man whose house in the suburbs needed extra cleaning once a week. That was either Sundays after church or sometimes Thursdays. All together, she consistently made just less than she and Rachel needed. Cecil closed the gap.

She found herself sleeping again. Rachel could kick and jerk in the bed beside her, yet Vonetta would sleep almost the whole night through. Nothing had really changed. She had lost her own bed where she had been free to study the blue light of half moons through the window, or recall a day's events through the slow drip of unexplainable tears. She had dispatched herself from the womb of her own wee-hour moods into this, sleep. All because he had been the first footer that year, the ad in his hand and paid two months in advance. Beyond that nothing had changed, except that what was hers got unmistakably smaller.

II

In his eyes, Vonetta had the look of a Negro movie star in the making. Thin, medium height with a red-bronze complexion that stayed bright no matter what, Vonetta could pass for unattainable whenever it pleased her. She kept her eyebrows arched under her black bangs, and they grew thick suddenly where they almost met above her very certain eyes. Her face was tight, high cheeked and diamond shaped with a pointy chin and plum-colored lips. Fond of close-fitting dresses cut at the knees or pretty two-piece outfits, Vonetta knew she looked the part. Cecil knew it too. Their shared knowledge of her attractiveness could threaten via assumptions of attitude. He thought she had too much of it; she questioned who he was to think so.

The only rub for him was Vonetta getting into his business. He never brought it home, which was why he was done with flop houses and wandering and part of why he answered her particular ad. But once his business was out in the open, Cecil was afraid it would stay out and he would have to live with it. It got out, and that was the cause of their first fight one day in the second month, long after Rachel had gone to school.

"Mr. Richards," Vonetta asked him. "Don't you think it's about time you out with whatever you're hiding around here?"

His face didn't change. He looked down into his pocket for his cigarettes, pulled one out of the packet and tapped it twice on the box. "I've nothing to hide from you that's not mine to keep, Miss McGee."

They were standing in the kitchen, her by the window and him by the door. "Look, I don't want to play games with you, Mr. Richards. You seem like a nice man and all, but you've got to understand."

"You seem like a nice young lady yourself, so there's no reason to start trouble, Miss McGee. I paid you through this month. You and your daughter don't have to be trippin' over my dirty drawers in the bathroom. Ain't sneakin' girlies up in here after dark. So, I don't see the reason for your questions."

"All of that is just fine, Mr. Richards, but none of that explains how come a man who's supposed to be a photographer goes to work and leaves his itty-bitty, half-broke camera on the dresser all day, unless maybe his customers are phantoms who enter at nighttime and don't make much noise—"

"Please don't go in my room when I'm not here," he said, sharpening his eyes.

"It happens to be my room," she squinted back.

"Not now, Miss McGee. Not when I'm payin for it." He was very serious. The idea of her in the room when he was away seemed to change everything about the conversation. He even stepped into the kitchen, and he pulled his cigarette from his face.

"Well, I need to know the truth about how you paying for that room, Mr. Richards, because I work too hard to keep mine and that child's life clean. I just do." Vonetta didn't waver. This is where being the same height played a hand.

Cecil looked at the steps leading down to the building's front door. He leaned back against the wall, one hand behind him, the other around the cigarette, and calmly crossed his leg. "Policy, Miss McGee. I don't mean no harm to you and your nice girl. That's how I pay for the room. I write paper." He watched a slight strain of shock squeeze the space between her eyes and her lips, then pass. "I am also a photographer, just not a professional photographer yet."

It didn't hurt as much to hear it as she thought it might. Vonetta played the numbers all the time herself. It occurred to her as her eyes scanned the floor between them that having a numbers runner around just might improve her luck in the game.

She pressed him why he had so many suitcases, then, why they were so full, why he wouldn't keep any in the basement and wanted them in the room with him. Why didn't he unpack them? His face never changed but he was irritated by the interrogation. Books, he told her.

"Dream books maybe?" she asked hopefully.

"No, sister. No dream books. Don't sell 'em, don't use 'em. Don't nobody need them."

Other things were for his "art," he said. Nothing was dangerous. Nothing was stolen. Nothing he wanted to share with anyone, including her or Rachel. "I'm pretty strict about that, so you need to let me know," he said.

Vonetta nodded, but wasn't going to let the tables turn just yet. She still wanted to know exactly who Cecil was running numbers for. There were different outfits, some more reputable than others. Some just took people's money and if you hit, maybe they paid, maybe they didn't. She played with Cherokee Henderson's organization, because they were top dog; a runner named Monkey faithfully took her bets on Mondays and Wednesdays. Cecil wouldn't give up anything, though, and she should have known better than to ask. It was worth a try. But by asking, Vonetta had already made pretty clear that he was unlikely to lose his room for such activity. "Just don't bring that stuff into this house, mister. We certainly don't need that kind of traffic comin' through here. Especially with the baby."

Cecil started to leave, then whirled around. He caught her looking at his waist. His waist was quite thin in proportion to his bowed legs and wide shoulders. That instant disclosed a notion in her eyes, not a look, but a notion. "I myself was wondering something about you," he said.

"Let's hear it."

"Your daughter. Your little girl don't seem to favor you much." Cecil's lips were so full that they weren't easily disturbed. But when they were, like in the moment after he made the comment, they momentarily betrayed his all-business aspect with a wide invitation to play. "She's not that little neither," he added.

"Rachel is not my born child. Her mother was a friend of mine. She died three years ago just about, and I've had her since then. Anything more you need to know, Mr. Richards?"

He looked thoughtful for a minute, then mumbled no apologetically. But he wouldn't leave the doorway. The silence grew awkward.

"Mr. Richards, it seems a little curious to me that a young, single man like yourself, you know, being in your line of work and all, why wouldn't you be more comfortable a little closer into town?"

Cecil's eyes woke up smartly. "Stay in the ghetto, you mean? I might ask you the same thing, Miss McGee, but I won't because it ought to be obvious. I used to. I used to quite a bit. Then I figured it out. The ghetto is a colony that white men put up to keep Negroes in their place. I'm not interested in that, so I came out here."

It's all right, she told him, sort of quiet. But it wasn't long before Vonetta circled back to the colony part, hoping Cecil would explain that.

"It's a place where the powerful keep the weak, so they know where to find them when they need them." He explained it as if he were reminding her how to make pudding. "Draw the boundaries, round up the folks, decide what they can and can't have, make them work, put in a police force to make sure they don't go nowhere. Like Africa," he said. "Most of the motherland is some white man's colony or another."

"I see, Mr. Richards, I see."

"Feel free to call me Cecil."

HIS CUSTOMERS CALLED HIM CEE. A QUARTER, FIFTY CENTS, A DOLLAR, twenty-five, I need to get rich, Cee, they'd tell him. As Cee, Cecil had the face of a listener when he wasn't really listening, eyes looking around at the bettor as if he cared when he didn't. He was hiding their number in his memory, whatever it was. The first three digits of a baby's birthday. The middle of a phone number. An address heard on the news. His customers called numbers out of any quantifiable corner of a conversation, a sign or a life. Cecil hid it. He could hide most numbers in his head. He had been arrested once when he was younger, years ago, foolishly carrying paper and greenbacks. He would be picked up many times more by the Cleveland police for this, for that, but never for numbers. They knew what the billfold implied, but without the numbers on him Cecil just looked like another lucky son of a bitch.

So, the cops were not his trouble. Of all the rackets, police went easy on policy unless something really bad happened. A knifing. A big hit and no pay out. Revenge crimes or setups between competitors. That was rare. The day to day was Cecil's block by block and face to face. The trembling hands of an elder Joe Little on Monroe Street, watching the lines on his long fingers fumble for the dollar, perhaps his last, cataract eyes feigning a smile, nurturing a hope, as the money reaches Cee's hand. Two hundred eighty-seven, the month and year of his birthday, he thinks. Cecil hides the digits, the cash amid the sound of barking dogs so regular there at that time of day, each day. Or Rhonda Williams's big middle. The five dollar bill hidden in her bosom or her waistband while he stands in the doorway. Her great heaving chest, surrounded by huge arms, always bare, that big middle where the five comes from. Behind all the flesh of her midsection, the shadowy light from down the long hallway leading in. Never the same number. Back down three flights of stairs into the street again. Or Clyde Samuels, a barber, bald, a man among mirrors, head and shoulders above other men, who daily puts just a quarter on the number of an interstate from which he'd traveled years ago, plus one more, a digit that would seize him with a loud giggle as Cee approaches. To Cecil, none of it was funny, all of it was foolish. He pretended to listen, because it was part of his business. While forgetting their tales, he remembered their numbers, the name of the game.

Colored Cleveland spread itself out for Cecil. He walked in it, and it all became his rhythm. It got so he could see around corners and through the walls of houses. Certain streets walked better slow, narrow ones fast. There were blocks where the eyes on you came from upstairs. Others were strictly stoops and porches, storefronts and benches. The busiest streets were choked with rivals, loyalties were thin and false. Over by the post office the street opened up a bit, relaxing his strides, and again near the park. Cecil covered the ghetto, sometimes twice a day. His steps crossed like the hands of time, stitching places together day after day.

But because he was not this place or that but a runner passing through them, Cecil wandered. A few times, he occasioned past Vonetta's section to a small park where a Negro could lie easy and unnoticed in the shade during summer and not be moved along. He didn't know the name of the park, and for some reason it took him a long time to pinpoint it exactly in his mind. He'd get lost. That excited him. He wasn't known in this part of the city, and he could be who he wanted. By Thanksgiving he had it down as a favorite getaway, but it was starting to get cold. He decided he should live there if he could and started reading the ads for boarders.

Cecil was right, not because the park was close by, but because he had found Rachel. If Rachel's eyes could open any wider, she would see backwards. For that alone, he could love her. She had never placed a bet on chance, nor earned a dime nor been with another. She was big and gangly and never in love. All she wanted to know was everything. She didn't even know what to be afraid of. Not the least his books, which Cecil pulled from one of his bags to show her once. Soon Rachel would come home looking for him. She wanted him to show her the art books, the photographs in black and white. It wasn't the subjects so much. They were faces of white people looking foreign and broke and lonely in a silly way. Or New York City scenes cast in shadowy grays. Mostly she was interested in Cecil's long explanations of them, there in the kitchen, her and her man alone, caught up in the explaining.

"When you gonna show me yours?" Rachel asked.

He had to think hard about it. He decided she couldn't tell the difference between them being as awful as they were or as good as the ones in the art books, which she didn't like. So he showed her a few from a roll taken in the fall. The subject's name was Andy. "Turn on the radio first."

Rachel dutifully got up from the kitchen chair. Her body seemed shy as she crossed past him to the radio. She smiled and turned it on.

He smiled back but made them listen for a while first. Rachel's eyes wouldn't leave him. She began to snap her fingers to the music. It was an upbeat song, swinging with a nice beat. Rachel wasn't even old enough to know what little powers she was trying out. She just knew she could make him smile again, and watched his lips flatten and stretch thin across his face. "Don't wanna get your things just yet?"

"Not yet. You know who this is playing?" he asked her. She shook her head.

"Ray Charles, sugar. That's Ray Charles."

"I like it," she said, got up and started dancing a little at first. Cecil clapped on the downbeats and looked down at her hips approvingly. She danced a bit harder. Rachel didn't mind the spotlight of his gaze. She stepped into it and shook her thing. Then giggled, "Don't know how to dance?"

Cecil could dance. He had moves worked out in advance for this particular song and got to them. "Ooh, you could dance good!" she said.

When the song finished, he went to get his pictures from his room. When he came back, Rachel had cleared the art books from the table so he could spread out his work.

"Who's the guy?" she asked, peering up from a photograph of a young Negro standing against a brick wall, wearing a dark leather petticoat.

"That's Andy, a guy I know. I asked him to model for me. This here is a series I was trying out. Think of it as sketches. It's not the real thing I'm working to get at. It's just the idea."

Rachel tried to think of them that way, but it was forced. "He has great lines."

"You're right, good eye. That's why I picked him."

The next picture was of Andy on a bench at a train depot. He was looking down in an unfriendly way, and the camera was looking up at him from below the wide spread of his knees. "Where's that?" she asked.

"Columbus depot, over where they put the coloreds."

The last was Andy in a room under a light wearing just a white t-shirt and not smiling again. The shadows made the lines of his eyelids and his lips pertrude. Rachel studied it carefully for a while. "Is it hard to do this?"

"I think so. Sometimes it's easier than others."

"How long did it take you to learn?"

"I'm still learning."

"How'd you get the camera?"

"Collecting a debt."

"I thought you said it was all cash, all the time. That's what you told me last week."

"I told you that?" She nodded. "This was the one exception I ever made."

"I suppose you're getting ready to be famous, huh?"

"Same as you, Raycharles, same as you."

Her eyes turned up as the sound registered, and she smiled. "What'd you call me?"

"Raycharles."

And it stuck.

III

Vonetta's trips into blue light wondering were less regular since Cecil came to live with them. She had little room to drift alone into the aching moods, and she had more to manage. Instead of thinking about her life as much, she worried about Rachel's, whose own life became obsessed with merging into Cecil's, breasts first. It might have been through talk with girls at school or things she'd seen in a magazine or even on Vonetta, but Rachel decided to emphasize her breasts around the house. She broke the brazier rule more often than not. She'd gotten hold of a look involving a man-size white cotton shirt with a dress collar and no pockets. Her flesh darkened the white, and her large nipples peaked and pressed from behind the fabric. The shirt was too small for her. But by finishing the look with the length tied into a knot against her belly, Rachel achieved the impression of a swollen bandage. By the middle of the second month, the idea was to suggest the need for fixing, and only Cecil's hands could do it.

Vonetta had other things to manage, too. Namely, her first lawsuit. Back when she was dating men often, there was one man in particular, Elvin. Elvin was a high roller, much older than her and established. Their love was quick and suspicious. Despite the doubts, they served each other's purposes for a while and they did it dutifully. Because they had a deal, a deal Vonetta believed she had the good sense to make. She satisfied his needs, covered for him, looked the part, and Elvin did what he needed to do on the side; it didn't matter that the side was so big it became the middle. He could do that; it wasn't that kind of love. But in exchange he had to take financial responsibility for her, at least enough to help her keep the house, the things in it, and carry on a little style. She didn't mind working at times, but he had a role in making sure whatever she had amounted to success and not simply survival. That was the bargain. They each came out ahead of where they would have been without the other.

Elvin got into trouble with some local men, specifically a man named Baby Blue who ran numbers and a private sporting house. Baby Blue rolled higher than Elvin; Elvin knew it and left town. That was two years before. Vonetta got nothing, except the chance to work with Gwendolyn at the phone company, the chance to get fired from there, the chance to become a cocktail waitress, and the chance to meet a third man, Sylvester Treaster, this one white.

She met Sylvester at Pharoah's where he came after work for a drink before making the drive to his home in the northeast suburbs. They became friends but not really, the friend an acquaintance subordinate hopes to be. A change occurred where they stayed the same kind of friends but without much attention to the differences in their races. Only the differences in their sexes seemed to matter after a time; yet he was older and married, and she was attractive and fighting mad about an ex-husband. They finally became friends. Vonetta had started cleaning his house once a week. Driving her home one evening, Sylvester asked her what ailed her, and she told him about Elvin's skipping out. Then he made a strange offer: He said he knew a lawyer and he'd pay for her to hire him. That way she could sue Elvin, the bastard, and she could start again.

So, the lawsuit became a basis for the friendship and little to do with the law. The lawyer, another white man named George Waters, handled it. Occasionally, he asked Vonetta to come to his office to discuss particulars or to give statements. But that part didn't last long and after that not much ever really seemed to happen. It was just good to have a place in her mind where the right people were working for her, and the wrong people were probably going to get theirs one day. She didn't know when, and she stopped hurrying. All she had to do was manage the fact that one day a trial would occur, and she would get to face Elvin and remember that she did not love him anymore and teach him he could not afford to forget her.

By the end of the second month, Vonetta's full attention was on Cecil and the Raycharles number he was playing on her daughter. The swollen bandage of breasts habit was something she could deal privately with Rachel, who could be ordered to stop. The problem was telling Cecil he'd better not do something he may not have been out to do. Ordinarily, the speculation could not last long, because Cecil, a man, would show his stripes, make a move. But Cecil had a stomach for restraint, though not in a gentlemanly way. After all, Cecil noticed without trying to hide the fact. Rachel might make a few passes near the front room where he was sitting with a cigarette. Pretty soon, a conversation would start up and she and her display would be right in the middle of things. Many was the time Vonetta watched Cecil's eyes follow Rachel's swathed chest forward march her whole body back and forth across any given room in the house. But he kept his thoughts to himself. So, she prayed. And she made a wish, until such time as she had reason to confront him. The wish was, "Rachel my touch not do Cecil Please," and she said it to herself twice a day.

Until one day. One day Vonetta got her reason to tell him. It was ten P.M., she was just getting home from work. They didn't hear her come in. She came up the stairs, and not hearing them, she quietly looked into her old, now his, room. There they were on the bed together, Rachel and Cecil, their backs to the door, looking at a book of photographs. It was a moment for the grand halls of memory, a scene set between the marble pillars of the unrepeatable past: Rachel's long legs growing out of the back of a hiked skirt, flattened against the mattress, hanging off one side; Cecil's short legs still in their tight black pants, hanging off the other side of the bed; their torsos coming together in a triangle at the pillow; he in just a white T-shirt, big arms at his sides, she on her side facing him, naked breasts beaming at him through the familiar white cotton. They were talking about the book, which they were in the middle of. Vonetta announced herself, told them to get up from there, never to do this again, scolded them angrily, and scared Rachel with the size of her eyes and the pained thrust of each breath. Rachel ran out of the room, and the two adults stared bitterly at each other for about a full minute.

"RAYCHARLES, HAVE YOU EVER HEARD THAT A PICTURE TELLS A thousand stories?" Cecil asked her a few days later, while they were sneaking some time together in the front room. Vonetta was again working the evening shift and wouldn't be home until late.

They were studying a photograph of the Flatiron building in the rain. "Yeah. As a matter of fact I have. But I don't think it's got to be a thousand exactly. It depends on whether there are people in the picture. If there are no people in it, like this one right here, I doubt there can be a whole thousand, you know?"

He looked at her from his left side, and the bottom half of his face opened up to reveal the end of a grin or the start of a smile. "Maybe so. But I'll tell you what. It's not a true statement no matter how many people are in it. Because the truth is that a picture tells one story, and that's all." Again, his voice was certain and gentle, and he didn't seem to expect much disagreement. Then he added, "But you'll discover that people will find a thousand different ways to *tell* that story."

She was skeptical and glanced back down at the page between them. "What's the story here?"

"Raycharles," he gave her a look to show how obvious it was. "It's the story of how a giant triangle building takes up a whole block in the middle of a street in New York City—in all kinds of weather."

She laughed hard with her eyes closed. "To you maybe. To me it's the story of how you feel when the sun gets blocked out by tall buildings and nobody's left but raindrops."

Cecil thought long and hard about that. "Nope," he said, staring at the page. "That's a nice way to tell the story, but that's just another way of talking about this big triangle building in the middle of this block. You just decided what it was you want to tell about it. You and I could do that all day."

"Up to a thousand?"

"Up to a thousand, Ray."

She looked up from the book and rested her cheek on her hand. "Hey, Cecil. What's our story?"

"Yours and mine?"

"Yup."

"Hard to say." He stood up from the couch casually and stretched. She was lightly slain by his motion. It was his waist, so small and the rest of him so wide, like a bow tie, and the way he twisted the middle just then touched her deep inside. "Eventually, you'll let me shoot you, and we'll look at it, figure it out. How's that?"

"How old are you?"

Cecil crossed his arms, squeezed his biceps over his shirt and laughed. "Thirty six years old." She was crushed at first, but tried to hide it by imitating his stretch. Rachel yawned almost the length of the sofa. When she regained her composure, they smiled at each other. "Why you so curious all of a sudden?" he asked.

She sat up and her eyebrows got serious. Part of her was very calm, yet part of her trembled from the fingertips. She was wondering to herself if age mattered. "I think we have a nice thing going, don't you, Cecil?"

He walked over to the mantle where his cigarette box lay. "No doubt about it, Raycharles." He lit a cigarette and tossed the burnt match into the fireplace. "You could be the girl for me," he smiled, but it didn't seem to come from quite the romantic place she thought it should.

"You really mean that, Cecil?" she asked. He nodded. "You think I'm pretty? I mean you said I got delicate fingers and all, but that doesn't mean you think I'm pretty."

"You're a beautiful girl, Raycharles, and a very nice person."

"I think you're just good at telling a girl what she wants to hear." She blushed magnificently. Cecil also blushed, a wide, spontaneous, royal flush of a movement across his face. "Come back over here for a second, OK?"

Cecil walked over to the couch and sat beside her. "What?" he asked into her growing eyes.

She turned in the seat to square her shoulders with his. Rachel was trembling slightly. "I want you to be my steady, Cecil." Her eyes implored, but they were poised to celebrate.

"Oh, baby," he started, struggling for words all of a sudden. "I could never give you the love you deserve."

"Why not? You already do. Have you got a girlfriend? I'm not too young, Cecil. I'm grown."

He tried to calm the panic that had reached her arms. "It's none of those things, Raycharles." He sighed and searched her eyes. "I'm just not that kind of man, Ray. I can love you, but not that way."

"Why not? What's wrong? What's wrong with me?"

"Nuthin'. Nuthin's wrong with you, nuthin' with me neither." Cecil leaned back into the sofa and stared off for a second. "I'm a different kind of man. If I like a woman, I like her as a friend or family. She's my sister, my cousin, like that."

"What if instead you loved her?"

"Same difference, sugar. My love is mostly saved for men."

[167]

Rachel's mind blinked. "For men?"

"Pretty much. That's how it's been."

Rachel didn't quite know what to do just then. She stared at her knee for a while and wouldn't look at Cecil. Cecil wanted to get up and leave the room. He was very hungry all of a sudden. Rachel looked up at him once and held him in a long, impatient stare. Then she turned away again and began to cry quietly. He waited, kissed her on the forehead and went off to the kitchen.

IV

Like her exchange of pure sleep for the sleepless twilight of her old bedroom, Vonetta had gotten her wish by Cecil's disclosure. It explained as much about him as it embarassed her about thoughts she'd had. By the start of the third month, she had few real worries and had to conjure them just to keep a full load. Rachel was safe, though heartbroken. She herself was safe, though Gwendolyn downstairs was disappointed. There was nothing new in the lawsuit. Vonetta might have just carried on. The first footer of the year was a man who brought some measure of prosperity and nothing else. Except that Cecil's homosexuality remained like a visitor in the house, speechless and unspoken to, but always there, even when Cecil wasn't.

Cecil himself drew inward again, back to the way he was in the beginning. Although Rachel stayed Raycharles in his mouth, they spent less time in each other's sight. He was busy with work and home less often. Out of a rivalry came tensions between two numbers games, the one he worked for and Baby Blue. There were accusations and counter-accusations of who was dirty, who stiffed bettors. Some of it was true. Most of it had to do with particular number runners, not who they worked for, but few picked over the distinctions for long. Nobody was entirely clean. Now, because of a string of jilted bettors going back to Christmas, things were starting to happen to people. For Cecil, it was just an opportunity to make more money. While others had to lay low, he stepped out. By stepping out, he was able to remove himself from Vonetta's and Rachel's magnifying lenses.

But it would have been a good time to want to go home. The ghetto was heating up and made endless demands for attention out of every corner of his eyes. It got so he was watching his back so much that he practically twitched. Plus, he was writing so many bets a day that he couldn't even think of taking photographs. The sooner he got back out to Bleeker Street, the easier Cecil's mind would feel. That was the hunch that brought him out that way in the first place. Now, just when he needed it, something had interfered with that peace.

It was the end of the third month, a week before rent was due, that Cecil decided that the way to get back his place in the house was through Vonetta. He brought wine for the occasion and caught her after Rachel had already gone to bed. It was a Thursday, the day she went to the suburbs to clean Sylvester Treaster's house. Vonetta was still in her cleaning whites, slumped in the big chair facing the mantle, eyes closed, her arms wide at her sides like she was in midflight of a jump off a rooftop.

His voice broke the silence like deep sounds out of her childhood, notes rising between a string and a bow. "You know the day just gets longer unless you finish it with a glass of wine." She twisted her head to see him by the doorway holding a bottle of something dark.

It was hard at first to believe this. "Cecil? What have you got there?"

He eased off the doorway and into the room a little ways. "Happened by this bottle of red wine. I know for a fact it's good, and you're welcome to some."

Vonetta remained suspended in free-falling fatigue. "Wine, Cecil?" Nobody she knew was inclined to treat a long day with wine, and the idea had to catch. Vonetta was not much of a drinker. Then she remembered his homosexuality was in the room with them and sat up. He was smiling, both lips, intently. "OK, Cecil. I think I will. Thank you."

The wine tasted heavy and good all the way down her throat.

Pretty soon she was telling him about getting to the suburbs. This bus, then that bus. The wine reached her head without delay. Cecil showed just what a good listener he was. He kept up his eye contact and nodded at all the natural moments.

"But this is what you have to do, I guess, when you have obligations." She said it like it was one of God's truths, good for him to know too, but one that she was still convincing herself of.

"I hear you," he said.

"I know you do," she said, sipping again.

"Say, Vonetta, I been wondering, if you feel like telling me, how'd you get this place?"

Vonetta almost knew better than to answer, but the wine sat her back in her chair right after she had risen indignantly. "You really wanna know?" A sneaky look dawned on her.

"If you'll tell me." He leaned forward in his chair.

"Strike me down, Cecil," she announced, drawing upright for dramatic effect, "if I didn't hit the number October 10, 1955! Yes, I did." Vonetta knocked the side of the wood coffee table twice with her knuckles. Then she and Cecil fell out laughing.

It felt good to laugh that hard. Vonetta hadn't laughed with anybody about the fact that her luck had carried her so far. She was busy worrying about the lawsuit, or wondering whether a time might come when she'd need to take another job. But the fact remained, the house became her trouble only after she hit the number that day. Here it took her boarder to appreciate the fact with her for the first time in a long time.

"So, you, Cecil, you must play a little something, huh?" she asked, winking and giving a friendly elbow in his direction.

"No, ma'am."

"That's all? No, ma'am? Why not?"

"It's a bad racket for Negroes. I'm glad for you and all, but it ain't good business for us folks."

"I know *you've* got to be kiddin'," she said in rapid fire. "Much money as you probably made off *us* folks."

He looked down and twirled his glass against the top of the table. He was blushing slightly. "Choice of evils though. I have no business with Mr. Charlie. I don't punch his clock, I don't follow his instructions, he don't know my name, and still I'm paid. Just cause I won't take his money doesn't mean I'm gonna throw mine away on the games."

"Well, who do you think pays out if it ain't Mr. Charlie?" her voice was getting a little louder. "You better believe it ain't *us* folks working the top."

"Why not? It's us folks' money. It doesn't take a whole lot more. I'm not sayin' there's no white bosses; I know the mafia's in in some places. But they don't run it all, is what I'm saying."

She shook her head. "Oh, then I guess you hate me, because I take nothin' but the white man's money. I'm trying to specialize in it." She stared at him for a second and then noticed that her glass was empty. "May I?" she said, pointing to the half full bottle. Cecil nodded quickly. Vonetta poured herself another full glass. "As a matter of fact, I got a friend who pays my legal expenses while I'm trying to get back my money from a nigger I used to be married to!"

Cecil's lips belied his interest. "A friend?"

"Yeah. A friend from where I work at." She corrected herself. "A friend whose house I just got through cleaning. Actually," she paused, "I clean this white friend's wife's house." She giggled to herself. "The house is white, too, if you can believe it."

Cecil registered something like shock, something he'd never figured, or given Vonetta credit for, and it all showed on his lips. "Say what? You sayin' this white guy you know from a bar pays you to clean his house and pays your legal expenses?"

She rested both elbows on her knees. "Just as you say," Vonetta answered, then twice knocked the side of the wood table with her knuckles. "Wanna toast?"

They toasted, though Cecil reluctantly.

The morning after saying too much held some shame for Vonetta, which she charmed away in a hurry. Cecil seemed to be over his bother about Sylvester Treaster and woke friendly. Vonetta paid the matter of his disdain no mind anyway. Instead, she wondered all day about the night before and how much she had to admit enjoying herself and the wine. In the days that followed she warmed up to Cecil when their paths crossed in the house. She even cooked extra when he wasn't around and occasionally left notes for him, letting him know there was food if he was hungry. Then, on rent day, after nothing was said about the little niceties passing between them, Cecil left Vonetta an envelope on the kitchen table. It contained the fourth month's rent, plus another half month's worth. She discovered it after dressing for work and stood by the kitchen window, peering down the street as if to find him and ask him about all the bills she was holding in her hand. But he was long gone.

She found him at the table late that night. Rachel was still up. They were sharing a small book about photography, reading together. Rachel's heartbreak had thrashed and fought within her for almost two weeks, and it seemed now to be dead and forgotten. So was the white shirt and the buldge and the knot. Vonetta stood in the doorway and smiled at them.

"There's food on the stove for you, mama."

"Thank you, darling."

Vonetta's shoes crossed the floor with woodblock sounds, and she peered over the pots to see what was made. Rachel scooted her chair back and announced she was going on to bed. For many minutes Vonetta and Cecil occupied opposite ends of the silence. She fixed a plate. He read. She ate quickly in small bites. He dragged long on his cigarette and blew the smoke into the hallway. Vonetta pulled back from her food and sneezed to the right, dabbed her nose with her napkin and lightly tapped the wooden table twice with her knuckle.

"Salut," Cecil said.

"Thank you, Mr. Richards. Pardon me."

"Is my smoke bothering you, Miss McGee?"

"No. Not at all."

"How was your day?"

"Fine and yours?"

He nodded. "Why you hit on the table like that?"

"Same reason I don't sneeze to my left side, I guess. Bad luck."

"What's the table got to do with it?"

"Spirits of gods inside, I believe. It's not the wood. They're in the trees the wood's cut from."

"You think it works?"

"You're sittin' in my good luck, fella." They laughed together. She scraped the plate, even though it was empty; he puffed though his cigarette was down to his fingertip. "I owe you some money back, Cecil. You gave me too much. Oh, and I appreciate you being on time with it and all."

"No, no. That wasn't a mistake what I paid you. I want to make the rest out as a donation to your fund. I don't know, maybe we can call it your liberation fund."

Vonetta heard him correctly, but when she looked at him she could only see the homosexual visitor. "Mr. Richards—Cecil, let me get this straight now. You trying to take care of me for some reason?"

At that moment the sweetness of her voice began to mean something to him it never meant before. It was irresistible and, together with the way her eyebrows arched with her words, made him blush. "If there's reasons to keep it in the family, then I got a reason."

"Oh, I'm not sure that will do, Cecil. Not as reasons go. I mean, men who give women money and all. That usually means something else." She understood the power of her eyebrows and began slowly to murder Cecil with them. "Now, I was pretty sure I knew you were not that kind of a man."

"It's not what you think, Vonetta."

"I don't know what to think, Cecil. Just what would you like me to think and I'll consider it, because this is very strange? I mean, I'm flattered, but . . ." She left it there.

"Well," he straightened up in his chair, "it occurred to me how it's not easy to take care of your business. You work hard, might feel over your head sometimes. Thought you could count on your husband, found out you can't." Vonetta nodded approvingly as he spoke. "Now, some white man, calls himself your friend, wants to slide you some cash here and there after you take care of his house someplace," Cecil pointed in the direction of the window. Vonetta stopped nodding and her eyes tightened. "I'm able to do my share a little more, so you don't have to take that kind of money. That's all."

"That's all. That's all?" She turned her head to the side and let Cecil see all the exasperation rushing to the veins in her neck. "I'd like to take your money, Cecil, but I don't appreciate what comes with it. Here you are trying to buy me out of living my life the way I wish? No thank you. And what about you? Let's talk about what's right. What do you think God has to say about how you do your life?"

"A lot less than he'll probably tell you about all your table knocking and rabbit feet and dream books."

She pulled back angrily and caught her bottom lip in her teeth. "Just a minute. Just wait one damned minute, Cecil. I don't know what you think you are doing coming in here and trying to direct traffic. You are my boarder. You are not my minister, my father, or my friend. But we sure can finish this right here, right now if you think your little twenty-five dollars a month buys you as big a mouth as you wearin'."

"Look, sister, I didn't mean to hurt your feelings like that. But you gotta know there ain't a white man in this world who's gonna have you serving him scotch and cleaning his floors and driving you home and paying your bills without wanting and taking something in return." He was gesturing, which Vonetta had never seen him do before. "If that's what you wanna do, well, go on and do it. If that's what you *have* to do, well then let me be a proper black man and help you instead."

Her eyebrows suddenly splashed across her forehead. "Black?"

"That's what I said. Black."

She'd never heard a Negro use the term just so, but he used it on himself. "Mm hmm." Vonetta rose and carried her plate slowly to the sink. She faced him, rolled her tongue around in her mouth, and rested a hand on her hip. "What you know about bein' a man, Cecil?"

She expected to draw blood. She even figured it was best to be near the sink and the drawer with the knives at the ready. But Cecil just reached for another cigarette. "More than you, Vonetta, and enough to get by."

After that, she couldn't remember seeing that visitor again.

V

During that fourth month, Cecil became a full-rights member of the house. He hung a few photographs on the wall of her, now his, bedroom. He kept his toothbrush in the bathroom opposite theirs, instead of always carrying it in with him. He ate their food and they ate his. Wine bottles, empty and full, occupied their own place in the pantry. But the main thing was a boldness about his body. Now it was visible, to himself, to them, and displays of the flesh and what they signified were no longer an exclusively feminine affair. He showed; the dark nipples of his open chest, the curvature of his upper thighs, what his tiny curls looked like just wet out of the shower. The rules were changing.

This somehow didn't present the usual trouble for Vonetta. The bargain she struck with sleep once Cecil arrived worked nicely. All of his man stuff was helping out. Whatever wasn't wanted, she discarded. And best of all, Cecil could get to Rachel better than Vonetta could on some things. Especially men. He didn't just warn her not to trust what boys her age said, Cecil could explain why certain things were a lie and had to be. He could answer her questions and question her answers. The summer was coming up and clothes were coming off. Rachel wanted honest appraisals of her look, what a man might see, how to keep him from hating you, maybe how to make him love you. Vonetta simply lost credibility on some of these issues, because she didn't date, anyway. Cecil came from the other side. He was an informant, an ally and a protector. Rachel trusted every little thing he said.

This might have been trouble all by itself, Vonetta losing Rachel's ear, except that it probably kept Rachel there. Rachel was nearing the age when Vonetta left home. The feeling had swept over Vonetta like a sudden reckoning, making no sense when she was asked to explain it, but all the sense once she'd done it. It could arise in Rachel at any time too, which worried Vonetta. Rachel had become the man in Vonetta's life. She took her in at twelve years old; they went through Rachel's puberty together. Not long after that, they went through Elvin's leaving and Rachel's own father disappearing. Now they slept in the same bed. Vonetta figured she might never need another man, though wanting one was possible. More often, she was just happy to let Rachel do the wanting, which Cecil could temper and balance, dragging it out, she hoped, until maybe getting and leaving with one would never actually happen.

Early in the fifth month, Vonetta got a call from the lawyer George Waters about the lawsuit. She had to go down to his office to meet with him, because he thought maybe there was going to be some activity. Elvin's lawyer wanted to speak with her, and once they got it all scheduled, they would probably meet at Waters' office downtown. Vonetta suprised herself by thinking to ask Cecil to come with her. She didn't. The meeting was called off at the last minute. Relieved, the first thing Vonetta did was spill all her fears about a trial to Cecil. Cecil listened and listened, and in the end promised he'd go wherever she needed him to go. That was over wine.

Wine slipped back into their evenings after the night they fought over money. He was drinking it, and she walked in. They talked until there was just one glass left in the bottle. Then he offered it to her. After that, wine became regular.

Cecil was full of beliefs he wanted to share, beliefs expressed through words and gestures. For the gestures alone, Vonetta could listen. But also because nobody she knew talked the way he did; maybe her father, once, long ago, but doubtful. Cecil said the main thing for Negroes was to be economically independent of white people. If you have your own money, they have to respect you and if they don't, you can leave. Europeans who came as immigrants, Jews, and even Japanese, they were always quietly making their own money from each other and leaving again for Europe or Israel or Japan when they got fed up. The Koreans would be next, he warned. Nobody Vonetta knew painted a world so complicated and evil and interconnected. Cecil could go on all evening sometimes without so much as mentioning Cleveland; or he could talk all night about things she didn't know existed in Cleveland.

But one subject never got away from him: white supremacy. Those were his words, made for his lips. He always spoke them with purpose and slowly; he had great faith in them, and the meaning of the two words together would expand across the evenings. When Cecil said white supremacy, Vonetta got ready to be despised, not just disliked, more than hated. She had suggested dislike once in a conversation and another time hate, but both times Cecil wanted to correct her. They truly despise Negroes, he said, each of us and all of us, our families and our children; in the South they're finding ways to replace us on the land and in the North they want us on as little of it as possible. The more locked up we are, the better they think it will be for them. It's not like it used to be. Things are only gonna get worse.

Vonetta was not always a great listener. She loved to hear Cecil talk; she heard in his gentle sermonizing an affection for more than being Negro, but for darkness, even blackness, which was unusual and courageous and even funny. Yet, he could go on so long that she had a few times woken up the next morning to find that she had fallen asleep while he was talking. Most of Cecil's beliefs didn't really move her. She kept doing what she usually did. She looked at some white people a little differently, but not a lot, not enough to stop cleaning Sylvester Treaster's house in the suburbs. Sylvester did not seem to despise Negroes. He often mentioned sympathetic things about them; the only reason she took less of his money was because the lawsuit was stalled over something and there were no fees. However, Vonetta did start to feel a little self-conscious about her superstitions; maybe that was Cecil's effect on her. And she decided to stop playing the numbers for a while. Cherokee Henderson's people got drawn into some of the trouble between Baby Blue and Cecil's boss. That made her wonder about Monkey and what if he found out about her living with Cecil. So, Vonetta saved a few more dollars every week, but she never told Cecil.

BY CECIL'S SIXTH MONTH IN VONETTA'S HOME, SHE HAD GROWN TO miss him when his days ran overlong. He seemed to relish what was happening on the streets, the new faces and their hands and signals and numbers; or maybe he had other reasons to be gone so often. Whatever it was exactly it decreased her time drinking wine and unraveling across the living room furniture together, which made Vonetta feel a little empty. It wasn't something she could justify or tell about. Rachel was the best cure until she went to sleep. Occasionally, Gwendolyn stood in, but Gwendolyn was not as interesting as Cecil anymore. It was just same old with Gwendolyn, who made herself more and more unavailable anyway because of a man named Darryl she was seeing.

So, Vonetta found herself drifting by the doorway to her, now his, bedroom just to smell his cigarette odor. She had never connected on the photography, but now she reconsidered. One night she stood in the center of the room, listening to Rachel's light snores from the next room, feeling a bit like a trespasser. The pictures on the walls were placed there neatly, even though each had been torn from a book. Nobody was in them. The first was the Brooklyn Bridge in New York City, but just the span and its cables from a distance, no people. The second was a storefront of a small shop in what looked like a small town; there was a hanging Coca Cola sign and a dog, but no people. The last was a curb and a fire hydrant standing prominently in one half of the frame. Vonetta stared at it quizzically, then giggled to herself.

She came back a few nights later. The bridge picture appealed to her; the lines carried her eyes off the page in different directions. Vonetta decided she could stand to see more. Being in her, now his, room felt less like trespassing and more like a room in her house again. Cecil must have taken her seriously that first day, because he still hadn't unpacked all of his things. Two bulging suitcases leaned against the far wall, hidden partly from view by the bed. Rachel once mentioned that the books were in the bags, so Vonetta went to the first one and opened it up. It was full of books, mostly the large hardcover ones she'd seen Cecil and Rachel looking at, but also some smaller paperbacks. She pulled out a picture book and sat at the edge of the bed. He kept his room pretty orderly, so she had to be careful not to disturb anything. The book bored her with pictures of furniture and objects on tables, so she put it back in the bag. She was going to walk away when the title of one of the paperbacks caught her eye, *The Night Rider Never Sleeps*. Something made her curious if this might be a book about risky doings.

On the cover was a drawing of a building with the word hotel above the doorway. Above that was a window, and in the window was the shadow of what looked to be half of a man and a woman lying down. Vonetta began to read and the story hardly got started before a man named Hank Connor was described from head to toe about to have his way with a blonde lady named Ginger. Ginger was afraid to say how badly she wanted Hank; the town was small and word about her husband's whereabouts was sketchy. Maybe she was a widow, maybe not. He might have been killed in a gunfight; he might be striking gold. If he was killed in a gunfight, it must have been a stranger that did it. Hank was a stranger and had a thick mustache. He let his actions do his talking, and soon they were engaged in carnal pleasures.

Back when Vonetta was about Rachel's age, there were unexplainable moments of physical embarassment. They were oily panties days. Something inside her desperately wanted to rule, and things outside savagely attacked the urge. The result was a war of embarassment and the oily stain in her panties. The moment was just that—a certain boy talked to her, or later when she was thinking about him on the bus ride home—the moment was quick, but the effect was a daylong event, or until she could change her clothes. Until Cecil's book about Hank Connors provoked such a moment. Vonetta stopped herself and took a deep breath which became a giggle. She hid the book in the bag again, figuring this was a discovery for slow consumption. If Cecil caught her in the room, she would just say that she had to come get some of her clothes out of the back of the closet.

But she didn't go back right away. She took time out to wonder about Cecil. Maybe he wasn't homosexual after all. Or maybe they didn't make books like those for homosexuals. If they did, she figured Cecil would be the guy who could find them. But whatever the case, he had brought these things into her house with Rachel. Rachel could find them as easily as she did, if she hadn't already. Vonetta also recalled vaguely that certain sex stories and dirty gadgets were against the law to have. For a few nights, Vonetta went back to not sleeping and worried instead about what she was going to do.

Nothing, she decided. She decided to leave it alone with Cecil, mainly because she could not imagine winning the argument. Vonetta also found that what became of Hank Connor grew into an all-day obsession for her. She would daydream at work just wondering. Within days, she was back at Cecil's bag, reading on his bed. The following day might be an oily panties day, and so it went.

There were four books in all, and Vonetta eventually made it through each one. The best was *Visits from the Stranger*, about a ladykiller from Italy and his travels. This book opened up many different parts of the world, all in the name of love. The stranger was very smooth and sincere, but easily deluded by beauty, the book said. Vonetta liked it especially because some of the love affairs were with women from all over the globe, including one from Africa, a Nubian princess.

The other two disturbed her curiosity. The storylines made her uneasy about how to react, and the dryness of her undergarments disappointed her. *When the Curtain Falls* told of an actor named Ruben, who played the lead to many of the most beautiful actresses of his day. But the action always concerned his backstage friendships with other male actors, even stage hands. How he knew their eyes were on him as he undressed, the excitement of having a bath prepared by a youthful attendant, the body proportions of a well wisher. The distance Vonetta felt from the book made it harder to ignore the fact that she was intruding in Cecil's things; no other book had done that. Yet the last one, *Perfect Angels*, disturbed her even more. These characters were nearly all ladies, fine country ladies, who dressed impeccably and who attended great balls at grand estates. They were young and rich, and their good manners could not hide their critical nature when unworthy gentlemen called. *Perfect Angels* was full of descriptions of how the rose-cheeked ladies prepared themselves to go out in the evening, exactly the clothes they wore, what was done to their hair. Vonetta had no trouble getting through it, but she couldn't help thinking about Cecil between each paragraph. A man so self-possessed as him, so gonna-take-on-the-world, so nothin'-from-Mr. Charlie kept books about his enemies' private parts in bags by his bed.

BY THE MIDDLE OF CECIL'S SEVENTH MONTH ON BLEEKER STREET, HE was still very much involved in the heavy goings on of what was going down in the numbers games. Days passed without Vonetta or Rachel seeing him. From the condition of the kitchen, it didn't even appear that he'd eaten there. But his things in the bathroom had gotten some use. Then he'd be gone again early. Vonetta tried drinking wine alone one night, but it wasn't the same.

Vonetta made one of her rounds to his bedroom after Rachel had fallen off and much to her surprise found that Cecil had moved the bag with the art books and the paperbacks. Immediately, she figured he must have discovered some trace that she had been in his things. She grew frantic, pulled at her fingers on one hand and walked around the bed to the closet. She saw the bag behind some of her summer dresses and breathed a heavy sigh. He couldn't have known or he wouldn't have put them near where she might innocently come upon them. She sat back on the bed. The other bag, the one she never opened was still there, only it had been moved closer to the bed and half of it was covered under the bedspread. The thought occurred to her. It even ran in a ripple from her chest to her hips. She stared at the buckles and tried to summon all her good sense quickly before it escaped her. The time. Sounds from the front door. What if Rachel woke. How long it would take her to react if she had to conceal what she was doing. What she could say. Whether Cecil remembered the exact placement of the bag, its contents and the bedspread hanging partially over it.

She turned off the light at the side of the bed and relied on the bulb from the hallway between the bedrooms. She went to the closet and pulled out a summer dress just in case. Then, taking a breath, she calmly opened the suitcase. Inside was a black binder made of thick cardboard or wood. It was neatly packed but worn. When she lifted it completely out of the bag, loose photographs slipped and one fell to the floor. She quickly picked it up and opened the binder, trying to find the place where it had fallen from. That photograph was just a sepia-colored snapshot. It showed a Negro man and woman with four children, dressed in church clothes. Neither of the adults smiled and their gaze veered to the left of the camera. The children, two boys and two girls, smiled broadly from behind wide, heavy lips, and all but one of the girls looked into the lens. The older boy looked to Vonetta like Cecil, only many years younger.

Vonetta put the picture on the bed beside her. She turned the pages of the binder. The first few pages contained the photographs of the model Andy, which Cecil had shown Rachel. Vonetta recalled Rachel's descriptions as they lay in bed. Andy pictures went on for a couple more pages. But on the page following the series of Andy wearing a T-shirt Vonetta found pictures of Andy in the nude. All the young daring in his face from before had turned to the coy smile of a child as he lay on his back, his skinny legs spread out atop a sheet; one thin arm half covered his forehead. Vonetta's eyes trailed over his small body, from those coy eyes to his slightly protruding ribs, to his large penis lying limp inside foreskin. She studied the penis in amazement until something in her neck started to lock. In another picture, Andy stood by a window, a profile silhouette—penis of a man, legs more like a child. Vonetta grew a little dizzy and blinked hard. Her palms were wet and her fingers shook lightly.

The next pages showed a different naked man, this one white, who looked to be in his forties. The name Ruben lit up in Vonetta's mind. These photographs were different, smaller, a little scuffed at the edges, and appeared to be taken by a different kind of camera. They looked professional. Ruben had big muscles and a part in the middle of his hair. He stared straight into the camera, as if he were about to wrestle with the photographer. In one picture, he looked over his shoulder at the camera, his little eyes appearing like dots along the width of his broad back. But in another, Ruben sat on the arm of a large parlor chair, naked, legs open, pectorals inflated, and, if Vonetta was not mistaken, his penis slightly erect. Vonetta stared in the dim hallway light, and the oily presence returned beneath her.

His footsteps seemed to march to the front stoop. The key entered the lock. Vonetta almost lost her mind. She scrambled to put the pages back into the neat order in which she found them. Then she closed the binder quietly and placed it carefully into the suitcase again without taking a breath. She closed the bag, got up and smoothed the bedspread where she had been sitting. Then she grabbed the summer dress from the bed, closed the closet door again and stepped into the hall just as Cecil was closing the door behind him. Not wanting to see him, Vonetta took a long stride she almost tripped over, and was in the bed (clothes on) with the light out before Cecil had made it up the stairs.

VI

In late July, the whole front of somebody's house was burned out on Maple. Word was the house was one of Baby Blue's, and it might have been a bomb that did it. It was an understandable likelihood around colored Cleveland that Baby Blue would want to kick some ass in revenge. The battle had to be won by somebody some time. But what surprised many of the regulars to the action was that Baby Blue had so much pull with the Cleveland Police Department, and the police quickly became a rearguard to Baby Blue's own people. Each had agents out shaking people down and hunting for snitches. Pretty soon after it happened, it became a race to see which one was going to find who did it. That's when Cecil decided he was leaving the house on Bleeker Street.

"Why?" Vonetta asked him. She really wanted to beg him. Just the one word, why, started one way from her mouth and left as a desperate cry. "Why do *you* have to leave? You didn't do anything. Isn't that just gonna make it look suspicious if people know you're movin' around?"

Cecil was back to his old face, no royal blush of the lips, no smile, a lockdown look and eyes out of the corners. He was standing in the kitchen doorway, smoking and holding his toothbrush in the other hand. It was noon, before Vonetta's shift. School was out and Rachel was off at a little job she had gotten herself downtown. Cecil wasn't acting like they were friends at all. "It's not safe. No reason to bring that down on Rachel."

Vonetta was stuck by the sink with her hands together in a pleading position. She was trying to get a handle on it so she could do away with the situation, but his calm made it difficult. "Cecil, I ain't heard anything about you. I've been listening too. I hear a lot." The words didn't seem to move him. She felt like a visitor from another state and what she might know was irrelevant. "I did hear about Darryl. You know, that man Gwendolyn's been hanging around? I heard his name get messed up in this stuff, though I can't be sure."

Cecil just smoked and looked down. His eyelids held his eyes so tight they were barely open. "Well, all that may be so. If it is, y'all should be careful who people see coming in this place. But, me, I have to go."

"When?"

"Today. Right now."

Vonetta wanted to scream. Her face shook and the muscles in her neck hardened. "Cecil! You can't."

Cecil looked up, a hint of surprise in his eyes. "Of course I can, Vonetta. I paid you up, don't want nuthin' back. I'm not gonna wait around here 'til something happens to me or y'all. What's the sense in that?"

"You comin' back?"

He looked back down and didn't answer for a while. Just dragged on his cigarette. "Nah," he whispered. "I don't think so."

Vonetta softened a bit and took a few steps toward him. "Why not, Cecil? You're like family." She smiled, fully expectant that this truth and this smile would finally sway something hiding inside him to return.

But it didn't. "I'm afraid not. You broke my rules, Vonetta. I didn't break yours, but you decided to break mine. So, I gotta go."

"What are you talking about?" she asked, lowering herself into the chair in front of him.

"You've been in my things while I was away." He said it like he couldn't say it.

"No. No. What do you mean, Cecil?"

"Don't lie to me, Vonetta. You been in my cases. You been in my pictures, my books, my things. You been in my things." The cool in Cecil's face was melting; the clarity in his voice was starting to choke. So, he took a long drag. As he let it out, he said, "You left a picture out. It was laying on the bed."

Vonetta gasped and dropped her head. She put both hands over her face and began to moan quietly. "I'm so sorry, Cecil. I'm so sorry, I really am."

"That's mine!" he said, almost angrily. "You can't be going in my goddamned things. I told you that before. Naw. I *pay* for that room; that room is *mine*. Those things are mine. You better get my per-*mission* to come through there!"

Vonetta looked up at him and tears mixed with black eyeliner streamed down her cheeks. "You right, Cecil. You absolutely right. I only just peaked a little. I promise I didn't look hard." At that, he cast her a strange look and winced. "I mean, oh, Cecil." She turned away, put her hands over her knees and rocked a little. "I don't know what I mean." She turned back to him and gave him all of her eyes. "Cecil, please don't ever think I think there's something wrong with you for having those things."

Now he wanted to scream and maybe to cry. Should he say something? Put this cigarette out, light another? Walk? He lit a new cigarette, dropped the other butt to the floor and twisted it under his shoe, daring her to object. She didn't. He took a puff and said, "You got nuthin' on me, Vonetta. That's for sure."

"What's that supposed to mean?"

"Ask me when you get through with your sugar daddy."

She snapped back in her chair. "You wanna start this again?" she asked gently. "You already a faggot, Cecil. Don't nobody care if you got pictures of it."

He smiled. "That makes you a bitch, Vonetta." He turned away. "I'm gone."

Cecil headed to the bedroom. Vonetta remained stuck in the chair, her mind racing. Nothing she could think of sounded like words to say now. She could hear him pulling clothes out of drawers. Vonetta took a deep breath, walked to the bedroom, and stood in the doorway where she felt a wave of security come over her. He would have to cross her to leave.

"Cecil. You have no cause to be angry with me. I'm just no good at this, that's all." She looked up at the ceiling and sighed nervously. "Let's see. I told you we already think of you like family, Rachel and I. Raycharles loves you. You know I care about you." She giggled to herself. "I only came in here after your things 'cause I was lonely to have wine together like we used to." He stopped packing, though he kept his back to her. "All I meant by the other stuff was that it don't bother me that you like men, just like it don't bother me that you keep those pictures."

Cecil turned around; all the composure had returned to his face.

"That's not the thing to me, Vonetta. Not to me. Being what I am, you could sooner kill me than change me. But the other stuff, going in my things, that's different."

That's embarassment she thought she detected on his face. Not a blush, nor a smirk, nor a smile, something new. Like a wall come tumbling down inside him. He finished packing. It had to be several, if not many, minutes, and Vonetta couldn't find a word to say. She daydreamed at his feet, occasionally watching them shift near the closet, then back to the bed. Nice shoes, she even thought. She hoped Rachel might walk in unexpected. She would know what to say. But nobody came. Vonetta simply stood by the border of Cecil's embarassment, feeling its tug at her own toes, stuck in guilt. Then she stepped quietly aside and watched him cross past her down the stairs.

Through the railing that stretched along the upstairs hallway, she caught his eye. "Let me know how we can reach you, OK, Cecil?"

"OK."

After a good cry, Vonetta was relieved to find one of Cecil's suitcases in the closet along with some stray clothes. No temptation could make her look in the bag this time. When people leave personal belongings behind it usually means they plan to be back eventually. So she believed.

VII

Two Cleveland police officers showed up to the house on Bleeker Street early in the morning on July 11, a Friday. They were two medium-sized men, one blond, the other dark haired. The dark-haired cop assumed the lead up the walk, and he was the one who rang the bell. Gwendolyn was home downstairs, but she didn't answer because Darryl was in the bed asleep. Vonetta looked out the kitchen window, saw the policemen, and came down the stairs. The cop would not let go of the bell.

"Good morning, officers. What can I help you with?" she asked through the glass.

"Are you Miss Vonetta McGee?"

"Yes. Yes, I am."

"You live alone, Miss McGee?"

"Uh, no."

"Is the owner of this property present with you?"

"I am the owner, officer. What's the problem?"

"You can start by opening the door, ma'am," said the dark-haired one. The blond one rolled his eyes.

Vonetta didn't answer right away. "Look, it's just that nobody here called for the police, and I need to know what business you have before I open my door. I'm sure you understand, officer."

What they had before was a mask compared to what their faces became. "No, you open this goddamn door this minute, ma'am, or you'll be making a lot of extra trouble for yourself. This is a police investigation. Now open the door."

Vonetta looked down at her feet and took a deep breath. She could see their belts hugging their uniforms, the bullets lined up, the guns in the holsters, just a few inches beyond the glass. "Well, just a minute then, please," she said. Vonetta turned and walked slowly, then hurriedly up the stairs. She ran to the phone in the kitchen and dialed the number for George Waters' law firm. While she waited for him to come to the phone, she could see the black and white sitting cockeyed at the curb, but the policemen below were out of view. The conversation with Waters seemed to last too long, but she couldn't hear what he was saying. She was rushing him, yet she wasn't taking in what to do. Finally, Vonetta hurried back down the stairs.

"Officers, do you have a search warrant to come in here with?"

Instant proof of the power of those words was their two faces, surprise, then the way bitch came flying off the hard curvatures of their lips. They cussed, and she held her breath. She watched them back off the stoop and confer. Their hands gestured for a bit. Then they went back to the cruiser and talked on the radio. Moments later, they drove away. Vonetta had to go to the bathroom bad.

Waters called back, wanting to know what happened. She told him and he laughed, said they probably wouldn't be back. Gwendolyn ran upstairs and Vonetta told her about it. She ran back down, woke Darryl, and rushed him out of the backdoor. Vonetta called Rachel at the store, but they wouldn't put her on until her break. She didn't know what to do; leave, stay, maybe call Sylvester. But she had never done that before; it didn't seem like something in their arrangement. Instead, she went to Cecil's, now her, bedroom and collected the things she was holding for him. She carried them down to the basement and put them inside a trunk. Then she covered the trunk with old clothes and a broken table and chair.

Gwendolyn came upstairs to tell Vonetta she was late for work. Vonetta asked her if she had anything in her place she shouldn't have. Gwendolyn thought hard and said no. She wasn't gone five minutes when police began to arrive.

This time there were more of them, three or four cruisers and a black maria. They parked in a semicircle around the house. Neighbors started coming to their windows. Kids playing on the sidewalks were sent inside. Vonetta saw them approach from the kitchen window, dropped her jaw and prayed to God. Just then George Waters pulled around the corner in his blue Buick. The distance between him and the four approaching police officers was about a hundred feet, and he tripped over himself to catch up. A new lead cop, bigger than before, leaned on the bell. Vonetta walked slowly downstairs.

"Son of a bitch is probably long gone by now," she heard one of them say to the other. "Open the door this minute, Miss McGee. We have a warrant, and we're coming in."

Waters tried to tell the lead cop that Vonetta would let them in if they produced the warrant. The lead cop didn't even look at him. The one closest to Waters, the blond one from before, put up his hands to back Waters off. Waters didn't like it, but he didn't move either.

"May *I* please see the warrant?" Vonetta asked. The words had only just occurred to her, but if they had to have a thing in order to come back, she wanted to see the thing.

He smirked, then reached into his vest pocket and flashed a small white piece of paper. "Now you're about to see the back side of my hand if you don't open this goddamn door right now."

Vonetta didn't move and the policeman didn't wait. He wrapped a handkerchief in his fist and smashed a hole in the glass pane. Vonetta screamed and jumped back as he turned the knob and opened the door. Two of them stormed in behind him; one stayed back for a moment to put his hand in Waters' face and keep him out. Vonetta saw the white piece of paper still in the cop's hand and grabbed it. There was no writing on it, so she stuffed it in her bra.

"No, you black bitch! No you sure don't." The second cop immediately pushed Vonetta down against the landing and climbed on top of her. He pinned her elbows to the floor with his knees while another one grabbed her breast, squeezed it hard, smiled for an instant standing over her, and grabbed the white piece of paper.

In no time there were policemen all over the house. As two held her against the stairs, she could hear their heavy shoes banging the floorboards above her. Furniture fell and glass broke. She could imagine them in each place sound came from, knocking and slamming and ripping. Three came down from upstairs and headed for the basement door. As one passed, he stepped hard on her naked foot. When she screamed, one of the cops holding her pressed his weight harder against her. When she asked to speak with her lawyer outside, the other yelled to shut up. When she wouldn't, they dragged her by her arms and led her down to the basement. There, the three cops tore up all they could find. She watched them huff and pant and grab at anything they could hold, opening old handbags and shirt pockets and every latch in sight. Until the trunk appeared. All five cops seemed to see it at once. One flung the furniture pieces away, while another opened it up. The dark-haired cop from that morning found Cecil's case. That was all there was to the trunk by now, so the others just watched him open it. He didn't know what he had for a few impossible moments while Vonetta held her breath. With a curious expression on his face, he inspected the title of each paperback. A second cop picked one up and leafed through it. They both squinted at the writing. Then a curly haired cop reached deeper into the case and pulled out the black binder and opened it up. Vonetta's heart raced and a fear of death ran through her.

"Well, I think you might be interested in this, Sergeant," the curly haired said.

He stood up and took the binder from the man. His jaw opened wide, then closed to emit a whistle. He turned one page, then another, then another, and stopped abruptly, slamming the binder shut again. His neck delighted in the slow, deliberate turn of his head as he faced Vonetta. All three locked eyes on her in a moment wedged between the marble pillars of her memory, one's tongue licking at his bottom lip, a second one taking a long, slow look down the length of her body, stopping at her breasts to grin, catch her eyes, and continuing to her midsection. But the dark-haired sergeant showed a disgust so complete, only divine intervention could rescue her from the cellar that afternoon.

"This is one nasty bitch, gentlemen. Bitch, *you* are under arrest."

Vonetta didn't have to stay long in jail that day, thanks to George Waters knowing what to do and who to know. The police found what they called policy paraphernalia in a drawer in the bedside table. These turned out to be a few betting slips she got from Monkey, as well as her all-time best luck hit that got her the house. Nothing from Cecil. They couldn't hold her on the paraphernalia, because gambling was just a misdemeanor. So, Vonetta went home to worry all weekend about the pictures of naked men.

"Whose pictures are those, Vonetta?" Waters asked her on the way home.

"What difference does it make?" she said, exhausted and leaning her head against the window frame. Cool July evening air rushed her nostrils and closed her eyes.

"Do they belong to you?"

"No."

"Then we need to let them know whose they are. You don't need this mess. We have enough to deal with." He just talked; she listened.

[191]

"It's not gonna make the case against Elvin easier if the other side hears you were convicted for keeping a pornographic library in your basement. I mean, there's a law in this state that makes it a felony for possessing what they call obscene materials." Still, he got no rise from Vonetta. "It's stupid, sure. I think so. You think so. A lot of things are stupid that put people in jail or ruin their lives or both. Here's one of them, and it's pretty serious business. You possessed them, no question about it." Vonetta kept her mouth and her eyes closed, even though they had turned onto Bleeker Street again and there was no more wind. Waters stopped the car and turned to her before she got out. "Whose stuff is it, Vonetta?"

"A boarder left it behind, Mr. Waters. Some guy."

"You know where we can find him?" She looked away. "This is not your affair, Vonetta. I mean, a guy like that, you know, and you've got the girl to take care of. This isn't your concern."

"I don't know where he is. I have no idea."

"What's his name?"

"Not now, Mr. Waters. You've been extremely kind today. You really helped me out. I'm here, right?" she managed to laugh. "Let's take this up another time, if that's all right."

THE PROSECUTORS BROUGHT THE CASE. THE CASE WENT TO TRIAL. Sylvester Treaster paid for George Waters. George Waters lost. The jury came back and found Vonetta guilty. The judge gave her the maximum of seven years imprisonment. Waters asked the judge to keep Vonetta out of jail while he appealed the verdict. The judge said yes. Cecil never showed up to claim his things and Vonetta never told.

VIII

As an idea out of Waters' mouth, the appeal was swift and sure. As a fact, it was no such thing. They couldn't even do it until after the judge decided a second time that he meant what he said the first time: Go to jail. So, Vonetta was imprisoned by worry over the many months while the appeal was happening. And it happened without her being able to do a thing; Waters did the appeal in her name. Vonetta just heard about things. Mostly how people talked about her on Bleeker Street and beyond. It was wrong the way she got treated by the police, people thought, but even so, that didn't mean having smut and underworld seamy stuff, the things that were rumored, prostitution, and white slave trade information, was right. Not for someone who carried herself like Vonetta used to try to do. Not with Rachel in that house. Not in that house on that street.

All Vonetta could do besides try to go on was pray and wish. The wish was simple, "Back come Cecil." Twice a day she said it, usually with Rachel too. Cecil had been a reliable wish in the past. As a first footer, he brought prosperity and friendship. Next, he put the ultimate end to her worries that he would try to get on Rachel. And for all his secrets, he had a lot of beliefs that he held strongly enough to demand others hold too. Cecil would come through. News would travel to his hiding place. Every rumor told on her would reach his ears where the falsehoods would burn. Maybe not right away, because he was angry and scared, she figured. He didn't seem to have family; she couldn't recall a single word about a brother or sister. He never even mentioned where he came from. But she and Rachel would weigh on him like family does, and he would be drawn back.

While days of work and school days past, Vonetta was waiting. By the end of Cecil's first year away, she had lived the full blue light return of a sleepless mood. Her bedroom staged a comeback gloom as willful as any in the past. It usually began with the lawsuit against her, which was nothing like what being the plaintiff on the attack against Elvin felt like. It was a terror. What it said and who it said it to and what it meant. Seven ceased to be a lucky number. Seven was only the number of years attached to the judge's lips. She felt the accusation start to wear upon her, and she picked up a condemned gait when she walked, dragging a bit, chin a little lower. Charm departed her repertoire. Some days she woke to see a hollow face stare back at her. And Vonetta's lawsuit against Elvin finally ended with a dismissal. She wasn't damaged by him, the judge said. Or not enough to matter.

Just why don't you tell me his name, Waters kept asking through it all. It was a dumb ritual. He would ask to ask. But at times he really meant it badly, and the question would lift him out of a chair or get his voice near screaming over the telephone. Vonetta's no was the same old no, brief and resolute in order not to show the weariness behind it or the wonder of how much longer or the doubt. After enough time had passed, the second year of Cecil's absence, even Rachel caught the question. She had decided to be a photographer, but Cecil's hold on her had otherwise slipped. And she was getting older, better to understand what seven years was like. But Vonetta held out for his return. She could still explain both sides of the situation to herself. Vonetta made the wish alone. Cecil still had a point.

After they lost the appeal in the courts of Ohio, Vonetta thought for sure that Sylvester Treaster would stop paying her legal bills. The only hope remaining was Waters' idea, probably spoken drunk, to take the case all the way up to the U.S. Supreme Court. Vonetta could not even bring herself to wish for that. A wasted wish will haunt you. Lawyers will say what they must, but by now she was learning how pitiful such powerful talk could be. He told her to wait and to have hope. Sylvester said the same. All the while they called Cecil "that son of a bitch," both of them, as if they had met together and decided to.

They caught the men who bombed Baby Blue's house. One of the guys who did it got beat up badly in prison; the score was settled. Those who laid low rose up again. Everybody who was in business was back in business pretty much as before. Rachel had her eighteenth birthday in June, right after graduation from high school. She finally tired of fighting Vonetta out of her bed and left the house on Bleeker Street for a place with some girlfriends downtown. If he was going to come forward, the time had sure come.

The wish became no kind of wish at all. Instead, Vonetta just wanted to talk to him. The dark blue light of deep funk and suicidal wonder produced stale questions that hung in the air. Everything Vonetta's eyes roamed across in the bedroom late at night repeatedly asked, How could you let this happen to me? How was it possible to forget about us? Why should I be punished so long by you? No more wish, just a case she wanted to make to his face if ever she got to see Cecil again. Me, I am nothing but the bitch in this, and I'm given whatever a bitch gets in their eyes. You are the perverted son of a bitch. The son of a bitch walks. That ought to be problematical for your special brand of son of a bitch because *you* like to be a proper brother, even want to say a *black* man. Just because I strayed into your almighty privacy don't mean you can watch me die some eternal bitch death, does it really? I'm sorry you came. I'm sorry I knew you. I'm sorry for you.

In twelve black robes and so many words, the Supreme Court said this perverted bitch should not go to jail unless the police have words with a judge's say-so on that piece of white paper. The judges' decision had nothing to do with the law of dirty pictures and nasty books. It made no sense to her. She was there when Waters spoke to them and all he talked about was how stupid the obscenity law was. It was some other guy who got up to talk about how the cops had no right to treat her like a bitch without a warrant. She took the victory anyway. And Vonetta went back to her life and worked on her walk and tried to get her charm together again and paid off that house enough to some day soon sell it and forever leave the place that changed her name so bad.

IV

THE BLACK METROPOLIS

Tell About Tellin'

I WAS ON THE MAIN LINE AT THE TIME THE RIOT WENT OFF, UPTIGHT like a kite and groovin, baby. That blind pig by Clairmount, one over the Economy Printin Comp'ny, I was there cause I was sposed to get me some pussy that night off a big-legged chick name Sissy. Was a Saturday in July. Sissy didn't wanna gimme none, so my boy T-Bone told me—no, somebody told me get to T-Bone over at the pig and I could score some skag. I go on a T-Bone mission. Get to the pig, went upstairs. They drinkin after hours, shootin craps, Georgia Skins, big, *big* crowd, full a big shots. Here come T-Bone. Gimme *my* shit. By two A.M., I'm fixed, baby, slowin down like a mo'fucker. Got stung back behind a store on Taylor, just around the corner there. I'm so nice. Orange, slippery, sweet. Couldn't go no place. Crazy in a blue cloud, mistin' and lopin' and cool like rain. My sky opened up, turned orange again. Can't say when I been so nice before.

I'm still trying to find out just what all the fuck this is finally done happen to me.

Good thing Sissy say I stink or else I mighta been up in that pig wit her when the fuzz come and threw all them fools down the stairs. The alley is my girl right then and I'm in love wit the bitch. Little road is all mines, got walls, ain't no dogs, think I see a moon above. Like a patio. Like I won the new patio behind Door Number Three. Just ain't got no lawn furniture. You could hear sirens on the Strip. Cops tearin down 12th Street, lots of 'em, just keep comin and comin, so close I know they be up in the pig. I listen, listen, hear some bangin, clangin, rain in my veins wash over me, and I'm so good and slow all a sudden, I can't hear nothin but the moon. I'm goin, goin . . .

Later, I come back outside wit the crowd, musta been about sunrise. Coulda been. They mad now. They on the Clairmount side, up in front by the entrance to the pig. Cops, cop cars, Buicks mostly, lots of 'em, carting away niggas after niggas after niggas, pretty niggas too, shovin and punchin 'em. Me and look like it's a army of people come to see what's happnin, hoes and pimps, johns, winos out there, some regula brothers too, just watchin and growin on the street, arms and legs and faces gettin swolled up. But I'm nice. There go Sissy wit her big legs on, honky pig motherfucker pushin her in the patrol car. But I'm nice. Then the brick came, I think. That's the next thing to know. Youngblood dropped a brick on the Man. Bang! Right through the back window. All them heads and arms and folks looked ready to run, but *the Man ran*! The Man got in *his* car and *all* them motherfuckers rolled. After that it was on. After that it was definately on.

Twelfth Street went wild. Heavy, I felt it, mostly young dudes, younger than me, and some sisters too, teenagers that live on them streets near there. Clairmount, Hazelwood, Blaine, West Philadelphia. All up in there, they was smashin shit, just fuckin up the stores with big-ass sticks and poles, beatin off the locks with tire irons, breakin' the glass. Not the junkies. It wasn't none a us right away. It wasn't hardly nobody who do b'ness on the Strip. These brothers and sisters had to be from the houses 'round there. I don't know. My grandparents live way over on Petoskey. My pops is up in Highland Park. I think first it was a neighborhood thing, not a nigga thing yet. Could see the sun risin. It was Sunday. They tore it up, tore up the stores on 12th, most of 'em if they had food or liquor or clothes. They shook 'em like trees and the fruits fell down.

I wasn't movin when the fuzz came back. I was groovin, sittin on the curb, leanin on the hydrant, just checkin out the scene, fucked up as I wanna be. Here they come rollin up and down, up and down. People just watchin 'em, slow motion. Dude standin there wit a brand-new radio in his hand, cops roll by, look straight at him. I figure this about to be a dead nigga. But the pigs don't stop. They just keep rollin. I saw that happen twice or maybe three times. Then niggas start runnin in the stores, comin out with a chair on they head, lamps, tables and whatnot. Saw a brother with a hi-fi from Jefferson Furniture, took the Jews in there for four hundred dollars,

I'm pretty sure. Another brother carryin half a shoe store a shoes. I saw 'em take rings and jewelry and diamonds and minerals from out the window box at Kaufman's. Christmas, baby. It was just hollerin and screamin and liftin shit, so much shit you keep hearin it break, shit fallin on the sidewalk, all out across the street like footprints behind all them happy motherfuckers breakin wild.

Wanted mine no doubt but murderized by bliss I couldn't move. The morning air sucked on my dick so good, I had to stay for a while. On my curb. I was nice. Idlin' like a Buick Wildcat, V-8 power steerin, black. I'm sittin back and black for once, *my* people, this be our street, not like what happened over on Hastings when whitey tore up the stores in Black Bottom for his highway. This be *our* street again. The soul brothers was takin the shit over and the Man wasn't gonna do nothin 'bout it. I been in they heads. I been in they eyes while they takin shit down the block. Watchin, peein, warm on my leg too—I was peein on my damned self just watchin, smilin, I remember I yelled, "Take that shit home, brother! Careful don't fall, sister!" 'Cause I been in they eyes, seen how the stores inside look different, seen 'em take over a toaster or a TV set, same shit used to have the power on you when you can't afford it, shit you got to keep in layaway, shit on credit you worryin 'bout forever. That shit's comin home now. I stayed out there a long time.

Until I started walkin. I walked right up on a fedora, green felt wit a white ribbon, said damn. Shit was just sittin there on the walk waitin for me. Could feel both of my legs again. Still nice, still beautiful. Everything was groovy out on 12th. Action every which a way. I'm a soul brother now, in my bad fedora, cool as a mo'fucker. Bang! A window. Bang! Another window. They started burnin the stores they finished wit, unless it was owned by Negroes. That day I think they let 'em alone if they was black owned. Niggas was out putting up signs sayin "Afro All the Way," "Very, very, very, *very* black."

Twelfth is a great big ol' wide street when they ain't no cars. I walked through the middle of it. Smoke risin up, clouds all over, day turned night. I felt like Malcolm's ghost, Detroit Red only browner. I felt like Jesus walkin on water. I felt like Moses partin the sea.

Wit asthma. I was startin to race too, I could feel smoke down in my chest. I needed somethin, a crew, but I looked around and wasn't nothin there. Nobody I knew was out there. I could name a hundred cats I figured to see. Cats that ran wit me sometimes, Quincy, Calvin, Frenchie, Junebug, Skee, Nano. Cats I used to hang wit from North-western High School, Auburey, Carl, Dizzy. Them niggas. Nobody. I couldn't see nobody but ten thousand motherfuckers with they arms full. I wanted mine. That's only natural. There go Castle's. My pops used to take me into Castle's Appliances on Pingree. That's not true, once he took me in there. I wanted everything, daddy wouldn't say nothin. Man there looked at me, looked at my father. The man waved at him, then he puffed, walked away. That's some jive shit, but he knew my father wasn't gonna buy me nothin in there. Daddy grabbed me by the neck and we went outside. Told me, "Work all week, pay your bills, come out on Saturday to spend what you earned, and the man act like your money ain't just as green as his. Dirty cracker motherfucker, c'mon boy." That's what he told me. The door at Castle's was wide the fuck open. Half the shit was gone out a there and I was sure as hell gonna take somethin off that jive-ass honky. It wasn't burnin yet. Didn't have no lights on. Glass broke all under my feet. Took me a transistor radio had nineteen bands. Got me some 9 volts too. I was very, very, *very* black right then. Woulda liked to see my pops roll up. We woulda laughed before I had to kick his ass.

Don't like to go too long without a score when I'm shootin. Had just enough for a fix, but I needed to know where T-Bone was at. I don't know if he got busted over at the blind pig or what. Everything was stone crazy, nothin was where it sposed to be. Went to a alley I like to stay at on Euclid just off the corner from 12th, close to the niggas where I could keep an eye out, maybe see T-Bone or somebody from a crew I might could roll wit. But I had to get stung first.

I sat in the grass by a cleaners, next to this guy's house I been scopin. I like to watch him from the alley there. I know he work at Chrysler. When I was wit Ford, I heard about this brother in the union over at Chrysler. I think he a steward. Got a nice car too. I was fixin to take that shit, but not today. That day I didn't go down the alley neither. I just sat in the grass next to his house and the cleaners. Like a patio. I got mellow like a motherfucker. Played my radio. One time it was Aretha Franklin—bitch *is* the queen of soul, sang *Respect*. What we want. I thought I was dreamin. Sat in the grass and started laughin. Maybe I was dead. Maybe I was sleep. How come I couldn't even feel the needle? Figure 'cause I was a black bird of paradise, that's why. Didn't even have no more asthma. Only better thing woulda been Sissy's titty in my mouth and grabbin her big ass. I'm so nice. I think I spanked one right there in the grass, right on 12th next to the cleaners. I don't know. Was Sunday. We was free . . .

Cletus Haynes, my pops, is a motherfucker. Said I'm done wit the nigga and kicked my ass out his house 'cause I'm gonna kill him. He got hypertension and I'm the tension, he said. That ain't why. Nigga don't ever wanna say nothin. Just want you to do this, do that, work like a nigga, pay for his damn house. I'm ten years old. No. I'm eight years old. He bought me the truck. A yellow crane little truck moth-erfucker with a scoop and a reel on it to pulley up dirt. Hell yeah it makes noise when you turn it, it's supposed to make noise, you dumb motherfucker. *He* bought it. Yes, but I played wit it too long. He told me once. Quit it, Billy. Can't always keep track, havin fun. *He* bought it. Not a word. He come from the kitchen, grab up the toy, walk over to the front door and stepped outside. Truck screamed. Saw daddy make a muscle wit his arm, cocked the truck back and threw it fifty yards. Bam, bam, bounce, bounce, break, break, all the little pieces dancin off into the street, then they stopped. Quiet. No more truck. Don't try to say nothin, no, no. Don't do that. He likes to leave it quiet. If you talk, he don't think his lesson lasts. Here come the smoke again. Smoke is comin down 12th Street from Highland Park. It ain't likely, but I do hope the motherfucker's burnin up. That was a bad-ass truck, wheels made a real rubber.

They was through lootin the cleaners 'cause it was on fire next to me. The crowd was just walkin past, like it was my porch. Some of the brothers knew that's near where I like to stay at when I ain't at Granny's. Carl Cooper. I thought I saw his ass go by. "S'appnin, Billy?" He said. "You fixin to burn up over here?" Carl had a crew he liked to hang wit. I just let him go. He didn't ask me to run wit em. Maybe I laughed. I was so damned nice. It *was* hot. Smoke started to get all in my lungs. I saw T-Bone then. He had on bad-ass threads, seven watches, sharkskin shoes. I still had me some bread from my compensation check. I was gonna hold it for somethin to eat, but wit all this jumpin off, well. Gimme *my* shit. T-Bone threw out his hands. Say he outta smack. "You lyin." "Wouldn't lie to a brother. Closed today. Check me tomorrow, slim." Carl and his dudes come back around, saw me cryin in the grass. "Get away from the store, junkie motherfucker. You 'bout to get burned up." He a kid, but he right.

The cleaners started to burn so bad it was catchin on Chrysler brother's house. I didn't see no car in his driveway. I broke into the basement windows on the side. Decided I was gonna find me somethin to eat. I don't think there was no power on. Brother had a nice crib too, but I couldn't hardly see nothin. Refrigerator didn't have no light. I'm makin a sandwich outta cheese and some beef rump. "Get out my house, sorry-ass nigga." I didn't see him or nothin. Got a piece in his hand though and he cocked it. He was carryin shit in the other arm. Over by the door tryin to get his stuff out the house 'cause it was burnin up. I see him and the gun, then smoke, then him again. "Take the food and get the fuck out, junkie." That's just what I done. I didn't say nothin. Brother had tears comin down his face. I dropped the sandwich 'cause I fell down the front steps.

Somebody like a muslim or the militants said Detroit was for the black man now. That's how it sounded. Heard sirens wailin and wailin they jive song, but couldn't hardly see no pigs. Fire trucks racin down Woodward Avenue, but the honky firemens wasn't hanging off them ladders the way they like to. Sposed to have snipers out, shootin at firemen. I still couldn't find me no dope. Maybe not my grandparents, but a whole lot of niggas decided it was time to be black. Whitey too. I saw whitey smashin stores. I saw whitey puttin mattresses on top they car. Detroit was burnin so bad.

I'm slowin down again. I'm losin colors. I wanted to get on Belle Isle, but the pigs was there. First pigs I saw really doin somethin. They wouldn't let you on the bridge. Down by the river I fell out. That dude Carl had no cause to call me a junkie like that, for real. We sposed to be celebratin. We sposed to be black now. How's a black man gonna be a junkie? Shoulda let me run wit him and his boys. That's fucked up. Shoulda hurt the motherfucker. I fell asleep down by the river. Detroit side. Free as a bird.

II

What happened next didn't happen to me right away. It happened to other cats when I was out tryin to squeeze a fix. Wasn't no fix to find. So, I went lootin. I was lootin and lookin to score and lootin, and things was gettin faster 'cause I couldn't stay high and I'm in a war.

Whitey came back.

They wanted Detroit like they want 'Nam. Man, it was funny in a way, coon gooks, gook coons, same thing. I was lootin. They started shootin. You could hear 'em tell it on my radio. The mayor, the governor, the president. They called they boys out to take everything back. Mayor said So be it, shoot the niggas. The Man tryin to act like the Man again.

I started hurtin just when it was fixin to get real. Come Monday, that's when I really dug smoke everywhere. And the sound of tanks. Sirens, tanks, squad cars, wagons, trucks, vans packed wit soldier motherfuckers. National Guard, army, state troopers. All the motherfuckers that didn't have to go to Vietnam got sent to Detroit, armed to they honky teeth. The Detroit pigs was packin pump action shotguns. Guard dudes had machine guns. Army had submachine guns. They carried rifles and had on white helmets or green ones.

They was startin to be hundreds of 'em, hundreds and thousands, maybe a hundred thousand. Whitey was good to go. I been in they eyes, and it wasn't like before. Lettin some cat climb out a store wit his hands full. They was shootin now. Pullin brothers out the smoke, jackin 'em up, haulin 'em to jail, and makin 'em bleed on the way.

One of them got kilt. He was a cop or a trooper. They said he had on blue so I know he was one of them. Plus, it was a shotgun that tore a hole right through his stomach. That was Tuesday. He died on the street by the A&P. They said a looter made it happen. After that a nigga didn't stand a chance. 'Cept me, only I couldn't get a fix. I could *not* get a goddamn fix. Motherfuckers was everywhere. That's how come the little girl got kilt. It was the commotion. Tanks and cars zippin this way and that, scared about a sniper and tryin to outrun each other, shootin at anything dark that moved; she moved. Up in her window, I heard. They don't see her size. They don't wonder. She human, right? She the wrong color shadow, right? A straight line, any line, the window pane, the curtain, any line look like a rifle barrel to them. She moved, and that was the end. I'm seein through they eyes; that's how come I could get past them with my radio. Whitey was scared. He so scared he gonna get hurt takin his city back he shootin at himself. But he just kept missin and missin me.

Nobody could get to nobody if they had to. I saw my boy Quincy, jacked up. He got a big gash on his head where a soldier beat him. Quincy said couldn't nobody in jail call out. He told me they got thousands of niggas in jails, put 'em in gymnasiums. Had 'em out in the ladies bathhouse cross the river at Belle Isle. Couldn't make no calls, couldn't pay no bail, thousands of motherfuckers, mostly just cats walkin by when the truck rolled up. Out past curfew. They put a curfew on. Quincy said his family didn't answer the phone when he tried to call 'em. Damn, I said. Man, let's go see about gettin some shit, I'm jonesin bad, I said. Was Wednesday, I think, 'cause what happened to me was on Friday or just about. Me and him was on Grand River by Warren. Quincy said he knew about a dude had some dope up in the Algiers Motel. I said where's that at. He said off Woodward, by Virginia Park.

I knew where it was at. That's where one of Carl's boys was stayin, cat named Auburey I knew 'cause he was close to my age. I think he was a grade ahead a me at Northwestern when I left out. Guy could use his fists real good. Kicked my ass outside the 20 Grand once. Auburey Pollard. He all right. Cats like that got money, always be in the 20 Grand. They got little jobs or big jobs whatever, maybe got union cards. I think Auburey was in the union at Ford wit me for a time, maybe. I knew for a fact they was pretty clean dudes. That's how come I couldn't run wit them fellas. They was just tryin to be men away from they daddy, I'm pretty sure. Stayin' in motels and shit.

It was like the jungle in Vietnam tryin to get to Virginia Park. Had to be two miles 'cause Quincy be one them crazy yellow motherfuckers. All the way he talkin about the black man's revolution. Then bullets be flyin and the motherfucker get quiet. I don't say nothin 'cause I don't know yet about all that. Just gimme my shit. That's my mission. Junebug told me T-Bone's in jail. So Quincy and me go haulin ass over fences and down alleys 'cause a nigga couldn't hardly walk on the street. They had helicopters and shit. Tanks shake the ground when they roll by too fast. By time we get to the Algiers you couldn't get in it. The fuzz had it roped off. Somethin was up. I was hurtin bad. I knew right away somethin was dead wrong about the whole situation. I looked into the hotel, wasn't nothin but broken windows. Quincy said let's go back in the back where they got another building, close to Euclid. Quincy wasn't about to give up on some dope even if the fuckin U.S. Army done captured the place. I went right around wit him. But the back was worse than the front. All the windows was shot out and I could see spent shells all over the damn parking lot. Somethin was up in there.

Fuck outta here now, niggers! That's what a Guard told us. He could see me. Had his rifle up. That straightened me up, seein that. Seein that barrel raised up like that cleared my head right up, and I thought about my grandmother and when would she know and how would she find out I was no more. I never worry too much about me and death. My only plan is to be clean when it happens. Blowin my head off ain't clean. I don't know how, but I got the fuck outta there. The Man wasn't playin. He was scared too, you could tell.

Quincy ran 'cause he a dumb-ass nigga. Honky pig motherfuckers had him on the ground right at the corner, start kickin him. If he'd a turned the corner runnin like that, I'm pretty sure they'd kilt his ass. I pretended I couldn't see nothin, just coolin it, headed up Woodward the other way, but I could see they boots in his face. He was screamin and pantin like a wet baby, but they didn't kill him. They just took him to jail for runnin.

Just then a soul brother named Kenny Brown saved my life. I'm shakin, ain't had shit to eat since Sunday, can't breath good, damn near ready to black out. Seein what happened to Quincy, I stay on Woodward past the high school and turn in on Owen. Kenny Brown had a sister live over there. Soon as I turn in the block, I hear the Man screech 'round the corner behind me. Siren starts screamin, tires gettin close. Somethin tells me I gotta run, so I run, but already I think I'm shot. Everything is burnin inside, and I'm all wet outside, runnin, runnin, probably goin in a circle. But I can hear them runnin up behind me, and I'm afraid if I turn 'round I'm gonna catch the bullet in my face and my granma can't leave open the casket. I run and run behind a house, the only one that wasn't brick, and a dude says, "Stay down, brother! Come in here." It was Kenny. He a friend of Auburey's and Carl's and them cats. At least I know him and Auburey be real tight. Same motherfucker who watched Auburey kick my ass at the 20 GRAND. He let me slide in the back door, and the pigs didn't see me.

Kenny was *all* fucked up. They had beat his ass but good. I never seen nobody after such a stone whuppin, 'cept maybe one time I was doin ten months at Iona when the guards let two dudes finish it. First thing he asked me was did I have a piece on me. Nah, man. Somebody got to die, he said. Kenny wasn't gonna kill nobody. He wasn't a killer. I seen killers in jail, dudes who killed by accident and dudes who were just warmin up. Kenny wasn't neither. He was scared though. He had blood dried up on the side of his head coverin two holes and it looked like somethin wanted to come out of 'em. Plus he was dirty, the kind of dirty you can't clean, not even your sister can clean it, 'cause your skin ain't human like; it got rips and cracks and dents. Like he been stretched by evil. Parts of Kenny was purple, other parts pink. I owe you, brother, I said, 'cause I felt sorry for him. I asked him did he want my radio and he couldn't hardly look at me. His sister come in the room, pretty chick had a skinny waist and no kind a smile. Looked like she was in shock. Both of 'em. She didn't want me in there. I could tell she didn't want no more trouble and I know I looked like it was following me 'cause it was. But he asked me did I want some food. *He* did. I said I did 'cause I did. She went got me a piece of chicken but forgot to bring me no hot sauce. Halfway through I wanted to marry that bitch. Sounded like bombs goin off outside the window.

Kenny wasn't gonna tell me nothin, I wasn't no kind of friend really 'cept seein him 'round Auburey, until I mentioned Quincy and the Algiers Motel. Motherfucker's eyes got awful big.

They kill him? he said. He dead? Quincy dead too now?

Fuck you mean dead too, man? They just busted his fool ass tryin to run. Who dead? I asked him.

They all dead, Billy. He said it like a whisper.

Say what?

They all dead, Billy. I seen it. Over at the Algiers. I was stayin there too.

Well, who the fuck is dead, nigga? Kenny looked straight at me. Under the dirt and the holes and all, his face is young, like Auburey's. He a boy, kinda big, but Kenny ain't no man yet. Carl the same way. Dudes like Quincy and Junebug and me, I think we been locked up more, went 'round wit the Big Four a few more times. These younger bloods got families. They ain't tryin to be dopeheads. Who dead, Kenny?

That's when he told me. Auburey Pollard, Carl Cooper and a cat I never heard of, Fred Temple. That's all, he thought. That's all that didn't come back from when they was stayin in the motel and the cops come bustin in. He said maybe they kilt the white girls but he didn't think so.

White girls?

Hoes, he said, young ones, seventeen.

None a y'all but seventeen, nigga, what you sayin?

Think what you want, he said.

Hoes? I said.

Hoes, blood.

They ain't got no white girl hoes up in there, do they? He just looked at me. They did last night.

Kenny said there was a bunch of brothers stayin at the motel wit Auburey. Carl and his main man Lee, Michael Clark, and himself. Fred Temple was somebody else they met there, who was stayin over 'cause he couldn't get home. He was hangin with some cats from a singin group that decided to room there 'til the buses started runnin again. Kenny said the cops came through the first time in the morning lookin for snipers, searchin 'em and pointin rifles in they faces. Auburey got beat up. Auburey always talk too slow, and he's big and real dark, look like he could do some damage. Makes pigs real mad quick. But they couldn't find nothin. Wasn't no guns or dope or loot, wasn't nothin. When the cops couldn't find nothin, Kenny said all the brothers had to laugh. Some of them went swimmin in the pool that day. They was 'fraid to go out, didn't want to try to go home. Kenny said some of 'em was even callin they mamas so they wouldn't make 'em worry. When the cops left, they started laughin even harder. After that, they was just shootin the shit, playin cards and watching TV. Kenny said he was scared. He said they was all kinda scared.

The cops came back that night. They was firin up and down the building, lookin for somethin. Kenny said they shot everything, everywhere, just bang, bang, bang! Brothers was jumpin and duckin in they rooms, tellin each other where to go, how you better kneel down, put your hands on your head so they don't shoot you, tell 'em where you is, tell 'em don't shoot, hollar so you don't surprise 'em. Kenny said they come in like animals, eyes look like they was on a hunt. They come in shootin holes in the walls and on the ceilings, shootin into closets and bathrooms and any door they couldn't see into. They had the boys line up against the wall, then they start interrogatin 'em. Where's the gun, ya fuckin pimp-ass nigger? You like white girls? They had two white girls there, come out a room wit a brother, a war vet, Kenny said. Dude still had his discharge papers on him. Kenny said it was pigs, maybe Guardsmen, but mostly pigs that beat 'em. They even beat the white girls too, beat all of 'em upside the face, beat 'em down to the ground and beat 'em back up again. That's how come Kenny got his worse scar.

One pig broke his rifle over Auburey's head. Kenny said Auburey say, 'Oh, I'm sorry I broke your gun.' Pimp-ass nigger, they called him. You better pray to your maker, pimp-ass niggers, they told them. And we prayed, Kenny said. We all got down and begged God to rescue us, you know? He whisperin. He don't want to sound too much like a punk. Auburey started beggin for his life. Auburey begged the one that was hittin on him to please don't shoot. Kenny said Auburey's face was near beat in. Them honkies beat him so one eye was hangin out his head. He had to beg, 'cause they was on him special. That's when they took him in one of the rooms. It was a game they was playin, sort of. Kenny said they take you in a room and start shootin buckshot out of they 12-gauge. Don't say nothin, nigger, they tell him so the others will think you dead. But the cop they got in the room wit Auburey, he maybe didn't know it was a game. Kenny said his buddy ask him if he wanna kill one too. That's when they heard Auburey beg some more and cry. Then came one blast, and Kenny thought he heard Auburey hit the floor. Then another bang and no more sounds.

Kenny got took in the room next. Same room. He said he looked over and Auburey didn't have no chest left. His insides was everywhere, and half his arm was gone. Kenny said his eyes was still open. 'What you see?' cop asked him. I see a dead man, Kenny said. 'No you don't, nigger. You don't see nothin.' Kenny said all kinds of soldiers and whatnot was comin in and out of the motel, goin up and down the stairs. Nobody knew where Carl Cooper was at. He'd gone downstairs when all the shootin started, tryin to get away 'cause he was scared. That's the one they got first, Kenny said. The soldiers told 'em, you niggers better keep your hands on your head and walk out the back door. If you look back or run, we gonna shoot your black ass. They was mostly just wearin they drawers. Fred Temple asked someone could he get his shoes. Pig said OK. But Fred never come back. All the rest of 'em got away. They passed Carl when they was leavin. He was dead, all tore up. There wasn't nothin left of him, not no kind of front. That's what buckshot will do.

What was I supposed to say? I stopped eatin 'cause I meant no disrespect. Damn, man. That shit is wrong, I said. Kenny didn't say nothin else for a while. I kept lookin at the last meat on that chicken bone. His sister brought me some cold pop, so I drank that. But wasn't nobody sayin nothin. Pretty soon I start to laugh a little. He still don't say nothin. Can't hold it and I start laughin harder. His sister come to the doorway and looked in on us. The fuck you laughin 'bout? he said. I didn't say nothin, I was still laughin. I knew his sister was watchin me.

Nah, nigga, what's so funny, man?

You, I said. Y'all was laughin. I'm laughin 'cause y'all was laughin.

What you mean, blood?

You said y'all was laughin after the first time the cops busted in the motel, right?

Oh, he said. You mean in the mornin yesterday when they first come in there lookin for shit?

Tryin to find a sniper, I said.

Yeah, he said, tryin to find a sniper. Kenny smiled.

Like you niggas got rifles, I laughed.

Yeah, he said. That was the National Guard, Billy. They some dumb-ass motherfuckers. Worse crackers than the Detroit pigs. Dumb and mean. Check this out. They got glass doors at the Algiers when you come into the back where we was stayin'. Well, the Guards come up the steps tryin to get in. I'm there with Lee and Auburey and Michael. Maybe Carl was there too. We had the door locked, 'cause the motel dude said keep it locked. So, the Guards come up with machine guns. They pointin at us through the glass, you know, through the curtains, see-through curtains, dig? They come marchin up like they gotta storm this here village, you know, 'cause we the Cong, dig? Motherfucker yells 'open this fuckin door!'

Nigger, right?

Yeah. Everything is always nigger wit them. Nigger for days. We don't move.

I said, why not?

'Cause the crazy motherfuckers got machine guns, man! You got ten kamikaze motherfuckers wit machine guns and you can't get through a glass door? So the littlest one up front, he about to shoot us. He got the gun right on Michael through the glass. Just on the other side. Michael said he saw death comin. Then another soldier say, 'Don't shoot him!' He lowered the gun. Then the little guy took the handle of the thing and breaks the glass, only he cuts his fuckin hand opening the door knob! We damned near died, Billy! We dyin laughin lookin at this punk motherfucker!

I laughed too. We both laughed. You could tell it hurt Kenny to laugh 'cause it stretched his cuts, but we was rollin. I said, that's why I'm laughin, Kenny. That's some funny shit. Kenny kept laughin. His sister went away. Y'all was laughin after they left too, right? Yeah, he said. Yeah, well, I said. You shouldn'ta done that, blood.

What you mean, Billy?

I laughed some more, but alone this time. You dumb-ass niggas shouldn'ta been laughin at the Man like that. Kenny's dirty little purple face got real serious. That's how come they kilt y'all, blood. You didn't have no b'ness laughin at 'em.

How you gonna say some crazy shit like that, Billy?

Be cool, youngblood. I'm just tellin you. Maybe you shoulda given up them hoes, you know? What'd y'all expect, brother? You had to be doin somethin up in there.

Kenny got mad. You better take your punk ass the fuck on outta here, Billy junkie motherfucker, talkin that jive shit. You just a fuckin junkie. Git yo stink ass out ma sister's house, and take that silly motherfuckin hat off the table. Gwon. Git out 'fore I fuck you up. Shoulda been your dope ass that got blown away in there.

I SPLIT OUTTA THERE IN A HURRY. KENNY SAID I WAS LUCKY I WAS LATE comin 'round wit Quincy. Groovy. Groovy, 'cause what happened to me next was I was lucky again. I caught a fix. I was lucky and found Calvin and Frenchie over by Joy Road. They was hawkin some shit they looted. Prices was goin up. I took clothes like they had and didn't get but five dollars for four dresses. Frenchie was gettin five dollars a dress. People was gettin scared to loot now. That's how come the prices musta went up. Frenchie was tight with T-Bone. Frenchie's into cocaine mostly, a little Mary Jane, but he had some skag for me. Calvin too, he like skag. So I got with them. Smoked a joint. Calvin had some jelly donuts. Niggas was startin to loot the black stores by now. The donuts hurt my teeth 'cause they too sweet and my teeth ain't so good. Donuts come outta a black party store, Frenchie said.

The problem was I told Calvin I seen Kenny and how he saved my life. Calvin had a lot to say then. Didn't even wanna shoot up right away. Calvin knew Carl, Auburey. He didn't know Fred Temple neither. Calvin knew Michael Clark too, another one of them dudes over at the Algiers when it happened. Calvin said Michael told him the dudes that got away had to tell the dead ones' mothers, 'cause the pigs didn't want nothin to do wit it. Mrs. Gill, Carl's mom, tried to call, pigs say if she try to come by the motel they gonna shoot her nigger ass too. Calvin say at the morgue, Auburey's moms went wit his big brother Chaney to claim the dead. I knew Chaney. Chaney was my age about. But I knew for a fact he was in Vietnam. I don't know how they got him back so quick. Calvin say Chaney saw Auburey's body and went crazy right there. He was ready to shoot all the people around just 'cause they was white. Chaney say Auburey looked worse than if the Cong did it. Right after that Auburey's pops was cool. Mr. Pollard, Calvin say he just try to go down by himself to the Algiers and poke around, find shit out, talk to people. Calvin said they all 'bout to go crazy.

I was through waitin on them motherfuckers and I started shootin up. Calvin I know had the clap once and I sho nuff didn't wanna share no needle wit him anyway. He over there talkin 'bout some pretty creepy shit. Calvin said he wish he could hear the pigs tell each other about how the other pig got kilt. Why come? Frenchie said. That's how you need to protect yourself from the Man, Calvin said. He said it was 'cause the white cop got a shotgun blast in his stomach by the A&P, that's what they told each other. They told how the nigga reached for the gun and it went off and kilt the other grey. Brothers was gonna have to die for that, and that's how they was gonna die, that same way, aimin at they stomach. Calvin start tellin 'bout all these other cats got blowed away in the riot, and the pigs shot 'em in the stomach too. That's what happened to Auburey and Carl both. Calvin said if every nigga heard it like the pigs was tellin each other, if they had it on nigga radio for us, maybe there wouldn't be no accidents. He said if Smokey Robinson came on and said watch out for your stomachs, wouldn't have so many get blowed away.

I didn't care and I split away from them niggas, or I got stung and they didn't do none and pretty soon they was gone and it was just me again or somethin. It was nice all right for a while. Wasn't no patio. I was somewhere, off behind some people's backyards. The smack was different. The high was some kind of different color, like brown mostly and red around the edges, too dark and had like a licorice taste. Got a li'l cramp in my stomach. Gettin nice. I was mellow, draggin, but somethin was up wit the cut. Somethin wasn't just right.

Never want my mama no more like I used to; why should I? Never covet the dead. But I wanted her then, crouched down in them weeds back there. Not like a child or a baby, 'cause I was a baby when she died, or she was gettin ready to have a baby and died. Anyway I was little. Right then I just thought I should see her and tell her about the riot happenin and how I ain't laughin at no peckerwood wanna point his shotgun at my gut. Mama be beautiful. She used to eat wit her fingers sometimes, daddy said. He said she got long fingers and long fingernails, looked like fine silver at her lips but brown like me. He say that so many times, I can hear the suck sound her fingers make. Could get me hard thinkin on it, the way he say it. That's *all* he ever say about my mama. Mama be beautiful.

My pops, Cletus Haynes, is a motherfucker for sure. Cat always comin from Kentucky, been twenty-five years but always just gettin here, comin and comin from Harlan County, where a nigga does this if he wanna live, where a nigga do that if he gonna eat. Motherfucker can kiss my ass, workin in the coal mines. Down South, down South. The fuck they do to a nigga down South they can't do in Detroit? Cletus ain't shit. Coal mines. Now he works in the factory at Ford. *I* worked in the factory at Ford. What nigga can't git a job up in there? All us young cats did that shit, like it's gonna do some good. Cletus scared the Man gonna quit him. He scared, I know he scared the Man gonna close it down. Cletus wanna live next to him and sing wit him and pray and tip his hat to Ol' Missy Ann. I say fuck that bitch. Henry Ford can suck my dick, too. That shit ain't cool. That's not how come cats like Auburey and them be workin for the union. They gonna lay us off all the time anyhow. Compensation checks. Gettin paid on Friday. That's how come. Don't matter who. Cletus don't understand once you step out the Man's line, he got the same thing waitin for you up here as down there.

Carl had a '63 Grand Prix. I think he worked over at Creedmore Cap & Gown. Carl used to wear some bad-ass vines. He stitched pretty good too, I think. Auburey was at Ford. Then he split, wantin' to be a welder or some shit. No, Auburey was gonna be a artist. He all right, Auburey. His pops, Mr. Pollard, he used to take Auburey and his brothers swimming over at Belle Isle. All a them like one crew, 'cause his pops is cool. They was all like brothers. His pops could box too, that's how come Auburey could fight so good. Learnt that shit at home. Cletus woulda *never* done that. I'd a dropped that motherfucker if he tell me to raise my fists. And Cletus can't swim neither. Auburey would back you up, I know. I said some shit to his kid brother one time, Tanner. That was the time outside the 20 Grand. Now Auburey dead. For laughin.

I'm nice, but I can't get away from it. The brown and the reds creep back in my eyes, and it's like a forest I'm stumbling through. My legs don't feel right and every time I stop to fix 'em, I come up on Auburey and Carl inside the Algiers Motel room. Fred Temple be off a little ways, lyin like a blob I can't really see good. One minute Auburey got his fists up, one minute he pass me in the union hall at Ford and nod, one minute he beggin 'Don't kill me! Don't kill me!' Mostly I just see he ain't got no stomach left, half a arm on one side like Kenny was sayin. Kenny said the cops shot him and laughed, talkin 'bout the nigger didn't even kick. How you sposed to kick? Carl don't have no front. If you ain't got no front, they can't bury you open casket I heard 'cause the fluid gotta be able to go everywhere. Calvin said Carl ain't got no dick neither.

I ain't never had no high like that. After a while, nothin was sweet to me. My tongue start to drop down into my throat and had thorns on it, diggin inside my neck. I kept seein Mrs. Gill. I like Mrs. Gill. She used to feel sorry for me 'cause I ain't have no mother when we was all young. Now I'm pretty sure she gotta be crazy, tryin to look on your boy and they ain't nothin left of him. Calvin could be right. It could be how the cops told the story about they dead one, not the laughin. Lookin for the right niggas to take they buddy's place. Carl and Auburey both got a lot of brothers and sisters. If it was me, well, my granma couldn't probly pick me out if they took her down to the morgue. She don't see nothin but God nohow. God's will. Our father. Cletus, that motherfucker would not come, I know. He'd pretend it'd kill him to see me, talkin 'bout he through wit the nigga, and now the nigga through. It wasn't probly 'cause they was laughin. Kenny was right. It coulda been me got to the Algiers wit Quincy and not those boys gettin kilt. Maybe we be the snipers. Maybe we get paid back for somethin else we done or somethin we was fixin to do. It probly shoulda been me that died.

III

Thas a funky hat you got on, brother. Where you goin?

Up Highland Park way, I told Frenchie. That shit you sold me was tilted, motherfucker.

Fuck you, nigga. I got some new stuff.

Not now. I'll be back for you later.

What the fuck is your jive ass gonna do?

Nothin. I don't never do nothin. I don't never hardly say nothin neither. But I was on my way to do somethin 'cause I had somethin to say all a sudden. Was Friday.

Cletus, the motherfucker, owed me somethin to say: Would he claim me at the morgue if they shot up my front, too? I wanted to know. He don't have to go crazy or give a shit. I just had to know if he'd go there. It's not my fault the truck made noise. *He* bought it for me. I'm sorry, square business, for his hypertension, but I ain't got what it takes to kill that man, I don't think. I coulda hit a ball twice instead a once if only he pitch it slower. That time he just pitched the ball too damn hard. That's all. I was nothin but a kid, don't play for no damn Detroit Tigers. He didn't have to leave it there, leave the ball out there where he was standin, and just walk away. Make me follow him home. No talkin. How you gonna leave the ball out there when your boy is tryin to hit it wit concentration? Don't make enough sense. I don't wanna know about him neither. I don't care about no Kentucky and how they came. Martin Luther King don't care 'bout that shit neither, I'm pretty sure. I just gotta know if he come for me when they shoot my front out. Do he wanna see me then. He wouldn't never worry on me when the pigs arrested me for bein someplace and throw my ass in jail. Picked up all them times on "investigation" for B&E, drivin witout a license, jaywalkin and shit. Cletus ain't done nothin. The one time the Big Four said we was bunchin up too much 'cause there was five of us on the street and they hurt me so bad I had to go to the hospital, he said I shouldn'ta been smart. I ain't try to be smart wit 'em, stupid motherfucker! Every nigga know that. Still and all, would Cletus come to the morgue, I wonder?

I walked up Linwood by Central High and cut across the field. People be on they porches, smellin smoke. Some blocks didn't have no light 'cause the power was down or the police shot out the streetlamps on account of snipers. I like the Elm trees and always have. Tuxedo leads over to Hamilton where I gotta go to see my father. He up on Ford. For a minute sometimes you don't see no tanks or hear no sirens. Pass by places I know ain't got no niggas. You forget what's happnin. Just looks like Detroit. Even Hamilton was all right some places. This thing went where it want to go and not where it didn't. Up there they got a little more money but only for a minute, and maybe that's how come it didn't seem to be so much lootin. Just depend where you are. If Auburey be up here when the shit broke, he still be gettin ready to be a artist maybe.

My pops got special locks, say I ain't gonna rob him again. He don't know that. His car ain't in the driveway. He ain't home. Motherfucker probly out wit one a his girlfriends. How you doin, Mrs. Wilson? She old. Used to bake cookies. I could use some lemonade she used to make. The front lawn got a slope in the grass, and that's where I wanted to be when Cletus ass drove up. I know people saw me from they porches. If that bitch over there wanted to tell me where my daddy gone, she coulda. I ain't got nothin to say to her or the one over there neither. Every time my stomach growled, I could see 'em again, Auburey and Carl, dead in a pool of theyselves, Fred a little ways over. This musta been the start of what happened to me.

Lotta people on the street after a while. It got dark. Kids playin. Just looked like Detroit summertime, only I'm startin to itch some. I'm tryin to stay nice, but I ain't high really. Just tryin not to go too fast. Wait on this motherfucker and see what jive he got to lay on me when I ask him. I know some dudes from 'round that way called

Dougie and Raymond. Them niggas saw me out there, come 'round to check me out. They down wit Junebug.

Sappnin', Billy? Dougie said. I told him I was waitin on my pops. Raymond said he seen the nigga drive off that mornin. He had bags in his trunk. I said now how you know he got bags in his trunk unless you got X-ray vision. Raymond ain't too smart. He say he mighta saw him put some in. Mighta. Ray all right. Where's Junebug at, I asked 'em? Junebug walked right up, eatin a sandwich. I know Junebug since we was little. I asked him could I have a bite a that sandwich. He wanna know what I'm doin up here. Seein my ugly motherfuckin pops, I said. I guess that was the right answer 'cause he didn't want his sandwich no more. Right on, I told him. And all three of 'em waited wit me to ask my dad would he claim me in the morgue if I didn't have no more front, only they didn't know about that.

Just like that this dark blue Chrysler comes slow 'round the corner. I got springs in my back made to bounce when the Big Four roll up. So do these nigga I'm wit. The car stopped at the curb, but I ain't jumpin. Even the driver got out. All a them. By the time the last door slammed Dougie was startin to back up toward my daddy's front door. Show 'em your keys, Raymond said. Yeah, man, show 'em your keys, Junebug said. I ain't got no keys, I told 'em. Aw shit, Billy. They got up, but I stayed down. It looked like a problem to me right away, 'cause the Big Four don't got but room for maybe one or two niggas in they car, big as these redneck peckerwoods was. They won't put you up front wit they shotguns. That's where they keep they tools for beatin ass. We stayed pretty cool. Four brothers on my daddy's lawn in the middle of a riot. This ain't what it was before. They was gonna have to choose. Maybe they was gonna have to drive away.

One started to say move it along the way they like to, only the others was already out and walkin up. Once they out, they past move it along. One had red hair. He said, you live here? to all of us. Nobody said yes. Raymond pointed up the street to his house, tryin to get his words out. He was scared as a motherfucker. Dougie too. Pigs probly ain't kilt a nigga all day. One redneck motioned for them two to step aside. Junebug sure was my ace and boon coon for standin up. I don't know what he was thinkin. He smarter than Quincy though. Quincy woulda run and git shot. The blond one was the lead. He comin right for me. I knew it. He had a stick, a club, I don't call it billy club, but it shoulda been a shotgun. I heard the story the way Calvin said they got it. This honky for sure woulda put buckshot in my gut. That's all he wanted to do right then. Shoot me. Let him, I figured.

Y'all on my daddy's lawn, I said. I didn't think of that. It just come out that way, but I sat there like I liked it, 'cause I did. White boy kept walkin up on me. Sometimes they like to smile. None of them bastards was smilin. This here is my house, I said.

Show me some I.D., he said. Ain't got none, I told him back. Don't need none. We just hangin. This here is where these fellas live. We ain't doin nothin, man. We ain't robbin no one.

This nigger is filthy, he said. You been out lootin all these days, forgot to take a bath, nigger? Take your ass downtown in an ambulance before I let your filthy ass in my car.

My motherfuckin punk-ass father was not comin home. I saw us gettin kilt right there. I got on my knees and started yelling loud as I could. They tryin to kill us for sittin out here! They tryin to kill all the niggas! I was screamin so loud I surprised myself. I saw people in each direction start comin out they houses and standin under Elms and lookin at us surrounded. Made me bolder. Don't let em kill us! We ain't done nothin wrong!

Nigger, he said, calm the way crackers like to do it. Get your dirty ass up and come with us. Red took his handcuffs out and stepped on my radio.

Go in yo houses and get yo guns! I was screamin. I heard a little girl cryin I was yellin so loud. It got good to me. Get yo guns, black people! This is what Carl would like to say, I know. Get yo guns and kill these redneck motherfuckers! Kill 'em, y'all! You can kill 'em like they be killin us!

After that it was nothin but me gettin jacked the fuck up. Red kicked me in my face wit his boot. I lost teeth I couldn't hardly use anyway. The blond guy liked to slap. They put me in cuffs and picked me up. Wouldn't even let me walk to they car. Just carried me, two of 'em, they couldn't wait. The brothers watched, glad it was me and not them. I was glad too. But didn't nobody get a gun after them like I said to. They just watched me get fucked up on the way to the car. The pigs tried to throw me in the back, but they missed. My head hit the side of the car and I damn near passed out.

Hold on to my hat, I yelled back to Junebug. And tell Cletus he a motherfucker! Tell Cletus he gonna get his next!

IV

I didn't need no heroin at the big jail on Belle Isle 'cause I had the riot in me. The riot happened to me, and that's how it felt for a lot of brothers in the place we started callin Belcatraz. I was the riot and part of it, one part of thousands, was me. White boys, the few a them in jail, they wanted out of there worse. We wanted out, but we knew what was up. They stayed together, scared most of the time, like it was all a mistake. They not the riot. Just got the feelin to loot on accident. Brothers was supposed to be there. They think all a nigga wants is survival. I always saw that. Every night I ever spent in jail was a nigga night. Every time I been to Recorders Court we the ones gettin but never givin. Now everybody could see it. Only this time I wanted to see how the Man was gonna do his thing. This time I thought about sayin somethin and what I would say. I never used to have nothin to say. Brothers was definitely thinkin about what they was gonna say to the judges this time.

That's how I beat the shakes really, thinkin about what to tell the judge, and Junebug. He was the next one to save my life. My body held up pretty good. The pigs picked up Junebug, but they never charged him for nothin. Maybe he was just in there long enough to see me through, then they let him go. He did my hurtin for me, could keep me still, keep me from bitin something off. I needed him sittin next to me when I was dryin out and my dreams wanted me dead. Every dream I died in. I'd see Auburey over and over lookin at me wit his open eyes. I'd see down through the big hole in Carl's stomach and see a sky falling. Usually I couldn't wake up and the dream went on all day and night. Junebug called it hallucinatin and he knew how to grab you by your eyeballs and make you see outside the dream. Then I started thinkin by him messin wit my eyes I was lettin Auburey get kilt again. So we'd fight. Junebug kick my ass. Then after a while, it all went away. Next day he split. He told me my hat was safe at his mama's house. I ain't takin it back.

Belcatraz got like a reunion. All I saw was men. I know women was there; we could hear 'em sometimes, want 'em, but never see 'em. Every brother came in jacked up. Most cats was my age, but there was lots of older guys too. Guys who had no business there, plain old assembly-line guys, people's uncles, grandfathers, neighbors. Dudes ain't even thinkin 'bout civil disobedience let alone gettin beaten down for bein niggas. Everybody. Hundreds and hundreds just like Quincy said. Quincy was there too, 'til he got moved some place else. I saw T-Bone for the last time before he got shot, saw Frenchie, Calvin, Nano, Skee. Each cat knew other cats I'd get to know, like Carlton, India, Al, Watt. You had to say another brother's name a lot 'cause otherwise we didn't have no name. Couldn't phone out. Nobody knew where you was, if you was dead. They said forty people died in that riot, probly fifty or sixty. You could be in the hospital. You could be anyplace. First they decide you shouldn't be in a bunch of brothers, then they put you in a bunch of niggas. In the processing, where they set the bail, that's how I knew they didn't know my name. And couldn't nobody afford bail the way they set it. They keep you or release you, hard to know why.

Cletus never came and I think my granma musta forgot. Six weeks I was in there before they took me back to court. If you was like me and didn't have nobody lookin for you, they had monitors who started comin 'round to check on you, see if you was not bein beat up too bad or gettin food. Some came from the churches. Nice people. And that's how I got a lawyer, a black lawyer, the first I ever talked to. Norman Harris. Brother Harris said they got me for inciting a riot. They got Raymond and Dougie for that too. It didn't make no kind of sense. How they gonna say I started the riot, I asked him?

The thing about Brother Harris was how we looked past each other. Brother Harris looked like he understood the law, and I surely do not. He looked like a regular brother too, but light skinned and mad the way they like to get, the way Quincy could get about the situation for the black man. Always fixin to get outrageous, but playin it cool on the surface.

"You don't have to start the riot. When they mean riot, they just mean startin shit out in public."

They started the shit wit me, I said.

"I know the cops approached you first, Billy. I'm not agreeing with them, I'm just explaining how the charges work. Inciting a riot is based on what you said when the policemen approached you."

Nah, it don't. It got to do with the fact that it was four of us sittin on my pop's lawn and we didn't move like they told us to.

"They say it was more than four of you. They need a bigger number according to the law."

People started comin over after I started yellin at 'em.

"A crowd?"

Hell yeah. A big crowd.

"There you go, brother. That's their number."

Nah, baby. Them motherfuckers *live* there. They ain't down wit no riot. They just come over to see a nigga get beat down. It was me that helped make it so the pigs could teach more niggas a lesson.

Brother Harris didn't want to but he laughed when I said that. "They're calling this a felony, Billy. The judge called you a militant, my man. The prosecutor has four white cops who want to testify that you and your partners urged black folks to kill them for their race. If we don't take a plea and go on to trial, you probably lookin at some real time."

I didn't want to hear all that. I got a motherfuckin right to say shit, don't I?

"First Amendment gets better than that. Says you also got the right to assemble brother to brother. But, Billy, I'm only telling you what it *says*, man."

Well, what does the law say *I* can say?

Brother Harris looked funny at me.

I wanna say I got a right to hang out in a black part of Highland Park with my black brothers in front of my black-ass punk, motherfuckin father's house sayin what I got to say witout four honky pigs tellin me who I can sit next to and when and how soon I gotta move it along, ya dig? I told Brother Harris we should say that they can't put the riot on me 'cause I was just speakin up for myself before somebody got misunderstood. The riot was already incited. The riot is bigger than me. I may be the riot but the riot ain't me. If every nigga is the riot then they might as well put half Detroit in jail. Let's tell 'em that and see what they got to say. We could tell 'em 'bout my father and how he ain't shit. We could tell 'em what happened to Carl and Auburey and that other fella and all the motherfuckers they decided to drop and see why I had so goddamn much to say back there. Shit. After this they need to just leave the black man alone, I told Brother Harris.

"The problem with what you're sayin, brother, is that you just comin up wit it now, *after* the cops busted you up and brought you in. We have to convince the judge that at the time the cops approached you all, you knew you were exercising your rights, not comin up with excuses later."

Bullshit, I said. Just tell the motherfuckers I was talkin. I was assembled. Tell 'em the pigs interrupted me.

I THINK WHAT HAPPENED TO ME WAS I WAS MISUNDERSTOOD, EVEN BY Brother Harris. Another brother, a very righteous cat named Abdullah, showed me how. The only difference between Brother Harris and Brother Abdullah was Brother Abdullah told me I better get to testify at my trial. He said the only tried and true when you have to tell about tellin is to make sure you the one that tells it. Brother Harris said that's not wise. Bein wise meant lettin the lawyer say what I had to say. Too many brothers arrested in the riot testified, and they lied, they try to play it too cool, and they got all fucked up. That's what he said some of the guys from the Algiers Motel did. Brother Harris said the black dudes helped out the cops with the things they said. He didn't think nothin would ever happen to them cops that kilt those brothers. Well, Brother Harris was the lawyer, and Abdullah is just a muslim in county jail. Abdullah don't even call it a riot. He call it a rebellion.

It was almost three months before my trial came up. They moved me to the city jail 'cause they started makin room there. My granma come to see me once with granpa, and she was so happy about how I looked she said she'd get up a collection for my bail. By now I had a·afro. She don't care for that, but she liked me wearin my hair in cornrows even less before. Brother Harris didn't let me testify. He was pretty good on his feet, never looked scared. He knew the cops that beat me was Big Four cops, and I could tell they knew he knew. He questioned them mean like he could tell when they was about to make shit up, and the judge had to step in. Still he got his outrage out. Me, I knew I was gonna lose, and I did. Judge Barnes said I might got a right to talk, but not what I said when I said it. The police were overworked and under fire. Crowds could mean more trouble. It wasn't my property we was on. That was that. I never got to say what I really had to say inside, but I was goin to jail.

I told the dude he shoulda let me testify. This time I could see through Brother Harris's eyes about me. He figured not taking the plea was enough, not to win it, not to get my freedom, but justice enough, better than the nigga he would never have to be, better than what a brother like me could expect. Maybe so, back when I didn't have nothin to say, but this time I did. I could at least tell about how come I had something to tell.

He said we could appeal my conviction; Brother Harris said the higher courts got smarter judges, dudes who ain't competin to see who could throw the most brothers in prison. Could I testify? I asked him. Sorry, that ain't the rules, he told me. I know he worked hard for me and I didn't pay him nothin. But square biz, sometimes I couldn't stand to look Brother Harris in the face.

Raymond and Dougie got acquitted. They lawyer was a white guy. Pretty soon after they started the appeal is when granma got enough money to get me out. They wasn't gonna let me go. Said if my pops wasn't dead, he needed to come down and vouch for me. Oh, he dead all right, I told the judge. Right there in front of my granny. She didn't even say nothin after I lied on her son. Maybe she knows. Petoskey where she and granpa live changed a lot while I was gone those months. They moved the police station. A mosque opened. Shit that burned stayed burned down. It changed everywhere. For sale signs on all the lawns. Over by 12th Street, lot a black folks who owned they homes was sellin. But the whites especially was gettin out. Each month you be drivin down streets you know, you see moving vans, trucks haulin white folks away. They went further west and out to Dearborn. They went up past Seven Mile, to Eight Mile. I didn't know they even had a Twelve Mile, but they do. White folks was mad and offended by niggas after the Motor City burned. They said somethin like this wasn't never gonna happen again. Pretty soon wasn't gonna be none of them left to see if it do.

We was still waitin on the appeal when Martin Luther King got kilt. I'm pretty sure Cletus was busy somewhere integratin when they kilt his boy. I never did see him, but I know he sold that house off Hamilton. The motherfucker's probly thinkin now what? Punk-ass negro truly ain't shit. And if my front got shot up, well, I got my answer.

Just like they did Carl. They kept pretendin to go after the cops that did the worst shit in the Algiers Motel. I saw Auburey's moms on TV a couple a times tearin it up, cryin and carryin on about justice. Calvin was right. All the Pollard men had trouble after Auburey died. The cops busted Tanner for some li'l shit and sent him up for a few weeks. They put Chaney in a mental hospital in California. Robert, the littlest one, he got three to ten for stealin seven dollars off a newsboy. Mr. Pollard left. He just split. I saw Fred Temple's people on TV too. They just like most folks, tryin to get a little someplace, been twenty-plus years at the same plant. Couldn't get no justice for they son. I heard one a the cops that did it kilt two other dudes that week. White folks was finally real mad at us. They forgot all about Carl. Nobody accused nobody of killin him. Nothin happened about it. It was all Auburey and a little Fred. Carl just plain died by hisself. When things calmed down after King died, the jury let the one cop go that kilt Auburey. They believed him after he changed his story and said it was self-defense. He said Auburey went for the shotgun and it went off. Believe what they wanna believe.

Brother Harris was wrong, too, I'm pretty sure. I was twenty-four years old by the time he lost his appeal in 1970, and I started serving my two to five along with Abdullah. Brother Harris was wrong about me bein late wit my defense. He had to be. I was tryin to say what I could when the Big Four stopped me. I wanted to testify, but he wouldn't let me. That means I had to be sayin somethin back up on Hamilton. They wouldn't send me away unless I was sayin *somethin*. I'm still sayin it. Probly ain't shit to say really, but I keep tellin myself when I get the chance. And I tell Abdullah I know I had a hell of a riot, but a punk-ass rebellion. First time I see him smile, he says try again.

Love Space

THE FIRST THING I DISCOVERED WITH HIM WAS THE POSSIBILITY OF nighttime. Before his lanky presence happened to me, I wasn't aware of my thing about nighttime, especially dusk. When the sun ebbed to a certain angle on the horizon, all that orange glint and shadow spelled death. It unsettles me into activity, anything to avoid being swallowed up by the end. Tomorrow isn't promised to us. So, my feeling was, you get up, get things done, go straight home, turn on all the lights.

I hired Theo into one of two additional community organizer slots made available to me by the head of the community development department, Arthur Robinson. If Theo is anything, he is tall, probably six feet five inches. He's taller than any of my brothers. Theo is so tall he's always above you, sitting, standing, kneeling; he's taller than you and always at one with any tree in the vicinity. He wears a little goatee that doesn't come all the way flush into a beard; there are gaps below the sides of his lips. His eyes are brown, clear and tucked under eyebrows so even they look groomed. And of course, Theo is white.

He told me during his interview that he is a scientific socialist. This alone nearly won him the job, not because he is one. I think he's just a liberal trying to pass as something more. But his complete lack of inhibition and his proud assertion of his difference, even when it wasn't really relevant, convinced me he might be good at representing poor tenants before the city agencies they have to go before. He's also older. It's hard for me to tell with white guys how old, but he was about thirty-four. I never heard anybody over thirty call themselves a scientific socialist. I thought in this country most people outgrew that by then.

Well, we're walking together out of the Mac Center at the end of the day. He's walking me to my car, and that evening I'm especially thankful because every little pre-thug-aspiring-con-junior-brother seemed to be out there ready to use me to prove some tragic point to, as far as I could tell, some invisible elder. Theo is talking about some project when all of a sudden he interrupts himself to point out the sunset coming down the street. That's how he put it. Look, he says, after everything else today, the sun itself has "arrived on this corner to genuflect before us." It struck me as such an unnecessarily grandiose way of announcing that the day was over, but it was real sincere. That's what made me actually notice what inspired it. The sun really was right there at the end of the street, perfectly sandwiched between the buildings on either side, washing everything, not just the red and brown bricks of the buildings, but the black asphalt, the brown faces, the green and blue buses, metal cars, everything, in an infinite amber that for the first time looked nothing to me like death. It looked like another face of spring.

I'M ALWAYS BEING JUDGED BY PEOPLE IN THE BLACK COMMUNITY *here, but right away Charlotte didn't do that, which was almost inappropriate given the position she's got. What the feds are doing by pouring money into places like the MacMillan Center is essentially buying a mainstream black power base, led by bought-out radical militants. Not that Charlotte even pretends to be one. It's just that, if anybody, she understands that what she does and who she hires has more to do with black people getting a foot in the door (or in the ass) at City Hall than with making the demands of tenants known before the Neighborhood Council or shit like that. Hiring me doesn't help that, yet still she was interested. Which is outta sight, because I really wanted this job. I really needed to be dealing with folks at the grass roots. And I admit that by 1972, I was drifting. I'm also very behind to Jill on support payments for Chrissy.*

None of that is to say that I wasn't also very enamored of Charlotte's legs and almost instantly wanted to screw her. I did. She's got big Diana Ross eyes that see everything. Her face is round and her hips are too wide for her Volkswagen. And she posed this incongruous challenge about liking nighttime.

THEO HAS A CHILD AND AN EX-WIFE AND THE WRONG JOB. AND THEY have the wrong names—Jill and Chrissy. When he told me that his little girl's name is Chrissy, I almost asked him how he could ever do such a thing, which seemed so painstakingly white to me and just very bewildering. Before I could even get into it though, he upped and said it was his ex-wife's decision to name her Chrissy. Still, I figured that wasn't really why they were apart. They were apart because of the jobs Theo, scientific socialist, liberal grassroots organizer though he is, takes. That made him immediately ineligible for me. Not that it really mattered. I wasn't looking, except in that slightly always looking sense. He was tall. But he has almost no butt, which if you take the position that *they* design pants to fit *them*, made him look cruelly pathetic in dungarees, which he bleached in a tie-dye effect that he wore every day. Every single day.

Still, I love his voice, which is even clearer than his eyes, deep and faithfully lyrical. Especially his voice near the end of the day when he's returned from fieldwork. It's full of notes accumulated over the hours of words and reactions. He's got perfect pitch.

LOOKING INTO THE WAY A PROBLEM IS TOLD WAS MY NEW DISCOVERY. Charlotte was more compelling. Charlotte at dusk could do something so forever, everything else was but a stop on the line to the real thing. It helped that the spring had finally come after a long, depressing winter. During my afternoon out talking with some women at the Dilmar Homes project, I was trying out my discovery. I tried to look into the way my clients tell their problems. Clearly, it's not just the fact that the place is infested and the paint chips fall from the ceiling into the cribs almost strategically (they don't seem to land anywhere else). More than that, you listen to these two women, Cecilia Pickens, Yvonne Walker, and if you give them a chance to just get down to it in their own terms, the infestation starts to look like and go along with their need for child care, the hours child care might bring look like and go along with the lack of any way to organize an effective job search, which sounds like the rude tones they hear down at the welfare office, which looks like the discomfort they feel when they're not in the ghetto. They don't see their lives in terms of bad housing, fucked-up schools, dead-end jobs, or hostile assistance from a system bent on ridiculing them. They don't break up living. They talk about it like I think about my own, all one thing. And seeing that, seeing how they explain what's not coming together helped me see where I need to bring some needle and thread, and it changed my life a little.

That's where I was coming from when I got back to the Mac Center and saw Charlotte stepping out onto the street. This woman is daylight savings time. She is the reason for it and the savings, I'm convinced. She's passing in front of me in a spring dress, a print dress full of indigo, lavender and crimson flowers afire against her caramel skin, smooth skin streaked with the sun across the bone of her calf. You're suddenly in the grip of all the hormones long pent up through the winter, but not just yours, hers too. Otherwise, she would probably think better than to wear that short dress, thin fabric so light it turned each breeze into a splash. It wasn't really warm enough for that. But just the things you retain in your double take is worth being alive forever: That part of her neck behind the ear under her little afro; or the high flesh of her thighs when a shock of wind blows the short skirt up before she can get her hands on it; or her breasts of honey pushing into the street against the wind. She meant it to be hot and it was so; she meant to be hot and she is. And I was meant to be there, a reminder to stick around, look around, but don't stand around. Go get some. Go get her.

So, I awkwardly pointed out the sunset coming down the street and somehow managed to ask her if she felt like walking to the park instead of heading right home.

I REALLY STARTED TO DRESS BETTER, POSSIBLY SEXIER. THAT WAS THE first sign that I might want to test my chemistry with Theo. He had a great apartment to hang out in. Lots of comfy chairs. The first few times I visited, his words had this way of filling up the living room like reclining figures. Sentences casually came off his tongue and sat in the deep chair by the lamp or on the oversized couch. But each wanted to be a large presence like Theo.

He lived in Jefferson Estates, which is an all-white housing project right in district 12. I don't get up to district 12 a lot. It's the smallest one; it's all white and located on the county line, right across the interstate actually, from the northwest suburbs. The suburbs there are also all white. Theo hangs rugs, which I liked instantly and stole the idea. Rugs on the walls make everything you say sound safe. It's good for a voice like his too, because with rugs around, those gently spoken words come out dressed in smoking jackets and silk pajamas.

Mostly we'd talk about his life, while I would be thinking of my own. I didn't talk as easily about myself in his house. I was happy to listen. I enjoyed that very much, but not to talk. One thing was I didn't really like Jefferson Estates, the whole idea of it. I find it strangely gratifying to see white people struggling in poverty, despite the fact that you already know lots of them do, and you're trying to help them get out of it. But on the other hand, they always looked a little closer to getting out of poverty to me, which seemed unfair. An all-white housing project like Jefferson Estates was ten times nicer than all-black projects like Dilmar Homes, which was unfair. Plus, I saw them as dangerous and unpredictable people around black folks. So many American flags. Most of them believe Nixon doesn't know anything and ought to be left alone. So, when I started going up there with Theo, I never much looked them in their faces, except their children. I walked through the lobby and the hallways as if I were conducting some routine inspection, some kind of field visit. And I asked Theo several times in different ways why he lived there.

What he would say never made much sense to me, I think, because it was confusion even to him. Escaping his own upbringing. Being close to people he considered real, yet forgoing the challenge of living in a black project because of judgments he thought people were making about him. Saving money he didn't have. I liked all that pure honesty even when it seemed a bit unreasonable. Theo just was not afraid to spill the half-eaten morsels of his personality. It made his whole manhood more available, something to be shared and not shrouded in broodish mystery getting ready to explode.

The problem then was not so much that I didn't feel comfortable talking about myself in his place, it was that Theo never seemed to notice that I never told *my* stories. So busy impressing me with his stuff, for a long time I didn't think he was even interested in mine. This was especially wierd, given the fact that I was still his *boss*. I mean, if you're gonna hang out with your boss and try to put a little move on her too, shouldn't you at least pretend you wanna know where she's coming from?

I HAD NEVER SMOKED REEFER WITH A BOSS IN ANY JOB I EVER HAD, and I've had several where I knew for a fact the guy got high. But all the organizers who technically work under her, the ones at Mac with us as well as those at the MLK Community Center nearby, are pretty tight. Charlotte is easy with anybody if she knows they're on board. But it's a delicate balance for her sometimes, 'cause of the age thing. The race thing is really mine to worry about, because they're all black—Rashid, Mwenda, Gordon and another woman who sometimes comes around, Wilhemina. Gordon is at least my age. Charlotte must be the youngest one and, like me, she's not originally from here. But Charlotte's the only one with a degree from a college anyone ever heard of, and I think she finished a masters in sociology. I'd bring them up to Jefferson so they could pretend to check in on their white clients. They'd smoke up my reefer because it's invariably better than that Mexican skunk weed you get in the ghetto.

Charlotte and I were very high the first time we made love. I was stoned. She'd gotten into a very serious debate with Mwenda about whether we should be talking to our clients about welfare as a temporary solution or as a guarantee, a right. Mwenda, I think, was way off base, treating it like it wasn't a right at all. Charlotte was trying to bring her back, trying to show her some balance, but Mwenda was getting mad.

The rest of us just listened, until Mwenda said she had to go. Rashid didn't want her to go off alone mad so he offered to go with her, and pretty soon Gordon realized his ride was with them. That left me and a very excited Charlotte, who was speaking in rapid fire sentences, really juiced up.

She started talking about her life a bit, trying to put her comments into context, like the fact that she grew up poor, she knew about the need for welfare and all despite knowing hard work. That kind of stuff. I wasn't listening very carefully. I was overcome by her beauty. The closer I came to her face as we sat on the couch with our red wine and cigarettes, the more passionate she seemed to speak. I wasn't feeding off the words so much as I was moved by the energy. Coltrane was on, and I remember the song Naima *playing. Charlotte was wearing beads and lots of heavy bracelets that looked to be copper and brass. They kept making tinny sounds when she gestured, signals to look here at her slender wrists, there at her neck, follow her neck down past the slanted edge of her daishiki collar. The saxophone began sounding just like her voice. She and Coltrane would blend and match moods, little giggles, rises, lows. I don't know much about music, but I know that the way* Naima *starts is an arch, and Trane comes back to it again and again. This arch is high and it sounds like the way to say "I" with a horn. Charlotte was riding the arch of the "I"s he played, exposing herself, bending over backwards, stretching into the archs. Well, I wanted to be on that arch with her and pretended that she was asking me to climb up.*

Of course, I was already quite up, physically. I was profoundly erect. So I got up and put the song back on the phonograph. Then I came back and leaned over toward her. Before that I had never studied the power of a cheekbone from so close above it. I never admired the fullness of hips turning into the sofa like they did under her body weight. Coltrane was all heavy and brown and full. So was her forehead, her cheek, the edge of her lip, her naked breasts exposed inside her top, each thick dark nipple in command.

I never wanted somebody so much. I felt like a child at the edge of the world. If called upon to speak, I would have squealed, begged. I would have begged not to have to speak, only to be naked, to stumble upon her skin or be tumbled upon by her. I didn't believe for a minute that I could please her. I felt very pink and unnatural actually. I was so hungry I didn't want to have to explain. I just wanted her to believe me. And even deeper in the back of my mind, I thought of Clyde Frazier, and I hoped to God that Charlotte would not measure me against that man.

THE FIRST TIME THEO AND I HAD SEX WAS NOT LOVE AT ALL. I WAS really just fucking him back, until I made the mistake of waking there the next morning. Some of us, community organizers and I, were sitting around at his place getting high and listening to jazz. We were having a good time, until Theo took over. It becomes a lecture on revolution. The audience is me, Mwenda, Gordon, and Rashid. Gordon is probably forty years old, a brother who I'm pretty sure is a communist and was getting ready to go cut cane in Cuba as he does every spring. Yet *he's* not saying shit. Mwenda's boyfriend Rashid, another brother, is there too. He's very good looking, politely righteous, respectfully inarticulate in the presence of whites, especially men, and not too *scientific* with his rage. Says not a word. As usual, Theo misinterprets this as interest in his gospel. Maybe it was for them. For me, it's the one aspect of his zeal and honesty that makes me want to clock him: he thinks he knows everything. His confidence is definitely powerful, even sexy. But when he goes ideological, I can't hang. Every time he mentions "the black community," what the fuck is "the black community"? He keeps saying it over and over. We're all looking around, wondering when he's gonna stop and it never hits him. Mwenda, who's about my age and a committed sister but a little jealous of me, starts going off about welfare in an effort— for which I remain eternally grateful—to rid us of Theo's lecture on revolution.

Maybe out of frustration, I find myself getting into it with *her* a little. The disagreement was honest enough, but I was not really

debating Mwenda as much as I was thinking up how to get through
to Theo short of using poison. It got away from me, that's all.

THE ANSWER TO MY BEING HORNY AND BEING TOO TALL FOR THE
moment was to slide onto the floor and begin kissing the bare skin of her
calves. I think she giggled. I know she stopped talking shortly after that.
When I got to her knees, she hesitated. Her thighs tensed up, so I put my
hands on her muscles. Jill had no thigh muscles to hold. Charlotte relaxed
and her legs parted just lightly. Her smell wafted into my nostrils, and I
looked into the dark crack expecting to see her vagina, which of course I
couldn't see under her skirt. I inhaled deeply all up and down the inside
of her thighs, hoping to smell more of her. Jill smelled like nothing, unless
powder is something. As soon as Charlotte moaned, I felt welcome. I
found out black women's toes bunch more. The spaces between them
resisted my tongue at first. Charlotte stretched her feet into my mouth.
Then Charlotte pulled her underpants off.

    The smell was more than a welcome to Charlotte herself, but a sensory
passport into the lies of my imagination. It was thicker and more pungent
than the spit and the odor of "nigger" spoken from my uncles sitting
around. It was sweeter than forbidden, and I tasted her in my gums for
days afterwards. When Charlotte came in my mouth, I belonged some
place after wandering around. When I watched her naked body dance
over my chest with her eyes closed, I copied her expressions 'cause I wanted
to be taken somewhere totally unfamiliar. I admit that. She moved just
to move, while I always moved to thrust and parry and eventually come,
as hard and as long as I could. I spent that night in awe, I guess. I didn't
know a woman's ass could form such curves in rapture. The shape of her
breasts. The anatomy of her collarbone, all the way up to her shoulder.

    But I had private misgivings about her pubic hair. Hard and wiry
and unfeminine to the touch. That was a problem for me.

JUST BECAUSE A BLACK MAN RARELY GIVES HEAD DOES NOT ALONE
explain why it was so important that Theo do it to me that night. If

he had not, we would not have connected because by then I was so annoyed by his grandstanding that I needed signs of submission. He really had to eat me out. For him I'm pretty sure it was exotica. I had been talking about myself, finally. I was partly trying to penetrate the look in his eyes that said he was listening only insofar as he was thinking up his next long-winded comment. My voice broke out that night. For once I enjoyed hearing my own reflections about the work we do and where I come from. That much Theo was able to create for me, for us, by being the keeper of the place, showing interested eyes, the necessary ears. And yet it was absolutely clear that he wanted the evening to end in bed. I had already decided that I could do that. I had slept with two white men before in school. It was no big deal, at least in retrospect. I always saw myself with a stone cold soul brother, but because that raises as many issues as it solves, especially the stone and cold parts of it, I was OK with the idea of screwing this decent man and the possibility of nighttime he offered. But it was a delicate balance. He had to show me that he could listen to what I had to say about things. Really listen. And want to. Like the expectations he had of others when he talked.

Theo clearly had not been with a sister before. Ever since that dusk in front of the Mac, the perpetual gaga in his eyes during not-too surreptitious glances at my breasts was clue enough. No, if we were gonna groove, I felt like I needed the connection of his tongue inside my vagina. I could get with the shape of that from a cosmic standpoint, looking down from the heavens at two human beings, seeing them in conflict over commitment to the work, the love, struggling to be close. Yes, she's a little distant, but mainly they're apart because of a distance he creates. He really wants to bridge the distance. She wants to bridge the distance, yet not relinquish her ground. They are in *his* place, among people who claim a similarity with him. In order to connect, he needs to submit to another role, transforming that big mouth of his into a pleasure-giving act of quiet, patient kindness, while she demonstrates her trust in turn by opening up her womb to him. They take the shape of intersecting triangles. His tongue inside her vagina between her legs. Sucking my toes was extra.

Theo is tender. Theo finally stopped talking and thinking about talking. It was not love making because it was not love. I really had been annoyed with him. I didn't even want to have intercourse that night. In my eyes, his naked body still reminded me of his conversational tone, and I wasn't ready to find it attractive. Being on top made it easier to avoid looking at his details, plus it feels better to me. The trick was falling asleep there. The trick was waking up in Jefferson Estates next to Theo's pink body and crooked toes and camel knees and slightly hairy back and feeling at home, actually falling back to sleep at the moment I might have slipped out and into my Bug and driven home. That wasn't supposed to happen. But leaving his sleeping body had no appeal. It had moved me, deeply and unforgettably. I wanted to see it awaken again. I wanted to be back in his lanky presence.

Only accidental glances at the top of his butt aroused my suspicion. Otherwise Theo was beautiful.

THE PROBLEM OF THE TEXTURE OF CHARLOTTE'S PUBIC HAIR WAS CAST *as Jill when it was really Doris Day. Jill is not blonde. Jill is not an actress or famous for anything in my view except apathy and disagreement. But she was the best I could do as far as fulfilling the quest for what we used to call My Girl. My Girl was known to every member of my family, with uncanny consensus. My mom knows her, dad winks, my sister loves her/hates her, and everyone on our street who had eyes wanted to look into hers whenever they could, described her as if she were just about to enter the conversation. Their expectations were designed according to how perfectly she'd fit into the plan. Nobody ever really got her, but it was normal to keep trying. Except in the TV show "I Dream of Jeanie." But the air force major guy totally misunderstood the fact that he practically owned her in Barbara Eden, had her as any man could hope to have her, yet he was understandably blinded by the fact that My Girl in his case was a genie. Jill was the closest I could come, until years into our marriage when we finally met each other and discovered our error. (I was not the air force major guy she needed.)*

I may have loved Charlotte's aftertaste in my mouth all day the next day, but it was a long time before I could open my eyes when I ate her. The feel and sight of her pubic area could shoot waves of repulsion through me, not because she was black, I don't think, but because I could not find any recognition of My Girl there.

I figured Charlotte had to feel something like that too. I definately hoped that she did so that it would be equal. I thought of Clyde Frazier, whose picture seemed everywhere available to me, on TV, at newsstands, billboards, radio, as much if not more than Doris Day or Barbara Eden. I thought Clyde was the black prince, acceptably so, serious with conviction, popular yet nobody's fool, superfly but not a pimp or a hustler. Cool at my height.

THEO'S LOVE CAME TO ME HATCHED FROM A GOVERNMENT CONspiracy, which I'm sure is how we could later sue that same government. First, we were paid federal funds to make the city do right by its own poor people. Then, we were paid to go everywhere at night and plot.

Sunset is at its most earnest by a river, I learned. Light gathers in the lips of the current's million waves and changes colors twice a second. We watched it shimmy and glisten from the boardwalk near the bridge. We kissed beneath the bridge. We bridged the blue in the sky with the yellow on the horizon. We turned red together as the sun dropped out of sight.

It surprised me that Theo thought I would be a basketball fan. I wasn't. My brother Eric always wanted to play professional basketball, and he used his wish to concoct a totally selfish world of his own rules about what he had to do and what I, a little girl sister with no such singular dream, was supposed to do around the house. Unfortunately for him, the basketball dream never happened, which left him prepared for a life of fame and play but very little else. For him, I ignore the games.

That's why it took me a while to uncover what Theo was worried about with Walt "Clyde" Frazier. Walt Frazier was an expert basketball guard for the Knickerbockers, who had led them to a world championship recently, was threatening to do it again, and for all that they called him Clyde. Theo explained that the Clyde part was because he wore "bourgeois style full-length mink coats," long sideburns, platform shoes, gangster hats, and drove a "Ruling Class Royce." Typically, I never got to tell Theo just how distasteful all that was to me before he confessed that he'd actually bought and read *two* of Clyde Frazier's books. Theo figured all us black girls wanted to ride Clyde or the next best thing. He understood if we did. I suggested maybe it was he who wanted to ride Clyde. He didn't appreciate that in an embarassed way. I consoled him by saying that my brother actually resembled Clyde, so I would be mentally unable to cross that line.

But I was beginning to have a recurring dream of carrying Theo's penis around with me in my purse when we were apart. And I thought it was encouraging that the dream action always took place somewhere at *night*. I was beginning to have a regular Theo thing in general. It was probably love, but it was also daring, which intensified the feeling of everything. I couldn't wait for dusk.

WHAT HAS EMBARASSED ME IS THE VIOLATION OF MY POLITICAL *beliefs represented by the marriage of Doris and Barbara and Clyde in my thoughts. These are not just my thoughts. My thoughts I think. These truths and comparisons and feelings operate automatically. I only manage them as best I can. You can share things like that with Charlotte and laugh about it. That wasn't the case with Jill or any other woman I knew. Charlotte is much stronger than any woman I've ever been this close to. She works harder, to the point of selflessness, I think, plodding on and plodding on. She can spend twice as much time in meetings run by other people than I ever could, honestly. She's driven in a kind of black-woman way that I used to think of as possibly compensating for something else she lacked, but later thought of as special. The black community has been situated differently in the capitalist economy, demanding that black women more than men exploit the opportunities available to them in defense of their families. This is probably why Clyde seems so out of my reach.*

But how I really managed my latent preoccupation with bourgeois labels was Raquel Welch. Raquel Welch, I had to admit, was not only more beautiful and desireable than Barbara Eden, her dark hair and ravishing brown eyes and great tits and meaty legs and foreign first name put her right on the line between My Girl and Charlotte. It is a bit late in life to admit that, but in any case it soon made Charlotte's pussy one of my favorite places to rest my head.

BY MID-SUMMER, YOU COULD SEE THE PROBLEM WITH DISTRICT 12 coming. It was no less a problem between Theo and me. I learned of a September 15 deadline for submitting an application to the federal HUD office in order to get a one million dollar grant for our area. They call it CDBG money—community development block grants. My idea was to build new housing, which everybody knows my area desperately needs, especially in the slums of district 10 where mostly black folks live. The idea was also to use a building site that was right on the border between district 12 and district 10. That way, we could promise that blacks and whites would actually live in affordable housing together. The problem was, in order to get an application in, it had to go with the support of the Neighborhood Council, which has four nominal members (only one of whom is black) and a chairman, who does whatever the hell he wants. His name is Nicholas Vittorini.

NICKY VITTORINI IS NOTHING BUT A FAT-CAT BUREAUCRATIC SCUMBAG *who serves at the pleasure of every corrupt city official appointed by the devil to maintain inequality between the poor and the chosen white folks forced to live in a world with them. He wears a Dick Nixon watch he bought in Disneyworld, and he only cares about the Neighborhood Council on two occasions: To say yes to a friend in need of unrequited patronage, and no to anything progressive.*

VITTORINI, OF COURSE, OPPOSED THE APPLICATION. HE CALLS IT NONsense when I show him how black families in district 10 can't get benefits that poor whites in district 12 reap just by being white and being next to the suburbs. Feed 'em welfare, he says. He can't stand the thought of race mixing no matter how the resources get spread around, because Vittorini's in the pocket of the county legislators from the suburbs. They play golf together. He says I should mind my business. He thinks the community development department wing that I head up, Organizing Initiative, has nothing to do with building housing anyway. Housing requires planning, he says, and "appropriately belongs" to the planning wing. Well, the head of the planning wing happens to be a guy named Murphy, also a hundred years old, also more interested in golf than seeing poor black people get a little equality. I tell Vittorini that the people I work with are organizing for habitable housing, and I'm just trying to help them. He waves me off, calls me radical behind my back, and plans a vacation until a few days before the application deadline. I try one more time, this time in private, to get him to understand that this is actually what the government pays us to do. He makes an off-hand joke about who really pays, young lady. They may be your pot of gold, I tell him, but I offer the rainbow. We hate each other so much we both leave laughing.

JEFFERSON ESTATES IS THE ONLY HOUSING PROJECT IN DISTRICT 12 with families instead of old people. Old people are the best poor people, because they vote, stay quiet and don't advocate overthrow very often (or if they do, not effectively). Families are a pain in the ass, which justifies use of excessive force to deal with them. The guy who built and manages Jefferson Estates for the city is a clever redneck named Olsen. He is, quite naturally, a close personal friend of a close personal friend of Vittorini's. Olsen told this friend who told Vittorini that Theodore Cox is a nigger lover, and that I frequently invite said niggers up to my pad for illicit activity. Vittorini mentioned to Charlotte that she had been rumored to be in and out of Jefferson Estates at hours unbecoming a lady, even a black lady.

First, I go to Olsen to confront him about what's being said behind my back. I let him know what was said, how he and I have a different understanding of what the term nigger lover implies, but that coming from him I would consider it enough provocation to answer him any time he's ready. Olsen got, as they say, gentlemanly very quickly, rising up in his office swivel chair, tugging at his beard and warned me, for my own good. He said he couldn't tell me, another man, how to live my life, but he said I knew better than to undo the hard work my father had plainly done on my name. I reminded him he didn't know my father or where he might find him, that the name was mine to do with what I wanted and that I was getting tired of talking. He said that as far as he was concerned we were through talking. He admitted he said what he said, but he wouldn't say it again. If I had a problem with what he'd said, he was only speaking for the neighbors, who were likely to act beyond his control if I didn't change my ways.

That's when I moved into Dilmar Homes.

Before I did that though, I attended a hearing of the Neighborhood Council at which Charlotte was scheduled to address the full panel. District 10 residents spoke in support of the new housing. I got a few district 12 residents to speak favorably, too. Charlotte got into a polite but heated exchange with Vittorini while the four blocks of wood at his side petrified. Then the public was given time on the mike. I took it and began to describe what I knew about Vittorini's vicious rumor mongering as well as what the council's refusal would mean to the city. I told them that refusing the money only worked to choke off the poorest section of the city into an alienated, isolated industrial reserve army of folks at the mercy of ruling-class interests, which would someday make them even more dangerous than they already are. If the council really felt threatened by the idea of organized poor people, they would be wise to throw them a bone now. New housing, in my opinion, was a bone.

THEO JUST PLAIN OLD TALKED TOO FUCKING MUCH. AND WHAT HE would say was often out of touch. Black people were not dogs to whom bones better be thrown before they come roaring out of their doghouses to lunge at the master's neck. Vittorini wasn't interested in poor folks being isoltaed from the means of production. He probably never even thought of that. That was just talk Theo liked to hear come out of his own mouth. He has a great voice. He loves it. He likes to contrast it with the local accent in public. But the problem we have is race. Vittorini doesn't want to upset racist suburban voters obsessed with lower property values and integrated schools. If Vittorini actually wants anything, it's simply to make black families disappear. You listen to Theo and you'd think it has nothing to do with people and their beliefs. To him it's just class warfare.

This became my cross to bear, because I love black families and I was falling in love with a man who talked publicly about throwing them bones. I'd hired him to help them realize their needs, yet he already had it figured out. It was all so damned white of him. To know it all. To control the debate. To grab the floor out of turn. Theo tried to tell me I took myself too seriously. He accused me of not getting beyond my own personal experience and into an understanding of "institutional dynamics." He saw the housing site as the place for uniting class consciousness. I saw it as getting scarce resources to black people.

We could disagree, no problem. The problem was feeling like Theo couldn't respect black people ultimately handling the situation. I didn't think he trusted our judgment. After it was clear that Vittorini wouldn't and probably couldn't move, I went around him and the regulations to my boss Arthur Robinson. Robinson was the head of the CDD anyway. If he approved the CDBG application in the absence of any vote by the Neighborhood Council, the feds might allow that. Arthur is black.

ARTHUR ROBINSON IS AN ESTABLISHMENT LACKEY IN SEARCH OF A pension.

ARTHUR HEARD ME OUT, WALKED OUT ON WHAT I'M SURE HE CONsidered a limb, and backed me. That's how we did it. That was my move to make. Theo wanted to know what I really did. He figured I did something he couldn't do. Not because I'm black. Theo swore he didn't, but I know he did: He insinuated I did something with Arthur. *To* Arthur.

This was our problem, Theo's and mine, and it was real serious. The sun no longer set on us. For weeks, I didn't want him in my apartment, and I thoroughly enjoyed the idea of his six foot five inch frame creeping alone past the dopeheads at Dilmar Homes. But mostly I went back to our places, the green meadow in the park, downtown to the theater district and its brightly lit sidewalks and the river. I thought about how Theo is duped every day by a world that never looks askance at him or questions his right to be there. It was bad enough he was treated as if he were always entitled to be heard anyplace on earth, but Theo *knew* it and *demanded* it without hesitation. I felt disloyal to my own then. I felt badly for Arthur Robinson as I would for my own father, who is also a bit timid and overly cautious yet is still degraded by white men behind his back. I felt for my own brothers, my big strong brothers. Theo can walk into practically any public place and feel at home. They *automatically* cower in certain places. Their *bodies* tell them to adjust pride downward for the moment. But Theo flaunts permanent rights of passage wherever he goes, and up to the moment of being disrespected by him, I felt like I'd been trying to ride piggyback.

SHE BELIEVED MY ARROGANCE AS IF IT CARRIED HALF ITS LYING weight. All I really wanted Charlotte to see was my dedication to her and to the people we work for. I just thought I'd be guilty of being a white liberal if I broke it down that way. I figured it was safer to speak in terms of principles.

But Charlotte didn't think I respected her authority. She had to remind me that I worked for her. She really did. I had forgotten. I really had.

What I did to Olsen, despite what it didn't get me, what I said in that hearing room to Vittorini nobody black does or says. Not Gordon, certainly not Rashid, not even Arthur Robinson. For a little while I was proud of that. I was hoping Charlotte got a good look at her man. I was hoping that moment would resonate to applause in the busted-up hallways and broken elevators of the gargantuan Dilmar Homes complex where I am regularly scared shitless and half my rugs were already stolen off my walls.

I WROTE THE CDBG APPLICATION, AND WE GOT THE GRANT. VITTORINI found out about it, of course, and went after me. He went right over Arthur to Mayor Muckleroy. He told him about me and Theo, how we were seen corrupting the good hallways of Jefferson Estates, along with other Negroes seen on the premises. This "fratenizing" conduct, Vittorini told him, was what was really behind the CDBG application, not Organizing Initiative work for which I was paid. About a week later, Muckleroy demanded that Arthur fire me and Theo. For good measure, Muckleroy wanted Mwenda fired too. Arthur tried to resist it, but the mayor threatened his job too.

The day after we got fired, at nine o'clock sharp, Theo, Mwenda and I demanded a meeting with the mayor at City Hall. Surprisingly, Muckleroy agreed to see us. I tried to be fair with Theo, because technically I wasn't his boss anymore and also being heavy handed wasn't my style. But I promised him that if he opened his fucking mouth too soon, he and I would have a problem of considerable magnitude.

I spoke first. Our mandate, Mr. Mayor, is to assist our clients in pressing their needs to the responsible city agency. The housing proposal was in their best interests. My staff and I were doing our job under the Model Cities regulations.

That's not the issue, he told us. Your conduct is the issue. Our community here in the city and what we say is proper, that's the issue.

We're paid by Washington, I said, trying to avoid a campaign speech on local values. If the federal government wants the housing and will pay for it, why should we stand in the way?

But that's where Muckleroy wanted it to go. Vittorini was a respected local official, he explained, who stood between the "anarchy" advocated by local workers on the federal payroll and the community's values here, "where the rubber meets the road."

"Washington doesn't tell us how to live our lives, Miss Scott. I understand you're a very hardworking young lady, but that alone can't justify conduct by you and some of your staff that puts the work itself at risk."

How's that, your honor? Theo asked him.

"Complaints, Mr. Cox. Complaints from some of your very own district clients. They don't like what you're up to or the example you're setting. It's not responsible. Now think what you like of Vittorini. I'm not even saying he's the smartest guy in town, but he does have the pulse of the community, and he and others strongly believe that because of a pattern of misconduct with you all, the public trust has eroded to the point where you cannot effectively do your jobs."

That was really that. Muckleroy promised to get us other jobs, this time in job-skills training, which didn't pay as well but which we took under the circumstances.

SHE NEVER ADMITTED IT TO ME, BUT CHARLOTTE STILL CARRIED *around private concerns about me and her. The worst thing about getting fired for her was that it had the symbolic effect of her being exiled from the black community. It didn't matter that a white mayor acting on a tip from a white councilmember directed a black official to do it. That's just how it looked on paper. You could see if you looked close up in the corners of her eyes, Charlotte did the work for love of black people, her people.*

That was the connection that really mattered. It wasn't love of the Great Society or Model Cities or welfare rights. She's a defender of her community. Getting fired for loving me raised inescapable questions about her loyalty to them and her ability to do what she had to do to continue that work.

THERE WAS NO DENYING THAT THEO AND I WERE SEEN WHERE AND when we were seen, or that we were fornicating, as they say. I was in love. It probably showed (I hope it showed). I hear it showed. I never expected the world to agree with me. But I really had to do *that* work. There was no question about it. Once it had been taken away from me, I realized how sacred it was. That created a quandary for me, privately. Theo was precious. But without him I would probably suffer no loss of conviction. With him, I had lost the one job I really loved.

SHE WENT THROUGH A PHASE WHERE SHE WAS CALCULATING THE SUM of the benefits I brought to her life. She never admitted this either, but I know she was. No man had ever said this to her, she'd say. No lover had ever done that to her. After going through a number of things I did or didn't do, Charlotte would find some way to return to my outburst at the hearing, my white-man thing. We'd fight because by then I was tired of apologizing. Then, to gain the upper hand, she'd raise the "black community" thing again.

HE STILL USES IT. HE STILL TREATS IT AS A MONOLITH. YET I DARE HIM to refer to what the "white community" wants.

THE IDEA OF SUING THE GOVERNMENT MIGHT HAVE STARTED IN MY head, but by then I was too gun-shy to mention it to Charlotte. It became harder to express myself to her. She was in a chronic rage about losing the job. The fact that it was an injustice for which I instinctively demanded a remedy sounded in my head like a white response, like a privileged response, when she had already heard enough of that. The irony is that I probably developed my sense of what an injustice is by watching black people's struggles for civil rights. The whole thing took me right back three years to the summer of '68, right back. So I was in the middle of my own feelings, yet I was very, very hurt, especially for Charlotte, and we had to do something about it. We at least had to try.

THEO MADE A FAINT-HEARTED SUGGESTION THAT PEOPLE HAVE PROBably sued in situations like ours. I started to answer him like he'd just provoked another battle. I said something like, of course they would, they sue for being discriminated against because of their race, why not for discrimination based on the race of the people they hang out with? It's no different.

But then I realized he had offered this lawsuit idea so delicately because he was afraid of my sensitivity. He had already thought some about our lawsuit, but he was covering up. Theo was afraid of me. That was my doing. That couldn't be blamed on a bad situation. I had to stop to appreciate his tenderness again. This is how what separates us joins us too. I couldn't let the guy go small just to please me.

IT WAS ONLY A MATTER OF TIME BEFORE I HAD TO MAKE CLEAR TO Charlotte that I could not be the one to justify her love for me. But that I expected her to come around eventually. She should call first and bring good intentions and her own reefer for a change.

HE IS MY RIVER, CHANGING, CONSTANT, CHANGING UNDER THE throes of evening light. He licks at my lips, presses his fullness against my earth and washes me with time.

SHE BRINGS ME TO MY SENSES AND LETS ME GO WANDERING IN THE stuff of her resolve, her sweetness juicy brilliance, her roundness fruity energy, her hope-determined rock.

WE LOST THE FIRST LAWSUIT IN THE DISTRICT COURT, BECAUSE THE judge ruled that the decision to discharge us was based on an acceptable range of factors, not just one and not just race.

ABOUT A YEAR AFTER WE FILED THE APPEAL, THE HONKIES GOT IT right. The circuit judge called the first judge an oakie pig fucker who couldn't read the Constitution, and Charlotte got her job back.

AYESHA COX WAS BORN ON THE FOURTH OF JULY, 1973, TWO WEEKS before the appellate court ruled for us. She is the color of sunset and has a mane of flaxen curls like pubic hair.

V

NEAR MILLENIUM

The Monkey Suit

TOM BLAZIER SPECIFICALLY TOLD JORDAN IT WAS BULLSHIT FOR THE firm to waste his valuable time giving counsel to "thieves." Jordan worked with Tom. But the managing partner, Russell Wallace, had asked Jordan to volunteer time to the Lawyers to Rebuild Los Angeles, a group trying to redevelop the areas torn up by the 1992 riots, and it sounded like a personal request. Tom reluctantly agreed to let him do it for the time being and warned Jordan to just "be cool." But that Monday in South Central, a woman ended a meeting by calling him "white boy." It was hard to be cool then. All the drive home, Jordan, concentrating on the sixteenth-century Statute of Elizabeth, did his best to forget her.

Jordan had lately been working up a mastery of ancient fraudulent conveyance law. The Statute of Elizabeth had become a place to go. Its old perfect words. Deluxe meanings. Powerful enough to escape South Central's endless expanse of miles, bungalow homes, squat housing projects and billboards. In Jordan's spare time, he was somehow supposed to help bring the stores back, those that burned and those never built. Now he was supposed to endure being called a white boy by one of the community organizers. He didn't even say anything back, just got into his BMW and headed north again. He wasn't going to justify his blackness to her or them. He didn't feel guilty for not being from the ghetto himself.

Following the sun north took him back to streets narrower by design, avenues alive with the checkerboard facades of low-rise commercial buildings and neon merchant scrawl. First, he went through chaotic, mostly Mexican Pico-Union and the sunlit hordes of vendors. Then to the aspiring Koreatown, full of spanking new minimalls with souped-up facades. To the Santa Monica freeway at last, like sparkling water going down on raw thirst, where the possibility of width expanded again under the heavy rays, car curves beckoned like little wishes granted, and leased hopes turned strictly Anglo again behind blue mirror sunglasses. The place had name recognition in his thoughts, and he always felt a little excited there. Westward home at just five o'clock, Jordan was off early.

He lived month to month in a rented condo that belonged to someone else in a garden complex of upscale apartments. Someone was always moving in or out or being transferred or falling off but not far. Most apartments were spacious one bedrooms like his, with sunken living rooms and small balconies looking west toward the beach beyond the hill. There were some families in two and three bedrooms. He'd see them by the pool in the courtyard, shrill towheads nannied by Indian-looking women, or pass them in the garage that nestled half underground behind metal bars. The long slope of palm fronds, birds of paradise, cactus and ferns greeted Jordan's every entry with a casual neighborliness none of his neighbors could share. Except another black man, slightly older, who never talked long but might stop washing his '64 Jaguar long enough to offer a friendly wave or a word. Jordan didn't actually know his name, and he didn't know anyone else at all. No one spoke or even met his eyes, except women at night looking startled. He mailed his monthly rent to an address in Malibu, almost three years and counting.

Later, he tried explaining it over the telephone to his friend Rolando, who wouldn't get it. So Jordan repeated it, pacing barefoot across the living room carpet. "She heads one of the community groups down in South Central I'm supposed to be counseling on their nonprofit status. She called me white boy. Right to my face."

Silence. Maybe he hadn't quite heard it again. "Fuck the poverty ho bitch, J," Rolando said finally. "Anytime they see a six-figure nigga who isn't holding a microphone or an Uzi, they wanna call him a white boy. Instead of losing time behind that worthless shit you need to be working that deal for Blazier."

In another conversation, at another time, Jordan told Rolando how important the appearance of some community work will be when he is reviewed for partnership next year. Rolando was also a seventh year; he knew. "I am, Ro. I am. But how's she gonna say some shit like that to a black lawyer?" Jordan got a phone impression of Rolando reading or doing something else on the other end. "I was trying to tell them about not overcrowding the agenda. They'd get more done in those meetings if they'd settle on their deal points and commit. I wasn't, you know, trying to be critical. They talk a lot of shit in those meetings."

"Fuck it, man. They ain't about anything anyway. Looking for corporate handouts, government handouts . . . ."

Like Jordan Dudley, Rolando Wellman was a seventh-year associate at the L.A. office of an old New York law firm, Dixon, Barrett & Thatchman. Jordan practiced in the corporate finance department, which contained only nine lawyers and was headed by two rainmaker partners, Duane Waters and Tom Blazier. Rolando was in a different department, sports and entertainment, where he worked on the contracts of professional athletes and famous musicians. Jordan had graduated from Yale Law School and joined Dixon Barrett, as it was known. There he met Rolando, a UCLA grad.

When Jordan got off the phone he went straight for his cello, which he kept in a special corner of the living room, elevated by a platform, with a wooden stool. He'd been playing continuously since junior high school, usually without accompaniment. The same cello. Caramel hued and worn on the side where their torsos met, the instrument grew up with Jordan's body and spoke in his tone of voice. Most of all, it was a moment and a place to go where now, in classical bow strokes and earnest melodies, he could lose the white-boy comment and find the statute.

Jordan's image leaned in and out of a mirror across the large room, as he sat in his underwear playing the instrument. Under the crystal glow of hallogen light, his amber skin moistened. The little pectoral puff he got working out blinked and jerked each time his arm swung the bow around the strings. In the mirror, a sullen daze came over his rectangular face, thin mustache and sad cheekbones. He played, locked into serene low tones. After a while, sweat began to bead at the ends of his silken curls. Then, cutting through the calm, Jordan kept hearing Tom's admonition, words so unlike him and the world of billion-dollar bridge loans. "Be cool."

THE PLAZA IN FRONT OF DIXON BARRETT'S BUILDING WAS LINED WITH shallow stairs spread wide in a diagonal for hundreds of feet. He would climb them by the thousands, marching really, eyeing the plaza sculptures, shiny brass hulks threatening like angry amoeba, getting larger as he approached, until he reached the perfect fountain spitting dyed blue water into a triangular pool. He loved Century City. He loved that building, its tight skin of tinted glass and maroon stone, its muscle-bound girth tilted frontward against the sky. When Jordan first began working there, he found himself drawing its shape on restaurant napkins or dreaming it.

Every day, as he reached the building's bank of revolving doors, Jordan heard theme music in his head. It wasn't a song but an insistent rhythm, melodized into a simple, pounding crescendo, as if he were ramming a gigantic door in a mythic challenge to reach paradise on the other side. The ceilings in the lobby were cathedral high, arched in grey marble but illuminated by recessed flood lamps that threw light like spears against the slate interior. Behind the King Arthur-like guard's station hung a colossal canvas holding a vast mountain scene in dusk tones, only it was all set in space, like a desert portion of the earth carved out and set adrift in the galaxy. For all the ridicule it elicited, Jordan never tired of looking at it, the cosmic sight that daily prompted the end to the theme music playing in his head. Then he'd take the elevator up to the fifty-third floor.

Jordan told only his father that he heard theme music when he entered the building. Nobody else. His mother had only an abstract love for his work, but it was deep. It covered whatever he did, but not what he did. So, he had trouble discussing details with her over the phone, because she couldn't hear them through her pride nor see them through its blindness. Jordan's father would know it. Not personally. Both of Jordan's parents had worked in relatively senior administrative posts in San Francisco city government. His father knew through Jordan's quiet arrival the overwhelming sense of access he had once imagined vaguely for himself but only visited briefly. He wanted to go back. So, they went back together, through Jordan, who was still loving the look and the feel of it seven years after he got there. His father only wished there was a way Jordan could play the pounding music he described.

Jordan had many options when he decided to relocate to L.A., and he chose Dixon Barrett for its reputation as a traditional or white shoe leader of New York firms that had succeeded in aggressively building a global presence during the '80s. The L.A. office had over seventy lawyers on four floors. Three were black, Jordan, Rolando, and Jacqueline Spencer, a first year in the litigation department. Dixon Barrett was one of the last firms to hire black lawyers or to participate in any of the various *pro bono* efforts law firms in the city engaged in following the riots in South Central. That was partly why Jordan went to work there. You knew what you got. Dixon, Barrett & Thatchman didn't pretend to care about diversity or affirmative action. They simply made their clients money and safeguarded their enormous wealth. There was no question what they did, and there was no question why someone like Jordan was there. He could do the work. That's what you had to do. All the time.

Except moments like when Tracy Kim visited his office for little apparent reason. Tracy was still in the early part of her second year at the firm. She worked in corporate finance and had been in on just one deal with Jordan. She became the keeper of Jordan's fondest sexual fantasies at work, and she clearly knew it.

"You worked all weekend?" he asked her, as she slumped in the chair opposite his desk. She nodded without looking at him. He worked all weekend and hadn't seen her.

Jordan watched her from behind the mahogony depth of his immaculate desk. It was carefully decorated with brass paper weights and the start of a line of deal trophies, fist-sized monuments and orbs bearing a client's name and the transaction, which continued on a shelf that ran along the wall perpendicular to the desk. Tracy was sitting sideways in his chair, hanging her legs over the arm. He caught sight of the crease beneath her knees. The shape of her tight body's curl against the cushion barely suggested the lace border of her stocking beneath the line of her skirt, the muscle of her upper thigh, the smooth curve of calf. He faintly awakened. She seemed to notice and kept talking.

"I'm Coleman's slave," she said, a slight whine in her voice. Slavery was a favorite comparison among associates at the firm. "At least *he* fucking thinks so." Jordan nodded. Tracy smiled the coy grin of a very junior person taking advantage of a very senior person's time. "How do I get him off my ass?"

Anywhere, there, somewhere, when the time was right, maybe until forever, Jordan wanted to make love to Tracy's perfect body. Beyond the thrill of deal talk, due diligence and hard-boiled negotiations, Jordan treated himself to unrequited fantasies in which he tasted the full sweetness of her full lips, breathed heavy on her high Korean cheekbones and cradled the angel in her face. She enjoyed the consistency of his interest and, by whiling time with him, spelled herself from hours of the dry contract proofreading reserved for juniors. It was an understanding permanently on the brink. In her eyes, Jordan was present, but not physical.

Catherine Salzman came to his door, saw Tracy sitting across the chair, rolled her eyes and interrupted. "Hey, you're back. How was the LRLA meeting in South Central?"

Tracy was smart, unusually fashionable among associates and methodically sensuous. Catherine was probably brilliant but staunchly ordinary. Brilliant was a term tossed around the firm more casually than slavery, but Catherine was close to the real thing in an understated way. Only her large brown eyes revealed it; otherwise she was a medium-sized, medium-height, married Jewish woman on the level. Jordan was her only black friend, a fact that could bother her conscience without provocation. Of all his colleagues who might say they wanted to get together for more than drinks on, say, a weekend, perhaps only Catherine meant it.

"It was all right. Nothing is moving," he answered in a serious voice meant to exclude Tracy and her svelte thighs. "Did anyone at the department lunch yesterday mention where the deal is?"

"Tom did. Maybe Duane. No, Tom. He says it's tricky, that there may be some fraudulent conveyance concerns, but he sounded up. It's a lot of money."

"Seven hundred and fifty million. Did he happen to mention me?"

"No."

"Oh." Jordan was primarily responsible for the fraudulent conveyance research. As the senior associate on the deal, it had been his job to draft the memo advising the client about the risks of future litigation. Plus, he was reviewing all the contract drafts. Down the hall was a workroom stacked full of carefully indexed documents, every one of which was Jordan's task to read and understand.

"I'm not surprised the South Central work is stuck," Tracy said. She would have slipped out of the room if it weren't for the way Catherine controlled Jordan's doorway. Catherine was a fifth-year associate. "The area is too big for any one lawyer to do something for. South Central is sprawling. It's got to be like twenty square miles."

Tom Blazier suddenly appeared in the doorway beside Catherine and not much taller. "The problem is the people, not the place," he said from behind his dark, thick-framed glasses. Still wearing glasses meant he had interrupted himself from deep reading to come down the corridor of the fifty-third floor to Jordan's office. Tracy snatched her leg down and began a slow-motion move for the door. Jordan looked quizzically at Tom, and meeting his eyes offered a sympathetic smile. Catherine backed against the doorway and grasped the doorstop behind her, considered herself exposed and immediately crossed her arms over her chest. But Tom managed the silence with the awkwardness of someone hoping for a response; he wouldn't talk long, but he seemed to want to talk some. Tracy whispered excuse me and quickly squeezed out of the room. Tom's eyes just glanced the bottom of her skirt.

"How can you say that, Tom," Catherine said calmly, "given that you know neither the people nor the place?"

"Because we're entitled to be judged by our performance, which I do know about." He turned to Jordan. "Saw your memo yesterday morning. Why don't you come on down and we'll talk about it."

"Good. I'll be there shortly."

Tom nodded and pressed his lips, nodded again at Catherine as he turned, and walked back into the hallway. Catherine kept her arms crossed and studied Tom as he disappeared down the corridor. "Rolando was right," she said whether Jordan was interested or not. "He does walk on tiptoes." Jordan didn't say anything and began fishing in a drawer. "The South Central thing's really got you down, huh?"

"Maybe. I don't know. I don't know how it would look if it were working out, to be honest with you." He sighed, but kept fishing around the desk distracted. "I don't know anything about community development, you know, Catherine? I don't even know how to *know* how to come up with answers. This stuff is tough as cancer. You can't just sort of step out of your life for a few hours to cure poverty."

"Only because people can't stay committed to the poor without losing patience with them or blaming them for something."

"But it's still greater than my ability to make a difference right now. I don't mean to sound callous."

"No, you have work to do. I understand. This deal is a monster."

"And the guy doesn't even mention my work, huh?" he asked. She shook her head. "Then it's probably the memo," he decided. "All right. Thanks, Catherine. Go 'way. I gotta get ready."

"Don't rule out the persistence of evil, Jordan. South Central was no accident."

He wasn't listening. Seven years working with Tom and Duane, every time he was asked to go to one of their offices, he had to fight a little nausea, clear his head privately at his desk and pray. Jordan wasn't particularly religious, never went to church, dabbled in spirituality as it made itself more available. Catherine left, Jordan waited briefly, closed the door, sat back down and spun his chair toward the wall.

"I surrender to you, Lord. Hold my hand and walk with me."

Of all the partners, Tom was a teacher. Partners like him could make associates into lawyers. With Tom, it was intimate, variable, sometimes taking the form of pop quizzes, the sink or swim or some other approach. Although he found fault with everything and was never satisfied, you had to see his criticisms in degrees. He defied prediction, but if you survived you learned. Jordan's memo was supposed to put the phases of the deal through the statute, a test at each turn. Any single failure could mean a problem down the line or a lawsuit, which could blow the deal. Just the forty-page draft of the memo had cost the client $50,000 in Jordan's billable hours.

As soon as Jordan sat down in one of two hard leather chairs opposite Tom's desk, Tom reached across and dropped the memo in front of him. "I made some suggestions. Why don'tcha take a look."

From a distance, the page looked bloodied. Tom had written with a red pen in the margins, between the lines, over the black printed letters. His marks were everywhere. Jordan pretended to read, but there was too much to make sense of in a moment, with Tom sitting back in his chair, hand on his chin, swiveling slightly, and occasionally pressing his lips tight. The next page was red. So was the following. Every page, a meticulous pattern of lacerations, as if every line screamed first with fault, then with criticism. Jordan read snippets. The tone turned nasty quick. He had done nothing right. This hadn't happened to him since he was a first-year associate, if then. Jordan couldn't help relying on the memory of his last evaluation two months before. It was glowing. Even Tom's comments, which was unusual. The only real knock was that he did almost no *pro bono* and should consider picking it up as he approached consideration for partnership. He did everything he could to keep his face tight and sure, but it seemed an inadequate barrier between them.

"What the hell happened to you on this thing, Jordan? This had to go out. You knew that."

"I'm surprised to see this kind of reaction, Tom. I thought it was there."

"You've got to be kidding. You could sail a ship through the holes in your analysis, Jordan. You misstated the terms of the bridge loan—that much is sitting in documents in the workroom. It's not well organized. It reads poorly. It's substandard, and it's just not acceptable, Jordan."

"I'll study your comments, Tom," he said, visibly sucking it up. "I'll fill the holes. I'll do what it takes. And I'll call the client and tell him we'll have it turned around by tomorrow noon, Hong Kong time."

Tom's expression did not change. "It's gone already. I gave it to Steve yesterday while you were visiting the ghetto."

Jordan was shocked. "Tom, why didn't you just page me or leave a message on my voice mail? I would have left in a second. I wouldn't have gone at all." The rub at first stung more than it bruised. Jordan was not fond of Steve Cougat, who was a sixth year, well into the partnership track and more likely to make it if Jordan didn't. Steve was popular, especially with Tom, and white. "*I* would have liked to have seen your comments to my draft before they're shown around."

"What are you talking about, Jordan? This is *our* work. *We* review our drafts all the time. We better. The work had to get done. He was here. You were not. It's over." Jordan started to say something else. Tom waved him off with his hand. "It's over." He turned around to a separate desk where his phone sat. "Read my comments. Figure it out. Talk to Steve about what's next." Jordan started toward the door. Tom was punching in a number, but Jordan could faintly hear him muttering. "Stay out of South Central for Christsakes."

ONLY O.J. COULD HAVE DONE IT. OCCASIONALLY FLASHING A PENSIVE grin but mostly seated stoically, O.J. Simpson's image at the defendant's table occupied the middle of Jordan's living room late in the evenings of the new year and resurrected the possibility of the defensible accused. Murder and incompetence weren't equivalent accusations, but each seemed as impossible to Jordan. Sometimes it was just O.J.'s jawbone that saved Jordan, its solid strength and flawlessness, or the angularity of his profile, or the similarity of the waves they both wore in their hair. In the weeks following Tom's comments on the memo draft, O.J. surrounded by the men of his defense team, the seriousness that was obvious by their suits alone, the preparedness that masqueraded as control, reassured Jordan in a way nothing else could.

For others, protection was Johnnie Cochran, O.J.'s lead counsel. "Johnnie is most definately a bad motherfucker," Rolando declared one night to Jordan and Jacqueline. The three had left work together late and went to a bar to watch tape-delayed excerpts of the trial. Even the friendly white bartender nodded with approval. Hunching his athletic build over the bar, Rolando stared at the screen and said, "He has the brother's back. That's just all there is to it."

A smallish, twenty-something white guy in a blue suit, eavesdropping for some time, finally asked Rolando through a smile, "C'mon, man, don't you think Cochran's just a little melodramatic?"

Rolando turned his big eyes slowly toward the new voice. "I don't remember speaking to you. Man." The guy shrank a little on his stool. "You a lawyer?" The stranger, smile gone, shook his head emphatically. Rolando waved him off with his hand. "Then you just another white boy with a wish."

The stranger swallowed the slight, raised his eyebrows a little and looked into his long glass. Then he caught Jordan and Jacqueline staring at him. "Darden's opening argument was more convincing," he offered, referring to the black lawyer on the prosecution team.

Though just out of law school, Jacqueline was nominally a trial lawyer so she spoke up. "Darden was pathetic." The guy looked surprised. "He was unprepared, clearly outclassed, barely coherent. You just like him 'cause he's bald," she said.

Jacqueline was still an experiment for Jordan and Rolando, bringing a woman into their fold of confidentiality at the firm, making that fold a deliberate-looking threesome, making that fold a fold at all. In that she had instant equality, but in everything else she was a mentee. Most lawyers stayed at such firms about two or three years, a little less for black lawyers. By that measure they were two or three careers ahead of her. That evening it was even more evident. Jacqueline was worried about an incident with a partner, who was upset about mistakes she'd made in a memo. She'd forgotten to check on whether the cases had been overruled by higher courts, and two of them had.

"The fact is I knew better. I'd made a list of things to check, and I forgot that I still had that left to do. It was just a dumb mistake," she told them.

"Sure was," Rolando said. "Who was it for?"

"Peter Wisebroad."

"Oh, that's too bad," he said. "He's a rainmaker in your department. You better work on your resume."

Jacqueline's clear, brown face was youthful and round. She was twenty-five, in her first real job, wearing one of her first four suits, the proud peach Anne Taylor that stretched a little more under her large-boned frame as the stress of practice began to grow on her. Jordan didn't know litigation, but he saw his early going in her face.

"Don't listen to Rolando," Jordan said. "It's not about all that. Everybody makes dumb-ass mistakes in the beginning. *Everybody.*" Jacqueline's eyes brightened a little. "You know that. Did you make any excuses when he caught it?"

"No, actually. There was nothing to say."

"Good. Then it'll be all right. They hate the resistance. Let them say it and clear it from their minds. After a while, you realize you have to manage them a little. Just do better the next time."

"Then there's the little matter of your skin color," Rolando added. "Jacqueline, this is my third law firm and let me tell you something straight up, the same mistakes don't stick to white associates the way they do us. Partners *expect* us to miss details—"

"C'mon, Rolando," Jordan interrupted. "Maybe some, very few. Seriously. And I know Wisebroad. He's not that way."

"J, how the fuck do you know Wisebroad?"

"I've had dinner with him." That wasn't entirely true. Jordan had attended a function and shared a firm table with Wisebroad and eight other Dixon Barrett partners. "Jacqueline, the job is hard enough without putting everything through a race test. Don't waste your energy. They hired you because you can do the work. Just settle in and do the work." He was emphatic and Rolando's eyes drifted back up to the trial on TV. Jacqueline's smile was heartfelt. Rolando played too rough, Jordan thought, as he continued to hold her gaze. "Besides, what Ro's saying cuts the other way too. Since the riot, the state bar association put pressure on L.A. firms to hire more African-American attorneys," he added, though he didn't really believe it mattered. "So, the firm not only wants you, but it needs you."

Jacqueline looked relieved and confidence returned to her eyes. "Thanks, fellas. I gotta get home. It's late. How much of this is mine?" she asked, looking at the check.

"I got it," Jordan said.

REMOVING HIMSELF FROM THE TIME-CONSUMING FRUSTRATIONS OF the LRLA work, Jordan rarely left the firm anymore. He blamed his South Central visits for his apparent distraction with the Statute of Elizabeth memo. As the weeks passed, all he could remember of those meetings was the community chairperson, Halifu Andami, calling him a white boy. The moment might return to him as he stood in the stacks of the firm's library, or waited for his cup to fill over by the coffee machine. That was the last of that for him. The firm's commitment to the rebuilding cause had passed from Jordan to Jacqueline now.

As the weather cooled and rains occasionally fell, lawyers across the city found it hard to resist O.J. trial commentary, and their impressions with each other became boilerplate professional comradery. Russell Wallace and his never-the-same-ones-twice suspenders were rarely seen for long at the coffee machine, but one day the firm's managing partner was there with his own observations. "Darden reminds me of you a little, Jordan," he said, heaping sweetener into a mug with his back to him. "I mean that as a compliment."

"I hope it's not our hairlines," Jordan joked, catching Wallace full in the eye as he turned around.

Wallace, leather-tanned, fiftyish, bespeckled in Armani tortoise shells across his thick, strong face, met Jordan's eyes and then looked away as if to find his thought. "No, no," he laughed, "not the hair, but his command. I'm impressed by his dignity." Jordan meanwhile nodded in a humble thanks for the unsolicited praise. "Unlike Cochran who seems to me—I mean I don't know him well, I've met the guy, and you have to respect what he's done, but the histrionics, the appeals to the heart rather than the head." He paused, then aborted the thought left dangling. "Well, thank God that's not your style is all. This is a law firm, not a Baptist church. You're that other guy."

Off he went, back down the corridor, and in his wake left Jordan with a new feeling about O.J. The immediate effect was to suspend his identification with the defendant's quiet strength and perfect profile. Jordan hadn't thought much about the lawyers in the case. But Wallace had given him Darden, a man about his age, to think about. He found himself sitting at his desk, now working on other aspects of the deal that seemed to go on forever, occasionally wondering about Darden. Because it was all going on, all day and probably all night, the O.J. trial, a little ways across town, not for a billion dollars, but for a man's freedom, the families of the victims, the world constantly watching the lawyers at work.

"Well, whadyou think about the state's case?" Jordan once put to Rolando.

"For starters, Darden's a pussy and a lightweight. He couldn't put a po' Mexican in jail, forget about a rich nigga."

Nevertheless, what Wallace started with Jordan, others continued. People he didn't particularly like, as well as others he respected, made passing mention of some intangible similarity between him and the prosecutor. For a while during the prosecution's case in February,

Jordan would sit up alone in his bed watching the tape-delayed proceedings, vaguely rooting for himself.

He began to think he had to. The music in his head started playing differently in the morning climb up the stairs. The droning rhythm lifted dirgelike into his ears, not the usual triumphant march. He used to anticipate the uncertainty of a day's work. Suddenly, it could be wrong. The day could do more than challenge him. It could stump him. Like the fact that, since the exchange with Tom, he'd only spoken with him about the deal twice. The second time, Tom told Jordan to ask Steve, the sixth year, about what was happening next. Steve had accompanied Tom on a meeting with the client that Jordan neither knew about nor was asked to attend. But that happened sometimes.

"What's up?" Jordan asked Steve, standing in his office doorway. Steve was busy reading some document. His computer screen shimmered with the text of something. He was occupied, but Jordan couldn't wait to talk to him.

"Hey, Jordy," Steve said. Usually he would look up, but this time he didn't. Usually, Steve would be standing in Jordan's door.

"Tom suggested you could put me back in the loop on the raw materials projections, since you were at the meeting with Adnanian."

Steve's heavy eyebrows squinted under delicate gold frames. "Yeah," he said, still fixated on the page. He ran his hand through his short-cropped dirty blond hair. "Yeah, I'm handling that." Before Jordan could react, Steve finally looked up. The charm of his slender face returned, revealing the warmth of his light blue eyes. "I'm sorry, man. I'm just trying to finish this by two o'clock in the afternoon Hong Kong time. Can you give me half an hour?"

They met thirty-five minutes later. Jordan was back in Steve's office, sitting opposite Steve's desk, being told where Steve was on an aspect of the deal probably not large enough for two. So it happened. Once. The feeling of Steve coming around the side of the desk to point something out from above, Steve imparting, Steve's breath from slightly above taking liberties with Jordan's ear slightly below. It happens on big deals with many parts that unfold over months. But then it happened twice, and a third time, until he was taking directions regularly from Steve, who had spoken with Tom or, worse, met with the client Adnanian.

So the music could hold the tenor of uncertainty, and the uncertainty worked a mild terror on years of growing expectations. The downtime he spent waiting for clear signals atrophied his initiative. Jordan had worked on hundreds of deals but few as big as this one, which was why his performance would be so closely scrutinized when they considered him for partnership in the upcoming months. But worst of all for the time being, his billable hours dropped. Ordinarily, he billed about two hundred forty per month. But in the first few months of the year, he was down to about one hundred twenty-five. He'd stay in the office even when there was no work to bill, putting in face time, reading, playing solitaire on his computer, or talking on the phone.

Jordan's friends at other firms told him not to worry and figured his department must have reached a slow part in the cycle. Nobody keeps their black associates around that long only to hang them out to dry, they'd say. Nobody really had seventh-year black associates. Jordan's father thought differently. He heard in Jordan's description of affairs no reason to assume Jordan was being mistreated because he was black. But he did suspect something was not quite right.

"Who can you talk straight with?" he asked into the phone.

Jordan had to think. "Waters. Duane Waters, the partner. He's definitely got my back. He'd be straight with me."

"Who is he in the process?"

"He's chairman of our department. Ultimately, he has to know everything. He probably has more influence over my making partner than anyone. But, you know, we've worked together quite a bit, so he's real familiar with the quality of my work. He and Tom are close friends, too."

Mr. Dudley thought long and sighed. "I think I'd try to talk with him, at least to feel him out. I'm not sure what I'd say, Jor, but I'd make my commitment plain."

That seemed like a lead to follow. It was rare to demonstrate loyalty in the law firm world, and Jordan could remind him of his. He had checked in with Duane at other times in the past, and it always went well. Duane was more approachable than Tom, reflective and friendly, with well-rounded interests in the arts, snow hiking and philanthropy that he'd insert into conversations. But Duane had been away most of the time during the past few months, visiting Adnanian in Hong Kong and drumming up business across the Pacific Rim, which may have been an overlooked part of Jordan's problem.

"I surrender to you, Lord. Hold my hand and walk with me."

"Sure, talk to me," Duane offered, gesturing toward the soft, modern chair in front of his enormous but spartan desk. Duane's long body was atypical among partners there. Most were fairly short. Duane was angular, with a scholarly quality and inviting features that suggested a more grown-up version of Steve. Jordan moved awkwardly into the large room, glancing back at the door. "And please, close the door," Duane added. They both settled into their chairs, and Duane's look grew serious as he prepared to listen.

"With history as a guide, Duane, I typically demonstrate my commitment to the firm by my hours and the number of matters I'm carrying." That sounded convoluted coming out of his mouth, but it was gone and he'd have to build on it. "It's possible that my *pro bono* work had distracted me from the fraudulent conveyance analysis. I accept that." Duane looked down, then offered a little wave of his hand as if it weren't a big deal. "I respect Tom's critique of the memo. It's just that my role in the deal has seemed to fall off precipitously. A lot of it's gone to Steve. New matters have been slow to come to me. So, I just wanted to come to you to see if you could help me understand the situation and, you know, so that I can head off any problems in the offing."

All Duane had to say was that he didn't think there was "a problem in the offing" and asked Jordan to explain the facts of the situation in more detail. That set Jordan moving, telling about the inconsistency of using Steve in the role in which he was being used, the inefficiency caused by Tom not talking to Jordan directly, and his not getting any of the new work that was coming in. Duane seemed to listen with care and relish, never making excuses but sometimes seeking examples for clarification. Jordan was relieved to be getting somewhere. Duane often nodded his head or smiled, or both. This further energized Jordan, who had not in so many weeks had a chance to be himself, let alone restore his name to a partner. Duane even took notes.

Jordan had returned. Just the meeting alone made him feel a part of the place again, rejuvenating him, giving rise to small ideas he brought to minor tasks and new gusto to old business. He had to be patient before he actually saw a change, but the meeting gave him patience.

"You look great," Jacqueline said to him one day near the elevators. "I haven't talked to you in weeks, but from a distance you were looking sort of preoccupied."

"I was fighting one of those bugs that just won't leave your system. But I'm better, thanks. Nice of you to notice. How's South Central?"

"I love it, Jordan," Jacqueline gushed. "I really feel like I'm contributing something, you know, like I'm learning."

"That's good. I was a little worried for you because they seem to need transactional lawyers, not litigators as much."

"But that's OK. That's OK. Because whatever is needed I feel more comfortable trying to do. You know? It's not one or the other, it's just lawyering, you know, helping, being creative, advocating." Her face was painfully sincere, and her eyes seemed to glisten. "Halifu Andami, I'm sure you remember her, the chairperson. She's great. We had lunch together at Roscoe's Chicken and Waffles the other day. She's like a mentor to me."

Jordan experienced what he figured Tom might have been feeling about his involvement in the LRLA work: enough already. Jacqueline just went on and on, oblivious to the fact that she could overcook her commitment to *pro bono* and lag on the billable work for which she was hired. Still he was glad she was excited about something.

THE CHANGE JORDAN WAITED FOR CAME A WEEK LATER. HE WAS walking by Tom's office. The door was open. As he passed, he noticed Duane inside with Tom and Steve.

"Jordy!" Steve called to him, sticking his head out of Tom's doorway as Jordan walked down the corridor. "Tom wants to you to stop in."

They had been laughing recently, but there was work out, papers familiar to Jordan as part of the deal documents. Jordan took his cue from Duane, who looked relaxed sitting on the wide windowsill. He nodded and smiled casually. Steve was friendly and sat down in one of the modern chairs in front of Tom's desk. Tom was in a good mood.

"Just wanted to get your thoughts on an idea, Jordan," said Tom. Jordan stepped in a few more feet and put his hands in the pockets of his slacks. Tom had a small conference table made of glass that occupied a corner of the office. A large ficus tree enshrouded it in leaves. Jordan considered sitting in one of the two chairs beneath it, but decided instead to stand. "You know we're near to closing this deal in Hong Kong. Adnanian's coming to town next week, and Duane and I are scheduled to take him to dinner. Well, he's got another matter pending, but he hasn't made a final decision about his counsel. He may go with another firm they use sometimes. So, the idea would be to use this opportunity to court him with the talent we bring."

Duane started in. "Whaddya say we open the dinner up to a few more members of the department, people who have worked on the deal? The idea is to inform and impress."

Jordan was immediately comfortable with the idea and sat down in one of the metal chairs under the ficus tree. The combination of quick agreement and four male bodies spread out and occupying their own spaces in the room made for satisfied demeanors all around. "Who should be there?" Jordan asked.

"Do you want to script things?" Steve asked over Jordan's question.

"No. Not a script per se," said Tom. "There are things I want understood, but most of that, Duane and I will do."

"Right," Duane agreed, "But Steve's got a point inasmuch as specific associates played certain roles that they should carefully make known to Ariel." They went back and forth on the question to script or not. Finally, Tom agreed that there should be some type of script, and Duane agreed not to be too specific. "Back to Jordan's question," Duane said. "Beats me. Catherine?"

"I think so," Jordan said. "She's actually worked quite a bit on the deal." There was no disagreement. "How about giving Tracy a chance to meet a client?"

The momentary silence suggested the partners didn't know who Tracy was, at least not Duane. "Tracy?" he asked.

"Yeah, Tracy Kim. She's a first year."

Tom frowned and leaned his chin on his hand. His words came from the bottom of his throat and the end of his breath. "She's our O-ho, Duane, or at least she comes off that way. That's not how we're gonna impress Ariel, though he's not above a crude mood at times."

Jordan withdrew Tracy's name, and she was never invited. But Jordan took time out of the afternoon to find out what Tom meant. Catherine knew. It's short for Oriental whore, she explained over the phone once she'd closed the door to her office.

"Oh my God," Jordan said. A fleeting taste of something bitter rose up and out of his throat. Catherine was uncharacteristically quiet. "That's pretty fucked up. I'm surprised Tom would say something like that."

"You're surprised, Jordan? You've gotta be kidding. Haven't you ever noticed the way Tom looks at Tracy in departmental meetings?"

"She's very attractive."

Catherine sighed. "That's really not the point, Jordan." She took another long pause. "Let me put it this way. If there's one thing I've realized about anti-Semitism, it's that it's not complicated. If you hate, you hate. You debase, you debase. Tracy's gonna have a hard time being taken seriously."

That's when it made sense to him. "She's fucked."

"Pretty much."

"THEY'RE FUCKED NOW," ROLANDO DECLARED OVER A PLATE OF nachos in Jordan's living room as the two watched tape-delayed testimony of a white police officer deny to one of O.J.'s lawyers that he had ever used the word *nigger*.

"What the fuck is the 'n-word'?" Jordan laughed, a mug of stout beer in his hand.

"They gotta say that," Rolando said, his dark skin reflecting the light over his shoulder. "See, they play like their doing that for black folks, so we won't think they say that shit all the time. But, homes, they know if they don't give it that kind of word, they could start slippin' up, and niggas will see how natural the word rolls off their lips."

Jordan giggled and slapped Rolando's hand as he held it out for him. But he wasn't convinced. The showdown between the lawyer and the witness trailed on across Jordan's giant TV screen, the characters' faces larger than life but pinkened and elongated by the curviture of the screen. "I still don't think they need this." Jordan said to the screen. "I still can't tell you how O.J. did it. It just doesn't make sense." Rolando looked over at him, eyebrows squished, lips lopsided, as if he thought Jordan crazy. "They don't need the racist cop angle. It's gravy."

"Bullshit. They need it to make it real, J. They need to get a word into the heads of everybody lookin' at this thing and thinking about nothing but race. Rich nigga, white bimbo, heavy fuckin', co-caine, high rollin', prince white boy surfer savior rolling up, anotha brotha with a white bitch. *All* that shit. Everybody's thinking it one way or another. All that shit spells get him. *This* is the answer to that. It's like planting a voice in your head."

These discussions either devoured an evening, Jordan found, or the subject was effectively changed. But Jordan wanted it both ways. So, they watched for a while, listened to the chatter of expert commentary that followed, and then he struck.

"Has it ever occurred to you that the closer you get to partnership, the less you really want it? I'm not talking about the better pay, the leverage, or, you know, prestige. I'm really just talking about being partners for life with these guys, having your whole professional stake tied up with theirs."

Rolando smiled. The grin grew fatter and stayed there overlong. "I never thought you'd be the one to ask me that, J, sounding as if you have doubts."

"I'm asking you, though. Rolando, you don't like them."

"That's true. And you like them more than anybody gave you reason to, so we both have some basis for doubt."

Jordan walked to the bar, reached for two large brandy glasses and poured cognac into them. Then he pulled two cigars out of a drawer and dropped them into a large, diamond-shaped ashtray. "You down?" he asked Rolando, who nodded hard. "I've been with them longer than you have, Ro. I basically started with them, so there might just be more to my relationships than there is for you."

They sipped, stretched their legs across the plush white carpet and lit up. "That would scare me," Rolando said. "Not liking them is as it should be, because I'm not in it for friends or to be liked and I'm not. They like the idea of me—sometimes. They like the fact that I already bring in more clients than some of the mo'fuckin partners in my group do. They can't touch that shit. They can't even talk to the kind of acts and players I can get with. I bring a new market to their old game, homes. Not every nigga wit a contract is looking for a Jewish lawyer anymore, see what I'm sayin'?"

"You're bringing in that much work, dude?" Jordan asked, obviously surprised. Jordan had clients that preferred him, but only one, a very small one, that he was responsible for bringing to the firm.

"Damn skippy," he said, puffing through a cloud. "It's not about being indispensable. They don't make me a partner, hey, I'm a nigga with legs." They sipped some more and made loud ahhh sounds when the cognac covered the backs of their throats. As the drink began to warm them over, Rolando's talk of partnership grew vivid, describing new offices, new and higher grades of pussy, new and better-made cars and lots of ownership. "It's time my ass bought everything I keep telling all my dumb-ass clients to do. No more leasing, J. No more renting."

"I'll tell you something about that promised land, home dude. I been to the mountain top, see? Saw what was going on below. But I may not make it there with you, and I just—"

"Aw, get the fuck outta here," Rolando laughed. "What're you sayin', Jordan? You think there is some conceivable way they could deny *you*, JD the JD, home-grown high yella golden boy like yourself?"

Smooth cognac settled Rolando's comment in his gut, and Jordan nearly backed off his confession. "I'm just saying I don't know. Strange shit happens. The work's been slow. I could be wrong. I hope so. But something might be up."

Rolando stopped to check Jordan's eyes, both of them, which meant turning face front beside him on the sofa. "If you're for real, brother, then you need to get your shit tight in hurry and we'll take your show on the road. If you're serious, I'm quite serious. I can hook you up with some people who can get you into see folks who need what only you can offer." Rolando wouldn't let go of Jordan's eyes. He put out his hand and Jordan slowly reached to shake it. Too fast and he would have disturbed everything he held in check inside, like water behind his eyes and a tiny creeping foreign rage. "Watch it close, man. But if you think they're getting ready to fuck you, get the fuck out. Fuck 'em first."

IN A SUMPTUOUS CAVERN OF MAROON VELVET WALLS, INDIGO PILLARS dividing Irish linen-wrapped tables fifteen deep and three levels down, Ariel Adnanian drank thirty-seven-year-old scotch and listened to law talk from Tom Blazier, Duane Waters and five associates, including Jordan. Jordan wore a scarlet bow tie against a black suit. He sat across from the client, who was flanked by Tom and Duane, but next to Catherine where he was more comfortable. Adnanian also wore black and a gold silk bow tie. It was he who pointed out the similarity to Jordan's clothes, while mockingly contrasting the dress of the other men present, all of whom wore shades of business blue over unremarkable ties. At his insistence, they bonded over that coincidence, and through a British accent, Adnanian teased Jordan about his tailor with bright smiles that made his chiseled face crack gently. At fifty, most of his thick tussle of hair had greyed, and he stroked it regularly over the top of his large head with fatty hands that otherwise folded in and out of almost perpetual gestures. When Steve tried to steal from Jordan the explanation of just what a fraudulent conveyance was, Adnanian grew bored quickly and, focusing on Jordan as if they had been alone for hours, asked: "So much for the Harvard version. Might we hear from the Yale man. Just what is it, Mr. Dudley?"

"It's confessing nakedness when you're fully clothed, actually," Jordan said, intriguing him. "You pretend and pretend that you've lost all you've got to wear, but the unmistakable fact is, if you just look behind the ruse, you're fully clothed."

"Splendidly clothed."

"To the nines and to die for." They laughed. "But really, in the seeing-red eyes of your creditor, you've accomplished by sleight of hand the appearance of having nothing left to take, so he walks away. And by some arrangement, you manage to keep the benefits of whatever it is you pretended to part with."

The partners adjusted the script accordingly. Duane, more socially at ease than Tom and more familiar with Adnanian, made sure during dinner that associate testimonials about what they did, or special training they had, made a stop through Jordan, who became a punctuation mark separating accounts. Long after mahi mahi and deep into tiramisu, Catherine eased into conversation beside Jordan. She was tense at first, showing a suspicion for the whole evening's strategy. Her talk sounded deliberately staged, lifted straight out of the firm brochure. But she broke her rule about drinking with members of the firm, and the scotch made everybody friends.

Then, across the room, a black man walked in wearing a burgundy, double-breasted suit and joined by an attractive black woman in a long velvet evening gown and two white men with balding heads and dark suits. The maître d' fawned and smiled for the black man, and they displayed a late-night familiarity as the one discreetly passed the other a bill.

"That's Johnnie Cochran, isn't it?" an excited third-year associate named Paul exclaimed.

"It sure is. That's O.J. Simpson's lead defense lawyer," Duane explained to Adnanian, as the entire table turned eyes across the room to see.

"I don't think that's him," Jordan said, squinting but feeling more certain than he sounded. The guy had a crown of gray hair unlike Cochran, he was considerably heavier and, most apparent to Jordan from a distance, lighter skinned.

But the consensus quickly followed that the famed defense attorney was there at the same fashionable night spot with the firm's corporate finance department and their colorful client. "That's him, Jordan," Tom said. "He's still wearing that ridiculous suit. What is it they call those, sharkskin?"

Associates eagerly took Tom's cue to "go O.J." as such freestyle conversations were called around the firm. And they started in on the defense attorney's wardrobe. "Peacock," was one, "bizarre" another, followed by giggles and a general test of wit that in rapid succession resulted in "Superfly," "Mac Daddy," "Shaft," and Tom's own, "pimp-like." Amid laughter that could almost reach the party's table across the room, Duane shared a polite moment with Jordan's eyes, until the client spoke. "The chap is known as a bit of a dandy, isn't he?"

With Adnanian participating and Cochran in the house, the table entered a start to finish review of the Simpson facts. Faint embarassment no more evident than a low-grade fever nestled behind Jordan's face for a reason he could not go into at the moment. But the group was mainly amused by the latest antics in the trial, and his anxiety gave way to legal entertainment in which even he eventually participated.

"But, Jordan," Adnanian began with furroughed brow and gestures like a director drawing a scene for the cast, "I'm rather puzzled by Cochran's use of the race card."

The question was meant for Jordan, and he felt fortunate to get it. It was his own. "I'm curious to know what that is myself," he smiled.

"Well, really it's become a national pastime of ours, Ariel," Tom explained. "In the absence of meritorious arguments, you cry racism. It doesn't matter how thin the theory, what counts is the confusion you cause. It's the guilt you provoke. The ironic thing here is it's being used by the guilty to inspire guilt."

Catherine turned red, but her voice didn't change at all. "What difference would that make to a predominantly black jury, Tom? Why should they feel guilt if, let's say for example, a racist police detective planted evidence against a black murder suspect?"

Adnanian raised his hand to halt the exchange. "No, I'm afraid I know what the race card is. My question is why would Cochran deal it? I'm trying to understand how it's at all relevant."

Again the question was meant for Jordan. Others who wanted to answer had to turn gaze at him, but Jordan sat thoroughly phased. In the dawn of that moment, a million things rushed his mind. His conversation with Rolando two nights before. The image of himself as Chris Darden. Perceptions of his profile. Sounding smart, not being interrupted, having something forceful, yet careful to say. Tom's quips. Changing the subject. And his own question: How did Adnanian, a ruddy-complexioned Armenian whose family he said had escaped genocide to the safety of British citizenship eventually to make many millions in several Hong Kong ventures, know what the so-called race card was anyway?

"Well, I'm not a litigator, Mr. Adnanian, and I'm not on firm ground talking about evidence and trial tactics. But Johnnie Cochran and the team representing O.J. are pretty experienced trial lawyers, and I'd imagine they're just following the chain of evidence, you know, and trying to show the jury any gaps."

"Gaps lead to doubts," Catherine shot in. "Reasonable doubts lead to acquittals. They're just doing their ethical duty to their client."

"They may be doing their jobs," Adnanian answered, charm and curiosity all but gone from his wide face. "But it's hardly ethical."

The thick scotch wore thin inside Jordan. The subject finally changed, and laughter, both nervous and real, returned. Adnanian proved to be quite a partygoer, demanding that he be taken to a nightclub to dance. Although they did, Jordan gradually withdrew into silent smiles and apparent listening. Duane kept nudging him to step back up, but Jordan felt drained, too drained even to dance each time Catherine asked him. Instead, she danced with Adnanian, who had dropped both his millionaire scowl and his O.J. indignance and began flirting with her. The office seemed dangerously distant from this rare mood. Jordan watched the tangled swell of white colleagues dancing, watched them jerk and trip onto and off of the beat, their awkward bodies happy but tricked. He wondered what, if anything, Rolando would have done in that situation. He wondered if he himself had safely exited the moment. He wondered if anybody but him stopped to notice as they left the restaurant that at close range the man in the burgundy suit looked nothing like Johnnie Cochran.

THEIR AWKWARD BODIES PROVED A BALM IN DISTRACTED MEMORY. Driving to work, leaving it for home, Jordan started making a lot of the differences between his colleagues' bodies and his own since the Adnanian dinner. He loved his body, not because it was particularly impressive or cut like a running back's, but mostly because his father's comments affirmed it growing up, lovers smiled at it, and it could do most things he wanted of it. It looked good in casual wear. It was comfortable at the beach. It got bigger in his late twenties, remained under control in his early thirties. Ready at any time to play basketball.

The sight of his colleagues' bodies standing in doorways, bent over desks, or stepping out of rest rooms became a private source of joy. Compared to them, his difference was unmistakable and beautiful and unchangeable. It was never something he thought about before, but he began to need it. And more often he took it to the basketball courts at his gym, ignoring evenings with his cello. Jordan admired the curviture of his own thighs in shorts, pitied the thickness of white opponents' quadriceps and calves that seemed to slow them as he elevated past. He strayed from the whiter teams in pick-up games, wanting to join whatever number of black men assembled in the nearly all-white gym. Winning grew more satisfying and necessary, louder and much more physical than it used to be, and he got better at it.

Still he couldn't dismiss some worry about his clothes. The night he matched the client was just luck. Jordan figured he was a good, not great, dresser, but he was no Rolando, who seemed to master corporate chic. His ties became suspect, all the bright colors he loved looked flamboyant hanging beside his suits. Too many double-breasted suits for a corporate lawyer, even for L.A., he decided. So, Jordan went shopping. He reaffirmed a vow to conservative dress he first made in his last year of law school. There had been no reason but fabric to leave Brooks Brothers in the first place, except perhaps the slow service and occasional questions about his use of a credit card. He couldn't let that stand in the way of partnership. He bought in blues mainly. He went back until the salesmen had to recognize him and treat him promptly. He'd stay for hours, watching his African biceps and quads and buttocks protrude, relent, then disappear beneath a fit increasingly right the harder he tried. And he bought more bow ties.

When his work began to slow again around mid-April, Jordan decided to use his spare time trying to find clients of his own, preferably black ones.

"I'm not hip hop," he told Rolando, "so I'll go to this affair, but I've got to be for real. I won't front."

Rolando looked funny at him, and they drove on to an underground club in a large Japantown loft. It was mostly fabulous when they got there, camera-ready black women in black velvet dresses with long extensions in their hair. Bald black men with goatees, some wearing baseball caps, in fat-footed shoes and oversized pants with big shirts hanging out. The whites and Asians there were similarly prepared, usually smoking, and, while clearly belonging, not quite hip hop. There were no Latinos. In the way back on an upper level was a room for VIPs, and there Rolando introduced Jordan to rap artists of some repute, a few professional athletes, lots of doe-eyed women, but mainly producers, agents and managers who spoke from behind sunglasses about "projects" upcoming or in progress.

"I truly didn't speak the language, dad," he told his father that Sunday. "We'd be talking or standing around with people who were saying things about work they were doing, but I couldn't follow their thoughts to completion. Maybe it was the music. They were trying to do business in a room where the music was pretty deafening. I mean you could hear the bass in your nuts. But the funniest thing, dad, is that a favorite thing to say now is, 'Know what I'm sayin'? Know what I'm sayin'?' Sometimes you'd hear a sentence start out like that. And I'm tring to look real earnest and listen, you know, and maybe come up with an idea that intrigues them and then off we'd go, but when a guy keeps sayin 'Know what I'm sayin' —"

"And he hasn't actually gotten to the point of saying anything."

"Well, there you see my problem."

"That's 'cause I know what you're sayin'."

"OK, pops, now you're hip hop. Next time you're comin' with me."

"Next time why don't you meet with the black chamber of commerce?"

Jordan got a head start on that idea because of a moment during a departmental meeting shortly after the conversation with his father. Duane Waters had asked lawyers to summarize their ongoing matters. The Adnanian deal was about to close, but Adnanian had decided for some reason to use another law firm for his pending transaction, a blow to the firm. Next, Paul, the lone third year, mentioned that he was wrapping up a deal where Dixon Barrett was acting as underwriters counsel. The transaction was a public-private venture; Dixon Barrett represented a private interest, while a firm named Coleman & Associates represented the county of Los Angeles. Jordan's ears perked up. Coleman & Associates was a small black law firm that had been around for years. Coleman lawyers knew everybody on the black chamber of commerce. Jordan wanted in. Although Tom was supervising Paul, Jordan thought it odd that a third year was doing the work alone.

"Sounds interesting, Paul," Jordan said, pretending to be the encouraging senior associate. "I'd like to come by and talk with you about it some time." Paul nodded enthusiastically, and the meeting went on.

Jordan waited until late in the afternoon before stopping in with Paul. He figured it would be easy enough to learn the basic structure of the deal, the schedule and a few key names of the lawyers, so that he could look them up and arrange to meet them after the closing. At 4:30 he headed to the fifty-second floor to see Paul. Paul wasn't in his office, so Jordan asked Jennifer, Paul's secretary, to have him call him. She said he was with Tom.

Tom's office door was nearly closed and Jordan couldn't see who was in there with him. Loud talk occasionally escaped, and Tom was clearly pissed off about something. His secretary was not at her desk. So, Jordan decided to wait in the hallway a moment, at least to figure out whether Paul was the one inside being chewed out.

"No, no, Paul! That is *not* what I told you to do. You know the son of a bitch can't write his way out of a paperbag. I told *you* to write it. This is a small deal. It has to be done efficiently; it serves no one's interest to drag it out over illiterate drafts. *They* may do that. *We* don't do that. If Grigsby has a problem with that, let me know and I'll call over there. I'm sick of fucking around. Jesus Christ, this is not a spear-chucking contest!"

Something exploded in Jordan's legs, and he found himself hurtling down the hallway at invisible speed. In an instant he was back in his own office, sitting within the pounding of his heart, the door slammed shut behind him, Los Angeles and the Pacific spread wide before his eyes. "Jigaboo" had come up before. It had been attributed to Tom in rumors spread by a junior associate who had left the firm years ago. "Nigger" came up only once. Work like a nigger, a partner from Dixon Barrett's D.C. office once said on a visit to L.A. He didn't know Jordan was within earshot either. When Jordan brought the matter to the managing partner who preceded Russel Wallace, they said they'd look into it. Nothing ever happened. The guy was originally from Alabama, Jordan was told. He meant it as a compliment and didn't know better. That too was years ago. Before Rodney King and the riots, before the sensitivity training meetings offered by the state bar association, before LRLA and the commitment of firms like his to cooperative efforts. It might have been innocent, Jordan began to think. Tom might just have been talking, upset. The references weren't clear. It sounded like there were many representatives involved. He might not have been talking about Coleman lawyers. Grigsby. That's not necessarily a black name.

Jordan's telephone rang on his desk. It was Paul. "I understand you came down to see me?"

"Let me just ask you, Paul: Does a guy named Grigsby work at Coleman?"

"Yeah, you know Charles Grigsby?" Paul asked, sounding almost excited.

"Not really. He, um, went to school with a friend of mine."

Just to be certain, Jordan looked up the name Charles Grigsby in a lawyer listing. Sure enough the name had beside it all the trappings of blackness: membership in black bar associations, committee work for various "community" things, Democratic clubs, a fraternal organization Jordan didn't recognize and a zip code in Baldwin Hills.

The problem with his moment of discovery was the overwhelming conviction that there was nothing he could do, which gripped him at almost the same time. He was trapped as much by the circumstance of eavesdropping as by his chances to make partner. Information that comes that way comes wholesale and cheap. He knew it would be discredited, considered a little ridiculous and easily denied. Plus, what would it get him? Tom certainly wasn't going to offer Jordan an apology. Instead, Jordan figured in the long run Tom would remember it as Jordan's premature attempt to gain some equal footing with a senior partner—maybe accuse him of playing the "race card"—and deny him partner on that basis. That was as clear as Jordan could make out the situation. In any event, he'd have to sit on what he heard.

So, the moment sat on him, bearing down over a number of endless days at work, and afterwards too. Within his new knowledge of Tom's words, the music in Jordan's head could get unbearable. Every step in the direction of the firm, not only in the mornings but at any time of day, anywhere, just if it seemed like Jordan was moving somehow toward it, the music pounded its heavy chords against the side of his head. So, every night he played basketball at the gym. His game got better, but much meaner. Jordan threw elbows from anywhere on the court; it didn't matter. He drove to the basket against white men guarding him nearly every time he got the ball, and he drove hard. He cursed often, angrily, and Jordan started fights. It had always been his style to be sportsmanlike; it was a dimension of his game. Jordan forgot.

"HE WAS WRONG, BUT I'D RIDE IT OUT," JORDAN'S FATHER suggested, though he sounded a little sad admitting it. "Damn!" Jordan thought he heard him say away from the phone. "I find it hard to believe that the guy really thinks like that. I mean, there's plenty of racists in the world, but Tom Blazier just never sounded like one."

"Who says shit like that, dad?"

"Angry, thoughtless, perhaps ignorant people, Jordan. But they're not all racists."

"You're saying I should just leave it alone?"

His father was quiet for a while, then sighed long into the phone. "I remember working in Oakland in the shipping yards shortly after my father sent for us from Texas. This of course is long before I met your mother. None of the jobs I saw down there were particularly tough. Mine was very easy, move so many bales or boxes of whatnot onto the cargo hold per hour. Foreman gave you a quota. It was hard for black workers to get into the union, so there were just a few jobs we could do and you got paid less than union wage. Guy used to say to me everytime I lost my grip and dropped something, 'That's one, nigger.' Few hours later, I'd drop another and before I could grab it back up, I'd hear his voice, 'That's two, nigger.' You got three strikes. I don't know why, I can't tell you what possible difference it made, and the strike rule only applied to black workers. If you struck out, you were gone, no questions asked, no appeals, no nothing. It was sport to them. Guys who made trouble over rules like that—and, Jordan, they had any number of useless rules designed just to break you down—those guys found trouble. It was a very dangerous place to be.

"But, son, your situation is very different. We used to have to take that shit for eight dollars a day. You make that much riding the elevator between floors in that building. A lot has changed. Some indignities you ride out because you have to. Others you ride out because, well, in the scheme of things, they're not really indignities. They're just ordinary bullshit you have to put up with on occasion."

It was his mom who liked to apologize for the indiscretions of white people; she would offer the best explanations, until he had to beg her to stop. That's why he kept her out of these matters. But his father, in the face of obvious transgression, was missing it. The whole episode silenced Jordan.

"You know what I'm sayin'?" his father asked. But Jordan was already gone.

He'd sit up at night watching the defendant's profile and sulk, as if he were watching himself. He'd listen only for a strong word in his defense, a turning point, some reassurance before he could go to sleep. He'd wake up with worse skin than he'd had in fifteen years. The cello gathered dust. Jordan avoided all O.J. discussions with whites.

Work with Tom dried up entirely. While Tom's words and his face and his power continued to ossify in Jordan's thoughts at work, Jordan was all but frozen out of contact with him and any new business matters he brought in. They barely acknowledged each other when they passed in the corridors, but the misperception was always inventively executed—eyes averted onto a page held below; distracted by the intersection of somebody else walking nearby; suddenly turning off into a doorway. However it finished, the scene would repeat itself in Jordan's thoughts. He'd try to take it out on white guys playing pickup at the gym. But there in the office and within the sounds of that pounding rhythmic dirge, it was Tom's firm that Jordan suddenly felt left out of. The consequence of an impasse with Tom, even an unspoken one, clearly favored Tom. So, Jordan rode it out.

You never heard exactly how another lawyer got fired. Lawyers didn't get fired. Associates are let go, but even then the process seems indirect and murky to all who, for some reason or another, can't deny the possibility of it ever happening to them. The genesis is always a review, which, depending on seniority, occurs every six months or twelve. Exact words are not disclosed outside that meeting. But the associate starts looking for other work amid the ticking of some clock of professional courtesy. Eventually, under circumstances as mysterious as plausible, they are gone.

"He told me that it was unlikely that I can have any kind of future with the firm," Jacqueline told Jordan, once he had closed the door and returned to his desk. "He said the firm would give me the time I need to find something more suitable." She was wearing the same peach suit from before, and gently crying in the chair. She tried to measure her tears, but her nose betrayed composure and she couldn't control her sniffling.

"Did you have any sense of it coming? What do you suppose it was?" he asked, shocked, really, that the firm would ask someone at just the end of her first year to go. It was standard practice to let even a difficult person stay until their second-year review, unless the associate had committed some extraordinary wrong, like malpractice.

"No, Jordan. I had absolutely no idea. All he said when I asked him was I never owned up to that mistake I made on that memo. He said after that there was a perception among some of the partners that I went off and *indulged* myself in *pro bono* activity. I spent too much time in South Central, working with LRLA."

Jordan couldn't deny the old reaction, which was automatic: To view Jacqueline from the other side of a thick glass partition, separating those who could meet the standards of a large law firm from the multitudes who could not. The reaction didn't last. It was overcome by sympathy and bewilderment. But even its fleeting presence forestalled his suspicion about the firm, and made him wonder about her. It was possible, though unlikely, that the litigation partners saw some clear and unmistakable pattern emerge in her work, which his own distant impressions missed.

"What are you gonna do?"

She wanted to tell him what a stupid question that seemed, but she decided instead to answer it. "I don't know. I'll talk to headhunters, I guess. I'll try to find a job. It's gonna be hard. The market really sucks right now. Plus, I look like damaged goods, don't I? I mean, who lets associates go after a year?"

He felt speechless, paralyzed and mighty lucky. "I'm real sorry, Jacqueline. It doesn't sound like you were treated fairly. Here," he added, sliding his chair around to his Rolodex, "let me give you the names and numbers of some reputable headhunters. And beyond that, I'll put the word out to some senior folks I know at other firms."

"Thanks, Jordan." Her lip quivered wildly and tears silently washed down her cheeks.

"You *will* recover from this, Jacqueline. This just may not have been your fit. That happens. Don't let it shake you. People bounce back from these things, only to make liars out of folks."

"Do people ever sue?" she asked out of nowhere.

The question surprised him. The answer seemed obvious, or at least the choice. But the very idea lost the fight for life inside him. "Not very often," he said sadly. "I've never heard of a successful lawsuit brought by an associate against a major firm for employment discrimination."

She listened attentively, controlling her chin as best she could and sniffling between his words. Then she gathered herself and left.

AROUND THE OFFICE, NOBODY SEEMED TO CARE ONE WAY OR THE other how the O.J. trial would come out. Lawyers talked about how effective something was, gave a condescending thumbs-up to one side or the other for some piece of evidence or plot twist, but they applauded only the tricks and tactics of the lawyer combatants without choosing a particular side. A little something started to happen during the closing arguments. The white attorneys for the defense and prosecution stirred minor interest over technical points about blood evidence and expert analysis. But the black attorneys, Johnnie Cochran and Christopher Darden, got the office talking about guilt or innocence. Sometimes it seemed a matter of the rhetoric used that day. Often it was their suits and their cadence that made a person say, "There's no way they're convicting him," or "He's gonna fry." All in all, it was preference, not conviction, that moved them.

Until the verdict announcement was officially designated for the middle of a work day. It was a Thursday. With such advance warning, the firm could prepare for it. Most employees were allowed to gather before a television set in the main conference room. Black secretaries and mail room staff avoided it. A carnival mood turned playfully hysterical, then recovered to festive, until a hundred pair of eyes stood riveted before the screen. Finally the jury, mostly black women with small educations, announced their verdict.

A day of silence was never declared. But after the initial impact settled, wrestled, erupted and then settled again inside, that's what it became around the office. Slowly locking silence and rapidly closing doors. You had to be right up next to a person to know what to expect from them. Paul, a gentle, boyish man, stood near a window in a conference room saying, "shit! shit! shit!" angrily, eagerly, over and over again to himself. Jennifer, his secretary, allowed a group of support staff to assemble behind her cubicle for a time, then asked them to go away so she could cry. Immediately after the news spread that the jury had acquitted O.J. Simpson, Tom Blazier leaped to the door of his office, began mouthing "ignorant motherfuckers" and slammed it shut for the rest of the day. Many people simply left early to mourn among family and friends. Jordan suddenly found himself the target of angry, suspicious looks that repeated simply, "How could you?"

He had learned from his mother, who left three voice mails before the actual verdict was announced and three afterwards. She was ecstatic, whooping and crying into the phone, "We did it! I'm so relieved. I don't want to be happy about that family's confusion, but it's justice, sweetheart! It's justice! Call me back." Which Jordan couldn't do right away. Besides, there were six other voice mails, all from black friends, all relieved, proud, cocky, or neutral. At first, Jordan was neutral, too. He figured there was probably reasonable doubt all along, and nothing had changed his view. He wasn't ready to get too excited with his mother about an understandable conclusion. Two innocent people were no less dead. But somehow, he was a little amazed.

"I say free the Simpson twelve," Rolando said, closing the door to Jordan's office behind him and sliding comfortably into a chair. "It's those motherfuckers who paid the price, sequestered for the last ten goddamned months. Oh, but they're gonna pay for it now, boy. White folks is straight pissed about these niggas. 'It's an outrage! We demand a recount! Hang the darkies!' Justice has truly taken them by surprise. It's right about time for them to kiss my ass, you know what I'm sayin'?" Rolando finally noticed Jordan looking flat-faced at him from the other side of the desk. Even when he repeated the question, Jordan's face didn't move. Rolando's smile made its way gradually from the back of his head until it was huge and familiar and undeniable. Jordan began to beam and they reached out for each other's hands, laughing aloud behind the closed door and slapping, slapping away, palms dancing in the verdict.

At that moment, Catherine walked in and closed the door behind her. It wasn't clear if the horror on her face had been there or was ignited by the sight of Rolando and Jordan. "How could they fucking do that, Jordan?" she asked cooly with the deadly aim in her eye fixed only on him. "You wanna tell me, honestly, how could seven black women in their right minds vote to acquit a wife batterer? The guy is a beast. What did I miss, Jordan?"

"Apparently the whole trial," said Rolando.

"I'm suprised by your reaction and your question, Cath," Jordan began. "Just weeks ago you weren't invested in any particular verdict. You said a lot of insightful things about racial inequities and whatnot. Now, in a case that could've gone either way, you're willing to tell black women how they should think."

"No, I'm not."

"Then at least you're asking me to defend it or explain it. I'm not in their heads. I don't go around asking you to defend everything the Israeli army does."

"Jordan, I really resent that. The analogy is offensive and dumb. I'm not disrespecting this jury any more than I was when I questioned the white jury that acquitted the cops who pulverized Rodney King. That was perverse. This thing looks perverse. They didn't follow the judge's instructions."

"You weren't there, Catherine. You didn't hear the evidence day in and day out. You didn't give up a year of your life. Give 'em a break."

Her expression softened. She even looked at Rolando, then at the window and back to Jordan. "OK." She took a break. "Let's just agree to talk more about it after some time has passed." He nodded. "I gotta go."

As soon as she left, Rolando turned serious and said, "We are not going down behind this shit, J, you hear me?"

Over the next two weeks, Jordan didn't exchange more than five words with Catherine. Opportunities to talk much to anyone began collapsing predictably, and he never discussed the verdict at work. He gained eleven pounds. Jordan's new Brooks Brothers clothes hung useless in his closet, as he was forced to return to a few reliable suits that fit him. The theme music that once moved him tormented him even in the office itself, accompanying every step he took in the corridors. Urinating in the bathroom, the rhythm would boom in his head as he anticipated an awkward encounter with an entering co-worker. Except for occasions with Rolando, he ate alone. For many the aftermath launched a tense, but short-lived search for things to return to normal. For Jordan it became a mere matter of time and letting things pass; he tried to respect his white coworkers' need for separate suffering, even if he couldn't understand it. He did his work; he did it with vengeance, giving no quarter to counterparts on the other side of deals. But if he was done by six or seven, he went home.

"WE NEED TO SCHEDULE A REVIEW," SAID DUANE'S VOICE ON Jordan's voice mail. Duane disliked the message system and rarely used it. Stranger than that, Jordan was not due for a review since his last glowing review eight months back. It only made sense if it was tied to special partnership matters. Then the message was a sign his advancement had begun. That's what he wanted to know when he finally calmed his heart enough to return Duane's call. Duane was cryptic, yet upbeat. Neither man was direct in his question or his answer. So when Jordan went into his Friday morning meeting with Duane Waters to hear evaluations of his work, he knew only that the head of his department had important things to address that might bear on a partnership vote coming up at some indefinite time in the future. Like lawyer schedules, these things were rarely precise. But the upshot, as Jordan put it in his mind, was that the word would come from Duane, a man he trusted and who liked him.

"I surrender to you, Lord. Hold my hand and walk with me."

They exchanged pleasantries and Jordan sat down opposite the desk. Duane's tanned face showed nothing Jordan could use, which probably meant this would be painless, informative and not without the firm's posing some challenges about minor things to improve. Duane told stories about his wife for a while, something about remodeling, the inconvenience, her silly preoccupation with finding someone gay to do it and laughs they were having over it all.

"Clarify something for me, will you, Duane?" Jordan decided to ask, feeling comfortable. "Why the review? I know consideration is coming up at some point, but unless this is that, I didn't think I was due."

Duane looked puzzled. He started to open a file full of odd-shaped papers, put it down and rested his hands on the desk. Then, in a flat, uncustomary voice he said, "I suspect you could tell me, Jordan."

Now Jordan looked puzzled, intentionally, resenting slightly the hint of gamesmanship occurring over his job. "No, Duane. I have absolutely no reason to speculate. Is there a problem?"

Between the impromptu question and the opportune answer launched the dawn of a moment that Jordan never dreamed would come. "I think that's the problem in a nutshell, Jordan. You don't see it?"

"I'm afraid not."

"Well, you seemed to be aware of it when you came to me a few months ago. In fact, your hunch was on the money, but you did nothing to correct it. At this point, you're facing some rather substantial criticisms of your work and your work habits. Let me go over the major ones with you first, then, as always, I'm happy to hear you out." Jordan felt huge in the chair, a bottom weight that seemed to drain his energy and attention away from Duane. He needed now to listen to perfection, put things together fast in his mind and, if the department had not already reached a conclusion, argue his case effectively. But something inside betrayed him. He heard only parts of things. ". . . hours are considerably lower than what's acceptable . . . show almost no commitment to community activity and dropped the only *pro bono* project you had into the hands of a first year, a *litigator* no less . . . client relations." Jordan couldn't believe it. The voice, the words, the music throbbing angrily inside him. ". . . fact of the matter is, you had a role in getting Adnanian's next matter and a role in our losing it . . . dropped the ball on bringing clients to the firm, which at the partnership level is so naive as to be inexcusable, Jordan, and I think you know that." Duane's eyes met his and, together with the tone of his voice, grew fatherly and stern and unbearable. These were lies, Jordan thought. If these weren't lies, why wasn't I told before now? Why create the expectation? I would be somewhere else by now. "And perhaps most troubling is your writing—" Suddenly, it was "them" and this was "their" favorite.

"I have consistently been commended for the quality of my written analysis, Duane, and I'd think *you* of all people can speak for me on that."

"Hey, wait a minute," Duane said with a force and a readiness Jordan had never heard him use with an ally. "First of all, you need to check your tone. I realize some of this may be difficult to hear, but that doesn't mean we let this conversation escalate."

Duane kept Jordan in his gaze and stilled the room in silence before he would let a breath resume. "You can't tell me to speak for your writing for the simple reason that I'm not familiar with all your written work and must rely on how others regard it. I can tell you now, it is *not* consistent."

"Duane," Jordan began slowly, restraining his voice carefully, "of course this is difficult to hear. You're right about that. You are the last person I would ever hope to escalate things with, and I appreciate that you're reporting what others have said. But beginning with the writing criticism first, the danger I see is that a single problem memo—about which reasonable people can disagree—may have come to define my written work over seven years. That to me seems unfair." The last word was the wrong one.

"Look, Jordan, please understand something right now. This is not a matter of fairness."

"It's Tom, isn't it?"

"On that memo, yes. I've seen it, and I agree with him."

"But you and I specifically discussed that already."

"What you did in coming to me, Jordan, was highly unprofessional. The proper thing would have been to go to Tom directly, which I'm fully prepared to do right now. Let's bring him in, if he's here. Let's air this out once and for all, because a lot obviously hangs in the balance."

Of course Tom was available. It was as if he had been waiting outside the door. A quick call and Tom was in the room, suddenly standing by the window not far from Duane. He was dead serious, although he started lightly. "How ya doin', Jordan?"

Jordan turned upward and forced a smile. They had at it. Tom reiterated everything Duane had said. He started with the same phrases, as though they'd prepared a single script. The unspoken conclusion was always the same; you have no future here. The more Tom talked, the more colorful he became, adding new phrases, growing a little angrier, suggesting some contempt here or there. "Partnership isn't something you're owed, Jordy. If *I* were to make a recommendation today, you'd either accept deferment until next year or you'd lose."

"Jordan, my friend," Duane said, softening his eyes at last. "So would mine." They let that hang in the air for a lifetime. Then Tom, looking official in the discharge of difficult duty, said he had something to return to and left. Jordan couldn't move or speak. He felt the moment wane in time yet become the skin wrapped tight around the hours afterward. Something inside was inexplicably lost. He'd seen something, but not this coming. "Jordan, the bottom line is time.

Nobody's saying it'll never happen. Nobody's saying we don't want you here. This is meant to be constructive. I, for one, have faith you'll make it." With that, it finally ended.

And what the meeting really meant began. Jordan returned to his office shaking mad. It took every restraint to close the door gently. With both fists he slammed the desk and folded his body into the thud. The fantasy of crushing bones rushed him and escaped. As he rose, a new one entered: To smash the window. He grabbed a deal trophy. Its feel and weight settled in his palm; he spun it in his fingers. He could hurl it through the window. It would explode the side of the skyscraper, hurtling the missile into the sky and shards of glass down to the plaza below. One piece could slice a lawyer in half. Jordan reached back like a pitcher and wound up his throw. His bicep actually tightened and his midsection coiled like a spring. He whipped his fist all the way around, but didn't let go the trophy. The rage couldn't move.

Seven years he'd worked at Dixon, Barrett & Thatchman. Given his seniority, it would be hard to find a comparable job someplace else. He'd have no time to come up through someone else's system. He'd never make partner. It would be hard to attract clients. He'd look like damaged goods. Jordan was breathing hard and dangerously close to acting out, even hurting somebody. They've never seen a wild black man, he sneered, impressing himself. They truly don't know just what the fuck that kinda rage can do!

He'd stayed in line because he was encouraged by Duane and others that he was on track for partnership. Each year for the last four years the message was clear. Everybody knew it. He and Rolando were the first black lawyers ever to go up for partner at the firm in L.A.; of the firm's four hundred seventy-five lawyers worldwide, there were only two black partners. If they each made it, the firm would double its numbers in a single year. Was that it? They would only make room for one? But if they deferred him, then he'd go up against Steve, their wonder boy. There was no way Steve was not making partner. As between him and Steve, choosing Steve would look fair.

They'd say that, "on the merits," Steve had him beat. Too bad, so sad. Steve can write and you can't. Steve's brought in his own clients, and you haven't. Steve's a team player, and you're a complainer. Steve never turns down work and puts in the time. You're too protective of your private time and your hours are low. Steve does *pro bono*, and you don't.

After sitting numb until sundown, Jordan left his briefcase, grabbed his jacket and, riding mercifully alone down the elevator, headed into the city. The BMW felt big, tenuous and stupid; getting a white one was a waste of color. Tom never liked the LRLA thing. But that alone couldn't explain it. Jordan reviewed the comments and episodes, wondering if they explained something. Calling the South Central residents thieves. Mocking Johnnie Cochran. Comparing Jordan to Christopher Darden. Demanding he explain the race card business. Calling the black firm ignorant, talking about spear chucking. It had all turned so gradually and without warning. Duane never gave you any reason to wonder. Firing Jacqueline. The O-ho stuff with Tracy. What else did they say? In the miniature of his life, what was happening to the O.J. jurors was happening to him, it seemed. The way people talked about how stupid they must be and how they were stuck in the limits of their racial cocoons, so was Jordan. In over his head.

He had no particular idea where to go, so he drove. There weren't enough streetlights, roads, or slow intersections to contain his feelings. But all the places where he might have gone on the West Side suddenly seemed products of a life dependent on his membership at the firm, and he couldn't go in. A general squeamishness overcame him and an impatience for his own panicked thoughts. If he were just unsure that he fit in at his firm, then conceivably he could try to find another firm. But if the belonging was rooted in his being good, if being good made him belong, and his not belonging now reflected a reality about just how good he really was, then all the world associated with important law firms and billion-dollar bridge loans, the restaurants, streetlife and bars, the cars, conversations and parking attendants, could reject him. He had been visiting when he thought he could stay.

"This is my home," he said to the young white woman in a calm voice that made violent wreckage of the silence near the mailboxes in his building's lobby. "I'm not at all interested in your fucking handbag. I bet if you didn't clutch it, I wouldn't even notice it." She said nothing, smiling a terrified smile, an acknowledgment of being knocked off the regularity of life as a neighbor there, and disappeared up a staircase.

Instead of reaffirming the love of his naked black body and his ancestral musculature, Jordan could only eat. He watched television and he ate mostly fried foods or chocolate in layers that soothed him with a half-blind fullness and suffocating exhaustion. Most of the waking weekend hours he slept or dozed. He snapped the cello bow over his thigh and refused to play it. In odd moments, he thought of things he was going to do to counteract what work would be like come Monday. But when Monday came, he couldn't go in and called in sick. He checked his voice mail twice, painfully each time, and by the end of the day only Catherine had called once, saying it wasn't important. She didn't know yet about his fall. In the mirror, his stomach seemed to bulge and above his waist rolls of flesh grew before his eyes. It wasn't just pimples on his skin, but blotches. It became a routine. Eat, check messages, feel feverish, go to the bathroom, fail, stand in the mirror, discover fault or weakness in his gaze, try again to move a bowel, sleep.

By Thursday Jordan was intent to return, because he had at last resolved to see for himself the real quality of his work. He had always succeeded in it. He'd always gotten it done well, in time, with a thoroughness that reflected clear and unshakable standards more than pride. He was disciplined, not passionate, although he was in love with his ability to do it well. So Jordan spent the better part of Thursday and Friday reading over every written memo, draft, letter or agreement he could find in four full drawers of deal files. He came in on the weekend, too. This was his corpus, a chronicle of how he'd spent the last several thousand waking hours, deals that made their way into headlines and now accounted for jobs, lives and dividends. Jordan kept an index and checked his inventory. He subjected each document to the scrutiny of time and distance; he promised to err on the side of finding error. And he did. Terrific and unbelievable and obviously sophomoric thinking produced pedestrian and humiliating errors in the writing, the presentation of the words, the analysis, the past and future. Even his handwritten notes were messier in retrospect. It wasn't that each effort was bad. It's that it could have been much better if he'd just applied himself differently. Although no one had seen what he was seeing now, the inescapable facts lay before him. A thought: What if this is why Dixon Barrett had hired so few black lawyers?

The trouble was Yale. He could remember raising his hand to speak in class, speaking at times—especially in the more corporate classes—for all black people, for their ability to participate in the discourse of sophisticated finance. Usually, the points were well-taken, said by objective professors to be real contributions. His grades were good. His grades were really good. But he also remembered distinct times in which a comment he made went without follow-up by anybody. In that moment, was there a silent chorus of laughter by white peers? Probably not, it was probably just a gentle, imperceptible shaking of the head that no, Jordan, fairly bright, willing and motivated, has once again gotten it wrong. But that's OK, because he's basically OK. Jordan slumped in memory. Had they been racists, they would have straight out and told him, using his vulnerability against him. Instead, they let it go, happy that he was close enough.

Jordan could go back through college and even high school and recall similar moments among classmates and teachers, well-intentioned people who wanted him to succeed, despite problems obvious to them but beyond his capacity at the time to understand, which is how it all starts to get away from you.

The only problem with the problem as he saw it became Rolando's success. If anything, it seemed that a black man like Jordan was supposed to succeed where one like Rolando would more likely fail. It didn't make any sense, unless Rolando was an exception to the rule. Nothing else could explain why the firm was so supportive of Rolando. For some reason, they must have *needed* an exception. It wasn't at all that he disliked Rolando. Rolando was one of his true friends. But Rolando did not go to Yale Law School and do well there. Rolando was, like Jacqueline, much darker skinned, with distinctly negroid features, and not especially good looking. He talked blacker with Jordan than he did around whites, but even still he did not speak as well or as white as Jordan could, would, did. He didn't know how, and pretended never to want to, which is another reason why his friendships at the firm were more limited. People had to cross a bridge to reach him. Jordan regularly crossed bridges *precisely* so that white colleagues would not be forced to. Thinking of Rolando made it harder for Jordan to accept that there really were serious problems with the quality of his own work.

But what had gone wrong was contained in a mystery combination of factors true and not true, right and not right, but shocking now in their subtlety and entanglement. And it was all just beyond his parent's capacity to comprehend, so Jordan didn't tell them. The image of them was at times comforting and not comforting. He tried to go back to his work, to handle each day at a time, until he could figure out exactly what went wrong and how to deal with it. But he couldn't help seeing his mother, her aching smile and perfect white teeth, the sweet regularity of her straightened hair, how short and diffident she could be. His dad was short too, not as short, sturdy but thinnish and getting thinner as he aged, impeccably polite, with a grey mustache and gently bluing eyes. If only they had stood a little taller in their pasts, they might seem more formidable to him now. If somehow Jordan's parents could have known of financial instruments and securitization, if fiduciary roles had not been so damned foreign, he might have had a backbone on which to rely when the tough questions first appeared. They stood by him, created for him and he was eternally grateful. But they also could be demanding about racial obligations. They prodded him to be ever aware of the attitudes of the white people around him, their ambivalence, impatience, tempers. Be aware. Check the pulse. Don't put them on the defensive. Yes, but whether his parents knew it or not (and he knew they didn't), that awareness comes from sharing in the knowledge of the others' world, which means you have to be able to keep up. They didn't keep up. They shrank from and worried about the distant world of white people instead of trying to just march in and learn the goddamned language. They left that for Jordan to do. Now he was fucked. Now things had mysteriously failed inside him, and it seemed, he hated to admit, to have started with them.

"YOU HAVE TO REMEMBER THEY'VE PROBABLY NEVER DONE THIS before," Catherine counseled him over a sandwich while they had lunch outside. "They still expect that you'll stay probably. You've been a part of the work for so long."

Jordan looked at her, sincerity in her large brown eyes, focaccia bread in her hands, but Catherine didn't seem to get it. "This time, *you're* kidding, right?" he asked. "If you know I'm being deferred, others know. It doesn't matter how well they act anguished about it, they blindsided me. What else did they say?"

Catherine put down the sandwich and studied his face for strength. "Jordy, just get the fuck out, man. This is no place to give your life to." She played with the bread. "I'm planning to get out soon."

He put his hands up impatiently. "Look, really, spare me patronizing consolation, spare me aplogies. Either tell me what else they said or don't."

She wouldn't look him in his eyes. She paused long enough to irritate him some more. "I'm your friend, Jordan, and I care about you, which makes it very hard to tell you things that I know would hurt *me*." He felt mercury drop in his spine and he stiffened up. "They don't take you seriously, Jordan. They used to, but I've noticed Tom and Duane change in the last year." She kept pausing too long for him. His eyes implored her to continue. "I can't explain it. God knows they don't talk to me, but I think it pre-dates that memo." She looked away and fiddled nervously with her fingers. "You do something with your eyes when you're listening intently."

"Right now?"

"No," she laughed. "You do something with your face that they've come to joke about. They imitate it, exaggerate the way you sometimes widen your expression. And the way you dress has become the butt of something really adolescent among them."

"Among whom? How do you know? What?"

"Well, clearly Steve. You know they just love Steve. He's a bright guy, no doubt about it. He does good work. But, I don't know, one time I rode down in the elevator with the three of them. They were laughing about something. It was a game, charades. This was a few months ago. Steve imitated your look. Duane did it too. Then Steve did something with his tie to make it look like a bowtie. The idea was to be ridiculous. I didn't know the reference, and they didn't want me to, so I just kind of smiled. But it occurred to me that you'd started wearing bowties around that time. Just as it was all coming to me, Tom, like he was the one who was supposed to be guessing, goes 'Monkey suit?' And they all started giggling hysterically. I was embarassed. Then we all got off at the lobby."

Jordan thought about taking vacation time. He thought about playing more ball, or going up to San Francisco to see his parents. He thought about doing a lot of things, even little things, for himself that he just couldn't do. He'd lay in bed at night. He'd try to feel himself under the covers, lie naked on his back and masturbate. But every image of a woman quarreled with him. He imagined Tracy, herself rejected, angry with him, repulsed. His body felt ugly, undeserving of pleasure, even in a fantasy. He stopped touching it. So, he worked a few, poorly focused hours each day. He ate and grew heavier. And he thought about Catherine's elevator ride constantly, up and down, as if he were there. Rage could make him dizzy.

Duane had given him the option of deferring partnership, and

Jordan finally decided to take it. He didn't know where he'd go or what he'd do, but at least there would be nothing immediately hanging over his hours at the firm. The whole momentous thing seemed to take no time to decide. He didn't consult anyone. He didn't even have to make an appointment with Duane or give him warning. One day he just stuck his head in Duane's office and asked him if he had a minute to follow up on the review. He'd caught Duane in an idle moment, but Jordan didn't even settle into the chair.

"I've decided to accept your recommendation and defer, you know, in order to preserve my position."

And that was all. He added the part about preserving his position spontaneously, not knowing what he meant by it, but hoping that it sounded strong or might develop future meaning. As moments go, the talk never rose to the level of the subject, a man accepting some awful, unacceptable fate. As a moment between two people, it hardly held meaning. Duane just nodded, smiled and said OK. It was a moment without a soul.

But once it was over, deferment gave Jordan a place to go and a thing to be, deferred. News would go out, there'd be private reaction, then he would go about the business of occupying an unfortunate, but nevertheless established category. He grew less excitable. When Jordan would pass Tom he'd offer faint-hearted hellos, which were returned in kind. The stiffness between them was genuine and the distance real, but still they managed to work briefly together. Steve, a clear victor, was also cordial to Jordan. It was the experience of mutual forgiveness when one works with someone dying from a terminal illness. The well are kind and delicate, relaxing their expectations in exchange for the condition of temporariness. The dying person is amiable and resolved, preparing himself for a peaceful exit from worldly priorities. The state of grace lasts but so long. For the time being, it worked for him.

Jordan had never thought of the cello as an instrument of his rage. Its notes, stroked long by the bow or carefully plucked by his fingers, were moans at best. Never roars. The cello's voice was the undeniable sweetness of love's inventions talking gently, humming powerfully, a mouth of sliding yawns waking peaceably and encouraging the new day. Which is why it stood unplayed and alone, not even in its special place, but forgotten in a corner and leaning strings first against the wall. But Jordan rediscovered its deeper voice. It can register a roar, a thump, a punch, or hard beats from the bottom. It can resound, wear boots, march heavy, kick and thud and pound the ground like the rhythmic crescendo of the theme music that tormented Jordan's thinking. And it did, night after night. Into an angry stupor he'd play.

A message from his mother said she was worried about him and she was coming down to L.A. soon to visit friends. In a few weeks or so. Jordan played. She didn't have to stay with him, but she'd like to see him. He played. She could possibly come to his office to meet him for lunch, which is always nice, she said.

Suffering the hours at work coolly and minimally, Jordan thumped his cello in the evenings. A card from Jacqueline said she'd found the job of a lifetime working with Halifu Andami in her organization in South Central. She wasn't sure if you could consider it lawyer work, maybe advocacy, she wrote. In any case, she was loving it and wanted to thank him for his efforts to help her find work at another firm, but she wasn't sure the money was worth it.

Then Rolando splashed across the dull wavelength of Jordan's hours at work. "Hey, man," he said, stepping into Jordan's office.

"Hey, man," Jordan replied the way he had every day for years.

Rolando dropped his body into the chair, kicked the door shut with his foot and leaned back looking fat and happy. "I'm gone, brother."

Jordan's muscles all braced at once. "Say again?"

"I'm taking my shit over to ECA. I'll rep the same accounts as an agent, mostly athletes, some music. Eventually, I'll produce some acts, albums, you know." Rolando watched Jordan's shock tighten across his face. He beamed. "It will be a *significant* increase in salary, bonuses *and* stock options. I held a motherfuckin' auction."

"How long have you been working on this?"

"After the verdict," he said, then noticed a jolt in Jordan's expression. "No, not *that* verdict really. Yours. When I heard about you, blood." Rolando looked away almost embarassed. "Been waitin' a long time to tell these bastards to kiss my black ass."

Jordan nodded gently and looked down. "When are you gonna announce?"

"I was just waiting to tell you. Now you're told. So, soon. Tomorrow."

Jordan played, standing, fingers climbing, whipping the rhythms around the cello's neck, humping it with his hips, pissing off his neighbors. He was glad for Rolando. He wished he could show that or, better yet, share in the ass whipping that it would appear to be to the firm. But he couldn't figure out a way. Having and losing two senior black associates and all of its black associates in one year could be somewhat embarassing news among law firms, but it wasn't a devestation. Next year they would replenish the number with fresh graduates, who would enter slightly wary but mostly lucky and confident and proud. They would dream of the maroon building with its stainless aching sides against the sky and draw its shape on napkins. The money would buy lovely things that were previously unattainable. The work would seem foreign and long, but upstanding and important. And in the mornings as they marched up the stairs to go to it, some would hear voices, sounds, even music accompanying the history they were making. A few would share that feeling of arrival with parents awestruck by the apparent glow of a miracle.

HIS MOTHER WAS A BEAUTIFUL WOMAN, WITH LARGE EYES AND SKIN like a coffee ground. They ate lunch by the fountain outside because she insisted on joining in his routines. Mrs. Dudley dressed for her son that day; she wore a pantsuit reserved for cool outdoor formals on cruises she and her husband occasionally took. Not her usual attire, not even when she was still working, but blue, vacation blue, almost powerful, almost but not quite fitting in with the suits of passing women lawyers in the plaza. The day was sparkling clear and a light September breeze spread the smog beyond the basin. He listened to everything familiar, like it was better than food. People at home. Stuff happening at church. Well wishers. Stories about his dad. Puzzling about poor blood circulation she started having recently. She asked about him, of course. Pulling large mushrooms out of the focaccia bread and neatly piling them in the cellophane, she listened while he lied about being OK despite some setbacks.

"What are we gonna do about all this?" she asked frankly, chewing, staring into his eyes.

"It's just something to deal with, mom, you know," he began to say, except that it wasn't in response to anything specific. She had figured out that there was a problem.

"Honey, you tell me what you think is necessary for me to hear and that's all. But I'm worried. I told you I'm worried. And I don't like the way you look, to be honest. If it's a deal, you usually say so. Clearly it's not a deal. It's something more." She left it at that.

"Oh, mom," he sighed. "You're not gonna like it. *You* are definately not gonna like to hear what's happened." She was supposed to flinch, but she didn't. "I've pretty much been passed over here, you know, for, um, partnership." She sat very quietly, her face tensed into one stern question, and listened. "It's a lot to tell. I'm not sure how much of it is worth going into." Jordan continued to tell it, all the details, all that was said, exactly who was who, while she listened with the same expression on her face. "That's Tom over there," Jordan said, pointing out a man in a grey suit as he crossed the plaza on tiptoe.

"That's the guy?"

"One of them," he answered. The anger rose like fresh acid burning up his temples, and as it reached his eyes, they swelled a little. He couldn't look at her, trying somehow to freeze the tears in a distant gaze.

She heard Jordan's teeth grind against each other and saw the protrusions in his jaw. Neatly and delicately, she folded up the remains of their sandwiches, gathered the drinks and the napkins, and took a brief look around the plaza. When she found what she was looking for, a secluded place beside the building, she asked Jordan if they could get up and walk over to it. He maintained his rocky face during the walk and met none of the passing smiles along the way. She tucked her arm under his and led his uneasy steps to a bench where they would be hidden from full view by short palm trees. There he cried while she held him.

"I'm sorry, mama," he said. "I'm sorry I let you down." The tears rushed over the words. As he shook, she reached her arm all the way over his shoulders and pulled him to her, shushing him, rocking, staring out at the perfect fountain and the spartan plaza.

"None of that," she cooed. "None of that." She patted him gently on his back, and that was his sign to pull it together. When he could lift his head again, she reached into her heavy pocketbook and fished inside for a tissue. He wiped his eyes, blew his nose, and she took it back and stuffed it in her pocket. "Jordan?"

"Yeah, mom."

"What are we gonna do about all this?"

"I wish I knew, mom. I'm still trying to figure it out. Right now, I gotta say, I feel, well, I feel like I'm dying."

That's when it became too hard for her to take. Mrs. Dudley rapidly searched his eyes, buckled her lip like she did when she was angry and a tear fell. But it was neither sadness nor consolation from which the tear escaped. Her eyes kept searching and fixing on his. Her back stiffened up and her cheeks grew tense. "Jordan, goddamn it, we'll sue them!" She studied his response, but none came. "Why? Why shouldn't we sue them?"

This time it wasn't Jacqueline asking, and he could not deny his mother. He struggled against the urge to find problems, reasons why not, low probabilities and enduring costs. How can you sue a law firm? But her eyes would not quit him, and she was not really asking. "Maybe we can," he managed to say.

"No, no, baby," she said abruptly, holding a finger to his face. "Listen to me. Listen to me very carefully, Jordan. You *must*!" The fury that used to terrify him as a child was back, this time in the shadow of powers that had humbled him but left her unmoved. "You *must* sue them. Your father and I did *not* work to do what we've done for you, we did *not* love you as we've loved you, so that some foolish man could come along and *fuck it all up!*" She paused. "Excuse me." She took several deep breaths and rubbed his knuckles for a minute. Her cheeks began to calm again. "There was a time when things like this you'd just ride out."

"Sometimes, mom, I wonder how much has changed. I really do."

"Well, don't. This ain't then."

AFTERWORD

THIS COLLECTION OF NARRATIVES IS PRIMARILY INTENDED AS A WORK of fiction, however, because the stories are all artistic departures from a set or composite of actual legal and historical situations, some readers may discern pedagogical intentions running through the work. These intentions are particularly apparent in the four stories that relate directly or indirectly to Supreme Court decisions. Other aspects of the stories relate to issues of legal scholarship that may interest ceratin readers. For these reasons, I offer the following explanatory notes.

NOTE ON THE USE OF SUPREME COURT CASES

The four stories that reflect Supreme Court decision making may be divided into two categories: those in which I deliberately tried to use the factual record in order to suggest something about the actual litigants (or retell aspects of recorded history) and those in which I did just the opposite. The two that fall into the former category are *For Love of Trains* and *Never Was*. These stories are based more closely on the facts as they are recounted in *Powell v. Alabama*, 287 U.S. 45 (1932),* and *Screws v. United States*, 325 U.S. 91 (1945), respectively, as well as in related primary and secondary sources. Although both stories embrace an idea suggested to me by the case and its place in history, these stories are experiments in explicit counter-narrative. That is, they are designed to challenge received readings of the cases in some manner or another. I chose, therefore, to use some of the real names of the people involved and to limit my interpretations to events that are described, if not attested to, somewhere in the public record of each case. This leaves room, however, for imagining the

---

*The other "Scottsboro Boys" decision of the Supreme Court is *Norris v. Alabama*, 294 U.S. 587 (1935).

feelings expressed by the participants. Hence, feelings attributed to Janie Patterson, for instance, are entirely made up by me. My hope is that an interested reader will find illuminating the comparison between the discussion of the right to adequate assistance of counsel in *Powell* and Janie Patterson's quest for justice in *For Love of Trains.*

Similarly, the multiple decisions in *Screws* concerning the constitutionality of a Reconstruction era statute may be superimposed on the narrator's conclusions about what really killed Bobby Hall in *Never Was.* Indeed, the perspectives couldn't be more different. The justices' abstract narratives focus upon the fairness due the law's prospective violators, while the story speaks for the victims from an expansive view of the real scope of injury.

On the other hand, my approach in the other two Supreme Court opinions is quite different, the connection to "fact" more indirect. I've used *Buchanan v. Warley,* 245 U.S. 60 (1917), and *Mapp v. Ohio,* 367 U.S. 643 (1961), as mere starting points for examinations into legal issues I consider more compelling than the ostensible conflicts. The stories inspired by the cases are *The Bargain* and *Bitch, Son of a Bitch,* respectively. *Warley* was an NAACP test case litigation, which challenged the constitutionality of Louisville's 1916 segregation ordinance. The Supreme Court ruled against the ordinance on freedom of contract grounds. For me, however, the contract issue necessarily involved relationships and the nature and terms of exchange—as does any situation involving segregation. The fact that the *real* relationship involved may have been set up only for the purposes of litigation negated the interesting relationship aspects of a dispute like that one (nor did it address the magical role that the Louisville city council seemed to assign to the earth itself). So, I deliberately broke with the facts and changed all relevant names.

The same is true with *Mapp.* Although it is a matter of public record that Ms. Mapp lived with a boarder and her stepdaughter in the time leading up to her conviction for possession of obscene materials, the Supreme Court's decision in her favor involves search and seizure rights to privacy under the Fourth Amendment, but fails to speak to the harm posed to the defendant by a conviction for a disreputable act. It also failed to address Ms. Mapp's implicit claims about her relationship with the boarder (whose belongings led to her conviction in the first place). Hence, it was important to depart radically from those basic circumstances—a male boarder who leaves behind pornographic material in a house with an adult woman and her teenage stepdaughter—and to try instead to explore how the experience of privacy might have played into such relationships. What if a very different violation of privacy was really at stake? What if some other privacy taboo was secretly at issue? Of course, beyond the skeletal facts, the feelings, beliefs and sexual proclivities of the invented characters are purely my own.

STORYTELLING SCHOLARSHIP

All of this can imply something other than creative recollection. The stories also speak to developments in scholarship about legal story-telling through the recognition of counter-narratives, as well as to exploring the possibility of reaching different legal outcomes as a result of their use. In the last several years, both critical legal theorists and law-and-literature scholars have criticized traditional legal insti-tutional thought for limiting what is allowed into legal analysis. These criticisms are both lengthy and divergent, but I will try to summarize them here. Through vehicles such as procedural rules and the doctrines of judicial restraint (and discretion), appellate courts, as one example, often construe law in ways that fail to take adequate account of subtle yet critical forces that affect how real people man-age their lives in a society riven by conflicts. This problem is espe-cially acute in lawsuits where power relationships are at issue. Thus, a court presented with a given controversy abstracts it too far from its context in larger societal conflicts, rendering a conclusion that is often superficial and incomplete because it has failed to address the complexities of the world in which the rule must now operate. Some-times such decision making merely deepens the conflict it was sup-posed to resolve. Some scholars go a step further and argue that the hierarchical structure of legal institutions itself (embodied, for instance, in the appellate decisionmaking process) works to resolve power conflicts in favor of status quo relationships—albeit through the mitigating language of a just and objective law. That is, they argue that it is often the function of legal elites to preserve class, gender and racial inequality through dominant narratives concealed as neutrality.

Law-and-literature scholars have contributed to these kinds of considerations by revealing how supposedly neutral forms of legal narrative function like literature to persuade, hide and construct versions of reality that advance a given set of results in spite of a judge's or a district attorney's stated objective of blindly doing justice. Complicating things still further is the fact that very little of this occurs by conscious intent.

These schools differ widely on how to address these limitations and, specifically, on how the use of narratives—fictional or non-fictional—can help. They differ about the various uses to which new narratives can be put, epistemological questions about how legal thinking works, and about just how far beyond traditional means of litigating, legislating and adjudicating our legal forms of expression should go before they cease to be "legal." Yet most of these scholars agree that the law—as it is currently practiced, as it has been historically wrought—needs the inclusion of new kinds of voices. Without them participating, interpreting and deciding, it lacks authentic scope and fullness. Whether these voices are nonfictional voices of experience, such as victim impact statements, or chronicles that straddle the line between fiction and nonfiction, such as the work of Derrick Bell and Richard Delgado, or merely broader perspectives on the law which incorporate excluded history, ignored psychological dynamics, or disregarded social science, new voices—nearly everyone agrees—need to be heard.

My work offers a range of voices that together provide an account of change amid the resiliency of ancient hurts and hatreds. This may be seen in the distance between the the first story, *Glow in the Dark,* and the last one, *The Monkey Suit.* Although their narrative formats are very different, the stories reach at each other from across more than one hundred fifty years of history. The social and material circumstances under which each protagonist lives and struggles could not resemble each other less. Yet, there are psychic bonds between them as black men stuck up against individual and institutional degradations which transcend the many fundamental shifts in the law over the last century and a half.

The characters, then, stand in as imperfect historical metaphors, rather than rigid rules. I tried to choose cases which prompted turning points in the development of important legal doctrines. But what I am also interested in is what these legal problems can mean in the lives of the nameless, faceless black litigants, who unwittingly assisted their formulation into the rules by which we live.

So, what joins John Henry and Jordan joins most of the characters in these narratives. The characters are people wrestling with their "something to say." Once that something comes to mind, if it comes to mind, they must confront external constraints on their ability just to say what they must. What they have to say could be seen as a defense to a legal accusation, an argument for the liability of an antagonist or the assertion of rights. The *legal* conclusion typically discounts or somehow discredits the account they would give in their own voice, even where they appear victorious. That voice—its apparent reasoning, feeling and sense of place—is a distinctive and in many ways superior narrative than what usually prevails through legal convention.

The final idea afloat among these tales is the possibility that fictional narratives of this sort might help actually to alter legal outcomes in the future. I'm far from sure about this, but I am hopeful.

Let me give two more examples from the book. The first relates to *The Bargain,* the story earlier mentioned that involves Louisville's segregation ordinance. Anachronistic as they now seem, the state-sponsored segregation schemes circa 1916 are directly related to those of succeeding generations. Residential segregation by race is nearly as deep in America today as it was back when southern border cities invented such ordinances during the rise of Jim Crow. *The Bargain* imagines that some kind of awkward friendship was involved, with rules defined by both custom and individual eccentricity. Out comes the ordinance with its rationalizing language and its notions of the races and their God-given spaces. It becomes a problem of absurd dimension. Unfortunately, the problem is hardly foreign to present-day debates about exclusionary zoning, regionalized government, gated communities and the like. The relationships, beliefs and rationales put forth at the start of the century are honored wisdom today. Something failed to move us. Ironic tales such as this one may reveal how the law's near fawning protection of contractual freedoms—an apparent good in its own right—nevertheless provides blind support for segregation.

A second example relates to how we conceptualize the rights of freedom of speech and association. *Tell About Tellin'* examines the Detroit riot/uprising of 1967 through the heroinized gaze of a young narrator. Most of the urban riots of the late twentieth century are regarded as complicated outbreaks by black folks fed up with police brutality and being on the political and economic bottom. To some extent, this story probably supports those readings. What occurred in Detroit and Newark and other cities in the late 1960s is equated with Los Angeles in 1992 following the acquittal of the police officers who savagely beat motorist Rodney King. But the story speaks from a different plane to less explored aspects of why some communities may erupt and what, if any, legal rights might attach to the members who do. Among the questions it asks are, How much is the ability to express prerequisite to the right to express freely? Who defines the scope of a right to associate? These matters remain as common as street corners, yet much of the law remains unclear. The story hints at the overlooked needs for democratic participation and psychic recognition that might one day be encompassed by legal remedies for police harassment and brutality.

Stories about cases and circumstances we think we already understand may reveal large gaps in accepted meanings of those and similar cases. Through fictions like mine, the legal community—and the rest of us—might be encouraged to alter standards, reinterpret legal interests, even recognize additional dimensions to existing rights. Cases like these could be known as much for the business they left unfinished as for the questions they seemed to answer. With these considerations in mind, I hope these stories nudge us to understand better even those matters we think are known.